The Friendly Guide to

MYTHOLOGY

Also by Nancy Hathaway

The Friendly Guide to the Universe
Native American Portraits: 1862–1918
Giving Sorrow Words (with Candy Lightner)
The Unicorn

The Friendly Guide to

MYTHOLOGY

A Mortal's Companion to the
Fantastical Realm
of Gods, Goddesses, Monsters,
and Heroes

Nancy Hathaway

a Winokur/Boates Book
VIKING

VIKING
Published by the Penguin Group
Penguin Putnam Inc., 375 Hudson Street, New York, New York 10014, U.S.A.
Penguin Books Ltd, 27 Wrights Lane, London W8 5TZ, England
Penguin Books Australia Ltd, Ringwood, Victoria, Australia
Penguin Books Canada Ltd, 10 Alcorn Avenue, Toronto, Ontario,
Canada M4V 3B2
Penguin Books (N.Z.) Ltd, 182–190 Wairau Road, Auckland 10, New Zealand

Penguin Books Ltd, Registered Offices:
Harmondsworth, Middlesex, England

First published in 2001 by Viking Penguin,
a member of Penguin Putnam Inc.

1   3   5   7   9   10   8   6   4   2

A Winokur / Boates Book

LIBRARY OF CONGRESS CATALOGING IN PUBLICATION DATA
Hathaway, Nancy, 1964–.
Friendly guide to mythology / Nancy Hathaway
p.   cm.
ISBN 0-670-85770-X (alk. paper)
1. Mythology. I. Title.
BL311 .H38 2000
291.1'3—dc21   00–034967

This book is printed on acid-free paper. ∞

Printed in the United States of America
Set in Galliard
Designed by Nancy Resnick

for George

Hail, Muse! et cetera.—

—Lord Byron

Acknowledgments

The longer a project takes to complete, the harder it is to construct a list of acknowledgments. I'll stick to the highlights. Jennifer Ehmann has been perspicacious and kind: a rare combination, and not only among editors. Production editor Jennifer Kobylarz, designer Nancy Resnick, and assistant production manager Grace Veras also merit praise, as does picture researcher Gillian Speeth. I am grateful to Rona Berg, Virginia Hooper, Jim Solomon, and everyone at the New York Society Library; to Helen Abbott, Sharon Bronte, and Diana Rico; and to Margo Kaufman, whose observations about writing (and everything else) never failed to make me laugh. Most of all, I want to thank Reid Boates and Jon Winokur, who have been supportive, entertaining, and helpful from beginning to end; my mother, Hannah Berman, who provided the drawings on pages 19, 66, 86, 91, 95, 103, 120, 162, 212, 217, 223, and 295; and my husband, George Sussman, who sustained me in every way.

Contents

Preface

When I started to work on this book, I found myself identifying not with Edith Hamilton or Jane Harrison or any of the other mythologists who inspired me to undertake the project, but rather, to my own dismay, with the juiceless Mr. Casaubon of *Middlemarch,* who "in his culminating age" (around forty-eight) marries the high-spirited and high-minded Dorothea Brooke and then does his best to subjugate her. One of his chief weapons in this endeavor is his book, *A Key to All Mythologies,* a never-ending labor of research that causes even courtship to feel like a burden to him. "I feed too much on the inward sources," he admits. "I live too much with the dead." As if to prove the point, he spends their Roman honeymoon in a library. His immersion in his subject, his ever-increasing collection of notebooks, and (no doubt) his advanced age turn his mind into "a sort of dried preparation, a lifeless embalmment of knowledge." It is easy to mock Mr. Casaubon, and to everyone's relief, he dies early on, his book unfinished . . . indeed, unbegun.

Dagon

Reading *Middlemarch,* I felt deeply sympathetic to him. True, he is a sour, unlikable man, and when he talks about his "new view of the Philistine god Dagon and other fish-deities," even the noble Dorothea can muster up nothing better than "fervid patience."

Though he seems pathetic, mean, and badly out of touch, I prefer to think that he is so enticed by the mystifying realm he finds in books that he just can't focus on the day-to-day reality of human beings and cottages.

After all, give him his due: the world of mythology found within the library walls is neither mundane nor arid. It is verdant, crawling, lush, an overgrown garden abuzz with life, and everywhere one wanders within in it, whether among the ancient Greeks or the Aztecs, the Egyptians or the Eskimos, one discovers the bizarre and the familiar, the gorgeous and the grotesque, the marvelous, the unsettling, and the raucously funny, all jumbled together. My theory is that Mr. Casaubon is one of those Victorians with a bacchanalian hidden life. He indulges himself at the library.

In contrast to Mr. Casaubon's unwritten tome, *The Friendly Guide to Mythology* does not attempt to dissect every mythology or to view mythology in one particular way. Unlike Mr. Casaubon, I do not believe that all mythologies are corruptions of a single tradition. I see mythology as an endless, Escher-like puzzle and an ongoing invention, not a static group of stories told by ancient peoples for purposes about which we can only hypothesize. Mythology is always in flux and the forces that reshape it are legion. Societal shifts stimulate new myths and alter old ones, with fresh interpretations arising to fit changing mores. Many myths disappear, leaving behind only tantalizing fragments that hint at their former complexity. On rare occasions, a forgotten myth returns to human awareness after a long absence, the way Gilgamesh, the bestseller of the ancient world, reappeared in 1853 with the discovery of clay tablets buried for almost two and a half millennia. And once in a while, a compelling mythmaker reanimates, revamps, or actually invents a myth.

Even when a myth is fully established, its details can be surprisingly fluid. Storytellers often clash over names, dates, and places, as well as the specifics of a god's birth, a monster's death, or a mortal's love affair. Consider, for example, the fate of Ariadne. After Theseus abandoned her, did she die or did she marry Dionysus? In the underworld, did Achilles wed the beautiful Helen or the murderous Medea? Choose the ending you prefer. Remember, too, that any attempt to bring myths up to date (or to retell them) inevitably distorts, for every individual views a myth through a personal prism and every age is dogged by the voices of censorship, taste, or political correctness, call it what you will. When Thomas Bulfinch, employed for thirty years by the Merchants Bank of Boston, completed his *Age of Fable* in 1855, he did not forget to eliminate from that volume "such stories and parts of stories as are offensive to pure taste and good morals." Nathaniel Hawthorne, though admittedly writing for children, acted similarly. In *Tanglewood Tales*, he justified his omission of disturbing episodes (such as the desertion of Ariadne) by calling them "a parasitical growth, having no essential connection with the original fable." In our own day too, every account is just a version. Like an iridescent bird whose color seems to change when either the bird or the observer moves, mythology looks different with each new theory, translation, archaeological find, and sociological shift; and the more standard a myth is, the more likely it is to exist in numerous, often contradictory, forms, each of which is amenable to interpretation. Homer disagrees with Hesiod; Ovid contradicts Pindar; a painted vase or a carved relief illustrates an incident alluded to nowhere else. Mythology is never written in stone, even when it is.

Similarly, mythological characters, human and divine, don't stay put. In the world of mythology, time is elastic and characters often wander from one story to another, making cameo appearances and intruding in surprising ways. Greek mythology in particular is a tightly woven web. It's as if all the characters in Shakespeare's plays were somehow related, as if Juliet turned out to be the younger sister of Lady Macbeth, who was friendly with one of the Lear girls, whose mother disappeared under peculiar circumstances involving Falstaff and was turned into a tree in the forest of Arden. In mythology, characters are interrelated, and major figures enter many tales, like players in a never-ending soap opera.

Mythological characters also evolve in interesting ways. Their personalities and positions mutate with history. For instance, in pre-Hellenic Greece, Hera was beloved. Ruling alone as an incarnation of the Great Goddess, she was the numinous center of an important and widespread religious cult (that word having none of the negative implications attached to it nowadays). By the thirteenth century BCE, her power was waning. She was linked with Zeus, philandering thunder god of the Indo-Europeans, and as her reputation devolved, she came to be known primarily as the goddess of marriage and the irritatingly jealous spouse of a randy god. Many mythologists have observed that the marriage of Hera and Zeus was quarrelsome because it was forced; the turbulence reflected the historical conquest of an indigenous goddess-worshipping society by patriarchal invaders. Nonetheless, as Homer suggests in a touching scene in the *Iliad,* the love between them was strong. So which image of the goddess is preferable? Though one is tempted to opt for the mighty pre-Hellenic goddess, the wife of Zeus was widely worshipped and memorably represented in literature and art, making her difficult to dismiss. Both images of the goddess are authentic for mythology favors no official version and boasts no orthodoxy. One telling of a myth gives rise to others, and each version twists, inverts, streamlines, or embellishes a previous rendition. The more you know about a myth, the more convoluted it gets.

There isn't even an agreed-upon definition of mythology. Its contents are as subject to debate as its meaning. Though few would dispute the mythological pedigree of deities such as Demeter and Apollo, other figures are harder to classify. Should we think of Buddha, Moses, Mary, or Mohammed as mythological? What about Paul Bunyon or the tooth fairy? How does mythology differ from legend, saga, fairy tale, folklore, fiction, and the stories that accrue around historical figures such as George Washington or Alexander the Great? Where does mythology end and religion begin? Is mythology simply someone else's religion? Or is it the intellectual detritus of the Ice Age, comprising a little distorted history, some bad science, and a thousand meditations on the mysteries of life, death, and the cosmos? We know that mythology is ubiquitous, springing into existence wherever civilizations develop. But why? And how? We can only speculate.

The pioneers of psychology maintain that mythology originates in the unconscious. Sigmund Freud believed that myths are projections of our repressed, infantile wishes and fears, and he called myths "the dreams of early mankind." (His disciple Karl Abraham turned the formula around, calling dreams "the myths of the individual.") Carl G. Jung rejected the personal unconscious as the source of mythology and looked instead to a universal energy he called the collective unconscious, a force so powerful, he wrote, that "If all the world's traditions were cut off at a single blow, the whole of mythology and the whole history of religion would start all over again with the next generation."

Other people dispute the notion that mythology is a product of the unconscious. French sociologist Émile Durkheim maintained that myths originate in the "collective conscious," which is similar for all human beings. French philosopher Roland Barthes described myth as a system of signs built upon language (which is itself a system of signs) and held that mythology arises in a historical context, not a psychological one. "It cannot possibly evolve from the 'nature' of things . . . ," he wrote. "There is no need of an unconscious in order to explain myth." Poet and mythologist Robert Graves agreed. Rejecting the Jungian view, Graves wrote that "a true science of myth should begin with a study of archaeology, history, and comparative religion, not in the psychotherapist's consulting-room."

Although the word "myth" in ordinary usage connotes a widely held yet false belief, myths are commonly thought of as metaphors intended to reveal larger truths. But do those truths concern natural phenomena, historical events, customs, religious rites or beliefs, ways of thinking, psychological processes, or spiritual needs? It depends on whom you ask. For well over two thousand years, theories have been flying.

Theagenes of Rhegion, writing around 525 BCE, perceived myths as scientific analogies. This approach, though never entirely out of fashion, reached its peak early on when Metrodorus of Lampsakos deconstructed Homer: "Agamemnon was the aether, Achilles the sun, Helen the earth . . . Demeter was the liver, Dionysus the spleen, and Apollo the bile."

Historical analogies have been in vogue periodically since 300 BCE, when Euhemerus of Messene proclaimed that gods are simply men who have been deified. Since then, mythologists who may not consider themselves Euhemerists per se nonetheless have found political upheavals and other historical events reflected in myths. For example, the eighteenth-century philosopher Giovanni Battista Vico suggested that the myth of Cadmus, who sowed the dragon's teeth and founded Thebes, describes a class struggle over agrarian laws, while Robert Graves, who compared myths to election cartoons, interpreted the same story as a chronicle of invasion and conquest.

Other mythologists believe that the primary function of mythology is to strengthen the cultural fabric of a society. Among these thinkers is the sociologist Bronislav Malinowski, who studied the myths of Trobriand Island, where he was marooned during World War I, and concluded that myths in primitive societies explain customs, reinforce beliefs, and encourage proper conduct. Neither symbolic nor intellectual, mythology, in his view, serves a purpose that is largely social and utilitarian.

French anthropologist Claude Lévi-Strauss disagreed. He saw mythology as a highly intellectual endeavor, a cerebral attempt to understand the disquieting contradictions found in opposites such as male and female, wet and dry, life and death. Adamantly refusing to denigrate mythology by describing it as primitive thought, he analyzed its structure and suggested that mythology, like language or music, is a logical system, cobbled together from separate elements like words in a sentence or phrases in a symphony.

The religious dimension of mythology has always excited interest. Historically minded mythologists are interested in how the ancients worshipped the deities who populate their myths, but that's only one approach. For centuries, scholars viewed classical mythology through the glass of Christianity. One such mythologist was Giovanni Boccaccio, author of *The Decameron*. After Petrarch convinced him in 1350, to give up imaginative writing in Italian in favor of Latin scholarship, Boccaccio spent the rest of his life writing *On the Genealogy of the Gods of the Gentiles*, which interpreted mythology as Christian allegory and was the most widely read handbook for two hundred years. Other mythologists took the opposite approach: rather than seeing pagan mythology as foreshadowing Christianity, they looked at Christianity as yet another variation on pagan themes. Two such thinkers were the second-century writer Celsus, who interpreted the story of Jesus mythologically and noted the similarity between the Virgin Mary and Danaë, a virgin magically impregnated by Zeus, and Sir James George Frazer, author of *The Golden Bough*, a multivolume tome that identified the dying-and-rising god as the basis of religion and, by implication, placed practicing Christians in a direct line with long-ago worshippers of the goddess Diana.

The most popular contemporary theories view mythology as a source of spiritual and psychological guidance and as a handy set of analogies to ordinary experience. None of this is new. The first-century Roman poet Lucretius, who committed suicide after being driven insane by a love potion, saw myths as allegories. He suggested, for instance, that the giant Tityus, who tried to rape Leto and was punished by being stretched out over nine acres with his liver eternally pecked at by vultures, reminds us of what it means to be infatuated, to "lie, in love, torn and consumed by our anxieties." Such comparisons are still being made and they still work (even if they sometimes diminish the myth).

In recent years, mythology has been reinvigorated. Only a few decades ago, it was to many people a sort of musty addendum to literature (and high culture in general), useful primarily because writers from previous centuries were evidently steeped in the stuff, and a contemporary reader ignorant of mythology was therefore in danger of missing references. Today, it has moved out of the library and into the lives of artists, writers, filmmakers, therapists, and regular people who have been influenced by two approaches in particular. The psychological approach, based in Jung and explicated most famously by Joseph Campbell, has created an upsurge of interest in mythology as an expression of something deep and abiding within the human psyche. Another influential approach to mythology has been championed by feminist scholars such as Merlin Stone, Riane Eisler, Marija Gimbutas, and Barbara G. Walker. Inspired by archaeological discoveries, they have illuminated old stories, revived ancient female deities long dismissed as unimportant or evil, and presented compelling evidence of widespread goddess worship that pre-dated Homer.

As a result, mythology has been reborn as the subject of scholarly pursuit, as a tool in the search for psychological insight and spiritual sustenance, and as a sourcebook for the entertainment industry. ("We should call him Jerkules," advises a character in Disney's 1998 animated musical, Hercules—a version of the hero's exploits that, unlike the play by Euripides, omits the part where he murders his children). During this upsurge in interest, Celtic and Native American mythologies have received a great deal of attention, while the Greeks have taken a few blows. For while psychologists, screenwriters, and French philosophers continue to see Greek mythology as a rich area of exploration, not everyone loves the Olympians. A century ago, the great Jane Harrison, who considered Sir James Frazer her mentor, dismissed them as "intellectual conceptions merely." In our own time, the mythologist Wendy Doniger O'Flaherty has called them "mythological zombies, the walking dead." And many people who like to think of themselves as spiritual pilgrims regard the Greeks as patriarchal and find greater resonance in Isis, Inanna, and anything Neolithic.

Yet as Marcel Detienne has written, "Rumor has it that we're not done with the Greeks." That has been my experience. Initially I intended *The Friendly Guide to Mythology* to be entirely multicultural, brimming with stories about characters such as Amaterasu, Quetzalcoatl, and Sedna, who are included, as well as Awonawilona and Sundiata, who are not. In the end, I was unable to tear myself away from Athena, Apollo, and the Olympian follies. They're just too engaging.

Even so, it wasn't easy to decide what to include. In making my choices, I kept in mind a cautionary statement made by Robert Ackerman, who pointed out that "Writing about myth and mythically inspired criticism offers as depressingly good an example of old-style *odium scholasticum* as one might wish." I've tried to avoid the odium (although not necessarily the scholasticum) by favoring the stories that exhilarate me, disturb me, or make me feel (as many myths do) weirdly gleeful. In an attempt to avoid the sorry fate of Mr. Casaubon, I have followed my intuition, obeyed the dictates of serendipity, and when stuck, appealed to the gods and goddesses for

Thoth, the Egyptian god of writing, knowledge, and the moon

assistance: to Hermes, storyteller and inventor of the alphabet; to Inanna, who hung on a meathook in the underworld for three days and made it out alive (surely every writer on deadline can identify with that ancient tale); to Athena, Greek goddess of wisdom; to Thoth, the Egyptian god of writing; and to whatever mythological figure I happened to be writing about at the time. Images of these figures heartened and sustained me. Or maybe I have just been beguiled, which is ultimately the purpose and the pleasure of mythology.

OVT OF CHAOS, VAST AND DARK

Tales of Creation and Destruction

Who really knows?
—the *Rig Veda*

How did the world begin? What was here first? And how did we come into existence? Every mythology addresses these questions. Whether these tales of creation start with something as vague as nothingness, as confusing as chaos, or as lowly as a turtle, whether they describe the birth of the infinite universe or limit themselves to the arrival of one particular tribe of human beings, they are the most basic of all myths.

In the grandest, most abstract stories, the Universe emerges from total darkness or unbounded light, from an endless ocean (amniotic fluid to some Freudian commentators), an abyss, a void—or, in the case of the Maori of New Zealand, nine different types of void, including the first, the second, the vast, and the delightful. Yet in these stories the emptiness is not as complete as it may seem, for in the midst of all that nothing, there is the spark of consciousness, often in the form of a deity whose method of creation might be as subtle as thinking, meditating, desiring, humming, or speaking (as in the Biblical story), as crass as vomiting, spitting, or masturbating (as in ancient Egypt), or as idiosyncratic as hurling a mat into the misty void, which is how the African god Mboom created the world. One way or another, the primordial creator sets the universe ticking.

Whatever the mechanism, creation *ex nihilo* is not easy to imagine, as anyone who has pondered the theory of the Big Bang knows. That's why many myths slide past the era of nothingness, chaos, or the void in preference for concrete, mundane images such as an animal, an egg, or a combination of the two, as in Sumatra, where a blue chicken named Manuk Manuk laid three eggs, which produced three gods, who in turn created heaven, earth, and the underworld.

> *O Thou, my Zero, is an impossible prayer,*
> *utter extinction is still a doubtful conceit.*
> *Though we pray to nothing, nothing cannot be there.*
> —Derek Walcott, *Omeros*

In the zoology of creation, large animals are strangely absent, but turtles, birds and other small creatures play a major part—and snakes and serpents are ubiquitous. Their ability to shed their skin and regenerate it, along with their venom, silence, and alarming, sinuous beauty recommended them to our ancestors as repositories of primordial energy. Whether good or evil, snakes generally appear in supporting roles (as in the Biblical tale). Occasionally, though, they are prime movers, as in Fiji, where the islanders say that the serpent god Ndengei created day and night by opening and shutting his eyes, or in ancient Babylonia, where it was reported that the body of the serpent Tiamat became the world as we know it.

Once the initial stages are complete, many creation myths come to resemble family trees. Greek creation is a prime example. It begins with an abstraction (Chaos) who creates offspring unilaterally and ends, generations later, with a vigorous group of gods, goddesses, and mortals who enmesh themselves in the surreal adventures and complicated relationships that characterize the most exciting mythologies.

The tales that follow, gathered from cultures around the world, tell the history of the universe in mythological form, beginning with a group of creation stories that rely on either dismemberment or mating, the fission and fusion of creation. Next comes a selection of myths about the origin of human beings, the history of civilization (a pageant in which the most dramatic event is often the great flood), the inevitability of death, the afterlife, and the possibility, however remote, that the world itself could come to an end.

Tales of Dismemberment

A man murders his mother-in-law and her intestines turn into aquatic vines. A warrior's decapitated head becomes the moon. A hero loses his leg, which is transformed into the stars in Orion's belt. These South American stories, recounted by Claude Lévi-Strauss, illustrate one of the strangest motifs in the lexicon of creation: dismemberment, whereby severed body parts, once connected to a primordial being, are transformed into every aspect of the cosmos, including plants, animals, celestial objects, natural forces, and all the geographical features of the planet on which we live. In these stories, which come from every continent, giants don't walk the earth, giants *are* the earth.

Marduk Slays the Serpent: A Babylonian Myth

In the beginning, there was only water. The fresh, sweet water was called Apsu while the salt water, which also took the form of a serpent, was Tiamat, the mother goddess. Apsu and Tiamat lived together peacefully and when their waters swirled together, Tiamat gave birth to several other gods including Mummu, the god of mist. In time, their offspring had children and grandchildren of their own. With several generations running around at once, friction was inevitable and hostilities began to mount. At issue was a perennial problem: Tiamat and Apsu could not tolerate the noise the younger deities were making. (For another Babylonian take on this theme, see page 35).

So Apsu, Tiamat, and Mummu resolved to attack the younger gods. For Tiamat, who loved her children, this was a terrible decision to make, and at the last minute she backed out, leaving Apsu and Mummu to conspire on their own. Their plans were foiled when Ea, the fish-tailed god of wisdom, cast a spell that caused Apsu to fall asleep. Ea chained him up, grabbed his crown, and killed him. He also tied up Mummu and strung a cord through his nose.

To celebrate his victory, Ea got married and moved into the House of Destinies, where his wife, Damkina, soon gave birth to the Babylonian god Marduk (also known as Bel or Lord). Full grown at birth, Marduk had four eyes and four ears, and flames flickered from his mouth whenever he spoke. Ea's father, the sky god Anu, was delighted to have a grandson, and he presented him with the four winds as a toy. Marduk was thrilled. He loved to use his new plaything to stir up the waves but the constant churning of the waters kept the older gods from getting any rest. They complained so vehemently to Tiamat that she set aside her hesitation and decided once more to make war against the younger gods.

Tiamat

To prepare, she gave birth to a scorpion-man, a fish-man, a bull-man, a horned serpent, a scaly dragon, a rabid dog, three storm monsters, and an assortment of demons. She also appointed her lover Qingu as leader of the troops, and she gave him the Tablet of Destinies, which conveyed all power to its owner.

Ea didn't want to enter combat against Tiamat. Neither did Anu. Only Marduk accepted the challenge. However, he told the other deities that if he succeeded, he wanted to be acknowledged as king of the gods. After a merry banquet, they agreed. Armed with a net, a mace, and a bow and arrows, Marduk set forth on his mission and came face to face with Tiamat.

The battle was titanic. Marduk encircled Tiamat with the net and let loose the winds, his favorite toy. They spun her around and around, and when she opened her mouth, she swallowed a hurricane. It roared into her belly, which became as distended as a pregnant woman's, and the winds blew so fiercely that she could not close her lips. Marduk shot an arrow into her open mouth. It pierced her belly, split her heart, and cleaved her body in two. Then he swung his mace and crushed her skull.

Marduk, armed for combat

And that is how the Marduk conquered Tiamat, the mother of the gods. In death, Tiamat became the universe. From one half of her body Marduk created the sky and from the other half, the earth. Her saliva became the clouds, the wind, and the rain; her venom was the fog; and from her eyes flowed the Tigris and Euphrates rivers.

To oversee all this, Marduk appointed a triumvirate of deities. Anu, his grandfather, was given rulership of the heavens. Ea, his father, became god of the waters. And Enlil, the great deity of the Babylonians, became the god of the atmosphere and the earth.

As for Qingu, Marduk wrested the Tablet of Destinies from him and killed him, along with the monsters and demons Tiamat had created. He promised to make Babylon the home of the gods. Finally, he turned his attention to one last problem: finding someone to work for the gods so they could relax. He solved the problem by taking the blood of the vanquished Qingu and using it to create human beings who, by design, were the slaves of the gods.

MARDUK: A CHRONOLOGY

1894 BCE	The First Babylonian Dynasty begins its 199-year reign. A central myth is that of Marduk, whose victory over Tiamat reflects the Babylonian conquest of a goddess-worshiping civilization.
1124–03 BCE	During the reign of Nebuchadnezzar I, scribes record the tale of Marduk on seven tablets known as the *Enuma Elish* (after the first two words, "When on high").
668–627 BCE	In Nineveh, King Assurbanipal fills a library with stories, hymns, books of divination, and epic poems including the *Enuma Elish*.
612 BCE	The Medes and Babylonians decimate Nineveh. The library of Assurbanipal is buried.
482 BCE	Xerxes, ruler of Persia, suppresses a revolt in Babylon and tears down the statue of Marduk, official god of the city.
1853	Archaeologists unearth the library of Assurbanipal.
1876	The story of Marduk reemerges as sections of the *Enuma Elish* are translated into English.
1990s	Marduk and Tiamat, reborn in Sweden as aggressive "death metal" bands, reenter the culture. Though acclaim is not universal ("derivative and uninspiring," laments one online reviewer), both bands survive into the twenty-first century.

P'an Ku Creates the World: A Chinese Myth

At the dawn of time, an egg floated in darkness. Within it, surrounded by swirling Chaos, was P'an Ku, the child of Yin and Yang. For 18,000 years he grew inside the egg, becoming taller and broader and denser until at last the shell cracked open and he emerged, his colossal body matted with hair and adorned with horns and tusks. The clear parts of the egg drifted up and turned into the heavens, while the yolk and the shell, being a fraction heavier, sank and became the earth. However, the difference between the parts was small and the heavens were pressed so tightly against the earth that there was no space for life to exist. So P'an Ku, like other gods in other mythologies, had no choice but to separate them. He stood up, braced his feet against the earth, and pushed the sky as far away as he could. Each day he grew ten feet; each day he pushed the sky that much further away. After 18,000 years, he was exhausted. He realized that the sky was so high above the earth that it would not collapse even if he were to stop holding it up, and he lay down to rest.

He died in his sleep. As his last breath left his body, it blew into the air and became the winds, and his voice turned into thunder. Blood gushed out of his body, becoming the ocean and all the rivers on earth except the Yellow River, which was fashioned from his tears. His head, arms, feet, and torso formed mountains. His flesh turned into soil and his bones and teeth were scattered everywhere, becoming rocks and minerals. The hair on his body turned into all the plants on earth, the hair on his head swept across the sky and became the constellations, his eyebrows became the planets, his right eye turned into the moon, and his left eye became the sun.

In the third century CE, about nine hundred years after P'an Ku became popular, mythmakers began to relate another story. P'an Ku's body, they said, was crawling with fleas and parasites. When the wind impregnated those tiny creatures, they gave birth to human beings.

Another Chinese story, at least seven hundred years older, credits the creation of human beings to the goddess Nü Gua. Her story is told on page 40.

The Frost Giants and the Creation of the World: An Icelandic Story

In the beginning, before the creation of Heaven and Earth, only hot and cold existed, each in a nebulous region of its own. Blankets of fog hovered above fields of ice in Niflheim, the kingdom of cold, while in Muspell, the domain of heat, flames and glowing embers warmed the air and caused the rivers to churn up a poisonous foam. For a long time, these opposing realms were kept apart by the yawning abyss known as Ginnungagap. But eventually the warm southern air mingled with the frigid air from the north, and the ice of Niflheim started to thaw. As it melted, it took on the shape of two creatures: the evil giant Ymir and the primeval cow Audhumla, whose milk nourished the gods. One night when the air was unbearably warm, Ymir sweat so profusely that a large family of frost giants climbed out of his leg, his feet mated with each other, creating one of his sons, and the first man and woman were born from beneath his left arm. (Something similar happened in Australia, where Karora gave birth through his armpits to both bandicoots and sons.)

Meanwhile, there were still no stars in the sky and the earth did not exist. Then one day the cow licked the salty ice and uncovered the hair of a creature locked inside. The next day, she exposed the head, and on the third day, she revealed the body of the giant Buri, known as the Strong.

Buri had a son (who knows how?) named Bor who in turn married Bestla, the daughter of a frost giant, and fathered three sons: Vili, Ve, and Odin, the god of magic, intelligence, war, and the dead. These three gods attacked

Yggdrasil, the cosmic tree. Sitting beneath its branches are the three Norns, the Norse goddesses of fate who determined the destiny of gods and human beings. Known in Britain as the Wyrd, they were the inspiration for the three weird sisters in Macbeth.

Ymir so viciously that blood spurted out of his body in crashing waves. It flooded the Abyss, formed puddles and pools that became the lakes and the seas, and drowned all the frost giants but one—Bergelmir, who escaped with his wife in a boat carved from a tree trunk.

Afterwards, Odin and his brothers dragged Ymir's corpse into the middle of the Ginnungagap, and created the world. They turned his flesh into earth, his teeth into stones, his hair into the forests, his brains into storm clouds, and his remaining blood into an ocean that encircled the world. To create the heavens, they lifted his skull into the sky and assigned four dwarfs, which they created from the maggots crawling on his body, to hold up the four corners. Finally they grabbed a few sparks from fiery Muspell and tossed them into the sky, where they turned into the sun, the moon, the planets, and the stars.

Looking around at their creation, the three gods claimed the land along the shore for themselves and allocated the middle region, which was called Midgard or Middle Earth, to humankind. To protect the inhabitants of Midgard, they surrounded it with a high wall made from Ymir's eyebrows.

Within that wall grew three trees. Two of them were transformed into a man and a woman. The third, a green ash called Yggdrasil, was the world tree. Its roots extend into Helheim, the land of the dead; its trunk runs right through Midgard, the home of human beings; and its branches stretch all the way to Asgard, the abode of the gods. Thus the world in all its complexity was created.

SOURCES: THE EDDAS

Northern European mythology comes to us primarily from two sources:

- The *Poetic* or *Elder Edda*. Composed around 850 and discovered in 1643 by an Icelandic bishop, it is an anonymous collection of verse about the gods and heroes of the north. Among its myths: the story of Odin.

- The *Prose* or *Younger Edda*. This assortment of stories about the Norse gods was compiled around 1222 by Snorri Sturluson, an Icelandic poet, historian, and politician, as well as one of the human heroes of mythology. For more about him, see page 62.

The Sacrifice: A Hindu Story

A well-known Hindu myth, one of that religion's many elaborate creation stories, tells how the gods sacrificed Purusha, the thousand-headed primordial Man. They molded his melted fat into the animals and they created the human population from his various body parts in a manner appropriate to their

> *When the gods spread the sacrifice with the Man as the offering, spring was the clarified buffer, summer the fuel, autumn the oblation.*
>
> —the *Rig Veda*

status. Thus the mouth gave birth to the upper-class Brahmin (as well as the gods Indra and Agni); the arms became the warriors; the thighs turned into farmers and other ordinary people; and the feet became the lowliest portion of the social body, the servants, as well as the earth itself. In this way, the caste system was born.

In another Hindu conception of the universe, the cosmic tortoise supports the elephants that carry the world.

Once that was accomplished, Purusha's eye became the sun, his mind mutated into the moon, his breath turned into the wind, his head became the sky, his navel was transformed into the atmosphere, and the seasons emanated from his armpits. He was so big that all this required only one quarter of him. The other three quarters rose into heaven, where they formed everything that is immortal. Thus the dismembered Purusha, like gods in other cultures who are sacrificed and

SOURCES: THE *RIG VEDA*

Completed in India around 1200 BCE, the *Rig Veda*, one of the sacred books of Hinduism, is a collection of 1,028 hymns. Among the deities honored in its pages are Agni, god of fire, Indra, king of the gods, and Soma, the elixir of immortality.

born again, is not dead. He is the world, he is immortal, he is us; he is both the worshipper and the victim of the sacrifice. As the *Rig Veda,* which was also created at Purusha's sacrifice, explains in all its elliptical glory, "With the sacrifice the gods sacrificed to the sacrifice."

Quetzalcoatl and Tezcatlipoca Attack the Goddess: An Aztec Myth

Before the earth existed, the gods Quetzalcoatl ("Plumed Serpent") and Tezcatlipoca ("Smoking Mirror")—great enemies in other stories—gazed down from the sky and saw sprawled across the waters a goddess whose body was dotted with eyes and strewn with mouths, every one of which was busy chewing and tearing at whatever food she could get. She was so ravenous that Quetzalcoatl and Tezcatlipoca were afraid she would consume everything in sight. To prevent this, they turned into serpents and pulled her in half. Her head and shoulders became the earth, and the rest of her body floated upward to become the heavens.

Although this angered the other gods, they made the best of a bad situation by creating beautiful parts of the earth from her body. They turned her eyes into caves, fountains, and wells; they made her mouths into rivers and larger caves; they shaped hills, valleys, and mountains from her nose and shoulders, and from her hair and skin they created trees, grass, and flowers, all to provide sustenance for human beings.

Yet the goddess, though dismembered, was not dead. Her mouths thirsted for human blood, which is why, every so often, she would withhold the fruits of the earth until her cravings were satisfied and she was fed the food she hungered for the most: human hearts.

> *Ah, Quetzalcoatl!*
> *Put sleep as black as beauty in the secret of my belly.*
> *Put star-oil over me.*
> *Call me a man.*
>
> —D. H. Lawrence

Ta'aroa Gets Angry: A Tahitian Tale

For a long time, the Tahitian god Ta'aroa lived inside an egg. It revolved silently in darkness for eons until the shell cracked open and Ta'aroa stepped outside. To his distress, he discovered that he was alone. Neither the sun nor the moon existed, and in every direction, he saw nothing and his frantic calls were answered only with silence. This made Ta'aroa so furious that he ordered the rocks and the sand to crawl out and provide him with a place to stand. Nothing happened. No movement occurred. Creation had not yet begun.

So Ta'aroa did what he could using the materials at hand. He angrily seized part of the eggshell, lifted it up, and turned it into the sky. Then he grabbed another piece of the shell and crumbled it into rocks and sand. Still he felt enraged. His anger simmered and burned, and at last he turned his fury on himself and tore his body apart. His flesh became the earth, his backbone became a mountain range, his organs floated into the sky and became clouds, his fingernails and toenails turned into the glittering scales of fish, his feathers became trees and bushes, his intestines became lobsters, shrimps, and eels, and his blood turned into the rainbow and colored the sky at sunset.

And yet he did not die.

And so today, everything has a shell. The sky is the shell to the constellations; the earth is a shell to plants, stones, and the seas; and woman is the shell to all human beings, who before birth are hidden within her like Ta'aroa in the cosmic egg.

Sky Woman Falls to Earth: A Native American Story

The Huron Indians say that in the beginning, there was only water below and sky above, where the Sky People lived. All else was darkness. When Sky Woman, whose name was Atahensic, contracted a mysterious ailment, her father, the chief, worried that she might die. Then one of the Sky People dreamed that if she sat next to the corn tree while it was being uprooted, she would be cured.

Her father wanted to dig the tree up right away but the other Sky People argued that the tree fed the entire tribe and he was putting them in danger. Undeterred, he directed them to dig. They hadn't been at it long when the tree pulled out of the ground with a terrible roar and toppled over, leaving a dark, gaping hole. A young man ran up to look. When he saw the tree lying on its side, its roots dangling in the air, he became so enraged that he kicked Sky Woman down the hole.

She tumbled through darkness toward the infinite sea and she would have drowned except that a loon caught her with its wings and Tortoise (without whom creation mythology would be quite different) let her sit on his back. It was sturdy but not nearly big enough. So Tortoise told the other animals to dive to the bottom of the sea and bring back a little earth from the ocean floor. Beaver went first but returned without a smidgen of earth. Otter also came back with nothing. Then Muskrat jumped into the water and paddled to the bottom of the sea. Tortoise and Sky Woman waited patiently for his return. When they

EARTH DIVER

A common motif in creation myths is that of the Earth Diver, an ordinary creature such as a toad, beaver, or turtle who swims into the murky depths of the sea and brings back a smidgen of mud that expands into the entire world. Although these myths are found everywhere, they are particularly numerous among Native American tribes.

finally spotted his little brown head bobbing in the waves, he was dead. Tortoise pried his jaws apart, peered inside his mouth, and

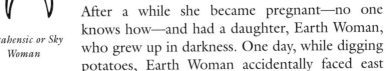

discovered a speck of dirt. He gave it to Sky Woman and instructed her to spread it around the edges of his shell. The more she spread, the more it grew, and soon that tiny clod of earth became a fertile island resting on the shell of the turtle.

Atahensic or Sky Woman

Now that she had land to walk around on, Sky Woman recovered from illness and built a lodge. After a while she became pregnant—no one knows how—and had a daughter, Earth Woman, who grew up in darkness. One day, while digging potatoes, Earth Woman accidentally faced east instead of west. As a result, wind was able to impregnate her (an effect the ancient Greeks also noted). Her body grew large with twins. When her time rolled around, Good Twin emerged from his mother's body in the usual way. Evil Twin refused and broke through her side, killing her.

Grief-stricken, Sky Woman buried her daughter and set about raising her grandchildren, although she could never bring herself to love Evil Twin. One day, Good Twin decided that he didn't want to live in darkness anymore and he dug up his mother's body. From her face, he formed a luminous sphere and threw it into the darkness, where it became the sun. From the back of her head, he fashioned a large glowing sphere and a handful of tiny ones. He flung them into the sky too, and they became the moon and the stars. Thus day and night were created. Soon Earth Woman's corpse, watered by Sky Woman's tears, became fruitful. Maize, beans, and a squash vine sprouted from her body. Life on earth became possible.

As for the rest of creation—the other plants and animals, the mountains and the lakes, and so on—Good Twin and Evil Twin managed it between them. Sometimes Good Twin got his way, creating towering maple trees and cool water. Other times Evil Twin was triumphant, forming treacherous mountains covered with razor-edged rocks. And on occasion, they forced each other to compromise. When Good Twin created rivers which flowed in two directions like modern roads, Evil Twin wouldn't allow it, even though it was easier to navigate on those rivers. Another time, Evil

Twin produced a mosquito as big as a turkey. Fortunately, Good Twin thwarted his brother's nasty intentions and shrank it down to its current size. In this way, our world came into existence.

Izanami and Izanagi: A Japanese Story

In the beginning, the world was like floating oil, drifting like a jelly-fish in a sea of nothing. Then invisible gods appeared. First came the Center of Heaven, followed by four other deities, one of whom was a reed. Seven generations of divinities followed, the last of whom were Izanagi and his sister Izanami. Their first task was to create something solid. They stood on the Floating Bridge of Heaven (it might have been the rainbow or the Milky Way) and dipped a bejeweled spear into the ocean below. When they lifted it out, drops of salty brine clinging to the tip of the spear trickled back into the water and formed an island.

Izanagi and Izanami climbed down onto the island and built a heavenly pillar and a palace. They lived there calmly until the day when they compared their bodies. The differences they discovered inspired them to invent a ritual. It had three elements: walking around the pillar in opposite directions, Izanagi to the left and Izanami to the right; exchanging compliments; and having sexual intercourse.

During their first performance of the ritual, something went wrong, for their first child was a leech, which they tucked into a reed boat and sailed out to sea. The gods decided that the fault was surely Izanami's, for in the ritual she had spoken first. So Izanagi and Izanami performed the entire procedure again, and this time Izanami was careful to speak briefly and only when spoken to. First they circumambulated the column; then Izanagi spoke and Izanami murmured a few words; then they went to bed.

Soon Izanami gave birth to all the islands of Japan and various deities, the last of whom was the God of Fire. As he was being born, he burnt her genitals so badly that she died. Nonetheless, she continued to give birth. Divinities sprang from her feces, her urine, and her vomit, as well as from the tears that her grief-stricken husband shed. Izanagi buried his wife on Mount Hiba and then took his long sword and slashed off the head of his son the fire god, whose blood also gave rise to more deities.

Time passed but Izanagi's sorrow was fresh. Missing her desperately, he decided to visit Izanami in Yomi, the underworld of Japanese mythology. When he found her waiting for him at the entrance, he told her he hoped to bring her back to life. She discussed this with the gods, who agreed to let her to return under one condition: Izanagi must not look at her until she was standing in the land of the living. He promised.

Like Orpheus, his curiosity got the better of him. Before

SOURCES: HEIDO-NO-ARE AND THE MYTHS OF SHINTOISM

Sometimes a single person keeps a myth alive. Often that person is a writer or an artist but in the case of Japanese mythology, it was a court woman with an extraordinary memory. In 681, Heido-no-Are was ordered to memorize the Shinto myths, which were rapidly being forgotten under the onslaught of Buddhism. Over three decades later, at the request of the empress, she repeated those stories to a scribe, who turned the material into one of the major books of Japanese mythology: the *Kojiko* or *Record of Ancient Matters*.

she had a chance to take a single step out of the underworld, he lit a torch and looked. He longed to be with her. But when he saw Izanami's body, with its rotting flesh and busy population of white maggots, he changed his mind.

This infuriated Izanami. As Izanagi ran out, she followed him. To slow her down, he dropped three peaches on the ground in front of her. In Greek mythology, Hippomenes used the same trick, slowing Atalanta down by tossing three golden apples in her way while she was running a race. Like Atalanta, Izanami lost a few seconds when she stopped to pick up the fruit. Thus Izanagi was able to escape from the underworld without her.

Either that, or it was Izanagi who stopped to pick up the peaches, which he found at the entranceway to the underworld. He flung them at the creatures who were pursuing him, including the eight thunder gods, the hags of Yomi, and a horde of warriors who fell back just as Izanami, still angry, emerged from the gates of hell. To keep her in the realm of the dead where she obviously belonged, Izanagi rolled a gigantic boulder across the pass, blocking her escape. That didn't stop her from wreaking vengeance. War broke out. Every day, Izanami claimed the lives of a thousand of her husband's offspring, and every day he gave birth to more than that. Soon he was so exhausted that he stopped to bathe in a stream and died. His breath became the storm god, Susa-no-wo. His left eye became the moon god, Tsukiyomi. And his right eye became one of the most important deities of the Japanese pantheon: Amaterasu, the goddess of the sun.

IF NOT GREEN CHEESE, WHAT?

Theories abound. The moon has been described as Izanagi's left eye, P'an Ku's right eye, Purusha's mind, and the Bolivian god Abaangui's nose. In Africa, the !Kung say that the creator !Kaggen hurled his shoe into the sky and it turned into the moon. The Hopi say that Spider Woman spun the moon out of white cotton fiber. One Oceanic myth reports that the moon was fashioned from fire; another claims that it was a mushroom; a third asserts that it was a snail. In a bloody myth from the Cook Islands, the moon was the lower half of a child who was sliced in two in a pre-Solomonic paternity dispute (the top half having become the sun). The Siberians tell a prettier story. They say that long ago, people knew how to fly and were so radiant that they shed light everywhere they went. Neither the sun nor the moon existed but after a while, people became dimmer and more earthbound, and the need for the luminaries grew. So one of the gods sent a spirit who dove to the bottom of the sea and found two mirrors buried in the ocean floor. He picked them up, swam to the surface, and placed them in the sky, where one turned into the sun and the other became the moon.

The Mating of the Gods

Many creation myths resemble family trees. These stories start with a solitary deity, often an abstraction, who creates offspring unilaterally. The first born are the basic elements of nature, often in matched male-and-female pairs such as heaven and earth, day and night, or sun and moon. As those deities, almost as vague as the prime mover, mate and multiply, their offspring grow less abstract and more particular. Soon the rudiments of creation are in place. That's when distinct personalities arise, ready to immerse themselves in the surreal adventures and recognizable relationships that characterize mythology.

An Egyptian Story: Variations on a Theme

In mythology, consistency is neither a goal nor a virtue. So it's not surprising that certain myths exist in many forms. In ancient Egypt, for instance, creation myths were numerous. Although they all began within a watery chaos called Nun, after that, the possibilities multiplied. Here are a few:

The supreme deity Amun. His headware features two large feathers, each divided vertically into two.

- the god Ptah, worshipped in Memphis around 3,000 BCE, found himself in the primeval waters where he used the powers of thought and speech to create the eight divinities known as the Ogdoad;
- or maybe the four male-and-female pairs of the Ogdoad created the primeval waters in the first place;
- or else the members of the Ogdoad, portrayed as snake-headed goddesses, frog-headed gods, or baboons, came together to form the cosmic egg which gave birth to the supreme sun god Ra (or Re);
- alternatively, the Theban god Amun (later known as Amun-Ra) may have crawled out of Nun in the shape of a snake and fertilized the cosmic egg;
- or perhaps Amun, who normally had the head of a ram but in this case took the shape of a goose, laid the cosmic egg,
- although it is also conceivable that the first deity appeared in

the form of a phoenix, a heron, a falcon, or a yellow wagtail bird.

- It's also possible that creation began when Ra emerged from the bud of a lotus and became a pillar known as the Benben;
- or the watery chaos of Nun may have given shape to Atum,
- or possibly Atum was born from a hill known as the Primeval Mound, later identified with the pyramids. In any case, we can stop there, because with Atum, the genealogy of the gods began.

Atum decided to masturbate. The hieroglyphics of the Pyramid texts (c. 2,400 BCE), spell it out explicitly: "I had union with my clenched hand, I joined myself in an embrace with my shadow, I poured seed into my mouth . . ." Moments later, he spat out his children: Shu, the god of air, and Tefnut, goddess of moisture.

Shu and Tefnut gave birth to two offspring of

THE OGDOAD

Kuk and Kauket: darkness
Huh and Hauhet: infinity
Amun and Amaunet: hidden power
Nun and Naunet: the watery abyss.

their own: Geb, god of earth, and the star-spangled Nut, goddess of the sky. It didn't take long before Nut was pregnant.

But the sun god Ra refused to let her give birth on any of the 360 days of the year. Fortunately, Thoth, the god of wisdom, magic, and writing, thought of a way to get around that by obeying the letter if not the spirit of Ra's imperative. He gambled with the moon and won a small portion—$\frac{1}{72}$—of each day of the year. Added together, those twenty-minute fractions equaled five extra days. On those special intercalary days, which were not regarded as part of the ordinary year, Nut gave birth to Seth and Nephthys, who hated each other (although they were briefly married), and to Isis and Osiris, who fell in love in

Osiris holding the crook and flail, twin symbols of power, and wearing his distinctive crown. (Credit: Hannah Berman)

DYING-AND-RISING GODS

Just as plants die in the fall only to be reborn in the spring, dying-and-rising gods like Osiris die young and are resurrected, thus offering hope of eternal life. Other dying-and-rising gods are Adonis, Attis, Baal, Tammuz (or Dumuzi), and Jesus Christ.

the womb. These nine deities—Atum, Shu, Tefnut, Geb, Nut, Seth, Nephthys, Isis, and Osiris—were known as the Ennead (from the Greek word for nine). They were all divine. But one was also human: the great Osiris, who was killed, revived, and resurrected in the under-world, where he became lord of the dead. His story is on page 91.

The Greek Creation

Like the Egyptians, the Greeks had a number of creation myths.

The goddess-worshipping Pelasgians, who supposedly entered Greece around 3,500 BCE, proclaimed (according to a myth reconstructed by Robert Graves) that creation began when Eurynome, the goddess of all things, arose from Chaos, separated the sea from the sky, and started to dance. As she whirled around, she generated the wind, which swelled into a giant serpent and mated with her, whereupon she turned into a dove and laid the cosmic egg. Then the serpent wound its body around the egg seven times and remained in that position until the egg was hatched.

When the shell cracked open, the sun, the moon, the stars, the earth, and all the plants and animals tumbled forth. Afterward, Eurynome and the serpent, whose name was Ophion, retired to Mount Olympus. It was not a happy move. Ophion tried to take credit for creation, and Eurynome banished him to an underground cave. Some time later, she gave birth to the Titans. Chief among them were Kronos and Rhea, who gave birth to Demeter, Hades, Hestia, Poseidon, Hera, and Zeus, king of the gods.

The eighth-century poet Hesiod tells a different story. In the beginning, he writes, there was Chaos—not a deity, not a personality, but simply a "yawning void." From Chaos came Earth (Gaia), Night (Nyx), Darkness (Erebos), the underworld (Tartarus), and seductive Eros, "who unnerves the limbs and overcomes the mind." Eros is not really a god, though. He's a quality, a kind of energy. Think of him as the force of attraction. But don't think of him as a character for he doesn't interact—at least not in the myth Hesiod tells. He reports that Gaia gave birth by herself ("without pleasant love") to the hills, the sea, and the starry sky, a deity named Uranus with whom she mated.

Gaia's body incorporates the entire earth in Michael Maier's alchemical illustration from 1618.

Her children with Uranus included:

- the three one-eyed Cyclopes: Brontes, Steropes, and Arges;
- the three Hecatonchires: insolent monsters named Kottos, Gyes, and Briareus, each of whom had a hundred arms and fifty heads;
- and the twelve Titans (see sidebar). The last to be born was Kronos, who attacked his father, Uranus, married his sister Rhea, and was conquered by his son, Zeus.

THE TITANS

Gaia and Uranus gave birth to twelve Titans: Oceanus, Tethys, Koios, Phoebe, Hyperion, Thea, Krius, Iapetos, Themis (Justice), Mnemosyne (Memory), Rhea, and Kronos. They paired off and had thousands of children, a few of whom are also considered Titans. They are:

- Atlas, Prometheus, and Epimetheus, the sons of Iapetus and an Oceanid;
- Helios (the sun), Selene (the moon), and Eos (dawn), the children of Hyperion and Thea;
- and Leto, the daughter of Koios and Phoebe, and the mother of Artemis and Apollo.

From the moment of their birth, Uranus envied what Hesiod called the "overwhelming masculinity" of his sons. Threatened by their mere presence, he imprisoned them within the earth, where they languished for years. At last Gaia figured out a diabolical

NIGHT

In Hesiod's creation story, Night (Nyx), daughter of Chaos, had many children. Two of them—Day (Hermera) and Aether—were conceived in love when she slept with Darkness (Erebos). But Night was so malign that otherwise, Hesiod tells us, she slept alone—which didn't stop her from giving birth. Her progeny, a forbidding lot, include:

- Klotho, Lachesis, and Atropos, also known as the Three Fates or Moirae. Their task is to spin the thread of each person's life, wind the thread upon a spindle, and snip it when that life reaches its preordained end;
- Doom, Death, the Destinies, Sleep, and "the whole tribe of Dreams";
- Blame, Distress, Nemesis, Fraud, Deceit, Incontinence, Old Age, and Strife, who in turn gave birth to:
- Work, Forgetfulness, Famine, Pains, Combat, Battles, Murder, Quarrels, Lies, Equivocation, Unclear Words, Oath, Folly, and Bad Government, the grandchildren of Night.

Followers of the Orphic religion rejected this myth. In their creation, Night mated with the wind and laid a silver egg that gave birth to Eros, a double-sexed, multiheaded creature also known as Phanes (Light). Or else Eros gave birth to Night, along with Uranus, Kronos, Zeus, and Dionysus, chief god of the Orphics. Either way, Night and Eros lived in a cave inside the earth and Night ruled the universe. Eventually, she slipped into obscurity, and Uranus, Kronos, and Zeus, sky gods all, lit up the heavens.

Nemesis. The goddess of retribution had the body of a vulture, as in this nineteenth-century engraving of a classical statue.

scheme to free them. She crafted a sickle from a gray, unbreakable stone called adamant and campaigned among her sons for someone to help her. Kronos volunteered. Gaia gave him the sickle, and the next time Uranus came around Gaia, "longing for love," Kronos popped out of hiding, sliced off his father's genitals, and flung them into the sea. Then, having conquered his father, Kronos freed his fellow Titans and turned his attention to his sister Rhea, who became his wife. Among their children were six of the Olympian gods, including Zeus. With them, Greek mythology blossoms into a thousand plots.

The Origin of Humanity

Thinking, dreaming, and other subtle actions are often enough to bring the world as a whole into existence. In contrast, creating human beings is a job that cannot be done with the mind alone. Raw materials, usually of the most prosaic kind, are required. In Corinth, for instance, human beings were said to be born from mushrooms. The Navajo report that First Man and First Woman were the children of corn. But by far the most common ingredients in the recipe for human beings are dust, mud, clay, and dirt, as in the stories below.

Earthlings

The Hopis say that Spider Woman created human beings by mixing four piles of earth—white, black, yellow, and red—with saliva, molding the mud into the shape of humans, covering the figures with a white cape, and singing them into life with the song of creation.

The Greek god Prometheus mixed earth with rain water or tears to make human beings, who are distinguished from the animals not by substance but by stance. For while other creatures stand on all fours and look at the ground, Ovid wrote, the beings made by Prometheus stand upright and gaze at the stars.

Other mythologies, less impressed with the nobility of man, offer dramatic explanations for the inequities of life. The Yoruba of Nigeria say that in the beginning, the high god Olorun ordered Obatala to create the world and its inhabitants. So Obatala packed up some earth and a rooster, grabbed a chain, and lowered himself from the sky into chaos. There he piled the earth up and got the rooster to scratch around in it. When its task was done, the earth was spread out over an expanse so large that the other gods could live there too. Afterwards, Obatala used a little earth to sculpt human bodies, but they remained inert until Olorun breathed life into them. With the two gods working in tandem, the people were perfectly formed. But in the midst of this great project, Obatala got drunk on palm wine and became careless. Naturally, his work suffered, and some babies were born crippled, blind, hunchbacked, or albino. Those people, sacred to Obatala, are considered his special children.

Chinese mythology also addresses the unfairness of life. Shortly after the world was created, the goddess Nü Gua felt lonely. Though plants and animals were scattered everywhere, she longed for the companionship of creatures with intelligence and the ability to reason. So she scooped up some wet clay from the banks of the Yellow River and pressed it into tiny figures like herself (except that where she had the tail of a snake, they had legs). When she impregnated each one with the force of yin or yang, the figures came to life. Those who received the breath of yang became men; those who were filled with yin became women. However, like Obatala, she found it tedious to model these clay figures one by one. To speed up the process, she took a thick length of rope, dipped it into the clay, and swung it around her head until the clay fell off in gobs. Those misshapen lumps also turned into human beings. The difference was that the individually molded figures became aristocrats, while those formed from the clay which dropped off the rope were born into poverty.

Skin, Bone, and More

In other stories, primordial protoplasm is generated from substances that are already part of who we are—like bone. That's what the Biblical God used when he took a rib from the first man and fashioned it into a woman. The Siberian Eskimo Creator acted similarly, tossing around seal bones that turned into human beings. And the Mexican creator Quetzalcoatl created humanity by mixing his blood with his father's bones.

Skin was the essential element in a Navajo story about Changing Woman, the mother of humanity. Like many mythological heroes, she was the child of one couple—Long Life Boy and Happiness Girl—and the foster child of another pair, First Man and First Woman. After they raised her, they travelled to the underworld and became the overseers of witchcraft and death. But first, they gave her a gift: a Medicine Bundle which contained the life force. Using this, Changing Woman rubbed little balls of skin from her own body and shaped them into four men and four women. The four Navajo clans are descended from them.

The Narrinyeri of Southern Australia, an irreverent group, say that the Creator used excrement to form human beings. Afterwards, he tickled them until they laughed and thus he brought us to life.

The ancient Egyptians would not have been amused. According to a Pyramid text, no sooner did the great god Atum spit out his two children, Shu and Tefnut, than they decided to go exploring. They wandered far away into the distant pools of the infinite ocean, and they were gone for a long time. Atum tried to find them but he couldn't see in the dark. Distraught, he sent his Eye in search of them. When the Eye returned with Shu and Tefnut, he was so relieved that he began to cry. Human beings were born from his tears.

Sex

Finally, in many stories the method of creation is something akin to plain old sex—except that there's usually nothing plain about it. For one thing, it's amazing how frequently women turn out to be initially unnecessary, even if, in the end, the myth opens up to include them. In an Eskimo myth, for instance, the survivors of the great flood are both men. One thing leads to another, and soon one of them becomes pregnant. A few magical words are intoned, the penis of the pregnant man splits, forming a sort of vagina, and the baby is born.

In a Hindu story, Purusha, the primeval male, feeling lonely and afraid, divided himself into a man and a woman. But the female half felt uncomfortable and decided to hide by changing her identity. When she turned into a cow, her male counterpart became a bull and mated with her; when she changed into a mare, he became a stallion and coupled with her; and when she turned into a ewe, he took the shape of a ram. On it went until all the species were created. Finally the two halves reunited as a man and a woman, and human beings were born.

In another Hindu tale, Prajapati, the architect of creation, miraculously gave birth through the power of asceticism to five children. Afterwards, his asceticism forgotten, he tried to mate with his only daughter, Dawn. When she leaped away in the shape of a doe, he became a stag and followed her, spilling his semen on the ground. It ran downhill and formed a lake which gave birth to various gods, four-legged creatures of all sorts, and human beings.

A variant of this story tells how Prajapati's four sons, Fire, Wind, Sun, and Moon, tried to follow their father's dictates and lead lives of austerity. It was an impossibility, thanks to their sister Dawn, a celestial nymph. At the mere sight of her, they spilled their precious fluids, which their father collected in a golden bowl. From that bowl a god arose. He had a thousand eyes, a thousand feet, and a thousand arrows, and one of his many names was Bhava: Existence.

The Ages of Humanity

Many mythologies report that no matter what substance they use to form human beings, be it as fine as gold or as course as stone, the gods had to make repeated attempts before they got it right, even when that meant wiping out an entire species and starting anew. In these stories, one form of humanity—or one mythological era—follows the next until, at last, we come to ourselves and the present day. Whether each "age" of humanity represents a historical epoch or a developmental stage such as infancy, adolescence or adulthood, this much is clear: the current crop of human beings is not the first and not necessarily the best but simply the most recent prototype of an evolving race.

A Tale from Borneo

Heaven and earth were newly formed when the two creators of the Dusun people of Northern Borneo—a goddess and a god who was a skilled ironsmith—turned their attention to human beings. Despite their success in creating the world, they had to try three times before they stumbled upon the perfect formula for people. The first time, they made people out of stone, but the stone people couldn't talk. Then they fashioned people out of wood, but the wood splintered, rotted, and fell apart. Finally, they took some earth from a termite mound and shaped it into a human being. The people of the termite mound are our ancestors.

The Greek Version

During the reign of Kronos, the gods of Mount Olympus created the first race of mortals. Hesiod says they were made of gold. The Romad poet, Ovid, a subtler writer, characterizes the time in which they lived as a Golden Age. Both agree that their lives were idyllic, for (as Hesiod says) "they lived with happy hearts/untouched by work or sorrow." They drank from rivers of milk or nectar and ate honey, cherries, strawberries, blackberries, acorns, and corn that grew of its own accord, even though the ground was untilled. They experienced neither sickness nor "vile old age" but died easily in their sleep. In those days, there were no laws and people were not harassed by judges with "bronze tablets . . . carrying threats of legal action" (Ovid's complaint, based on experience). Yet men behaved as they should, without fear or compulsion.

Eventually, Zeus overthrew Kronos, who was banished to the dark recesses of Tartarus, and the people of the Golden Age died out. Hesiod says that they still exist as spirits who give us wealth and keep us safe from harm.

The gods next created a silver race, inferior to the gold both in stature and in mind. Also at that time, the world changed. Spring was no longer perennial. The year divided into seasons and, for the first time, inclement weather caused people to seek shelter. Ovid says they began to live in caves, built dwellings out of branches and bark, and cultivated corn.

Hesiod's picture of the Silver Age is considerably stranger. Growing up, a child of the Silver Age "was raised at home a hundred years/And played, huge baby, by his mother's side." That long childhood was followed by a brief, anguished, out-of-control adulthood in which the denizens of the Silver Age injured one another. Worse, they failed to sacrifice to the gods, which angered Zeus so much that he got rid of them. The silver race was buried in the ground but, like the golden race, they still exist. They are the spirits of the underworld, "inferior to the gold," Hesiod says, "but honored too."

Zeus then fashioned a third race of mortals. Terrible and strong, the bronze people ate no bread, and they loved violence and war. Eventually they killed themselves off and went to Hades.

The fourth race was a definite improvement, for this time Zeus created the demigods, who fought in Thebes and sailed to Troy. Many of these noble heroes died and were buried. Others live a carefree existence in the Blessed Isles at the edge of the earth, where Kronos, having been released from his bonds in Tartarus, is king.

Finally, Zeus made a fifth race: the miserable race of iron, who work, grieve, grow weary and die. During the iron age, men began to sail in ships and to survey and divide the land. Crime, treachery, plunder, and greed appeared. Friends fought, brotherly love was rare, and according to Ovid, "Husbands waited eagerly for the deaths of their wives, and wives for that of their husbands. Ruthless stepmothers mixed brews of deadly aconite, and sons pried into their fathers' horoscopes, impatient for them to die." Things reached such a sorry pass that Justice, the last goddess to remain on earth, finally abandoned it and joined the other immortals, leaving behind only demigods, spirits, fauns, satyrs, nymphs, and human beings.

"I wish I were not of this race," Hesiod wrote. Like ourselves, he had no such luck.

A Hindu Scenario

In the complicated and mathematically precise system that belongs to the mythology of Hinduism, Vishnu creates, preserves, and destroys the world, over and over again. The repeating pattern includes (but is not limited to) the following ages or yugas:

- First comes the Krta Yuga, the age of truth. It is characterized by goodness, serenity, and an easy acceptance of dharma, the concept that there is a proper way to live that supports the social order. During this era, gift-giving trees fulfill everyone's needs, meditation is widely practiced, and sorrow does not exist. This golden age lasts for 4,000 divine or 1,440,000 human years.
- Next comes the Treta Age, which prevails for 3,000 divine years. People no longer spontaneously follow their dharma. Instead, they must learn to sacrifice, to perform certain ceremonies, and to act in an upright and moral fashion. The weather deteriorates so badly that people are forced to seek shelter in houses they must build for themselves. The gift-giving trees disappear and private property makes its appearance, as do greed, adultery, and anger. On the positive side, rain fertilizes the crops, and fruit trees decorate the earth with their pastel blossoms, bringing delight to all.
- In the Dvapara Age, which lasts for 2,000 divine years, desire, suffering, disease, and death become ordinary elements of human existence, and the decline continues.
- The last era is the Kali Yuga, a 1,000-year dark age characterized by dissension, war, strife of all sorts, and a shortened life span. During this terrible time, status is determined solely on the basis of what you own, moral virtue is nearly nonexistent, and pleasure is to be found only in sex. This age is our own.

Counting brief periods of twilight before and after each age, this cycle takes 12,000 divine years (or 4,320,000 ordinary ones). After a thousand repetitions, or half of a cosmic day, the great Vishnu unleashes the forces of heat, fire, and flood, annihilates all life, and falls asleep, leaving behind a single sign of hope: a golden egg. It floats on the primordial

In another myth, Vishnu brings the world into existence by sucking on his toe.

sea until the day is done and Vishnu awakes. A lotus springs from his navel, and Brahma—Vishnu himself, in his guise as the creator—emerges from the flower, observes that the universe is lifeless, and cracks open the egg, whereupon the process begins all over again.

The Fifth Sun and the Creation of Humanity: An Aztec Myth

In the creation cycle of the Aztecs, there have been five eons or suns, each with its individual luminary and its uniquely disastrous end. The first sun, also known as the sun of earth, lasted for 676 years (or thirteen repetitions of the astoundingly accurate fifty-two year Aztec calendar cycle), at which point calamity struck. The people were devoured by jaguars in a bloody attack that lasted thirteen years.

Next came the sun of air, which persisted for seven fifty-two-year cycles or 364 years, until a single cataclysmic day when hurricane winds roared across the land, battering houses, ripping trees out of the ground, driving the sun from the sky, and turning the people into monkeys.

During the third era, the sun of fire shone for six calendar cycles or 312 years. Then a rain of flames and embers destroyed the houses, the sun, and the people. They were turned into Pipiles, a neighboring group whose incomprehensible speech sounded like, to Aztec ears, the gobbling of turkeys or children.

The fourth sun, like the first, lasted for 676 year under the rulership of the goddess Chalchiuhtlicue. Then the rain poured down for fifty-two years, turning most of the people into fish. Fortunately, the chief god Tezcatlipoca (or Titlacahuan) wanted to save a human couple named Tata and Nene. He instructed them to hollow out a large log and climb inside it. Then he sealed them in with only a single ear of corn each. After they had eaten every last kernel, the waters began to subside. By the time they broke through the log and climbed out, they were ravenously hungry. The first thing they did was to catch a fish and roast it.

The head of Quetzalcoatl, carved on a pyramid in Teotihuacan, Mexico.

That was a mistake. Angered that the people made fire, Tez-catlipoca came down to earth, cut off their heads, and reattached them right over their rear ends, thereby turning people into dogs. And that was it for the age of the fourth sun.

The fifth and present sun was born after the gods gathered together and asked two of their number to volunteer—one to become the sun and one simply to be there as an understudy. The first volunteer was a wealthy god, Ticciztecatl; the second was the poverty-stricken, misshapen, scabby god Nanautzin. Both made offerings. Ticciztecatl sacrificed gold, precious jewels, and brightly colored feathers while Nanautzin brought hay, a few bloody thorns, three reeds, and a couple of scabs picked from his own body.

After four days of fasting, a bonfire was lit. The rich god was surprised to discover that before he could become the sun, he was expected to immolate himself in the fire. Despite the grandeur of his offerings and the strength of his desire for glory and recognition, he lacked courage. Four times, he tried to leap into the flames. Four times he failed.

Then it was Nanautzin's turn. With his unprepossessing appearance, he had never before been honored. Undeterred by fear or heat, he jumped into the blazing heart of the fire on the first try. As his paper garments distintegrated in the flames and his flesh cooked, he became the fifth sun. His example shamed Ticciztecatl, who found courage at last, cast himself into the conflagration, and became the moon.

Still, the Aztec people did not exist. So Quetzalcoatl traveled to the land of the dead to retrieve the bones of his father. After many challenges, he had the bones in hand when he stumbled and dropped them. As they scattered, a covey of quail fluttered down and pecked them to bits. Quetzalcoatl swept up the fragments, soared into the sky, and presented them to the earth goddess Cihuacoatl, who ground them into powder in a jade bowl. Then Quetzalcoatl and the other gods gathered around the bowl, drew blood from their penises, and stirred it into the powder. From that mixture, the fifth race of human beings was born. They are not destined to live forever, though. One day earthquakes will rattle across the land, and the fifth world, like the four before it, will come to an end.

THE CHRONICLE OF THE PLUMED SERPENT

Over the course of two thousand years, the Aztec god Quetzal-coatl played many parts. Also known as Kukalcan (to the Mayans), Gucumatz (to the Quiché Maya), and Nine Wind (to the Mixtec), he was a vegetation god, the planet Venus, the inventor of music, medicine, books, and the calendar (among other elements of civilization), and the primary creator of the human race, which he further championed by sacrificing snakes, birds, and butterflies instead of people. Sometimes described as the plumed (or feathered) serpent, and sometimes as a bearded man, he slipped from mythology into history in 987 CE when the Toltec king Topiltzin-Quetzalcoatl retreated from central Mexico to the Yucatan. In so doing, the man became identified with the god who, it was said, had been defeated by his rival, Tezcatlipoca, and driven to the sea. Quetzalcoatl sailed away on a raft of serpents but, like King Arthur or Jesus Christ, he was expected to return, most likely in a One Reed year, one of the fifty-two years of the Aztec calendar.

Spanish conquistador Hernando Cortés couldn't have asked for more. When he arrived in Mexico in 1519, a One Reed year, Emperor Moctezuma II took him to be the resurrected god. Within a few years, Aztec civilization was destroyed. (The population of Mexico before the invasion: 25 million. By the end of the century: one million.) Quetzalcoatl survived, becoming a symbol of ancient Mexico and a rallying point for revolutionaries and artists including Emiliano Zapata, Diego Rivera, José Clemente Orozco, and Sandinista poet Ernesto Cardénal.

Two Mayan Myths

The *Popul Vuh,* the mythological chronicle of the Quiché Maya of Guatemala, tells us that in the beginning everything was silent, motionless, and empty. Nothing existed except the sky, the sea, and a handful of gods including Tepeu, Gucumatz, and the god whose name is Heart of Heaven. They huddled beneath a blanket of green and blue feathers, and eventually they got to talking. That was when creation began, for no sooner did they speak of something than it sprang into existence, their words made manifest. Soon all the glorious details of the world were in place: the cypresses and pines, the valleys and mountains, and all the beasts, including birds, deer, serpents, pumas, and jaguars.

But when Tepeu and Gucumatz asked the animals to speak the names of the gods and praise them, the animals said nothing. To punish them for their silence, Tepeu and Gucumatz made it their destiny to be torn apart and sacrificed. They also resolved to create humanity in time for the first dawn, which had yet to occur.

In their initial attempt to make a human being, they used mud and water. That creature was so soft, absorbent, and limp that it could not hold its head up. Its face sank to one side, and although it could speak, it was totally mindless. They decided to try again.

After a minor disagreement over materials, they settled on wood. The wooden creatures resembled human beings, and they multiplied. However, they were stiff, expressionless, and unkind. They lacked souls and minds, walked on all fours, and ignored the gods. So the gods tortured them, flooded the earth with a black, resinous rain and annihilated them. The wooden people were so universally disliked that their dogs, who claimed to have been starved and beaten with sticks, attacked them. Even their household items, their pots and tortilla griddles and grinding stones, flung themselves against their former owners and hit them repeatedly on their faces. The few wooden people who managed to survive these assaults did leave descendants, though: the monkeys, who remind us of an earlier generation of men.

For their third and final attempt, Tepeu and Gucumatz used yellow and white corn and cornmeal dough to shape human beings. The first four men they created walked and talked like human beings and remembered to tend their holy altars and give thanks. But they had one characteristic that disturbed the gods: extraordinary sight. At a glance, they could see all of creation, from the curve of the earth to the tiniest speck of pollen floating in the midday sun. This vision made them almost the equal of the gods, and so the Heart of Heaven blew mist into their eyes. Their vision blurred, dimmed and narrowed until they, like us, could only see what was close to them.

Afterwards, the gods created four women who became the wives of the first four men. They gave birth to people who were black and white and belonged to tribes both large and small, including the Quiché Maya. All these people multiplied in darkness. The first day had not yet come.

When the dawn approached and the women saw the morning star rise in the east, they lit incense and danced for joy. Then the sun, which in those days looked like a man and was hotter than it is now, rose over the horizon. The wet and muddy surface of the earth dried, the Queletzu bird began to sing, and the most savage animals, those most dangerous to human kind, turned to stone.

This is not the only Mayan myth concerning the origin of humanity. In another story, the creator, whose name was Hunab, flooded the earth and then repopulated it. First, he created a race of dwarfs. That didn't work out, so he inundated the earth and tried again. This time, he made a race of people who behaved so badly

SOURCES: THE *POPUL VUH*

In 1524, Spanish conquistador Hernando Cortés sent an emissary to Guatemala for the express purpose of conquering the Quiché Maya. He executed their leaders, burned their capital to the ground, and scattered their population. The *Popul Vuh* or *Book of the Community* survived. Written in pre-Columbian hieroglyphs, it mixed mythology and history. Around 1550, a converted member of the tribe transcribed the Quiché text using the Latin alphabet. A century and a half later, a priest borrowed that book from a villager. After copying it in the original Quiché and translating it into Spanish, he presented his manuscript to the University of San Carlos. It sat there undisturbed until 1857, when a Viennese doctor named Carl Scherzer discovered it and published the Spanish version. Four years later, a French translation appeared, and in 1950, the *Popul Vuh* was translated into English. Each version has its own particular defects, and the original 1550 manuscript has been missing since the nineteenth century. The *Popul Vuh*'s extraordinary spirit—one in which stones speak, gods drink blood, and bones turn into boys—remains.

that they were known as "offenders." He flooded the earth once more and this time created the Mayan people. But even they are not eternal, for some day another flood will come and they too will be wiped off the face of the earth.

Tales of the Flood

Why are tales of the flood so widespread? Was there a mammoth deluge once upon a time, a rainy season that didn't stop? Was the destruction so awesome that, all over the world, people tell similar stories of near-universal punishment? It has been suggested that the people who lived on the banks of the flood-prone Tigris and Euphrates may have exported their myths of river rise and of a flood that devastated Mesopotamia in the third millennium BCE. Alternatively, the source of these stories may be found in a more global phenomenon—the great thaw that followed the last Ice Age, around 13,600 BCE. Or maybe the ubiquity of these stories is connected to the psychological symbolism of water. Whatever the reason, the repetition of narrative elements, ranging from plot (a mortal is told to build or board a ship of peculiar size) to symbols (the dove) to the names of characters (Noah in the Bible, Nü Gua or Nuwa in a Chinese tale), seems uncanny.

Enlil Can't Stand the Noise: A Babylonian Story

In Shurrupak, a city on the Euphrates, the inhabitants made so much noise that "the world bellowed like a wild bull" (or so says the tale of *Gilgamesh*) and the god Enlil could not get any sleep. This irritated him so much that he decided to destroy humanity. Ea, god of wisdom and sweet waters, found out about this and decided to warn Utnapishtim, the king of Sumer. While Utnapishtim was dreaming, Ea whispered to him through the walls of his reed house that he should tear it down, build a boat of specific dimensions, and load all living creatures into it. He also told Utnapishtim that if anyone asked why he was doing this, he should say that Enlil was angry at him and that, to protect himself, he planned to sail to the Persian Gulf and live with Ea.

So Utnapishtim and the members of his household set about building a ship that would be shaped like a cube seven stories high and an acre across. This task took six days. The children brought pitch while the men stoked the furnace, laid the keel, hammered the ribs and planking into place, divided the decks with bulkheads, raised the punt-poles into position, and caulked everything. Utnapishtim filled the boats with supplies and brought wine to the shipwright. On the seventh day, when the boat was completed, he anointed himself on the head. Everyone celebrated.

Ea, god of wisdom, wearing a fish.

Then Utnapishtim's relatives came on board, followed by the craftsmen and the animals, both wild and tame. The cube-shaped craft was launched—as one might imagine, with difficulty—and Utnapishtim battened down the ship in preparation for the ordeal ahead.

In the morning, the storm gods and the gods of the abyss let loose the forces of destruction. A black cloud lay plastered across the horizon, and so much rain fell that a man could not find his brother standing right in front of him and the gods in heaven could not see the people below. For six days and nights the storms ravaged the earth. The destruction was so complete that even the gods wept.

On the seventh day, the storm subsided. The sea was as flat and still as a roof. Utnapishtim opened the hatch, stepped outside, and cried, for he was entirely surrounded by water. Fourteen leagues away, the peak of Mount Nisir seemed to float above the water. He sailed in that direction and, like Noah, tossed out a dove. But the mountain was still so far away that, finding nowhere else to alight, the bird flew back to the ship.

He sent a swallow, but she also returned.

Finally he sent a raven, and the bird did not come back. So Utnapishtim knew that the waters had receded and land had reappeared. He made a grand sacrifice, burning wood, cane, cedar, and myrtle in fourteen cauldrons, which emitted a sweet, intoxicating smell the gods found irresistible. Ishtar, the queen of heaven, offered her lapis lazuli necklace as a remembrance of the flood and invited all the gods to the sacrifice—except Enlil, who was angry, for he had ordered the destruction of the mortals and yet they had survived. Ea tried to placate him. He said that Enlil had overreacted to the transgressions of mortals and he claimed that Utnapishtim had discovered Enlil's scheme through a dream.

Enlil accepted the explanation and calmed down. He blessed Utnapishtim and his wife and made them immortal. Then he sent them to live in paradise at the mouth of the rivers, where the sun rises. According to the clay tablets which recorded this story, Utnapishtim told this tale to his descendent Gilgamesh, who was the fifth king after the flood.

Zeus Gets Angry: The Classical Myth

When Julius Caesar was assassinated in 44 BCE, the violence of the act terrified people. Panic swept through the population and "the whole world shuddered," wrote the Roman poet Ovid (who was not born until the following year). That reaction reminded Ovid of the way the gods felt when they heard that Lycaon, the king of Arcadia, was scheming against them. No one, not even an immortal, likes to be the victim of a plot.

So Jupiter (Zeus to the Greeks) decided to investigate. He appeared at Lycaon's door and announced himself. Lycaon, doubting the stranger's identity, asked him to submit to a test. He sacrificed a hostage (meaning he slit his throat), roasted and boiled the victim's limbs and organs, and piled the steaming meats on a platter, which he set in front of the god. Jupiter detected the human meat immediately. It made him so angry that he turned Lycaon into a wolf and decided to destroy humanity and start all over again. Fortunately, just as he was about to let loose a barrage of thunder and lightning, he remembered the one force greater than himself: fate, which had decreed that at some unspecified time in the future the world would erupt in flames and the universe would collapse. Not wanting to spark that final conflagration, Jupiter decided to put the lightning bolts aside and destroy the world with another weapon: water.

That's Ovid's version. Apollodorus, an Athenian writer of the second century BCE, suggests another scenario. He reports that Lycaon had fifty sons (and he lists them by name). To test them, Zeus visited in the guise of a lowly traveler. Not only did the sons, who were prideful and impious, fail to recognize the god, they served him a soup whose ingredients included the innards of sheep and goats mixed with the intestines of a boy—possibly their brother Nyctimus. This concoction, like the mixed grill Lycaon gave Jupiter or the stew that Tantalus served to the gods, didn't fool Zeus for a second. He returned Nyctimus to life, transformed the other forty-nine sons into wolves, and returned to Mount Olympus so filled with despair that he flooded the earth, fully intending to eliminate the human race.

Or maybe Zeus flooded the earth because he was angry that Prometheus had stolen fire and given it to mankind, thereby granting human beings powers that the other gods didn't wish them to have.

In any case, Zeus let loose the South Wind, who flew into the heavens and crushed the clouds in his powerful hands. Sheets of rain pummeled the earth. The water rose so high that wolves, lions, tigers, and wild boars swam in the waves, dolphins knocked against the branches of oak trees, and the birds, unable to find a place to alight, fell into the sea, exhausted.

Everyone might have died were it not for Prometheus, who had warned his son Deucalion, the best man who ever lived. Deucalion constructed an ark for himself and his wife Pyrrha, and so they survived the storm. When the rain stopped and the waters receded, they came aground on the soggy slopes of Mount Parnassus and prepared to disembark. To their bewilderment, the goddess Themis told them that they must cover their heads and throw their mother's bones behind them. Both their mothers were dead, and besides, they didn't have the bones. They didn't know what to do.

As they ruminated over their situation, they realized that they might have interpreted the word "mother" in too limited a way. Perhaps it had a larger meaning.

With that in mind, they picked up stones—the bones of mother earth—and flung them behind them. Those that Deucalion tossed became men; those that Pyrrha threw became women. The earth, warmed by the sun and thoroughly watered by the flood, soon was home to an astonishing assortment of animals, some similar to those that had existed previously and others entirely new. In this way the world was repopulated.

Venus Saves Wainkaura: A Brazilian Story

The flood, the dove, and the ship, familiar to us from the Biblical tale of Noah, also appear in a tale told by the Sherente of Brazil. This story begins with Venus, who was wandering the earth in the shape of a man. No one would take him in because he was, in a word, disgusting. Bloody ulcers festered all over his skin, he stank, and a flock of bees buzzed in his wake like a dark, threatening cloud.

Nonetheless, when Venus came to the home of an Indian named Wainkaura and announced that he was lost, he was made welcome. Wainkaura gave him a newly woven mat to sit on and ordered that a pot of hot water be brought to clean Venus's body. He recommended that this take place inside—not outside, as one might expect—and he told Venus to sit on his virgin daughter's bare thighs. While Venus was perched in this position, Wainkaura gently washed his sores.

That night, Venus warned Wainkaura that the god Waptokwa was angry because the Indians had been slaughtering each other, even to the point of killing tiny children with arrows. Fed up with this behavior, Waptokwa was plotting to destroy the human race. Venus told Wainkaura if he wanted to live, he should quietly pack his belongings and kill a dove. Wainkaura set off on this mission.

When he returned with the dove, Venus confessed that he had slept with his daughter. He offered to pay for the privilege, but

Wainkaura refused. Then Venus took the dove's fragile carcass and turned it into a boat large enough for Wainkaura's entire family. No sooner did they climb inside than a whirlwind appeared out of nowhere, lifted Venus up and transported him into the darkening sky. As the clouds gathered, a distant rumbling grew to a crescendo and the clouds burst. Rain battered the earth for a long time and nearly all the Indians drowned or starved to death. Only Wainkaura and his family, snug in their little dove-boat, survived to tell the tale and to become the ancestors of humanity.

Nü Gua, the Gourd Girl: A Story from Southern China

A man was in trouble with the thunder god. To protect himself, his daughter Nü Gua (or Nuwa), and his son Fuxi, he built an iron cage in front of his house, armed herself with an iron fork, and waited. When lightning crackled across the horizons, the booming thunder god appeared in front of the house brandishing an axe. Fortunately, the man was ready. He prodded the thunder god into the iron cage and slammed the door behind him.

He intended to cook the god, but he needed some spices. So the next morning, secure in the knowledge that his prisoner was locked up, he asked his children to watch the cage until his return. Above all, he warned, they must not give the god anything to drink.

As soon as he set off for market, the thunder god begged for a sip of water. His whimpering touched Nü Gua's heart, and she relented. With the first sip, the thunder god broke through the iron bars and stood before them in all his scaly glory. Then he reached inside his horrible mouth and wrenched out one of his teeth, which he handed to them. Before he disappeared into the sky, he told them to climb inside the gourd which would grow from it. The children planted the tooth, which grew into a tree. Before long, a gourd dangled from a branch and tumbled to the ground.

When the children's father returned, he saw that things had not gone as planned. He built an iron boat, and as soon as the rain started, he stepped into it. At the same time, the children climbed inside the gourd. The downpour drenched the land. The waters rose so high that the man in his iron vessel and the children in their gourd were soon floating on the waves right outside heaven. When the man knocked on heaven's door, the banging surprised the king of heaven so much that he stopped the rain. The waters receded. The man and the iron boat fell a thousand miles to earth, as did the children in their gourd. When the iron boat hit the earth, it shattered into pieces and the man was killed. The gourd, on the other hand, merely bounced a few times. The children emerged slightly bruised but otherwise in good shape.

However, they were alone on the face of the earth, for everyone else had died in the flood. After some time had passed, Fuxi admitted that he wanted to make love to Nü Gua. Although this didn't feel right to her, she relented. She became pregnant and gave birth to a ball of flesh. When Fuxi saw it, he took an axe very much like one the thunder god had used to threaten his father, and he chopped the fleshy sphere into pieces so small that the wind picked them up and scattered them all around the world. Every place they landed, those bits of flesh became people. Thus Nü Gua became the mother of humanity.

NÜ GUA'S OTHER ACCOMPLISHMENTS

In addition to creating humanity, Nü Gua is famous for the following:

- She patched up a hole in the sky using melted multicolored stones.
- She cut off the legs of a giant tortoise and used them to hold up the sky.
- She marked the cardinal points of the compass with the tortoise's amputated toes.
- She burned reeds and used the ash to dam up the rivers during a flood.
- She instituted marriage and became the goddess of matchmakers and go-betweens.

Why the World Is Such a Mess: Tricksters and Troublemakers

In the beginning, the Winnebago Indians tell us, Earthmaker wanted the world to have structure and organization, so he assigned each species its own lodge. Then the trickster Wakdjunkaga came along and with one enormous fart blew those lodges apart and scattered living creatures everywhere. His uncouth behavior ruined Earthmaker's neat plan and created the world as we know it.

That's what tricksters do. They humanize creation (and mythology) by misbehaving, miscalculating, and making a mess of things. When greed, lechery, and outrageous behavior appear in a myth, when conflict, confusion, and chicanery show their faces, you can bet that a trickster is around. Impulsive, rebellious, entirely without morals, and absolutely guaranteed to make trouble, tricksters sow the seeds of discord with their fumbling ways and open the door to pandemonium.

Like certain people, tricksters have unlimited energy, enormous appetites, and no scruples whatsoever. Deceptive, anarchic, and capricious, tricksters break apart categories, create disorder, follow their instincts, and make us laugh. Their unruly ways subvert the status quo and irritate the self-righteous. They are incapable of delayed gratification, their judgment is bad, and their manners are worse. They fart, sneeze, fall into their own excrement, and do strange things with their bodily parts. Wakdjunkaga, for instance, burned his own anus, ate his intestines (they tasted delicious), put his penis in a box and sent it across the water, and suffered great pain when his right arm got into a fight with his left.

Like us, tricksters repeatedly get caught in traps of their own devise. Yet they inspire affection, for they are irrepressible. They often triumph, they never surrender, and they prove that sometimes it pays to lie—even if sometimes it doesn't. Carl Jung considered the trickster "a collective shadow figure, an epitome of all the inferior traits of character in individuals." Joseph Campbell saw the tricksters as a positive character, "the archetype of the hero, the giver of all great boons." There's something to be said for both views. On the one hand, tricksters are slippery, selfish, and occasionally evil. They lie, cheat, do stupid things, and cause trouble for one and all. On the other hand, they perform the essential task of bringing culture to humanity. They show us how to hunt, cook, and make musical instruments, they force us to work, and, like the African-American trickster Br'er Rabbit, they teach us to tell stories.

Tricksters exist virtually everywhere, although they are especially numerous in African, South American, and Native American mythologies. Here are a few of the best:

Inktomi

Imagine a spider the size of a man. That's the Lakota trickster Inktomi. He knew all languages, including that of rocks and stones, and he was a compelling speaker, although he was often loose with the facts. Many eons ago, for instance, human beings lived in an underground paradise. Everyone was happy—until Inktomi convinced them that life would be more fulfilling on earth. He spoke so glowingly about the possibilities that the entire human race left their Shangri-la behind. And here we are. Ha ha.

Coyote

Coyote, the North American trickster whose penis was so large he had to cart it around in a special pack, was a powerful creator. He killed the monstrous beaver Wishpoosh and used the corpse to fashion the peoples of the Pacific Northwest, making him the creator of humanity. But like any trickster, he also did many foolish things. One time, for instance, he watched the Chickadees throwing their eyes into trees and decided to join in the game. With his eyes in the treetops, he could see far, far away. Unfortunately, the birds stole his eyes, after which he had to fill his eye sockets with hot pitch (either that, or he borrowed two ill-fitting eyes, one from a tiny mouse and one from an enormous buffalo). Coyote's antics created work, sickness, death, pubic hair, Europeans, and other things about which one might have decidedly negative feelings. He was by no means entirely malevolent, though, for he was also responsible for the pleasure human beings receive during sexual intercourse.

Maui

Maui was an ugly god. When he was born, his mother thought he was dead. She wrapped him up in a bundle of her hair and threw him into the ocean, where the sea-fairies raised him. Eventually he found his true family, and one day he went fishing with his brothers. As the youngest brother, he was determined to show them that he could catch the biggest fish. When his brothers refused to give him bait, he baited his hook with his grandmother's jawbone, cast it as far as he could, and pulled up the Polynesian islands from the bottom of the sea. Another time, he stole fire from the fingernails of the goddess Mahui-Ike and gave it to mankind. He also lassoed the sun in a noose and slowed it down to lengthen the day, thereby providing more time in which to work. Despite these (and other) accomplishments, Maui was discontent, for he wished to be immortal. In his attempt to conquer death, he climbed inside Hine-nui-te-Po, the goddess of the underworld, while she was asleep. Unfortunately, a bird saw the whole thing and couldn't stop laughing, which woke up the goddess, whereupon she crushed poor Maui to death.

Eshu

Born of Oshun, the Yoruban goddess of love, Eshu helped human beings by conveying their sacrifices to the gods. But more than anything else, he liked to cause trouble. One day, Eshu decided to break up the long-standing friendship between two farmers whose plots of land were adjoining. Wearing a hat that was black on one side and white on the other, he walked along the border that separated their fields. To the farmer on one side, he seemed to be wearing a black hat. The farmer on the other side insisted his hat was white. Soon the argument became so heated that the king intervened. Once Eshu admitted his role in the quarrel, the king wanted to punish him. Eshu escaped, easily outrunning the king's men and setting fire to houses along the way. As people rushed out of their burning houses clutching their dearest possessions, Eshu offered to guard their bundles for them. He seemed trustworthy. But as soon as their backs were turned, he distributed the bundles to other people. Soon everyone's possessions were mixed up together, and he had achieved his goal: chaos.

Loki

In Greek mythology, the gods are by definition immortal. Not so in Nordic mythology, where the immortality of the gods is fragile and easily threatened, thanks to the trickster Loki. He could become a flea, a flame, a fish, a polar bear, an old woman, or anything he wanted. Yet he was careless with the lives of his fellow deities.

One time, for instance, Odin, Hoenir, and Loki were traveling when they stopped to eat. They stole an ox from a nearby herd and tried to roast it. But no matter how long they prodded the fire, the meat would not cook. An eagle watching from an oak tree—actually the frost giant Thjazi in the shape of the an eagle— offered to help if the three gods would share the meal with him. The gods were willing, and soon the meat was cooked to perfection. However, when they sat down to enjoy it, Thjazi took an unfairly large portion, which made Loki so angry that he picked up a stick and clobbered him with it. To protect himself from Loki's blows, Thjazi grabbed the stick and tried to wrest it out of Loki's hands. No matter how hard he pulled, Loki held on. At last Thjazi flapped his wings and flew into the air with Loki still clutching the stick.

Loki screamed to be let down but Thjazi was now in a bargaining position. He agreed to let him down only if Loki promised to get him something in return: the lovely goddess Idun and her golden apples of youth. Loki agreed. So Thjazi flew to Asgard, the home of the gods, and Loki disembarked.

When he found Idun, he told her that he had discovered some miraculous apples that were as delicious as her own. Naturally, she was curious, even when he told her that the fruit was hanging on a tree in the woods. Intrigued, she picked up her basket of apples and followed him into the woods. As soon as she was out of sight of the other gods, Thjazi swooped down, picked her up, and flew to Jotunheim, the home of the frost giants.

Idun was captive in Jotunheim for a long time. In Asgard, her absence quickly became a serious problem, for the gods were used to partaking of the apples on a daily basis. The apples kept them young. Without them, they started to age. Gray hair sprouted on their heads, their faces became wrinkled, their steps faltered, and they became afraid of death. Everyone wondered where Idun was, and Loki pretended to be as mystified as everyone else. Odin wasn't fooled. Knowing that Loki was to blame, Odin threatened to kill him unless he brought the goddess back. Loki had to comply. He borrowed Freya's magical falcon skin, took the form of a falcon, and flew to Jotunheim. When he arrived, Thjazi was fishing, which gave Loki the chance he needed. He turned Idun into a nut, popped her into his mouth, and flew back to Asgard. By the time Thjazi noticed that she was gone, Loki had a strong head start.

But eagles also fly swiftly, and soon Thjazi was right behind him. Fortunately, the other gods, desperate to get the apples back, were watching. Once Loki soared safely over the wall, they lit a bonfire, and moments later, Thjazi flew over the wall. The flames licked his feathers, scorched his flesh, and sent him tumbling to the ground, where the other gods killed him.

Equilibrium returned. And yet, by his actions, Loki established the possibility that even the gods can grow old and die.

THE SNOW-SHOE GODDESS

After the death of Thjazi, his daughter Skadi was distraught. To help compensate her for the loss, Odin turned her father's eyes into stars but she wanted more: specifically, a few laughs and a husband. The gods agreed to let her select a husband from among them on one condition: she had to choose solely on the basis of their feet. The gods lined up behind a curtain with only that part of their anatomy visible, and Skadi made her decision. She hoped to marry Baldur. Instead, she chose Njord, the god with the most beautiful feet.

Their wedding was a merry occasion. Loki entertained the guests by tying his testicles to the beard of a goat, and Skadi did indeed laugh. The marriage, however, was a failure, for Skadi and Njord were geographically incompatible. She was a mountain girl—Snorri Sturluson calls her the Snow-shoe Goddess—and the cawing sea gulls kept her up at night; he was a sea god who hated to hear the howling wolves. They tried spending nine days in one place and nine days in the other but in the end, Skadi returned to her father's old homestead, where she met her perfect mate: Ullr, the god of skiing.

Death, Destruction, and Apocalypse

Myths about death and the afterlife infiltrate every culture, offering whimsical explanations for why we die, horrifying accounts of what happens next, and once in a while, detailed visions of the end of the world.

Why We Die

You might think that mythological stories that address the question "Why do we die?" would be filled with images of journeys, seasons, and the opposite shore. You might expect death to be perceived as either grand or terrible and to be spoken of in a way that gave meaning and shape to everything that preceded it. Instead, the majority of stories on this topic reach a different conclusion. Death, they seem to agree, needn't have entered the world at all, except that someone miscalculated, got tired, misunderstood, made a bad call, or did something stupid. Death is nothing but a big mistake.

Who made the mistake? Sometimes—rarely—it was a man. For instance, in Burma, death entered the world because a man thought it would be amusing to joke with the sun god by pretending to be dead. Alas, the sun god had no sense of humor and soon death was all too real.

Once in a while a god's mistake resulted in death. In the Pacific island of New Britain, To Purgo, the stupid twin of a better, wiser god, was instructed to tell humanity that they would live eternally while snakes would die. Alas, To Purgo got mixed up and said it the other way around, with disastrous consequences.

Animals are often blamed for the existence of death. In an African story, Toad was assigned the task of carrying an earthenware jug. Be careful, he was told; death is inside. Toad held the jug tightly and was as careful as he could possibly be. Then along came Frog, wanting to help. Toad didn't want to relinquish the responsibility but Frog kept nagging. Eventually Toad relented and let Frog carry the jar. Needless to say, Frog dropped it. The jar shattered and death leaked out into the world.

In another story, told by the Zulus and the Wute of East Africa, the Creator, known as the Old Old One, asked a chameleon to give the people the message that we would not die. But the chameleon dawdled, ate berries, bought a new headdress, gobbled down flies, relaxed in the sun, and fell asleep. After a while, the Old Old One changed his mind and told the lizard—or the snake—to bring the people a revised message, which was that from now on, everyone would face death. The lizard arrived straightaway with the bad news. Not long afterwards, the lazy chameleon showed up. It was too late. Humanity heard the message that life ends in death, and from then on, that's the way it's been.

Despite the evidence of these stories, gods, men, and animals are not primarily the ones held responsible for the sad reality of death. That distinction goes to women. In an Australian myth, a swarm of honey bees took up residence in a hollow tree. Women were not allowed to go near the tree, but one woman, yearning for honey, disobeyed. No sooner did she chop into the tree than an enormous

WHAT'S WRONG IS WRONG:
A STORY FROM INDIA

Incest is unavoidable in creation stories. The problem is an arithmetical one: if you expect a handful of people to populate the earth, they've got to mate with each other, even if they happen to be related. That's one reason why, common as it is, incest goes largely unremarked upon in mythology. An exception occurs in the story of Tefafu, who created human beings in the usual trial-and-error manner. He tried this and that, and finally he got the details right. Instead of feeling pleased with himself, though, he envied his creations and decided to annihilate them. Rain drenched the earth and everyone would have died except that, as often happens in such tales, he saved two people, a brother and a sister. After the deluge, he encouraged them to mate. They didn't want to, for they were convinced that it was wrong to commit incest. He reassured them and they procreated.

But Tefafu tricked them. Incest is wrong, no matter who claims otherwise, and the fruits of such a marriage are inevitably subject to disease. And that is why sickness and death entered the world.

bat unfolded its wings and fluttered out of the trunk. It was the spirit of death.

The Dogon of Mali say that in the beginning, human beings did not die. They turned into snakes instead. One time, though, a young woman wanted to buy a cow from the god Amma. When she asked the price, Amma said, "Death." Not understanding, the woman agreed, and shortly thereafter, her husband died. She protested to no avail, and since then, death has been universal. After the first death, there is every other.

A story from Morocco explains that once upon a time, death was temporary. People would lapse into unconsciousness for a while and then they would return to life. One day, Fatima, the prophet's daughter, heard that the child of her rival had become ill in just this way. Feeling vengeful, she asked her father to make death permanent. And indeed, the child never woke up. Some time later, though, one of

Fatima's sons fell in battle. When she asked her father if her child would be revived, he told her no. For she had asked that death be made permanent; and he had prayed to god on her behalf; and the prayer had been answered.

Finally, in a classic tale told by the Blackfoot Indians, death came into the world after Old Man, the creator, made a woman and a child out of dirt and clay. The woman asked if they would live forever. Old Man hadn't considered that question, so he suggested that they pitch a buffalo chip into the water. If it floats, he said, people will die for four days and then return to life. If it sinks, death will be permanent. The woman didn't like the sound of this. Instead of casting a buffalo chip into the water, she suggested, let's throw a stone. If it floats, eternal life will be ours. If it sinks, life will end in death. Old Man agreed to go by her rules. He threw the stone into the water and it sank to the bottom. Ever since then, death has been our portion.

A Story about Stones

The association of stones with eternity is widespread. In Nigeria, it was said that God's earliest creations were human beings, tortoises, and stones. They were all immortal. When they got old, they were rejuvenated. But the tortoises wished to reproduce. God told them that if they wanted children, they had to accept death. The tortoises agreed to the bargain, and soon they were giving birth and dying. The sight of the little baby tortoises must have inspired the humans, for they made the same deal. But the stones, observing what was happening to tortoises and people, reached a different conclusion. They decided to forego the privilege of having babies. And so today, people and tortoises die but stones are immortal.

Hell and the Afterlife

Hell is other people.

—Jean-Paul Sartre, *No Exit*

What happens after we die? From the beginning of human history, that unanswerable question has engaged mythmakers, all of whom seem to agree that after death, existence continues—elsewhere. In early societies, the kingdom of the dead, generally located under the earth or far away in the west where the sun goes down, was often a place where human beings of all stripes mingled, regardless of moral or economic worth. Later on, the concept of reward and punishment began to reshape the infernal regions, confronting humanity with a selection of possible fates. Sometimes, as in the Christian conception, the afterlife was divided into only two or three parts, the most desirable of which could be reached by those who were born into the right group, behaved in the right way, were initiated into the right religion, or were fortunate enough to be buried correctly. The less desirable destination was more easily, and often more democratically, achieved.

In some cultures, the underworld was a complex, bureaucratic place with many subdivisions. The Japanese underworld has sixteen sections; the ascetic Jains of India picture a purgatory of seven sections which could be distinguished by the sort of sinner admitted or the type of the torture applied; and the Hindu hell boasts over two dozen departments, the Dante-esque horrors of which are suggested by their names: Horrifying, Most Horrifying, Dark, Utter Dark, Wheel of Time, Foundationless, Diarrhea, Forest of Sword Blades, Burning Vat, Thorny, Saw-Toothed, Dog-Eating, Pincers, Red Hot Iron Balls, Groat Gravel, Horrible, Ash River, Worm-Eating, Blood- and Pus-Eating, Sharp, Wheel, Drying Up, Endless, Slime-Eating, Pressing Machine, Scorpion-Eating, Feces and Urine, and Wolf-Eating (for "stupid backbiters and men who take bribes").

Here are a few other illustrations of the realms of the dead, with an emphasis on the infernal regions:

- Egyptian Hell. After entrance into the "Hall of Double Justice," the newly dead faced a simple procedure presided over by Osiris, the lord of the dead, Anubis, the god of embalming, Thoth, the scribe of the underworld, and forty-two judges who represented the forty-two Egyptian provinces and the forty-two separate parts of the conscience. Before these observers, the dead person's heart would be placed on one side of a delicately calibrated scale, while on the other side there would be a single feather, the ideogram of Maat, goddess of truth and justice. If the heart proved heavier than the feather, a patchwork monster, part lion, part hippopotamus, and part crocodile, would devour it on the spot. To avoid that fate, it helped to make offerings to Osiris, to be buried with the appropriate talismans and, once dead, to make a negative confession in which one denied having committed various sins while alive. None of that mattered, though, if the heart and the feather were not perfectly balanced.

Anubis. Typically pictured in a crouching position, the jackal-headed god is holding an ointment used in embalming, a process that he invented.

If they were balanced, one could be assured of eternal bliss amidst the gods and the mortal dead. However, even in the afterlife, canals and dykes needed to be maintained, and chores had to be done. To make certain that eternity was relaxing for the departed, Egyptians buried their loved ones with little statuettes that would do the work for them.

- The Mesopotamian underworld. The night before he died, Enkidu, dear friend of Gilgamesh, dreamed about the "house from which none who enters ever returns, down the road from which there is no coming back." This infernal residence was the gloomy palace of Irkalla or Ereshkigal, the Queen of Darkness. Within it, the inhabitants sit in total darkness, dressed like birds and eating dust and clay. The gods who controlled their fate included the handless, footless demon Namtar, Ereshkigal's messenger and vizier, who represents the evil side of fate and brings disease to human beings; Nergal, a plague god sometimes named as Ereshkigal's husband; Ningizzida and Neti, gatekeepers of heaven and the underworld, respectively; Belit-Sheri, keeper of the book of death; and the seven nameless sky gods who were banished into the underworld for their misdeeds and forced to be the judges of the dead.

- She'ol. An early Hebrew concept many contemporary Jews are unlikely to recognize, She'ol is a dark, dusty, despair-filled place. Located in the depths of a black pit at the bottom of the universe, this is where the dead, both good and bad, are bolted in to lead lives of quiet desperation. Unlike the Babylonian underworld, which was infested with demons, She'ol (a word which can also be used simply to mean the grave) was ruled by God, who also ruled heaven and occasionally allowed the worthy to make the journey from one place to the other.

- Gehenna. Initially a real, not imaginary, valley near Jerusalem, this was the site of a Phoenician ritual in which firstborn children were sacrificed to the god Moloch. Later on, the place became a garbage dump where the bodies of criminals and animals were burned. Eventually, the Jews, and presumably everyone else, came to associate the place with hell. Once it entered the realm of the mythological, it was said to be located under the earth, at the foot of a mountain, or beneath the ocean floor. Although Gehenna is a Jewish concept, the Islamic Qur'an features a memorable description of it in which Gehenna, described as an "ill resort" for the insolent, becomes a monster, a smoky, buzzing synthesis of hundreds of thousands of demons, each with thousands of rattling, groaning mouths.

- Niflheim. The Viking underworld was an icy, dismal land of fog and shadow, not unlike the underworld of Homer, but colder. Guarded by the dog Garm, whose duty it was to keep the living out, and presided over by the black-and-white decomposing goddess Hel, it was located beneath one of the three roots of Yggdrasil, the sacred ash which was the tree of the world. Very little happened there. In striking contrast to this boring place was Valhalla, the Viking heaven, a gigantic hall with 540 doors where by day heroic Norse warriors could enjoy the pleasures of combat (only, no death!) and by night they could companionably drink mead, which was served to them by the Valkyries. Women could enter this hallowed hall by volunteering to die (generally by hanging or strangulation) and joining their men on the funeral pyre.

- The Christian hell. Prototypically described by Saint Augustine (354–430 CE) in *City of God* as a bottomless pit featuring a lake of fire and brimstone, it offered a multitude of hideous tortures for the body and the soul. These torments served a double purpose by punishing the damned and simultaneously rewarding the residents of heaven, who had a clear view of the proceedings. Saint Thomas Aquinas (and others) believed that the sight of these gruesome yet entertaining events would cheer the blessed spirits of the higher realm and contribute to their happiness. Unfortunately, the likelihood of getting to enjoy this eternal Schadenfreude was slim, for at many points in the history of the church, the agonies of hell were deemed virtually unavoidable. In the fourteenth century, for example, Berthold of Regensburg preached that only one person in a hundred thousand could expect to be saved from its white-hot torments.

- Mictlan, the Mesoamerican underworld. The Aztecs believed that the manner of one's death determined the quality of one's afterlife. So all those who died in battle, in sacrifice, in childbirth, by drowning, by lightning, or by succumbing to one of the diseases sent by Tlaloc, the rain god, went directly to one of the thirteen levels of heaven. Everyone else had to travel through the nine levels of the underworld, a journey that took four years. During that time, the soul, accompanied by a yellow dog, had to overcome a series of challenges including clashing mountains, obsidian knives, and two kinds of sacrifice. At last the soul took the jade beads, hot chocolate, and tools with which it had been cremated, presented them to the goddess Mictecacihuatl and her husband Mictlanteuhtli, the lord of death, and gained entrance to Mictlan, the deepest level of the underworld and the soul's ultimate destination.

Mictlanteuhtli, Aztec god of the dead. From a basalt statue carved around 1500, shortly before Hernando Cortés landed in Mexico.

- Chinese Buddhist Hell. Although residence here is not usually eternal, in that most souls leave it to be reincarnated as gods, humans, animals, or certain kinds of demons, it features the full spectrum of tortures, the majority of which are clearly geared to the crime; for example, misers are forced to swallow molten gold and silver. This hell, like that of the Egyptians, also had a bureaucratic edge. Horse-Face and Ox-Head, two representatives of the king of hell, were expected to arrive at the scene of death with an official warrant and then to accompany the dead soul on its journey. Hell itself was subdivided into eighteen sections, each assigned to crimes which ranged from back-biting to eating human flesh. There were ten courts presided over by kings, each with a slightly different function, and a number of towns, including Feng-tu, where the courts were located, and Wang-ssu-ch'eng, the town of Those who Died in Accidents. Being sent there was not a good thing, because in order to reincarnate, accident victims (and suicides) needed to find their own replacements—and it had to be someone who died in the same way. So after three years in hell, during which time they subsisted as starving demons, those souls returned to the land of the living, but only to haunt the spot where they died in hopes of arranging a similar catastrophe for someone else.

As for the souls of the just, they might be sent to K'un-lun Mountain, the home of the gods, which was ruled over by the Lady Queen of the West from a nine-story jade palace. Or they might be sent to the Land of Extreme Felicity in the West, where all delights would be theirs except for the pleasure of sleeping late, which they could never enjoy because every dawn it was their duty to offer flowers to the Buddhas of all lands.

Ragnarok: The Final Battle

Most early mythologies subscribe to the doctrine of cycles and seasons. The destruction of the world and the end of time simply don't enter the picture they way they do in Christianity or Islam. However, there are occasional exceptions, most notably in the frozen north, where the long, dark winter nights gave people plenty of time to mull over the depressing possibilities. Norse mythology, which was highly influenced by Christianity, includes a detailed and dramatic scenario of destruction. The story of Ragnarok, the doom of the gods, like the conclusion of a great novel, ties up many stories all at once. It starts small, with wickedness and bad weather, climaxes with what can only be considered Apocalypse, and ends on a note of renewal, nostalgia, and hope.

The Doom of the Gods

Ragnarok, the last great battle of the gods, is destined to begin with an epidemic of bad behavior, followed by a three-year outbreak of strife, hatred, and war. Snorri Sturluson, the thirteenth-century politician who recounted this story, described this arduous period as an "axe-age, a sword-age, a wind-age, a wolf-age," during which brother will turn against brother, and incest and adultery will be widespread. Afterwards, Fimbulwinter, the ultimate global freeze, will descend upon the earth. For three years, snow, frost, and stinging winds will whip unceasingly through the air as a prelude to the catastrophes which follow. Then a wolf will swallow the sun, another wolf will swallow the moon, the stars will drop from the sky, and the world tree, Yggdrasil, will be uprooted.

The savage Fenrir Wolf, who is so big that when he opens his mouth, his lower jaw scrapes the earth and his upper jaw touches the sky, will escape from the magic ribbon around his neck. The Midgard Serpent, Jormungand, who is coiled underwater encircling the Earth, his tail in his mouth, will crash through the surface of the sea, stirring up tidal waves and spewing poison in all directions. And the gods, who are doomed, will fight side by side with the warriors in Valhalla.

A nineteenth-century engraving of Heimdall blowing the horn that will announce the doom of the gods.

The trickster Loki, after eons in chains, will burst free and set sail in a ship made entirely from the fingernails of the dead. With the help of the fire giants, his daughter Hel, and all the dead souls from her domain, he will cross the Bifrost Bridge, where Heimdall, who can see for a hundred miles and has such acute hearing that he can hear wool

THE WOLF FENRIR

Long before Ragnarok, the savage wolf Fenrir, one of Loki's children, threatened the gods. Although they tried to capture him, he broke through their chains. At last the dwarfs made an unbreakable ribbon by braiding together the roots of a mountain, the spittle of a bird, and the breath of a fish. The gods had a tough time convincing Fenrir to let them slip that frail-looking ribbon over his neck. He agreed only if, as proof of their good intentions, one of them placed his hand in Fenrir's mouth. Tyr, the god of war, volunteered.

*The wolf Fenrir,
son of Loki*

He bravely inserted his left hand between the wolf's jaws. As the magic ribbon slipped over his neck and tightened, Fenrir realized what was happening and bit off Tyr's hand. The other gods laughed but the ribbon held, allowing the gods to rope Fenrir to a rock and prop his mouth open with a sword. Not until Ragnarok would Fenrir roam freely.

grow, stands ready to blow his horn and signal the arrival of Ragnarok. He and Loki will fight; both will die in the encounter. The Bifrost Bridge will go up in flames and Asgard, the home of the gods, will be destroyed. The Fenrir Wolf will swallow Odin and be killed in turn by Odin's son, who will plant his foot on the wolf's jaw and tear it apart. Thor will slay the Midgard Serpent but will die himself, overcome by its venom. The one-handed god Tyr will attack the dog Garm, who guards the gates of the underworld. Both will die in the struggle. In the end, all the gods will die with the exception of the giant Surt, who will set all of creation aflame. Then the earth will sink into the sea, and the human race will perish.

Hope will remain. The earth, purified through immersion in the sea, will rise, greener and lovelier than ever. Although the gods will be dead, their sons will live. Baldur and his brother Hoder, sons of Frigg and Odin, will chat about times gone by and they will discover, hidden in the thick grass, the golden chessmen that once were the playthings of the gods. A new sun, the daughter of the first, will glow in the sky. And it will turn out that a man and a woman have hidden in a wood, allowing human beings to repopulate the earth and the whole process to begin again.

From the Annals of Mythology: The Legendary Mythologists

Despite what some people like to think, myths do not float into our minds from the ether, the collective unconscious, the oral tradition, or the misty recesses of our dreams. Myths are passed on to us by storytellers who commit their version of the myth to tablets, parchment, paper, stone, clay, or marble. These individuals, anonymous and otherwise, are our guides to those tales. Among them are Hesiod, whose work describes the Greek creation and the birth of the gods, and Snorri Sturluson, a sly thirteenth-century Icelandic politician who compiled the old Nordic myths about the death of the gods.

The Life of Hesiod

One day in the eighth century BCE, a farmer named Hesiod was tending a flock of lambs on Mount Helicon when the Muses appeared before him, handed him a sprig of flowering laurel, and "breathed a sacred voice" into his mouth. He described that event, along with stories about the origin of the world and the genealogy of the gods, in his first book, *Theogony* (from *theo*, the Greek word for god). Most of what we know about the birth of the Greek gods is derived from this source.

After that visit, Hesiod continued to till the rocky fields of Boeotia, northwest of Athens, but he also wrote. In addition to *Theogony*, he wrote *Works and Days*, *A Catalogue of Women and Heroines*, a brief work about astronomy, and a poem about divination by birds. As a rhapsode or wandering minstrel, Hesiod recited these poems at contests which then (as now) were an important element in the lives of poets. Legend has it that at one such competition in Chalkis, he triumphed over Homer.

Despite his status as a prize-winning poet, Hesiod's life was not easy. A dour man and a misogynist, he was particularly rankled by the wrong-headed ways of his brother, Perses, who, after their father's death, finagled the greater part of the paternal farm (possibly by bribing local officials) and nonetheless managed to get into debt. Rather than farming, Perses preferred to hang out in the market place, where he liked to "gape at politicians and give ear to all the quarrels." Hesiod could hardly stand it.

So in an attempt to set his brother right, Hesiod wrote *Works and Days*. In that poem, he recounted the stories of Prometheus, Pandora, and the ages of man, vividly depicted the labor of the agricultural year, recommended the best use to make of the days of the month ("The first ninth is a wholly painless day,/Good to beget both sons and daughters . . .") and handed out copious advice to Perses on such subjects as when to travel, when to sharpen his sickles, when to cut timber, when to tell his slaves to build barns and when to give them a rest, which deities to pray to before ploughing (Zeus and Demeter), what to wear while sowing seed (nothing), and when to pick grapes, a recommendation that relies on the ability to recognize stars and constellations, knowledge even the hapless Perses would have possessed:

> *But when Orion and the Dog Star move*
> *Into the mid-sky, and Arcturus sees*
> *The rosy-fingered Dawn, then Perses, pluck*
> *The clustered grape, and bring your harvest home.*

Unable to leave it at that, Hesiod permitted himself to give suggestions on matters far beyond the agricultural. Like Polonius, he didn't refrain just because his advice was thoroughly self-evident. He reminded his brother to be courteous to his neighbors, to shun gossip, to wash his hands before offering wine to Zeus, and to extend dinner invitations to "your friend, but not your enemy." "Don't be called too hospitable, nor yet unfriendly," he wrote, and he warned poor Perses against cutting his fingernails in public, being rude at feasts, leaving the ladle in the mixing bowl, and bathing in water "With which a woman bathed herself before; The punishment is awful, for a time." He gave his brother detailed instructions about where to urinate (neither on nor near the road, and not "in springs, or in the mouths of streams which flow Seaward. . . . And please, do not relieve yourself in them"), what kind of winter coat to wear (fleecy, with a "tunic to the ground, woven with thicker woof than warp"), and when to get married (around age thirty—although women typically married at sixteen).

His philosophy is clear. "If in your heart you pray for riches, do/ These things: pile work on work, and still more work." To make sure the message was clear, he reiterated: "You foolish Perses, go to work!"

Hesiod's moralizing is so irksome, his outlook so puritanical, and his beliefs so rigid that it's a relief to hear that his hypocrisy was eventually revealed. Among his caveats to his brother, Hesiod had written:

> *Also, he*
> *Who harms a guest or suppliant, or acts*
> *Unseemly, sleeping with his brother's wife,*
> *. . . He angers Zeus himself, and in the end*
> *He pays harsh penalties for all his sins.*

Precisely these sorts of unseemly actions, or the accusation of such, brought about Hesiod's demise. It happened after the contest at Chalkis, when Hesiod traveled to Delphi and was warned that he might die in "the fair grove of Nemean Zeus." On this basis, he decided not to go to Nemea. Instead, he stayed in Oenoë in Locri, a place which unbeknownst to the poet was also sacred to Nemean Zeus. It was there that Hesiod evidently seduced the sister of his host—a big mistake in a land where hospitality was a primary virtue and the relationship between guest and host was revered. Writing a thousand years later, Pausanias reported that Hesiod may have been wrongly accused, but the evidence went against him. It was said that as a result of her union with Hesiod, the nameless sister became the mother of the lyric poet Stesichorus.

Hesiod paid the harshest penalty for his dalliance, for he was murdered by the woman's brothers (an event described by Thucydides) and his body was tossed into the sea. Afterwards, Plutarch reports, dolphins carried his body back to land and the men who killed him were drowned. Some time later, when a plague assaulted the citizens and cattle of Orchomenos in Boeotia, a delegation from that tormented place went to Delphi to consult the oracle. They were told to sail to Naupaktos and bring back Hesiod's bones, which would be revealed to them by a crow.

And indeed, when they landed, they saw a crow sitting on a rock. A hollow in that rock cradled the bones, which back in Orchomenos came to be regarded much like relics of the saints in medieval Christendom. At last Hesiod was given a proper burial. "His name rang loudest on the stone of Wisdom," said the verse that Pausanias saw inscribed on his tombstone. "Hesiod lies here."

HESIOD ON THE JOYS OF SUMMER

But when the thistle blooms and on the tree
The loud cicada sits and pours his song
Shrill and continuous, beneath his wings,
Exhausting summertime has come. The goats
Are very fat, and wine is very good.
Women are full of lust, but men are weak,
Their heads and limbs drained dry by Sirius,
Their skin parched from the heat. But at this time,
I love a shady rock, and Bibline wine,
A cake of cheese, and goat's milk, and some meat
Of heifers pastured in the woods, uncalved,
Or first-born kids. Then may I sit in shade
And drink the shining wine, and eat my fill
And turn my face to meet the fresh West Wind . . .

Snorri Sturluson

The Icelandic poet Snorri Sturluson (1179–1241) is remembered for his literary contributions, but he led the life of a Machiavellian politician. Raised in privileged circumstances in the home of a chieftain who was a respected historian, he sought riches and prestige, and he found them, acquiring property, power, and enemies throughout his life. After marrying an heiress, he too became a chieftain, and a litigious one at that. He was so ruthless and arrogant that he even took his brothers into court. Nonetheless, his influence grew. When he was thirty-five years old, he was elected "lawspeaker," the highest position on the Icelandic high court. He held that position from 1215 to 1218. And that's when his troubles began.

On a trip to Norway, Snorri was able to deflect a planned invasion of Iceland by convincing the Norwegian king, Haakon IV, that with Snorri's help he could become king of Iceland. Haakon, who was fourteen years old, was pleased, and Snorri became the man of the hour. He returned in triumph to Iceland, was reelected lawspeaker, and plunged back into politics. He was conniving and vengeful, and like other members of his family (including his illegitimate son Óraekja, who was known for his rapacious methods of tax collection), he was drawn to intrigue.

Yet he was also a scholar, a historian, and a poet. He noticed that, although people were interested in the pagan myths, they didn't really know those old tales, a situation which was particularly embarrassing for poets and intellectuals. So around 1220, Snorri—he goes by his first name—began the *Prose Edda* (in contrast to the *Poetic Edda,* an anonymous collection written three or four centuries earlier), part of which is a poetic handbook explaining the intricacies of Iceland verse and part of which is a compendium of Norse mythology.

The timing was propitious, for pagan mythology was under assault by the Christian clergy, who were so anxious to eliminate all vestiges of the ancient gods that they even changed the names of the days of the week, eliminating Tuesday, Wednesday, Thursday, Friday, and Saturday (the days of Tyr, Woden, Thor, Frigg, and Saturn, respectively) in favor of Third Day, Mid-week-day, Fifth Day, Fast Day, and Wash Day. (Sunday and Monday, days of the sun and the moon, were allowed to remain). In that environment, the traditional myths were fast disappearing. Snorri collected the old tales and wove them together with numerous quotations from poetry. He did it with charm, humor, and a refusal to take it all too seriously.

Meanwhile, his political machinations continued. In 1237, nineteen years after his first trip, Snorri sailed to Norway once again. When he was ready to return to his homeland, King Haakon, who was losing faith, refused to let him leave. Snorri went anyway, which made the king his implacable enemy. Haakon called in several of Snorri's enemies, including two members of the family, and commanded that he be assassinated. On September 22, 1241, Snorri Sturluson was murdered in his home by his son-in-law.

If Snorri's diplomatic career ultimately came to naught, his literary and historical efforts were a resounding triumph. He wrote a biography of Saint Olaf, another of Egil, the tenth-century Viking poet of whom he was a descendant, and *Heimskringla,* a history of the Norwegian kings that begins with the god Odin and ends in the year 1184. His most famous book is the *Prose Edda.* The mythological section begins with a tongue-in-cheek warning that "Christians . . . must not believe in pagan gods," and concludes with a bemused shrug: "And now, if you have anything more to ask, I can't think how you can manage it, for I've never heard anyone tell more of the story of the world."

AN ABECEDARIUM OF
GODDESSES

magine the Ice Age, when wooly mammoths roamed the earth and agriculture wasn't even a dream. During that "remote and creepy time," as H. L. Mencken called it, life was short, harsh, anxiety-filled and, one might think, entirely unenviable.

Yet one aspect of that era causes many people to look back longingly. For in the dawn of history, they believe, goddess worship was ubiquitous. As evidence proponents of this theory cite the work of artists who carved a spectacular array of figurines, almost entirely female or of indeterminate gender, from bone, stone, marble, clay, antler, and ivory. Some of those ancient statuettes are round, sexual, with exaggerated breasts and buttocks; others are sleek, narrow, Brancusi-like. Some are birdlike, snakelike, fishlike, beelike, or inscribed with spirals, labyrinths, and crescent moons. Some look pregnant; others have strangely elongated necks and are clearly phallic. The most famous is a heavy-breasted, thick-thighed, limestone figurine small enough to hold in one hand, notable for being both cellulitic and curiously cute. Carved between 27,000 and 22,000 years ago, this Paleolithic relic, discovered in 1908 near the banks of the Danube, is known as the Venus of Willendorf.

Despite that evocative name, we know very little about this or any of the figurines found scattered throughout Europe, the Middle

East, and parts of Asia. We don't know if they were erotic images, religious icons, household objects, or charms meant to promote fertility. We do know that there are thousands of them. That abundance, together with the absence of an equivalent number of male figures, led U.C.L.A. professor Marija Gimbutas and members of the Goddess Movement she helped inspire to conclude that early civilizations revered women and practiced some form of goddess worship. Although many archaeologists vehemently dispute her conclusion, Gimbutas's 1974 book *The Gods and Goddesses of Old Europe* (later retitled *The Goddesses and Gods of Old Europe*) made an enormous impact. It created a vision of a peaceful, spiritual world in which the Goddess in her many manifestations was a supreme deity, a creator, the queen of heaven, the ruler of the underworld, Mother Earth, Mother Nature, and more.

> *We have a beautiful mother*
> *Her green lap immense*
> *Her brown embrace eternal*
> *Her blue body everything we know.*
>
> —Alice Walker

A Minoan snake goddess, c. 1600 BCE. A drawing of a figurine found in the palace at Knossos. on Crete. (Credit: Hannah Berman)

Thanks to luck and archaeology, a few specific spots have been identified as sanctuaries of the Goddess. Those places include Malta, c. 15,000 BCE, where inhabitants worshipped in massive temples designed around the image of the female body; Çatal Hüyük, a mud brick town on the plains of Anatolia in Turkey which flourished for eight centuries before it was decimated by volcanoes and fire around 5,700 BCE; and Crete, home of Ariadne, where goddess worship reached its zenith, and the citizenry created an outpouring of art so joyous that the Greeks envied them.

Despite compelling archaeological evidence from these and other places, the idea of the ancient Goddess continues to attract hostile criticism from those who contend that artifacts do not equal theology, that analysis is all too often a matter of wishful thinking, and that the extent and reality of goddess worship, even in places like Çatal Hüyük, is purely speculative. Nonetheless, in the minds of many, those ancient goddess-worshipping societies were a sort of utopia: egalitarian, artistic, life-affirming, and attuned to the cycles of nature, the rhythms of the body, and the aspirations of the spirit.

But nothing lasts forever. As the Paleolithic age melted into the Neolithic, the great Goddess began to weaken, while her son/lover, once little more than her consort, grew in statue and eventually became dominant. No one can say why this happened. One widely discussed notion suggests that Goddess worship went into decline after patriarchal invaders vanquished goddess-worshipping communities. Mythological shifts followed in the wake of military conquest, and the old myths were altered to reflect the new political realities. If this scenario is accurate, mythology as we think we know it is a revisionist narrative told from the perspective of the oppressor, who got the last word.

Or perhaps women were worshipped most fervently when childbirth was the greatest of mysteries and no one knew what induced pregnancy. (Three suspected causes, according to Robert Graves: the wind, swallowing insects, eating beans.) Women were venerated while men, deemed irrelevant, were treated accordingly. The shift came, H. L. Mencken proposed, "when some primeval and forgotten Harvey discovered the physiological role of the father. It was . . . the most profound and revolutionary discovery ever made in the world." Afterwards, the balance of power shifted—which may explain why goddesses like Durga and Kali, who once controlled the forces of life and death without benefit of male assistance, became the wives of Shiva, who was worshipped in the form of a phallus.

A third hypothesis, developed by Leonard Shain in *The Alphabet Versus the Goddess,* blames the demise of the goddess on literacy. He suggests that the spread of the alphabet, which favors the linear, logical, left side of the brain, doomed goddess worship, which relies upon intuitive, holistic, right-brain ways of thinking—and that the proliferation of images in the age of television and the internet is stimulating the right brain and promoting a return to the goddess.

No matter what caused the demise of goddess worship, there is widespread interest in the notion that, once upon a time, the Goddess ruled. That idea has been extant at least since 1861, when a Swiss criminal court judge named Johann Jakob Bachofen suggested that human development proceeded in stages, each of which he associated with a deity, a celestial body, and a form of social organization. Stage one, he wrote in his book *Mother Right,* was a time of rampant promiscuity: he tied it to Aphrodite, the earth, and natural law. Stage two was linked to Demeter, the moon, and matriarchy. These stages, both characterized by goddess worship, collapsed in the wake of stage three, which he associated with Dionysus, Apollo and the sun. Stage three is patriarchy.

Bachofen's theories have bounced in and out of fashion, influencing among others Freidrich Engels, Sigmund Freud, Carl Jung, and Jane E. Harrison, who suggested in her monumental *Prolegomena* (1903) that we have lost knowledge of the Great Mother Goddess who once reigned supreme. "The Great Mother is prior to the masculine divinities," she wrote. Before the Greeks, before God, there was the Goddess.

In recent decades, this vision of the distant past and the omnipotent goddess has blossomed, particularly within the worlds of academe, women's studies, and feminist spirituality. An astonishing array of study groups, ritual circles, workshops, Web sites, and consumer items proclaims that goddess worship, the religion of the Ice Age, has returned. Or perhaps it has merely arrived. For although primitive people may (or may not) have worshiped the great goddess as a supreme diety, it's also true that the goddess movement expresses a contemorary need and is in certain ways a modern creation. In any case, whether she represents ecological awareness, a rejection of patriarchal values, a harmonious way of living in tune with the cosmos, an aspect of the psyche, or an expression of the divine, the goddess has become a vital presence for many women (and a few men) in a way that would surely stagger the hunters and gatherers of long ago.

This much is indisputable: cast about in the world of mythology and you will come across goddesses of every stripe. There are goddesses of the earth, the moon, the sun, the stars, and the underworld, goddesses of birth, death, love, sex, war, and wisdom, goddesses zoological and botanical, cosmological and cultural, goddesses who weave and goddesses who worry. In the history of mythology, heroines who accomplish remarkable deeds are relatively few, but goddesses—eternal, earthy, transcendent, and yet recognizably human in their reactions—abound. All told, there are more than eleven thousand goddesses, a minuscule percentage of whom appear in these pages.

This section includes major goddesses like Inanna and Isis and minor ones like Jari and Uke Mochi. (It does not, however, include Greek goddesses, who are discussed in the next section.) Arranged alphabetically (which is to say, in no particular order), they form a chorus whose song dates from the earliest chapters of human history.

Amaterasu

The sun goddess Amaterasu, chief divinity in the Japanese pantheon, was the brilliant shining daughter of Izanagi and Izanami, she was born from either her father's left eye or her mother's menstrual blood. Despite that noble heritage, she had trouble getting along with her siblings. Her brother Susanowo was particularly troublesome.

To determine once and for all who was more powerful, they agreed to a contest in which the one who created the largest number of male deities would be declared the winner. Amaterasu grabbed her brother's sword, snapped it into three, chewed each piece, and spat it out, thereby creating three gods. Susanowo took his sister's fertility beads and using a similar method, created five male deities. Naturally, Susanowo claimed victory. But so did Amaterasu. When she argued that the deities he created came from her beads and hence she should be given credit, Susanowo lost his temper. He destroyed the rice fields, threw excrement around the palace, and pushed a flayed piebald horse through a hole in the roof of Amaterasu's weaving hall. When the horse crashed to the floor, one of the weavers—perhaps Amaterasu herself—accidentally hit her genitals against the shuttle of the spinning wheel and died.

After their contest, Amaterasu was so frightened of Susanowo that she retreated into the Rock Cave of Heaven and the world was plunged into darkness. Eight hundred gods and goddesses who lived on the Plain of High Heaven tried to convince Amaterasu to show her face and relight the world, but she wouldn't budge. Finally, one of them hung a mirror on a tree, and another, the goddess Ame-no-Uzume, performed an erotic dance that exposed her breasts and genitals. Her movements were so clever that the assembled deities couldn't stop laughing. Hearing their roars, Amaterasu grew curious. She peered out to see what was so funny, and her own brilliant reflection caught her eye. When she stepped out for a closer look in the mirror, one of the gods pulled her out of the cave while another took a magic cord and barricaded it so she couldn't retreat. In this way, Amaterasu, having been seduced by her own image, returned to heaven. Sunlight once again brightened the world, and mirrors became sacred objects.

As for Susanowo, the gods shaved off his beard, pulled out his toenails, and flung him out of heaven. He became the god of storms and disorder, and in time he moved to the underworld.

Bastet

To anyone who has ever been in thrall to a cat, the general absence of cat goddesses is inexplicable. Only the ancient Egyptians, who worshipped the cat-headed Bastet, seem to have recognized the ineffable perfection of that animal. Before 1000 BCE, Bastet was perceived as a sun goddess with the head of a lion and worshipped for her ability to heal. She was also the wife, daughter, or sister of the sun god Ra, as well as his protector. Every night, after Ra sailed across the sky in his little boat, he entered the underworld and was attacked by the evil serpent Apep, who represented the forces of chaos. Every dawn, the fierce battle came to an end when Bastet slashed the serpent's vertebrae and decapitated him.

(Credit: Hannah Berman)

Around 1000 BCE, Bastet's appearance and demeanor changed, especially in Bubastis, which became the capital of Egypt around 950 BCE Artists began to depict her as a cat or as a woman with the head of a cat. No longer a sun goddess, she became a lunar deity and was associated with love, sex, music, dance, and pleasures of all kinds. During the annual feast held in her honor, celebrants danced lasciviously, shook sacred rattles and, according to Herodotus, consumed more wine than during the entire rest of the year.

In honor of Bastet, the Egyptians also carved statues, mummified (and perhaps sacrificed) hundreds of thousands of cats, and buried them in special cemeteries. Bastet's popularity began to wane in the fourth century BCE, but the Egyptians continued to protect cats in ways that we can scarcely imagine. One Roman learned that the hard way when he accidentally killed one. "The populace crowded to the house of the Roman who had committed this 'murder'," reports Diodorus Siculus, a Greek historian of the first century BCE who traveled in Egypt and observed these events, "and neither the efforts of magistrates sent by the king to protect him nor the universal fear inspired by the might of Rome could avail to save the man's life."

Benten

Around 500 BCE, a traveler named Yu-kie told the Emperor of China about an amazing kingdom a thousand li distant where the women lived in fine palaces and married serpents, who conveniently remained in holes in the ground. However, when a dragon who lurked in a nearby cave was snatching up little children and devouring them, the kingdom descended into chaos. The goddess Benten couldn't bear it, so she floated down on a cloud of dust and married the dragon, although due to his revolting appearance and terrible habits, she did it reluctantly. Afterwards, peace came to the kingdom.

In the twelfth century, Benten became a popular Buddhist deity in Japan, where she is the goddess of music, eloquence, wealth, love, beauty, and geishas. Also called Benzaiten or Dai-ben-zai-ten ("Great Divinity of the Reasoning Faculty"), she brings luck in marriage, helps gamblers and speculators of all kinds, and prevents earthquakes by mating with the white snakes who swim beneath the island of Japan. Like many goddesses, she is also the queen of the sea, and as such is worshipped on islands and along the shore.

Her greater distinction is that she is the only goddess numbered among the Shichi Fukujin, the Seven Deities of Happiness and Good Fortune. They sail together on a treasure ship which pulls into port every New Year's Eve carrying a hat that makes the wearer invisible, a sacred key, an inexhaustible purse, a clove, a magic raincoat, and other lucky objects. Put a picture of that treasure ship beneath your pillow, it is said, and you are sure to have an auspicious dream.

The Lucky Seven

In the seventeenth century, a Japanese monk rounded up a group of immortals known collectively as the Shichi Fukujin, the Seven Deities of Happiness and Good Fortune. They are:

- Ebisu, a Shinto god of profit and hard work.
- Daikoku, a Shinto god of prosperity and agriculture, often shown perched on bales of rice.
- Bishamonten, a Buddhist god of war, protector against demons, and symbol of law and authority.
- Fukurokuju, a Chinese god of wisdom, popularity, and long life.
- Jurojun, a Chinese god of longevity and happy old age.
- Hotei Osho, a roly-poly Buddhist god of generosity and long life.
- Benten, the goddess of love, marriage, geishas, and wealth.

Brigit

When a new religion sweeps away an earlier one, often the old divinities do not die. Instead, they are fused with the new gods and incorporated into the new religion. A prime example is the Celtic goddess Brigit, who began as a fertility goddess charged with protecting flocks and ended up as the foster mother of Jesus. Originally, she was the daughter of the Dagda, the chief god of the Irish pantheon. Like many Celtic goddesses, she was a triple goddess comprised of three sisters, each named Brigit, each the mother of a son. One sister was the goddess of poetry, divination, arcane knowledge, and learning, one was the goddess of healing and childbirth, and one was the goddess of metalwork, weaving, and brewing. In this form, Brigit was so widely worshipped that Imbolc, one of the four major festivals of the Celtic year, was dedicated to her.

In the sixth century, Christians began to tell the story of another Brigit, the daughter of a slave woman and a Druid. Born at sunrise, she was fed the milk of a white cow with red ears, a color combination in Celtic mythology that indicates the creature is from the Otherworld. While Brigit was still a child, her father converted to Christianity. Nonetheless, when Brigit told him that she wanted to enter a convent, he was adamant that she should marry instead. To prevent that from happening, she blinded herself in one eye. (Either that or an old woman with one eye held her prisoner inside an icy mountain.) She eventually got her wish and founded an order in County Kildare. Her generosity was legendary. Her cows could provide a lake of milk every day along with many baskets of butter. She could turn water into ale and with a single measure of the stuff, she could satisfy seventeen churches full of people. When she walked, flowers and shamrocks sprouted up in her footsteps, and no matter how much food or drink she gave away, there was always more. Like other great goddesses, she came to be known as the Queen of Heaven. She was also incorporated into the Christian story as the foster mother of Jesus and the midwife of the Virgin Mary, and in those capacities, she was revered. Some years after she died in 523, her body was supposedly placed into the same tomb as Saint Patrick (who died around 461), and for almost seven centuries after her death, the nuns in her order tended a perpetual flame in her honor. That ended in 1220, when the Archbishop of Dublin put a stop to it. Her feast day is still celebrated on February 1, the pagan holiday of Imbolc.

Cerridwen

The Welsh goddess Cerridwen was a sorceress, a shape-shifter, a lunar goddess, and a hag so fearsome that she was symbolized by a white sow who ate the dead. She was also the keeper of the Cauldron of Inspiration and Knowledge, which she decided to use one day on behalf of one of her offspring. She had two children: a beautiful daughter named Crearwy and an ugly boy named Afagddu. To compensate her son for his unfortunate appearance, Cerridwen wanted to give him the gift of wisdom. She stewed up a magical potion in the cauldron, asked a blind man to kindle the fire, and set the cauldron over a low flame. Because it had to simmer for a year and a day, she asked a boy named Gwion Bach to watch the pot. He watched it dutifully for almost the entire time. Then one day, while Cerridwen was gathering herbs and casting spells, three drops splashed onto his finger and he instinctively licked it.

With that single gesture, Gwion Bach, a mere mortal, gained all the knowledge that had been intended for Afagddu and foresaw everything that was to happen. He also earned Cerridwen's ire. As she lunged after him, he ran away and the cauldron burst. He turned into a hare and she became a greyhound speeding after him. When he leaped into the water and became a fish, she took the shape of an otter, slipping easily through the waves. He became a little bird and soared into the air, whereupon she turned into a falcon. Yet still he managed to evade her. Finally, desperate to hide, he flew into a barn, dove into an enormous pile of wheat, and disguised himself as a single grain. She turned into a black hen and swallowed it.

Nine months later, Cerridwen gave birth to a baby. She knew it was Gwion Bach, but he was so resplendent that she couldn't kill him. Instead, as often happens with heroes, she wrapped him in a humble container—in this case, a hide-covered bag—and placed him into the water. The next day, May first, a man named Elphin found the bag in his father's salmon weir. He sliced open the hides, saw the baby's head, and exclaimed, "Oh, what a radiant forehead (tal iesin)." That child, named Taliesin, became the greatest poet in the Welsh language, while Cerridwen, keeper of the cauldron, became a goddess of wisdom, poetry, and fertility, as well as a muse who is honored by her devotees with wine, cake, games, and dancing.

TALIESIN

Taliesin, son of Cerridwen, occupies both the actual world and the world of myth. In reality, he was a sixth-century bard famed for the excellence of his verse, little of which survives. In myth, he was much more than a poet. A thirteen-year-old who appeared at the court of King Maelgwn (a historical figure) and extemporaneously composed such splendid verse that the other poets were struck dumb, he also freed his foster father Elphin, who had been imprisoned, found an underground cauldron filled with gold, sailed with King Arthur to the underworld, carried a banner for Alexander the Great, and knew Noah, Moses, and Mary Magdalen. Frank Lloyd Wright, who was of Welsh descent, used the name for his home in Wisconsin and his winter retreat in Arizona.

Coatlicue and Coyolxuahqui

When it comes to terror, the Aztec earth goddess Coatlicue ("Serpent Skirt") could compete with the best. Although she was the goddess of florists, she subsisted on a diet of corpses, and her image was not pretty. An imposing statue depicts her with two fanged serpent heads, a necklace of severed hands, hearts, and skulls, a vest of human skin, and a skirt woven of writhing serpents. She was married to Mixcoatl ("Serpent Cloud"), the god of hunting, and she had four hundred sons and one daughter, Coyolxuahqui ("Golden Bells"). One day when Coatlicue was sweeping the floor of the temple, a tuft of feathers fluttered down from the sky. She picked it up and tucked it into her dress. When she looked for it later, she could not find it, and she realized that she was pregnant. Her children, humiliated by what they saw as a disgraceful situation, decided that she should die.

Inside her womb, her unborn child Huitzilopochtli ("Hummingbird on the Left") advised Coatlicue to hide in a cave. His warning came too late. Her other children, with Coyolxuahqui in the lead, arrived at the cave en masse and killed their mother. As she died, Huitzilopochtli, the sun god, leaped out of the womb, fully grown and painted blue. Seeking vengeance for his mother's death, he decapitated his sister, let her body tumble down the hillside, and flung her head into the sky, where it became the moon. Thus day, ruled by the supreme god, Huitzilopochtli, triumphed over night, the domain of Coyolxauhqui.

To commemorate Coatlicue's slaughter and to sustain the triumph of Huitzilopoch-tli, Aztec priests practiced the art of human sacrifice. The most spectacular such sacrifice occurred in 1486, with the construction of the Templo Mayor in Tenochtitlan, now Mexico City. Using obsidian knives, the priests ripped

A statue of Coatlicue from Tenochtitlan, Mexico. Unearthed in 1791, the massive carving dates from the fourteenth or fifteenth century.

the beating hearts out of as many as 60,000 men, women, and children and heaved their lifeless bodies, in imitation of Coyolxuahqui's, down the temple steps onto a large circular stone carved with an image of the dismembered goddess. In 1978 a workman doing excavation stumbled upon the mighty stone, now on display for tourists.

Together, Coatlicue and her children represented the entire cosmos. Coatlicue was the earth; her daughter Coyolxuahqui was the moon; her four hundred sons were the stars; and Huitzilopochtli, the most important god in the pantheon, was the sun.

Cybele

In the year 204, BCE, Rome was in trouble. With hailstorms battering the city and Hannibal threatening to invade, concerned officials consulted both the Sibylline Books and the Delphic Oracle. They were informed that victory could be achieved only if Cybele, the

Cybele surrounded by dragons.
A sixteenth-century woodcut
by Jost Ammons.

mother goddess who was inspiring frenzied worship throughout the ancient world, came directly into Rome. Fortunately, Cybele, later known as Magna Mater, had fallen to earth in the form of a black meteorite. So a delegation of high-status Romans traveled to Phrygia (now Turkey), retrieved the famous stone, and ceremoniously brought it back to the eternal city. Curious inhabitants pelted the priests of Cybele with rose petals as the government officials installed the stone in a temple on the Palatine hill. Thus the Great Goddess, whose origins may date back approximately nine thousand years, to the Neolithic town of Çatal Hüyük, entered imperial Rome. Soon the threat was deflected, Hannibal turned away, and the cult of Cybele, the mother of gods and men, swept through the empire.

The myth behind the cult had as many variations as a theme by Haydn. Its two main characters were Cybele and her consort Attis. He was a vegetation god, born on December 25, nine months after the goddess Nana plucked a blossom from an almond or pomegranate tree—a tree that, in one of the story's more recondite versions, sprang from the severed male organs of Cybele, who was originally a hermaphrodite, making Cybele her son's father, mother, and lover. Like Zeus, Attis was abandoned at birth and saved by a goat. When he grew up, he and Cybele became lovers. (Or else he became her priest, pledged to celibacy.) Unfortunately, Attis made a fatal error: he fell in love with a nymph. Not one to be rejected, Cybele responded by driving him mad. In his delirium, he tore off his genitals and bled to death beneath a pine tree (or else he was gored by a boar, killed in a hunting accident, or turned into a tree). Filled with sorrow, Cybele carried his lifeless form to a cave on Mount Ida where Zeus promised that his body would never decay.

Cybele holding a bust of Attis. Her temple in Rome, taken over by Christians in the fourth century, occupied the same site as the Vatican.

The rites that paralleled this tale were memorable. Devotees fasted for days, priests—eunuchs all—flagellated themselves with whips specially designed for the occasion, and initiates were baptized in the blood of a bull. In an annual five-day festival in the spring, people wept copious tears as they mourned the death of Attis and carried his symbol—a fir tree wrapped in wool and bedecked in ribbons and flowers—through the streets; Cybele's high priest and a human representative of the goddess celebrated their "sacred marriage"; young men danced themselves into a frenzy and castrated themselves; and the faithful celebrated the resurrection of Attis in a celebration so jubilant and orgiastic that it was known as the Hilaria. On the final day of these observances, Cybele's worn-out followers carried the statue of the Goddess to a river and ritually washed it, perhaps as a purification or a rain charm, perhaps for a purpose beyond our knowing.

Roman officials, troubled by the same aspects of these rituals that bother us, refused to permit their countrymen to become priests of Cybele. For about two hundred years, only foreigners were allowed to serve in that capacity. Yet the Mother Goddess and her resurrected son continued to attract devotees (as did Isis, another foreign goddess). Two and a half centuries after Cybele's triumphal entry into Rome, the emperor Claudius made the cult an official part of Roman religion. Though the story of Christianity soon toppled the myth of Cybele and Attis, Cybele herself still ranks as the last great goddess to be officially recognized in the western world.

Durga

Vengeful and bloodthirsty, Durga ("Inaccessible") is one of the many forms of the divine mother Devi and one of the few Hindu goddesses who is more than simply the consort of a god.

She came into existence when a buffalo demon was threatening the gods. Despite their most ferocious efforts, the gods could not subdue it. Their weakness and ineptitude made them so angry that flames shot out of their mouths and a wave of fury, hot and palpable, arose in their midst. That wave grew, solidified, and turned into the goddess Durga. She seduced the buffalo demon, spurned its offer of marriage, and captured it with her noose. The demon bucked and struggled, straining against the rope, and turned into a lion, a man, and an elephant. Throughout each metamorphosis, she held on to the rope, and with each new shape, she attacked. When the demon returned to its original form as a buffalo, she pinned it with her trident and beheaded it with her sword.

Durga's role is to combat evil, to rid the world of demons, and to destroy ignorance. Typically shown brandishing a club, a sword, a bow and arrow, and other weapons in her many arms, she was so ferocious that she gave birth to the goddess Kali, who burst from her forehead when she was in the heat of anger.

Known by many names and titles, including Mother of the Universe, she is unapproachable but not petty, as this incident reveals: Like other Hindu goddesses, Durga is sometimes said to be Shiva's wife. She was a second, inferior wife though, and the great god didn't treat her well. In a story told in Bengal, Shiva, suffering from a surfeit of marijuana, sold her jewelry. Durga stayed with him anyway, ignoring his low-rent abusiveness and saving her deepest wrath for evil, not insult.

Finally, like every great goddess, Durga is complex, and stories about her are sometimes contradictory. Thus, while she loved bloodshed and is usually said to have been born in battle, an alternative account claims that she emerged from Vishnu as the power of sleep or creativity. And although she was born in anger (and gave birth in anger), she is also renowned for having introduced yoga to humanity.

Epona

Once there was a man named Phoulouios Stellos who hated women so much that he preferred to mate with a horse. That mare gave birth to a baby girl who was named Epona.

That solitary fragment, told by an obscure Greek writer named Agesilaos, is the only story we have about Epona, the horse goddess of the Celts. However, images of her are numerous. Typically shown riding sidesaddle or standing between two ponies, Epona was worshipped in the British Isles and throughout Europe. In stables all over the Celtic world, devotees erected shrines in her honor and decked them with roses. Alone among the Celtic deities, Epona was taken up by the Roman cavalry and given her own feast day, December 18.

Like other deities, Epona played many parts. Sometimes known as Regina (the Queen), she was also a goddess of the underworld whose concerns included the human soul; a fertility goddess, often depicted with fruit, grain, bowls, and a cornucopia; and a goddess of travel whose responsibilities ranged from the peregrinations of ordinary living to the journey of life and death.

Freyja

Freyja, the promiscuous Norse goddess of love, fertility and death, was a witch and a sorceress. She rode a chariot drawn by two cats, wore a feathered cloak which enabled her to fly, and owned a boar named Gullinbursti whose bristles glowed in the dark.

None of these attributes could save her from feeling downcast when her husband Od (about whom little is known) abandoned her. Weeping tears of gold, Freyja looked for him everywhere. Her pain was deep. It was also short-lived.

Freyja in her chariot.

To ease her sorrow, she took so many lovers that she was accused of roaming around at night like a she-goat among bucks. She slept with the elves and the gods, including her twin brother Freyr (who owned a ship so large that it could hold all the gods and so small that he could fold it up and put it in his pocket). However, that occasion proved an embarrassment, for the other gods surprised her in flagrante delicto and she became so flustered that she farted. Freyja even slept with mortal men, although she drew the line at giants. Her most famous lovers were four dwarfs who owned an object she coveted: the Brisingamen necklace, which they had forged (and which is sometimes said to be the Rainbow Bridge, the link that connects this world to the realm of the gods). The dwarfs refused to give it to her unless she slept with each of them in turn, and she happily complied.

All this irritated Odin, the king of the gods. He had wooed her unsuccessfully and he decided to seek revenge. He asked the trickster Loki to bring him the necklace. Although Freyja lived in Sessrymnir, a vast and well-defended castle, Loki easily gained access. He turned into a fly, flew past the ramparts, and found Freyja asleep in her bedroom. Because she was lying on her back, he could not unhook the necklace. So he turned into a still smaller creature, a flea. In that form, he bit her on the breast and she rolled over, allowing him to unclasp the chain.

Freyja is sometimes said to be the leader of the Valkyries. In that capacity, she is allowed to choose half the slain in battle to live with her in her palace in Asgard. Thus she is a goddess of death as well as love: a goddess for all occasions. No surprise then that, as late as the thirteenth century, Snorri Sturluson, "Homer of the Norse," stated that of all the gods and goddesses, she was the most famous and that in addition, she was the only one still worshipped, the only one still alive.

Frigg

Frigg, the queen of heaven and goddess of marriage in Norse mythology, has a story very different from that of Freyja, the goddess of love and sex. Yet their origins may be the same and they may simply represent two different aspects of a woman's life.

The wife of Odin, Frigg sat beside her husband on the heavenly throne. Like him, she could see all of creation as well as the past, the present and the future, but she carried a bunch of keys at her waist, the symbol of the housewife, and she never spoke about what she saw, perhaps because she was busy doing other things. Using a constellation for a spinning wheel, she spun multicolored threads and wove the canopy of the clouds. She also watched over mortal lovers, married people, and pregnant women. Most of all, she was a mother.

Her son Baldur, known as the Good, was particularly blessed. He led a life untouched by sorrow or anxiety until one night when he woke with a start from a terrible nightmare. In his dream, he entered Niflheim, the land of the dead, and was greeted by the goddess Hel, who had the face and torso of a living woman but the legs of a partially decomposed corpse. She embraced him and gave him a tour of her palace, a domicile so dark and miserable that it was named Sleetcold and her throne was called Sick Bed.

The meaning of the nightmare was self-evident, and he confided his fears to his mother. She went into action. To protect him, Frigg traveled all around the world asking each and every thing, living and otherwise, to vow not to harm her son. Fire, earth, and water promised not to hurt him. She asked every animal, bird, serpent, and plant, every metal and every stone, every poison and every disease to swear not to harm him. They all took the sacred oath, and soon Baldur seemed invulnerable. The gods, amused by his immunity to injury, invented a game in which they flung various objects at him and laughed uproariously as everything bounced off. All the gods enjoyed the game with one exception: the trickster Loki, who was jealous of Beldur and determined to bring him down.

He began by taking the shape of an old woman and cross-examining Frigg. Had she really extracted a vow from everything on earth, or had she perchance neglected something? Frigg admitted that she had made one insignificant omission: a humble mistletoe bush growing west of Valhalla. In no time at all, Loki found the little bush. He pulled it up by its roots, carved a twig into a dart, and returned to the hall of the gods, where the game was in progress.

Amidst the raucous laughter, one figure failed to participate. It was Hoder, Baldur's blind twin. Loki, the sly god, handed him the dart and offered to hold his arm and direct his aim. Happy to join in the merriment at last, Hoder heaved the mistletoe at his brother. Loki's aim was true. The mistletoe pierced Baldur's heart and he collapsed, dead on the spot.

Thus, despite all her efforts, Frigg failed to protect her son. Worse, she was partially responsible for his death. She watched as the gods piled his corpse onto a funeral ship along with the bodies of his horse and his wife Nana, who had died of grief. Then they lit the pyre and pushed the ship out to sea. Everyone mourned except Frigg, who refused to accept the inevitable. Determined to get her child back, she begged the other gods to ask Hel what ransom she would demand in exchange for Baldur. Her son Hermod the Bold, messenger of the gods, promised to find out. He mounted Odin's eight-legged horse, Sleipnir, and rode for nine days and nights until he reached the land of the dead. Because he was still alive, the gates of the dismal palace would not open for him. But Sleipnir leaped over the walls and Hermod was able to confront Hel. She told him that she would release Baldur if—and only if—everything in the world, dead or alive, wept for him.

Fire, earth, and water wept. Every poison and disease wept, as did every plant, animal, bird, and serpent, every metal and every stone. They wept for Baldur, the *Prose Edda* says, the way objects weep when they are taken out of the frost and into the warmth. Only Loki, disguised as a giantess who lived in the dark recesses of a cave, refused to mourn. Thanks to that one holdout, Frigg was unable to rescue her son Baldur from the underworld. Nonetheless, she was worshipped by women who wanted to get pregnant as well as by those giving birth.

Gnowee

Once when the earth was new and smothered in darkness, the Australian sun goddess Gnowee ventured out to gather yams with her son and in so doing became separated from him. She looked for him everywhere but couldn't see far in the thick gloom. So she lit an enormous torch. Yet no matter how high she held it, the blaze illuminated only a small area. Finally, hoping to shed more light and see further, she climbed up into the sky. With the torch held high, she could see hills, rivers, and fields in every direction yet she could not find her own son. However, she has not given up hope. Every day, torch in hand, she climbs into the sky and travels from one horizon to the other, and she does not stop searching until the day is done.

Heng-o

Once upon a time, all ten suns decided to rise at the same time. The sky was ablaze with light, and as the day wore on, the heat became intense beyond imagining. The Chinese archer Shen I, seeing that the earth was in danger of drying up, shot down nine of the suns. Afterwards he journeyed to the Palace of the Queen Mother of the West, who rewarded him with a pill guaranteed to convey immortality.

A less thoughtful person might have taken the pill immediately, but Shen I felt unworthy. He decided he ought to purify himself first, so he took the pill home and hid it. One day while he was gone, his wife Heng-o (or Ch'ang-o) found the pill and swallowed it on the spot. Her feet lifted off the floor and soon she was bobbing about the ceiling like a helium balloon. When she heard Shen I coming home, she was so afraid that he would be angry at her that she opened the window and drifted into the sky. He tried to follow her, but a hurricane wind roared between them and slowed his progress. She floated up to the moon without interference.

Once she landed in that cold, desolate place, empty except for a single cinnamon tree, she turned into a frog and coughed up the pill's dark coating, which spread over the lunar surface in the shape of a rabbit. (This mark, readily observable in the dark basalt seas that splotch the lunar face, is recognized by many cultures.)

Meanwhile, the hurricane blew Shen I to the home of the King Father of the East, who told him to forgive his wife and gave him a special cake which enabled him to travel to the moon. Some versions of this story claim that Heng-o, the lunar goddess, turned into a three-legged toad. Nonetheless, when Shen I arrived, he reconciled with her and built her a home, the Palace of Boundless Cold. He visits her there every month on the full moon.

Huitaca

In the beginning, according to the Muisca people of central Colombia, everything was dark, and all the light was hidden inside the creator Chiminigagua, a mysterious being a long ways away. When the light started to leak out of him, creation began. First, he created two black birds. They flew everywhere, carrying the rays of the sun with them and spreading a bright, shining wind. Then he created a woman named Bachué ("she of the large breasts") who waded out of a lake holding the hand of a small boy. When he grew up, she married him and gave birth to so many children that she is considered the mother of mankind (as well as the bringer of laws and religious ceremonies). After many generations, she and her husband were transformed into serpents (like Cadmus and Harmonia in Greek myth) and returned to the sacred lake.

Not long after, an old man with a long beard appeared in the east. This was Bochica, who taught the people how to build houses, cultivate the fields, weave, spin, and paint. He preached the value of hard work and sobriety, and the knowledge he brought was extremely useful. Unfortunately, he was also austere, humorless, and puritanical.

An equal and opposite reaction arose in the shape of the licentious Huitaca, the goddess of joy, also known as Chia (and said to be Bachué in another guise). A lover of laughter, intoxicating beverages, and everything that brings pleasure, she couldn't stand Bochica's unrelentingly earnest approach to life (though she married him anyway). To thwart his efforts, she teased him, caused the rivers to rise, and stirred up a huge flood in which many people died. In so doing, she infuriated the male gods in this story. What happened next is debatable. Maybe Bochica picked her up and hurled her into the sky where, like other goddesses who were thrown into the heavens by angry men, she became the moon. Or perhaps Chiminigagua changed her into an owl. Either way, from then on Huitaca only came out at night. She is said to be the weaver of dreams, and of useful ones in particular.

SOURCE: A MISSIONARY AMONG THE MUISCA

When Spanish conquistadors invaded Colombia in 1548, the Muisca (or Chibcha) resisted mightily but in vain. Their culture, which included goddess worship, legendary goldsmithing, and human sacrifice, was virtually obliterated. Fortunately, in the 1600s a Franciscan father named Pedro Simón researched their mythology. This story comes from him.

Inanna

Recognized throughout the Mesopotamian world and actively wor-shipped for almost four millennia, Inanna's prominence was immense. Called Inanna by the Sumerians, Ishtar by the Babyloni-ans, and Astarte by the Phoenicians, she was the Great Mother and the Queen of Heaven, the goddess of love and the goddess of war, known to tear into cadavers with the hideous intensity of a dog. In addition, unlike earlier goddesses with similar titles, her full story, complete with plot, character, and a generous helping of sex, is known. It was recorded around 1765 BCE.

Inanna in the Underworld

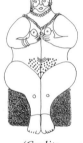

For one reason or another, every important mythological character must descend into the underworld. Inanna went there to visit her sister Ereshkigal, queen of the dead. Leaving behind her beloved husband/brother Dumuzi (Tammuz to the Babylonians), a shepherd whom she called her "honey-man," she abandoned her temples and prepared for her journey by fixing herself up. She arranged her dark bangs, applied eye makeup, donned her best clothing, and adorned herself with a glittering crown, a double strand of lapis beads, a gold bracelet, and a breast-plate so seductive it was named "Come, man, come."

(Credit: Hannah Berman)

She set off on her journey with her loyal servant Ninshubur but at a certain point she knew she had to travel alone. After telling Nin-shubur what to do should she fail to return, she continued on by herself. At last she reached the gates of the underworld.

At the first gate, the gatekeeper, Neti, told her that, before she was allowed to enter, she had to remove her crown. She complied. At each of the seven gates, Inanna was ordered to take off another piece of clothing. At last, completely naked, she crouched in front of her sister who stared at her with "the eyes of death," killing her instantly. Inanna's corpse was hung from a hook on the wall, and there it remained for three full days, rotting.

ROUNDTRIP TICKET TO THE UNDERWORLD:
EIGHT WHO MADE THE ULTIMATE EXCURSION

The underworld is a common destination for mythological characters because, as psychologist James Hillman has suggested, the underworld is the psyche and cannot be avoided. Yet every mythological character who journeys there goes for a different reason. To wit:

- Aeneas went to visit his father.
- Persephone was abducted.
- Orpheus made the descent to bring his beloved Eurydice back to life.
- Izanagi went to retrieve his wife Izanami.
- Odysseus sought advice from the prophet Tiresias.
- Theseus set off on a lark with a friend and ended up stuck to a chair.
- Heracles went to kidnap the dog Cerberus and to free Theseus.
- Gilgamesh ventured into the underworld in search of immortality.

Meanwhile, Ninshubur was waiting. After three days, she dressed up like a beggar and went into action. Crying out in grief, she beat the drum, circled the homes of the gods, tore at her eyes, mouth, and thighs, and went to the shrine of Enlil in Nippur to beg for help. "She who goes to the Dark City stays there," Enlil said, and he denied her pleas. In Ur, the god Nana also refused to help. Finally, Ninshubur reached Eridu, where Enki, the god of water and wisdom, offered assistance. He scraped the dirt from under his fingernails and shaped it into two creatures who were neither male nor female. After he gave the food of life to one and the water of life to the other, the two of them set out for the underworld. They slipped through the doors with no more difficulty than a fly and found Ereshkigal naked on the bed. As she lay there with her hair swirling around her head, she moaned, "Oh! Oh! My inside," and then "Oh! Oh! My outside," and she cried out in a similar way about her belly, her back, her heart, and her liver.

At each exclamation, the tiny creatures repeated her words. Ereshkigal was so pleased that she tried to present them with gifts, but they rejected each offer. Finally they asked for the corpse on the wall, and she gave it to them. When they sprinkled it with the food and water of life, Inanna came to life.

Her ascent from the underworld wasn't easy. With a crowd of demons or gallas surrounding her, she came face to face with the judges of the underworld. They told her that if she wished to return to the land of the living, she had to leave someone else in her place. At the gates of the underworld, the gallas offered to take Ninshubur in Inanna's place. Remembering her servant's loyalty, Inanna refused to make the exchange.

At Umma, the gallas suggested that they take her son Shara in her place. Inanna refused to send him to the underworld because he had trimmed her nails and smoothed her hair. She also said no when the gallas wanted to take Lulal, another son.

Then they reached Uruk, where her husband Dumuzi was sitting on his throne by a big apple tree. During the three days when Inanna was swinging from a meathook in the underworld, everyone had mourned—except Dumuzi. Hearing that news made Inanna so angry that when the gallas grabbed him by the thighs, emptied the milk from his seven churns, and beat him with axes, she did nothing to stop them. Instead, she gazed at him as Ereshkigal had looked at her—with "the eyes of death."

Luckily for Dumuzi, Utu, the god of justice, answered his prayers, turning his hands and feet into snakes so that he was able to escape. Fearful and weeping, Dumuzi nodded off, but his sleep was troubled. In the morning, he described a dream to his sister Geshtinanna. The signs, she said, were ominous. Sure enough, the gallas approached. Dumuzi hid, begging his sister and his friend not to reveal his location.

When the gallas asked Geshtinanna where he was, she refused to tell. She declined their gifts, and although they tortured her fearfully, pouring pitch into her vagina, she said nothing.

Dumuzi's friend had no such scruples, and soon Dumuzi was surrounded by the gallas. Once again he called out to Utu, who turned his hands and feet into those of gazelles. But he could not escape. The gallas bound his hands and neck and dragged him into the underworld.

Although Inanna had been angry with her husband earlier, she plunged into mourning when the gallas abducted him. The entire city grieved. His mother, Sirtur, was devastated, and his sister Geshtinanna was so distraught that she volunteered to take his place in the underworld.

However, Inanna had no idea where he was until an insignificant-looking

INANNA WEEPS FOR DUMUZI

Gone is my husband, my sweet husband.
Gone is my husband, my sweet love . . .
The jackal lies down in his bed.
The raven dwells in his sheepfold.
You ask me about his reed pipe?
The wind must play it for him.
You ask me about his sweet songs?
The wind must sing them for him.

—Diane Wolkstein and Samuel Noah Kramer,
from *Inanna: Queen of Heaven and Earth*

fly told her that Dumuzi was at the edge of the steppe, near Arali, on the way to the underworld. In exchange for this information, Inanna gave the fly a gift which its descendants still enjoy: free admission to beer houses, taverns, and anyplace on earth where minstrels sing or wise men and women converse.

When Inanna and Geshtinanna finally found Dumuzi, Inanna told him that for half the year he would reside in the land of the dead, and for the other half of the year his compassionate sister Geshtinanna would take his place. Thus the shepherd Dumuzi became a fertility god whose comings and goings, like those of Persephone or Adonis, were associated with the seasonal cycles of vegetation. His annual descent into the underworld was mourned, both in story and in historical reality. Throughout the Near East and Mediterranean regions, weeping women participated in ceremonies that mirrored the mourning of Inanna (or Ishtar) for her lover Dumuzi (or Tammuz). This widespread custom even appears in the Bible. Writing in the sixth century BCE, the author of the Book of Ezekiel describes a series of abominations. Among them: sun worship and "women weeping for Tammuz."

Inanna's Sacred Marriage

Just as it is shocking to learn that the fairy tales we remember from Disney or from children's books are G-rated, sanitized versions of the real thing (think of Cinderella's stepsisters, amputating their toes so that they can squeeze their bloody feet into those dainty slippers), it is surprising to discover how overtly erotic early mythology is. No better example of this can be found than Inanna, whose literature is filled with the most exuberant sexuality. On the way to visit the god Enki, she stopped to put on her crown and admire herself. "When she leaned against the apple tree, her vulva was wondrous to behold," reads the cuneiform text. "Rejoicing at her wondrous vulva, the young woman Inanna applauded herself."

Upon her arrival, she was served butter cake, cold water, and beer. Soon she and Enki were toasting each other, and Enki began to give his powers away. Over the course of the evening, he raised his cup fourteen times, and each time gave her five, six, or seven powers including the throne, the crown, truth, the art of lovemaking, and—a separate power—the kissing of the phallus. No sooner did Enki name the powers than Inanna replied, "I take them!"

As the goddess of fertility, her desire was unrestrained. "My untilled land lies fallow . . . ," she sings. "Who will plow my vulva? Who will plow my high field? Who will plow my wet ground?" Dumuzi volunteers. "Then plow my vulva, man of my heart! Plow my vulva."

In ritual, her sexuality found expression in an annual New Year's ceremony common to early cultures known as sacred marriage. First the people would prepare a bed with cedar oil and a fresh sheet. Then Inanna and Dumuzi—or their representatives in the form of the high priestess of the temple and the king or his appointed substitute—would make love, an act meant to ensure a fruitful year for the crops, the flocks, and the people of Sumer. Sadly for the participants, the rite was a sacrificial one. The figures representing Dumuzi and Inanna were killed. This aspect of the ceremony, which may have been performed every eight years, changed over time. Around 2,500 BCE, the king's entire court, along with a great deal of elaborate art, seems to have been dispatched to the underworld with him. Later, the sacrifice was performed symbolically and the king was merely struck on the cheek. If tears sprang to his eyes, the harvest could confidently be expected to be a rich one.

It was essential to conduct these rituals in the proper way, for the well-being of the community depended upon the continued goodwill of the goddess. According to the Babylonians, who worshipped Inanna under the name Ishtar, when the goddess withdrew, all sexual desire disappears. "The bull springs not upon the cow, the ass impregnates not the jenny," reads the ancient text, and it goes on to report that even in the privacy of their bedroom, the man sleeps alone and the woman lies on her side.

Isis

The Egyptian goddess Isis, queen of the gods, is arguably the greatest deity of the ancient world. Her story starts in the womb, where she made love for the first time with her beloved brother Osiris. When they grew up, they married. As king and queen of Egypt, they ruled together. They abolished cannibalism, built towns and temples, and taught the Egyptians weaving, spinning, cooking, agriculture, the alphabet, and writing, all of which Isis invented. Once that was accomplished, Osiris decided to bring civilization to the rest of the world. While he traveled to Asia, Isis ruled in his place.

Isis, wearing a tiny throne on her head, with Osiris. (Credit: Hannah Berman)

But Osiris had an implacable enemy: his brother Seth. When Osiris returned, Seth invited him and seventy-two of his wicked friends to a lavish feast at which he proudly displayed an intricately carved chest and offered it to anyone who could fit inside. Like Cinderella's stepsisters, one person after another tried to squeeze into it without success. At last Osiris stepped into the chest and lay down in it. He fit perfectly, for it had been contoured to his measurements. Seth and his compatriots slammed the lid down, nailed it shut, and threw it into the Nile, drowning him. (During religious festivals, women reenacted this event by tossing clay figurines of Osiris into the river.)

The chest floated out to the Mediterranean and washed ashore in Byblos in Lebanon, where it lodged in the roots of a tree. Isis, whose grief was so unceasing that her tears were said to cause the flooding of the Nile, had no idea where his body was. Desperate to find it, she wandered everywhere, accompanied only by the jackal-headed Anubis, whom she had raised.

When she arrived in Byblos, she visited the king and noticed a thick column cut from a fragrant tree. She knew by the delicious scent that this column encased the body of her husband Osiris. To be near him, she secured a job as a nurse for the queen's son. Like the Greek goddess Demeter, who took similar employment, she tried to make the child immortal by warming him in the fire each night. But she was still marooned in sorrow and her sad cries woke the queen, who rushed into her quarters, saw her son in the flames, and screamed. That broke the spell.

Afterwards, Isis revealed herself as a goddess and explained what she had been doing. Although the queen begged her to continue, it was too late. Isis refused. She did, however, ask the king to give her the pillar, and he assented. When the wood was chopped away, the sarcophagus was revealed, with the body of Osiris inside. According to the Greek writer Plutarch (46–120 CE), who visited Egypt as a young man and is the single greatest source we have for this story, Isis let out such a mournful cry at the sight that the sound killed the baby.

Determined to bring her beloved back to life, Isis carted the coffin back to Egypt. With the help of her sister Nephthys, she turned into a swallow. By fluttering around the corpse and flapping her wings, she stirred the air and forced the breath of life into his lungs. Thus Osiris was temporarily revived. She used those precious moments to conceive her son, the falcon-god Horus. To protect her child from the evil intentions of Seth, Isis hid the baby in a thicket of papyrus and continued to guard her husband's tomb.

However, her mind was divided, for she longed to see her child. One moonlit night, she visited Horus and briefly left the tomb unguarded. That was the opportunity Seth had been waiting for. He opened the coffin, hacked Osiris into fourteen pieces, and scattered them across Egypt. Isis retrieved all the parts of the corpse with the exception of the phallus, which had been swallowed by a fish, and she buried each part where she found it. So the body of Osiris could truly be said to reside in thirteen places—though in another version of the myth, she patched Osiris back together and brought him to the island of Philae where, thanks to Anubis, he became the first mummy.

His soul descended to the underworld and became King of the Dead. The Egyptians celebrated the death and resurrection of Osiris with a mock burial and the creation of tiny barley gardens planted in sand and moistened with the waters of the Nile. The barley sprouting from the dead sand represented the returning god. "Of all Egyptians, perhaps of all ancient deities, no god has lived so long or had so wide and deep an influence as Osiris," Jane E. Harrison wrote. "He stands as the prototype of the great class of resurrection-gods who die that they may live again." The influence of Isis, the agent of his revival, was greater still. She was considered a saviour.

King Horus

With Osiris in the underworld, the evil Seth became king. When Horus grew up, he challenged his uncle for the office. To determine the correct ruler, the other gods held a trial. Thoth and Shu voted in favor of Horus, but Ra, the sun god, ruled in favor of Seth. That was when Isis stepped in. Disguised as a lovely young woman, she got Seth to agree that it was wrong to rob a son of his birthright. Only then did she reveal her identity. Although Seth complained that he had been tricked, he and Horus both agreed to settle the dispute by way of a contest.

The Oudjat eye. Egyptian coffins often sported one on each side of the head, thereby enabling the deceased to keep up with events in the world.

The challenge? Each was to turn into a hippopotamus and stay under water for three months. Once again, Isis interfered. She tried to harpoon Seth. Instead, she accidentally speared her son. On her next attempt, she wounded Seth. But by then Horus was so angry that he cut off his mother's head. In response, Ra ordered Seth to tear out Horus's eyes. Or perhaps Seth sodomized Horus. Or maybe they sodomized each other. In any case, Horus castrated Seth, who turned into a black pig, tore out Horus's eye, and flung it beyond the horizon.

The world plunged into darkness. Thoth, the scribe of the gods, pieced the fragments of the eye together and in that way created the full moon. He also gave Horus the Eye of Eternity or *oudjat* eye, which had the power to conquer death. Horus journeyed to the underworld and gave this magical eye to Osiris, bringing him eternal life.

Still, Horus was not king. Unsure of what to do, the gods finally wrote a letter to Osiris in the underworld. Osiris replied that if Horus did not receive the throne, he would send demons to harass

THE EYE OF RA

Egypt is not the only civilization fascinated by the eye. The three Gorgons of Greek mythology shared a single eye among them; the Inuit goddess Sedna, who lives in the depths of the Arctic sea, is one-eyed; the Hindu god Shiva had a third eye; and the Scandinavian god Odin sacrificed an eye for the chance to drink at the fountain of knowledge and wisdom. But in Egyptian mythology the eye is more than a symbol or an attribute. It also acts as a character who often—not always—works on behalf of its owner. The Eye of Ra, for instance, figured in many incidents:

- It found Shu and Tefnut when they wandered off after the creation and brought them back to their father, Ra.
- It turned into a cobra known as Uraeus which the sun god wore around his forehead to frighten his enemies.
- And once, it almost destroyed mankind, at the request of the gods. Taking the form of the lion goddess Sehkmet, the Eye approached the slaughter with zest. The carnage was well underway when Ra had second thoughts. To slow down the destruction, he took seven thousand jars filled with red beer and poured it on the ground until it resembled a lake of blood. The Eye paused to take a sip. Soon, too drunk to threaten anyone, she turned into the cow goddess Hathor and humanity was saved. Sadly, death and disease came into the world at that time. But so did the custom of drinking beer at the Feast of Hathor.

The Uraeus.

the gods. So Horus became king, and Seth ascended to the sky, where he became the god of storms.

I am a Cowboy in the Boat of Ra

I am a cowboy in the boat of Ra,
sidewinders in the saloons of fools
bit my forehead   like   O
the untrustworthiness of Egyptologists
Who do not know their trips. Who was that
dog-faced man? they asked, the day I rode
from town. . . .

—Ishmael Reed

Isis the Healer and the Names of Ra

Many major deities have the ability to cure the sick and revive the dead, and Isis was no exception. When her weakling son Horus was born, she created special medications and nursed him tenderly, a scene frequently depicted in art and undoubtedly the origin of the iconography associated with the Virgin Mary. Later on, she applied the milk of a gazelle to his bleeding eye sockets and restored his sight (and thus was often petitioned to cure blindness). She knew the healing power of herbs, berries, and seeds, and she could concoct all kinds of remedies, ranging from a practical drug Galen described which could heal lesions and cure headaches to the elixir of immortality. Ovid himself prayed to her when his wife was dying from a botched abortion.

Despite her vast pharmaceutical knowledge, Isis didn't rely on herbs and potions. She could cure through the power of speech and incantation. Her name itself was believed to be a potent weapon against harm, and those who were troubled by illness (or infertility) might visit one of her temples to

Isis, wearing the disc of the sun between two cow horns, nurses her son Horus. Sigmund Freud kept a small statue of this image on his desk. (Credit: Hannah Berman)

petition her for a fee. After a few days in her temple, a period known as incubation, anyone, no matter how weak, could expect to be healed. Sanctuaries dedicated to her were scattered across the ancient world.

Yet Isis was not born with healing abilities. She obtained them from Ra after she created a poisonous snake which sunk its fangs into his flesh. The bite caused him such excruciating pain that he begged for help. She refused unless he revealed his secret names. Like other deities, Isis included, Ra had many names. He told her three of them. In the morning, he said, his name was Khepri; at noon he was Ra; and in the evening he was Atum. Unmoved by this paltry offering, Isis refused to alleviate the pain until Ra revealed all his names. When he capitulated, she incorporated them into a magic spell and his pain disappeared. Afterwards there was nothing that Isis couldn't cure.

The Rites of Isis

Isis had everything you could want in a goddess. Omnipotent and compassionate, she was the queen of heaven and earth, the goddess of the underworld, the Great Mother, the devoted wife, the Goddess of Ten Thousand Names and the One. Other goddesses were thought to be mere aspects of Isis. Always the protagonist, ever active, she was a personal savior made empathetic by her grief over the death of Osiris, and she was thought to live not on some distant Olympus but here, among us—which may be why the rites of Isis were the most popular mystery religion imported into Greece and Rome.

Romans began to worship Isis around 80 BCE. During the first two centuries of our era, slaves and aristocrats, courtesans, politicians, and other influential people were welcomed into her cult. Initiation included the following elements (not necessarily in this order):

- an eleven-day fast, during which the candidate refrained from meat, drink, and sex;
- a complete, biographical narrative confessing all sins in front of others;

- a dramatic evening service in which a halo of light appeared around the head of the priest and blazing sulfur torches were thrust into water but kept burning;
- a symbolic death by drowning, decapitation, mummification or burial in a sarcophagus;
- a symbolic journey through the upper and lower worlds;
- a baptism by water or fire, after which the initiate was "reborn" as the sun god and thus as a servant of Isis;
- an oath and a vow of secrecy.

In 378 CE the Christian emperor Theodosius I officially banned her worship. Throughout the Roman empire, her temples were destroyed and Christian churches were built upon the ruins. The cult of Isis faded from Roman life.

Yet the goddess maintained a hold over the human imagination. Some say that her worship continued in another form, namely that of the Virgin Mary. (At St. Germaine des Prés, built in 542 over what was once a temple of Isis, Parisians worshipped a black statue of Isis as the Virgin Mary until 1514.) But it isn't necessary to conflate Isis with other figures to find proof of her continued appeal. In the eighteenth century, the mysteries of Isis contributed to Mozart's opera *The Magic Flute.* In the nineteenth century, the Romantics held her in high esteem, as did Madame Blavatsky, who claimed to be an initiate. Even now, as perhaps the most powerful goddess in human history, Isis continues to attract devotees. In 1976, on the spring equinox, her followers formed the Fellowship of Isis, an international organization, based in Ireland, which numbered Jorge Luis Borges among its members. Its manifesto pledges democracy, freedom of conscience, reverence for life, religious tolerance, and communion with the Goddess, while eschewing secrecy, asceticism, and sacrifice, "actual or symbolic." By 2000, the organization claimed over seventeen thousand members in ninety-three countries, plus cyberspace. The temple of Isis can now be found online at www.fellowshipofisis.com.

Jari

Some myths illuminate the big mysteries of life, like how the universe was created or why we die. Others, such as this story from Papua New Guinea, focus on smaller, equally perplexing concerns: like where fire came from, how people learned to cook, and why men's genitals look the way they do.

The story begins with the ancestor goddess Gogo, who was a snake. She had a beautiful daughter named Jari who married and gave birth to a son. But Jari failed to mention to her husband that her mother was a snake. So when he discovered a giant serpent coiled around his child one day, he had no way of knowing that this was his mother-in-law. Had he guessed the truth, he might have greeted the snake and welcomed it. Wealth and fame might have been his. Instead, he killed the snake, chopped it up, and cooked it. When Jari learned what had happened, she fell into a vengeful rage and killed and cooked their son.

After that, she wandered around the island, criss-crossing the land with rivers and divulging the secrets of birth magic. When she remarried, she taught her new husband how to build a home, grow tobacco, and chew betel nuts. She took some fire from her genitals to teach him how to cook, and later on, after his breath became unbearably foul, she created an anus for him. One problem remained. Jari's desire to make love with her husband was continually frustrated because he lacked the equipment. So she gathered some betel nuts and breadfruit and used them to fashion a set of genitals for him. Then they could truly be lovers.

Kali

Kali, known as the black one, is one of the most gruesome goddesses in all of mythology. With her necklace of skulls, girdle of severed arms or snakes, long, lolling tongue, bloody fangs, and disheveled hair, she is also one of the most recognizable.

Several stories recount her birth. One begins with the Hindu god

Shiva, who was teasing his wife Parvati about her dark complexion. He was so relentless and she felt so humiliated that eventually, through the practice of asceticism, she sloughed off her skin, took the name Gauri, and turned gold (proving that mythology is not immune to racism). Her discarded skin became Kali, the goddess of death, destruction, and time.

Another story begins with the goddess Durga, who was dueling with the demon Raktabija. Durga was ferocious, but with every slash of her sword, the odds against her worsened because the moment a drop of Raktabija's blood splashed on the ground, it multiplied into a thousand new demons. Outnumbered and desperate for assistance, Durga thought so hard about what to do and was so angry that Kali burst out of her forehead like Athena from the forehead of Zeus or Shiva from the forehead of Vishnu. Kali won the battle. She swallowed all the newborn demons, pierced Rak-tabija with a spear, and, holding him high, swallowed every last drop of his blood.

Kali, wearing a necklace of skulls, dances on the body of Shiva.

Another tale reports that Kali was murdered right after she was born. With her hair still wet from the waters of birth, the evil king Kamsa swung her around and smashed her against the stone floor. She ascended to heaven. When darkness fell and ghosts roamed the night, she danced, laughed mockingly, and promised Kamsa that when it was his time to die, she would drink his blood.

Often depicted dancing on (or devouring) the sexually aroused corpse of her husband Shiva, Kali's nightmarish image makes it impossible to sentimentalize her. She is an embodiment of fear and a reflection of the wish to destroy, and her rites reputedly included human sacrifice. The professional assassins known as Thugs who preyed upon travelers for about three hundred years (until 1837) were said to strangle people as ritual offerings to Kali. Even now, at her temple in India, goats are sacrificed on a daily basis.

Kali's bloodthirstiness is memorable, but that's not why people worship her. Born to demolish demons who threaten the cosmic order, Kali reminds us that death is a part of life and that there is much in the here and now that needs to be destroyed, beginning with ignorance. She created the means to do that by inventing Sanskrit, the individual letters of which are represented by the skulls slung around her neck. Her iconography also suggests other positive aspects, for although in two of her four hands she holds such objects as a shield, a giant's amputated hand, a noose, or a sword, her other two hands are often empty, though not without meaning. Through the use of ceremonial poses, they offer reassurance and blessings to her followers and promise to allay their fears.

Like other Hindu deities, Kali goes by many names and can be thought of as one manifestation of the goddess Devi. If she exults in death, she also creates life, for just as Isis brings Osiris back to life, Kali reanimates Shiva by dancing on his corpse. As a symbol of the eternal feminine, she was even the wet nurse for Skanda, the six-headed god of war. With the universal syllable annexed to her name, she is thus a mother goddess, often worshipped as Kali-Ma. She represents more than one aspect of existence; she is the entire process from beginning to end.

Kuan Yin

The story of Kuan Yin, the beloved goddess of compassion, is one of the stranger tales in the annals of mythology. It begins with a bodhisattva or enlightened being named Avalokitesvara. In India he was said to have a thousand arms which he used to distribute alms and perform good deeds. In Tibet, where he is said to reincarnate as the Dalai Lama, he was famous for converting people to Buddhism assisted only by a monkey who was born in the palm of his hand. In China, Avalokitesvara had an identity so fluid that he became a goddess.

The transformation happened slowly. Kuan Yin, as he was known in China, could take many forms. His first sixteen appearances were male. Then in the fifth century CE, a monk who was translating the Lotus-sutra from Sanskrit into Chinese added seventeen new forms including a nun, a woman, a housewife, an officer's wife, a Brahman woman, a laywoman, and a young girl. After that the bodhisattva's appearances continued to be primarily masculine, but the scales of divinity were tipping. His identity fused with that of Matsu, a goddess who protects sailors, Sheng Mu, a popular Chinese deity who protects women and is known as the Holy Mother, and a much-admired martyr named Miao Shan. With that, her transformation was complete.

As is often the case with heroines in fairy tale and legend, Miao Shan was the youngest of three girls. Her father, the king, wanted his daughters to marry, and the two older girls were glad to comply. But Miao Shan wished only to live as a Buddhist nun. Hoping to discourage her, her father gave her permission to enter a nearby monastery. In secret, though, he asked the nuns to treat his daughter harshly. He thought this would convince her to return to the world.

It had no such effect. Miao Shan cheerfully did everything she was asked, and her father became so angry that he killed her. A tiger-shaped spirit carried her into the underworld, where she fed the hungry, administered to the miserable, doused the infernal flames, turned the instruments of torture into flowers, and made hell into a paradise. Then she returned to the land of the living and received one of the peaches of immortality, which assured her status as a goddess.

She also learned, to her distress, that while she was in the underworld, her father had been punished with a hideous disease for abusing his daughter. Only one remedy could cure it: a medicine made from the arms and eyes of a person who is completely without anger. The king asked his two older daughters, the Goneril and Regan of this tale, to donate their bodily parts. They declined. Miao Shan volunteered without hesitation. The remedy was made and the king was healed.

When he discovered that it was his murdered daughter who had provided the cure, he embraced her. Miao Shan, who proved that the love of a child for a parent transcends all circumstances and is greater than death, was transformed into Kuan Yin, the thousand-armed goddess of mercy and compassion.

Often shown carrying a willow twig and a vase filled with magic water, Kuan Yin in selfless, gentle, and immensely popular. As a bodhisattva, she chose to remain human even after she was enlightened, making her a divinity for this life, someone who can be invoked in times of ordinary need. She is known as "the One Who Hears the Cries of the World" because no calamity is too large or too mundane to deserve her attention. First and foremost, she comes to the aid of women who want children. In addition she restores health, reunites families, offers protection against fire, flood, falling, and storms, helps free prisoners from their chains, comforts the dying and the dead, and assists those who are worried about passing their examinations. Invoke her at a moment of distress, her devotees believe, or repeat her mantra a sufficient number of times, and she will respond—without judgment, without blame, and without delay.

Lilith

The myth of Lilith, all by itself, is reason enough to study mythology. Originally a storm demon, she was a sexual predator who ravaged men in their sleep, causing them to have nocturnal emissions and making it impossible for them to find satisfaction with ordinary women. She attacked women by causing barrenness, miscarriage, and difficulties in childbirth. She was even a threat to babies, for she loved to tickle their feet in their sleep, make them laugh, and strangle them. From those pernicious beginnings, she rose through the ranks until she became nothing less than the wife of God. Yet Lilith is almost entirely absent in the Bible. The one passing reference she receives, in Isaiah 34:14, is often translated as "screech owl," "night hag" or simply "demon." Yet in folklore, Talmudic commentaries, and the Zohar, the kabbalistic pamphlets of the thirteenth-century mystic Moses de Léon, her presence is vivid and unforgettable. Here is her story:

In the beginning, Adam was married to Lilith. Like Adam, she was created from earth but when God made Lilith, he used unclean dirt, with predictable results. Lilith was not a good wife. Whenever Adam and Lilith slept together, she objected to his being on top, noting that, as in chapter one of Genesis, they were created equally. He insisted. So she uttered the sacred name of God and flew off to the Red Sea where she cavorted with demons so promiscuously that she gave birth to over a hundred baby demons a day.

> *Wildcats shall meet hyenas, goat-demons shall greet each other;*
> *There too the lilith shall repose and find herself a resting place.*
>
> —Isaiah 34:14

Adam missed her tremendously. At his request, God sent three angels—Senoy, Sansenoy, and Semangelof—to convince her to return to her mate. After the angels threatened Lilith in various ways, they reached a compromise. She agreed that one hundred of her children, demons all, would be killed every day. She also agreed to forfeit her power over babies whenever she saw the names of those three angels written on a door or an amulet near a newborn. But she refused to return to Adam.

So God made Adam another wife. He constructed her from the inside out, starting with bones, adding various organs and muscles and blood, covering it all with skin, and then finishing it off with bits of hair here and there. However, he foolishly allowed Adam to watch. Adam was so disgusted by what he saw that God realized the match would never work. He took his creation away, no one knows to where, and tried again. This time he did it the easy way. He put Adam to sleep, removed a rib, and—as in chapter two of Genesis—fashioned Eve.

Eve was more docile than Lilith but she wasn't submissive enough, and when Lilith snuck into Eden in the form of a serpent, she easily convinced Eve to taste the fruit of the tree of knowledge. Adam and Eve were banished from the Garden of Eden.

As penance, Adam entered a period of celibacy that lasted 130 years. During that time he did not sleep with Eve but he could not control Lilith and other demons. They came to him in the night, coupled with him while he was dreaming, and gave birth to many demons. One of them was Lilith's child (or twin) Samael, who become her mate. To underline his opposition to the match, God castrated Samael, thereby forcing Lilith to continue satisfying her desires in the arms of sleeping men.

Lilith stands on lions and is flanked by owls in this drawing of a Sumerian bas-relief, carved around 2400 BCE. (Credit: Hannah Berman)

When the temple in Jerusalem was destroyed, God was shaken. In his despair, he turned away from his true wife, the Shekhinah, the female face of God, and embraced Lilith. Thus Lilith, once no better than a demon, became the consort of God. And that, thirteenth-century commentators tell us, is how things will be until the coming of the Messiah, when God will reject Lilith and return once again to the Shekhinah, his true mate.

Mary

Bright virgin, steadfast in eternity,
Star of this storm-tossed sea,
Trusted guide of every trustful pilot,
Turn your thoughts to the terrifying squall
In which I find myself, alone and rudderless . . .

—Petrach, "Hymn to the Virgin"

Technically, which is to say, theologically, Mary is not a goddess. Observation suggests otherwise. For centuries, while generations of Christian theologians debated the fine points of her divinity, millions of people have worshipped Mary, lighting candles, leaving votive offerings, invoking her in their prayers, and dedicating shrines and cathedrals to her around the world. The reverence for her, so similar to that accorded pagan goddesses, reminds us that mythology and religion overlap, and that divinity resides not in doctrine but in the heart and practice of the devotee.

Mary receives scant attention in the Bible (neither her birth nor her death are mentioned), and throughout the history of Christianity, the church has been ambivalent about her position and qualities. The church Fathers (there were no Mothers) saw that Mary, like the great pagan goddesses, was associated with the moon, with the sea, and most important, with a male god, her son and/or lover, who died (typically in connection with a tree) and was resurrected, often after three days. The church exploited these parallels by constructing churches in Mary's honor directly over shrines to Juno, Rhea, Minerva, Cybele, or Isis (who, like Mary, was known as the "Star of the Sea"). In the sixth century, even the Parthenon, once the preserve of the virgin goddess Athena, was rededicated to the Virgin Mary. In this way, the church redirected the power of the pagan goddesses.

As their power ebbed, Mary absorbed much of the affection that had been directed towards them and fulfilled the need for a Mother goddess. Titles that once belonged to other goddesses—Queen of Angels, Queen of Heaven, Queen of Peace—accrued to her, and people worshipped at her throne. Their devotion, directed as it was toward the female figure rather than the male god, made the church fathers profoundly uncomfortable. Epiphanius (c.315–403), bishop of the Greek island of Salamis, was forthright in his opinion: "Let the father, the Son and the Holy Spirit be worshipped," he declared, "but let no one worship Mary."

Nonetheless, during the twelfth and thirteenth centuries, eighty cathedrals were built in northern France, practically all them named Notre Dame in Mary's honor. Legends arose in which Mary (or her statue) performed miracles for her devotees. Thus a knight who was late to a tournament (because he was at mass) discovered that Mary had acted as his substitute, and a young nun who abandoned the religious life in search of romance learned upon her return to the convent years later that Mary had quietly covered for her. Many people also described encounters with Mary.

On of the most far-reaching encounters occurred in 1531, when Juan Diego, on his way to mass, saw a radiant, dark-skinned woman floating on a hill above a cactus. "I am the mother of God," she told him. She directed him to tell Juan de Zumárraga, the first bishop of Mexico, to build a shrine in her honor. The bishop, who the same year destroyed five hundred temples, twenty thousand idols, and every piece of indigenous writing he could lay his hands on, refused, perhaps because he knew that the Indians worshiped the earth goddess Tonantzin on the same hillside. He changed his mind when Juan Diego reappeared with a profusion of out-of-season roses wrapped in a cloak imbued with an image which the bishop himself identified as Mary, the Virgin of Guadalupe. In 1754, over two centuries later, the Virgin of Guadalupe was declared the patron saint of Mexico. In France in 1858, a series of visitations reported by a fourteen-year-old girl turned Lourdes into a shrine where five million pilgrims still go every year in hopes of being healed. Millions more travel to Fatima, which became famous in the tumultuous year of 1917 after three Portuguese children reported that the Virgin Mary appeared in front of them (and confided that she was worried about recent events in Russia). Some centuries have been richer in visitations than others. In the eighteenth century, only seventeen visitations were reported. In the twentieth century, more than four hundred sightings were reported, some in very silly places. According to one estimate, over the last thousand years, approximately 21,000 people throughout the Catholic world described encounters with the Virgin Mary.

All of which put Christian theologians in an awkward position. To assert that Mary, while admirable, was not actually divine, they had to make some fine distinctions. Logically inconvenient elements of the story, such as Mary's virginity, had to be addressed, for although many mythologies include stories of virgin birth, only Christianity seemed intend on taking it literally.

Today, after grappling with these matters for two thousand years, the Catholic church supports these official doctrines about Mary:

- Perpetual Virginity. She was granted this quality at the Second Council of Constantinople in 381, despite the fact that the Bible repeatedly mentions her other children.
- Divine Motherhood. In 431, a Church Council at Ephesus, once the shrine of Artemis, gave Mary the title "Theotokos" or Bearer of God.
- Immaculate Conception. This means that in addition to being a virgin mother, Mary was herself the fruit of a virgin birth, born without original sin, which arrives at the instant of conception. A story supporting this idea appeared in the second-century Protoevangelium or Book of James. It seems that for many years, Mary's parents, Anna and Joachim, had yearned for a child. When a high priest at the temple suggested to Joachim that his childlessness was a punishment from God, Joachim trekked into the desert to do penance. While he was there (for forty days, naturally), Anna stayed behind. One day she wandered into a garden and an angel announced that she would bear a child. Joachim received the message at the same time and rushed home. At the gates of Jerusalem, the two embraced joyfully, and Anna soon gave birth to Mary. This story was eventually dropped from the official church canon. The idea behind it, the Immaculate Conception, remained, and was made official in 1854.
- Assumption into heaven. How did Mary die? The church struggled long and hard with that question. The dilemma was that, if Mary was the mother of God and therefore without sin, surely she didn't die in the same way as the rest of us. Perhaps she didn't die at all. But that inconvenient omission would make her immortal, perilously like a goddess, and even greater than Jesus, who did die, even if he returned

later on. So although her death, like her birth, is not mentioned in the Bible, and there was no corroborating evidence (such as a tomb or a relic), it was essential that Mary die. During the first several centuries of the Christian era, many stories, often involving Jews, were told about her death. None were official, and the confusion surrounding her death remained. That uncertainty is reflected in the word used to describe the death of Mary: it is called the Dormition, or falling asleep. Ultimately, the notion developed that Mary died and was immediately reanimated and lifted directly into heaven, generally in a cloud or a chariot. Thus she was better than the rest of us, though still not a goddess. As the eighth-century theologian John Damascene wrote, "We do not celebrate a goddess, as in the fantastic fables of the Greeks, since we proclaim her death." The details about her death became official doctrine on November 1, 1950, when Pope Pius XII stood in front of a crowd in Saint Peter's Square and proclaimed that Mary was "taken up body and soul into heavenly glory upon the completion of her earthly sojourn."

- Queen of Heaven. In the Book of Revelations (12.2), these lines appear: "And there appeared a great wonder in heaven: clothed with the sun, and the moon under her feet, and upon her head a crown of twelve stars." That passage has been repeatedly illustrated with images of Mary standing on a crescent moon and wearing a star-strewn blue cloak. Like other goddesses before her, Mary is more than a mother, and her reign is global, lunar, astronomical. Her celestial role became official in 1954 when Pope Pius XII gave her the title Queen of Heaven.

Today, Mary is a peculiar figure. Adored by countless believers, she receives mixed reviews from feminists. On the one hand, she loses points for docility, passivity, and being defined in terms of a male. "For the first time in history," writes Simone de Beauvoir, "the mother kneels before her son; she freely accepts her inferiority. This is the supreme masculine victory, consummated in the cult of the Virgin." Other feminists celebrate the persistence of her worship, which they see as more vital than that accorded her son. They assert, with Elizabeth Gould Davis, author of *The First Sex,* that "the only reality in Christianity is Mary, the Female Principle, the ancient goddess reborn."

It has been claimed that Mary may be the Mother of God and the Queen of Heaven but, unlike the ancient goddesses, she is not the earth mother, and thus her position is diminished. That's an argument for theologians. Whatever church doctrine may be on the subject, the fact is that around the world, billions of people find solace in worshipping the Virgin Mary, Mother Goddess of Christianity.

> *Zeus rides thru Bethlehem's blue sky.*
> *It's Buddha sits in Mary's belly waving Kuan*
> *Yin's white hand at the Yang-tze . . .*
>
> —Allen Ginsburg

Niamh

One day when the great Celtic poet and warrior Oisín (or Ossian) was out hunting, the golden-haired Niamh, goddess of the Otherworld, rode up beside him on her silver-hooved steed and convinced him to climb onto the horse behind her. Soon the two of them were galloping over the waves to an island in the eastern sea called Tir na n'Og, the Land of Forever Young, a place where pain, sorrow, and old age are unknown.

During his sojourn in the Otherworld, Oisín and Niamh became lovers and she gave birth to a daughter named Plur na mBan, the Flower of Women.

> And Niamh calling *Away, come away:*
> *Empty your heart of its mortal dream.*
>
> —W. B. Yeats

Much as he enjoyed his new family, he confessed that he felt homesick for Ireland and wished to return for a visit. Although Niamh was not encouraging, he persisted. At last she agreed to let him borrow her magic horse on one condition: he must not dismount. To do so would be disastrous.

So Oisín got on the horse and rode to Ireland. When he arrived, nothing looked the same and he could find no one he knew. He soon discovered why: while he was dallying with Niamh, three hundred years had passed. Not long after learning that disturbing fact, he stopped to help a group of men move a heavy boulder, lost his balance, and toppled to the ground. Within seconds, his youth evaporated, he was ambushed by old age, and his body crumpled into dust.

That's one version of the story. According to another, Oisín aged horribly when he fell, turning from a vital warrior into a fragile, stooped old man. But he did not die. Instead, he met Saint Patrick, who engaged him in a long conversation about his father, Finn MacCool, and the pagan past. Those stories, along with stories told by Caolite, another refugee from the Land of Forever Young, were compiled around the year 1200 in *The Interrogation of the Old Men,* a classic of Gaelic literature.

OTO-HIME: THE JAPANESE VERSION

In the annals of mythology, Niamh's experience with a mortal lover is not unique. Something similar happened in Japan, where a fisherman named Urashima caught a turtle, threw it back into the ocean, and was rewarded when the turtle offered to introduce him to the Dragon Princess at the bottom of the sea. Urashima climbed on the turtle's back and held on until they reached the undersea paradise of the goddess Oto-Hime. Like Niamh, she was a beauty. Her palace was a marvel of pearls, coral, and shells, and her attendants were dragons with golden tails. Naturally, the goddess and the fisherman fell in love. But after a while, he became homesick and longed to see his parents. Oto-Hime tried to convince him to stay. When her attempts proved futile, she gave him a small box accompanied by the usual mythological injunction: Do not open.

Urashima took the box, climbed onto the turtle's back, and left the watery Eden behind. Back home, nothing looked familiar. Even the fashions were new, and he could not find a single person he knew. At last he spoke with an old man who dimly recalled Urashima's family as people who had lived in the area three hundred years before. Urashima was so perplexed by this revelation that, without thinking, he pried open the box. A wisp of smoke spiraled into the air, and as it dissolved, Urashima withered, aged, and disintegrated into dust.

Oshun and Oya

If there is one contemporary form that mythology most resembles, it would be soap opera. And if there is one specific mythology that might be presented in that form and still maintain its essential flavor, it would be the stories that the Yoruba of Nigeria and their descendants in the Western Hemisphere tell about their orishas, or dieties. Consider, for example, the goddesses Oshun and Oya, both of whom loved the fire-breathing Chango (or Shango), a handsome warrior, ruthless king, and powerful magician.

Oshun, the luxury-loving goddess of love, sexuality, healing, and fresh water, was an irresistible coquette who had many lovers. She married Orunmiller, the god of divination, and she was herself a master of prognostication. But the love of her life was the unpredictable Chango, who hung himself from a tree (like Odin) and became a storm god. Although she was attracted to him at first sight, he pretended to ignore her wiles. His indifference evaporated when she dipped her fingers into her gourd and spread honey over his lips. Soon they were embroiled in a passionate affair.

At the same time, Chango was deeply involved with Oya, the fierce goddess of wind, water, tornadoes, sudden change, and the River Niger. She was married to Ogun, the hot-tempered, industrious god of war and metal. Once she met the charming, seductive Chango, she abandoned her husband in a flash.

Oya soon discovered that men like Chango are seldom monogamous. One time, she tried to keep him away from Oshun by imprisoning him in his own house, surrounded by the dead. Her efforts failed, for Oshun, who is as powerful as Oya, crept past the guards, dressed Chango in women's clothes, and helped him escape. However, Chango left the house so quickly that he forgot to take his magic gourd, which held the secret of breathing fire. When Oya found the gourd and tasted the ground-up paste inside, her mouth burned and lightning leaped from her lips. After Chango returned, their relationship grew even more quarrelsome. Now whenever thunder rumbles through the air and lightning rips across the sky, people say that Oya and Chango are squabbling.

As for Ogun, he did not bounce back so easily after Oya left him. Like Hephaestus, the Greek god of metal who caught his beloved Aphrodite in bed with Ares, Ogun was devastated. The difference was that Hephaestus demanded justice, whereas Ogun withdrew and disappeared into the woods. With the god of work nowhere to be seen, people grew lazy and quit their labors. All building ceased. The other orishas tried to lure Ogun out of hiding but he wouldn't budge. Even Oludumare, the supreme deity, could not convince Ogun to return to the world. Something had to be done.

Oshun stepped in. She donned her most provocative clothing, tied five yellow handkerchiefs around her waist (yellow is her favorite color), and began to dance. Each day, she swayed a little closer to Ogun. Finally she was so close that she was able to dip her fingers into her gourd and smear honey over his lips. This technique had worked with Chango, and it was every bit as effective with Ogun. Smitten, he ventured out, and soon people picked up their tools and returned to work. Since then, Ogun occasionally retires to the woods, though never for long. He has lost his bitterness over Oya; he has never stopped longing for the love of Oshun.

Parvati

Parvati, like other Hindu goddesses, was a manifestation of the Divine Mother Devi. A self-disciplined ascetic, affectionate mother and highly sexual spouse, she was the daughter of the mountain and one of the many wives of Shiva, the god of creation and destruction.

Sweet and benevolent, Parvati married Shiva after the suicide of his previous wife, Sati. Chillingly translated as "good woman," Sati was humiliated because her husband had been excluded from a sacrifice. To express her outrage over that slight, she threw herself on a blazing pyre, thereby starting the Hindu custom of suttee. Afterwards, Sati reincarnated as Parvati. From childhood, she wished to marry the great

Parvati, daughter of the mountain, sitting on a bull.

god. To attract his admiration, she practiced extreme austerities such as standing on one leg for years at a time. Shiva too was pursuing the life of an ascetic, living as a yogi in the mountains. But Indra, king of the gods, did not want Shiva to withdraw from the world. He commanded Kama, the god of love, to shoot Shiva with one of the arrows of desire and thus to make him aware of Parvati's presence. When the arrow found its mark, Shiva was shaken out of his meditative state. His eye fell upon Parvati, and soon they married.

Their sex life was so earthshaking that the gods decided to interrupt them. As a result, Shiva spilled his seed on the ground. It ended up in the Ganges River, where it formed Karttikeya or Skanda, the six-headed god of war. As soon as Parvati saw him, her milk started to flow and she happily nursed him. (Kali is also said to have nursed Skanda.)

Nonetheless, Parvati was disturbed that Shiva had created a child without her. She balanced the scales by creating her son Ganesha entirely on her own. One day she wanted to take a bath but was unable to find anyone to guard the room. So she rubbed a few flakes of skin off her body and turned them into Ganesha. He promised to allow no one into the room. Even when Shiva appeared, Ganesha refused to let him enter. This time, Shiva was the one who felt slighted. He sent his attendants to fight Ganesha. They didn't stand a chance. Ganesha grabbed an iron club and soon there were severed body parts and bashed-in bodies everywhere. Thoroughly enraged, Shiva grabbed his trident and sliced off Ganesha's head.

The attendants rejoiced with hand drums and kettle drums. There was nothing to celebrate, though, for Parvati was so distressed by the murder of her son that she was ready to destroy the world. The seers and the gods begged for her forgiveness, and at last she relented under one condition: that her son be revived.

Because it was too late for Ganesha to return to his original form, Shiva instructed the gods to decapitate the first being to cross their path and connect its head to Ganesha's fallen body. The first such creature was an elephant. They cut off its head, attached it to Ganesha's body, chanted mantras over the corpse, and sprinkled it with holy water. Ganesha came to life, and the world was saved. With her child revived, Parvati and Shiva enjoyed a contented family life and are often depicted relaxing outdoor with their sons.

Like the Divine Mother Devi and other Hindu goddesses, Parvati appears in several forms. In addition to her previous incarnation as Sati, she became Gauri, Kali, and Uma, who was devoted to asceticism. Sometimes said to be one of Parvati's sisters, Uma received her name when her mother, upon learning that yet another of her daughters had renounced the world, called out "Oh! Don't!" or "U! Ma!"

HOW GANESHA LOST HIS TUSK

One of the most recognizable gods in any mythology, Ganesha, the son of Parvati, has four arms, a pot belly, and the head of an elephant. Close examination reveals, however, that he often has only one tusk. The missing one, it is sometimes said, was severed in a fight. A more common explanation has it that Ganesha, as the god of wisdom, learning, and writing, wore his tusk down by using it to record all 11,000 verses of the *Mahabarata*, one of the great Sanskrit epics. A popular god often depicted riding a rat, he is invoked at the beginning of enterprises and worshipped with red flowers, herbs, and small cakes shaped like figs.

Pele

Do many people today actually "believe" in gods and goddesses? In the case of the Hawaiian fire goddess Pele, the answer is yes. Her violent spirit is easily piqued and when she explodes in wrath, incandescent rivers of lava snake down the mountainside and blizzards of ash blanket the surroundings. Before a volcanic eruption, people say, she always appears nearby and when she stamps her foot, the earth rumbles. To prevent these disasters, Pele's devotees soothe her by singing ancient chants and by tossing sugarcane, strawberries, hibiscus, silk, brandy, and tobacco into the heart of the volcano.

Her story, an epic tale of love, betrayal, and sibling rivalry, begins on Tahiti, her first home. Some say that she left that island because her husband, Wahieloa, had been enticed by another lover. Others say that she drove her family to distraction and they forced her to go, perhaps because her sister Na-maka-o-ka-ha'i discovered that Pele had been consorting with her husband.

To escape from her angry sister, Pele stole her brother's canoe and headed north with her youngest sister, Hi'iaka. They sailed for a long time. But Pele couldn't find a good place to stop, and Na-maka-o-ka-ha'i was fast approaching.

When the two sisters met at last, a titanic battle broke out between them. They fought fiercely, but Pele was at a disadvantage, for Na-maka-o-ka-ha'i was assisted by a sea monster and in due time she triumphed. Which is to say, Pele died. Her spirit floated out of her body and settled in Hawaii, where she took up residence in Mount Kilauea.

With the crater as her base, Pele explored the world in various guises, typically as an old woman or a radiant young one. To make sure that her wandering soul didn't get permanently separated from her body, her loyal sister Hi'iaka would call her back after three days by singing a magical chant. Even when Pele fell in love with Lohiau, a handsome chief who lived far away, Hi'iaka called her back after only three days.

Longing to spend more time with her lover, Pele asked Hi'iaka to bring him to her, a trip that she estimated would take forty days. In exchange, Pele promised to tend her sister's garden. So Hi'iaka, fortified with magical powers, left on her journey. Along the way, she restored the hands of a girl who had none, cured a man of his lameness, and had other adventures. As a result, the trip took longer than anticipated, and by the time she arrived, Lohiau had been so devastated by Pele's long absence that he had hanged himself. Using her magical chant, Hi'iaka called his spirit back, forced it to enter his body by way of the eye socket, and thus restored his life. They began the journey back.

As they traveled, Hi'iaka and Lohiau became attracted to each other but Hi'iaka loved her sister and resisted the temptation. However, when they reached Hawaii, she learned that Pele had burned her sister's gardens in a jealous fit and killed Hi'iaka's friend, the poet Hopoe, who had taught her the hula. As an act of vengeance, Hi'iaka seduced Lohiau. They made love on the rim of the volcano, in full view of Pele. Pele retaliated by drowning Lohiau in a river of lava.

Dead again, Lohiau descended through the ten levels of the

underworld, and Hi'iaka followed. At the lowest level, Hi'iaka was about to open the floodgates and drown the world just to destroy her sister. But at the last moment, she relented and went to Oahu, where she discovered that Lohiau had been brought back to life by another diety. Overjoyed, Hi'iaka and Lohiau become lovers.

Not long afterwards, Pele met someone new: Kama'pua'a, the hog god. Amorous and bellicose, he could expand until his body covered an entire valley, shrink until he disappeared into the undergrowth like a tiny piglet, or take on human form. Soon Pele and he were lovers. Even so, her temper can never be truly controlled. She continues to punish those who anger her, which is why people in Hawaii, natives and visitors alike, still attest to the violence of her temper.

Quies

Whenever people seek parallels between the Roman divinities and those of the Greeks, the Romans invariably suffer. One reason is that Greek literature predates Roman literature by centuries. By the time the Romans were writing about their myths, they were thoroughly steeped in the legends of Olympus and tended to fuse the Roman gods with their Greek equivalents, even when the parallels were less than perfect. And who could blame them? The ancient Italian divinities played a role in religious observances but lacked personalities, and there were often no stories about them. Even major deities such as Janus, the two-faced god of doorways and beginnings whose name lingers on in the word January, lacked significant mythology. In addition, the Romans acknowledged a horde of utilitarian gods who had stunningly specific functions. Among them were Consus, who oversaw the wheat harvest, Silvanus, who reigned over the clearing of the land, Mena, the goddess of menstruation, and three minor gods who, like Janus, presided over the doorway: Forculus, whose role was to guard the door itself, Cardea, who oversaw the hinges, and Limentinus, who stood watch over the threshold. Not surprisingly, many of these gods simply disappeared.

In some ways, that's a loss. Because there are certain Roman dieties whom, if one were a believer, one might wish to invoke more often. Chief among them is Quies, the Roman goddess of tranquillity, who was worshipped at rest stops along the side of the road. Saint Augustine, no friend to paganism, noted that her temple was beyond the city gates and opined that this low-status location was "a symptom of an unquiet mind," proof that because the Romans worshipped "a mob of demons," they "could not dwell with quiet." The temple of Quies, he observed, never became a national shrine; the goddess received no public acknowledgment.

But why would she? The Romans were no fools. They knew that a goddess of serenity, worshipped for her ability to calm the soul, would seldom be encountered in the city or invoked in public. Her name lives on in the word "quiet."

Rhiannon

The Celtic goddess Rhiannon was betrothed against her will to Gwawl, the son of a goddess. However, she had her eye on someone else: Pwyll, the King of Dyfed, a kingdom in southwest Wales. To attract his attention, she dressed up in gold and trotted past him on a white mare. Smitten, he pursued her for days but she just kept on riding. At last, thoroughly exasperated, he called out, "Wait for me!" whereupon she stopped and declared her love. Pwyll responded in kind.

Not long afterwards, poor Gwawl was invited to what he thought would be his wedding feast. Instead, following a series of tricks and double crosses, he was trapped inside Rhiannon's magic bag of abundance and kicked around like a ball by the wedding guests. Rhiannon happily married Pwyll.

Soon she had a son. Six attendants guarded him. Nevertheless, on the first of May, one of the four holiest days of the Celtic calendar, they all fell asleep at once and he was kidnapped. To protect themselves from accusations, the attendants plotted to cast the blame on Rhiannon, who had nodded off herself. They killed a puppy, smeared the blood over her lips, and charged her with murdering her child. She vehemently maintained innocence, but the evidence against her was compelling, and she was sentenced to sit for seven years at the gate to Ardeth Castle. Every time a visitor arrived, she had to relate her story and carry that visitor on her back, like a horse, to the castle door.

Meanwhile, peculiar events were happening in Dyfed at the home of a man named Teyrnon. Every year on the first of May, one of his mares would give birth to a foal, which would promptly disappear. In hopes of clearing up the mystery, Teyrnon spent a watchful night in the stable. To his astonishment, the moment the foal was born, a giant claw reached through the stable window and grabbed it. Teyrnon was ready. He hacked off the claw with his sword and saved the horse. When he stepped outside a few minutes later, he found a baby on his doorstep.

He and his wife named the child Gwri ("Golden Hair") and raised him. In time he realized that the child must be the one stolen from Rhiannon, and he returned him to her. She named her son Pryderi ("Care"), and her period of punishment came to an end.

Years passed. Pryderi grew up and got married, Pwyll died, and Rhiannon married Manawydan, the son of Lyr. One day, while Rhiannon, Manawydan, and Pryderi were attending a feast, a pale mist settled over them. When it lifted, the familiar landscape had disappeared and they were adrift in a wasteland. They all set off to England. In the course of their travels, Rhiannon and Pryderi came upon a golden cauldron which was attached to the sky with four long chains. It was lovely to look at but the moment they touched it, their hands stuck to its shiny, well-crafted surface and they were unable to speak.

Manawydan had no idea where they were. He didn't even know where to look. Instead, he busied himself by trying to cultivate a field of wheat. He had an adversary, though: a field mouse who kept stealing his grain. When he finally captured the mouse, he was so angry that he decided to string it up on a miniature gallows and hang it. Fortunately, a right-thinking bishop arrived and talked him out of the execution. In exchange for the life of the mouse, Manawydan obtained the freedom of Rhiannon and Pryderi.

Rhiannon is often identified with Epona, the horse goddess worshipped by the Romans.

Rhiannon's story is told in the *Mabinogion,* a collection of medieval Welsh tales, the earliest of which was written down in the eleventh century. The stories, including several Arthurian tales, were translated into English in the nineteenth century by Lady Charlotte Elizabeth Guest.

Once, after a man she had been kind to tried to rape her, she turned into a horse and broke his thighbone with a kick. Nonetheless, her emblematic animal is a trio of magical birds. Their song was so strong that it could rouse the dead and so sweet that, even heard from a distance across the open sea, it could cure insomnia and deliver the balm of sleep.

Sedna

Sedna, the Inuit goddess of the sea, was a beautiful young woman who rejected all her suitors and refused to wed . . . until the day she lost her heart to a bird-man.

He was a fulmar, an Arctic seabird noted for its foul smell. For a long time, he had been searching for a mate among the other birds. None struck his fancy. Then he saw Sedna and fell in love. He assumed human form, cut and stitched a luxurious parka for himself, and proceeded to woo her in the classic way. "Come live with me and be my love," he said, or words to that effect. She would live in luxury, he declared in a cozy tent made of soft furs and exquisite feathers, and he promised her an ivory necklace, delicious food, and all the supplies she could ever want. She decided to cast her fate with the bird-man.

As soon as she arrived at his home after a long journey by kayak, she realized that he had lied to her. The tent was covered not with thick animal furs but with the thin, scaly skins of fish, and the cold wind whipped through them. Instead of a bearskin rug on the bed, she had to sleep on leathery walrus hides. And the jewelry was nowhere to be seen. In her misery, she called out to her father to rescue her, but he was far away and couldn't hear her. She spent months in that desolate place. At last, winter turned to spring, and Sedna's father showed up to visit his beloved daughter. When she told him how unhappy she was, he was so angry that he struck the bird-man and killed him. He and Sedna climbed into the kayak and began to paddle home.

Trouble followed. When the other seabirds discovered the lifeless body of the bird-man, they sought revenge. They flew after Sedna, surrounded the boat, and flapped their wings viciously, churning up the water and the wind. They kayak rocked and turned in the high waves. As storm clouds gathered, Sedna's father grew afraid. He loved his daughter. But he knew that sooner or later the boat would capsize and he would be sucked beneath the waves—and all because of her. Not wanting to drown in the frigid sea, he took the only action he could think of: he tossed her overboard.

Sedna clung to the side of the kayak. The birds continued to flap and caw, and the little boat bucked and rolled in the crashing waves. Sedna's father was distraught. He knew that until his daughter sank beneath the water, his own life was in danger. So he took out his fishing knife and hacked off her fingers one by one at the first joint. Her fingertips tumbled into the sea, where they swelled into whales and swam away.

Yet Sedna still clung to the side of the boat. So her father attacked again. He chopped her fingers off at the middle joint. And those bloody segments of her fingers dropped into the water too, where they were turned into ringed seals and paddled away. Then he cut off the bloody stumps of her fingers, which turned into bearded ground seals, and her thumbs, which became walruses. All these animals swam away, and yet Sedna using her wrists, clung to the side of the boat. Finally the seabirds stopped their commotion and wheeled away.

The storm subsided. With her father's help, Sedna climbed back into the boat. But she was furious with him, and though they sailed for a long time, her anger did not subside. Back in the village, she sought revenge. As her father slept, she called her team of huskies and directed them to gnaw on his hands and feet. He awoke in agony to find the dogs chewing on his extremities. He cursed and screamed, and as he did, the earth trembled and shook until the ground gave way beneath them. Sedna, her father, and the dogs plummeted to the bottom of the sea, where the underworld is located.

Sedna lives there still. As queen of the underworld (and chief diety of her people), she can reward hunters with animals or threaten them with terrifying storms. There is only one thing she cannot do, and so a shaman seeking her assistance must journey in spirit to the bottom of the ocean and help her comb her magnificent long hair.

Tatsuta-Hime

In the Japanese pantheon, Tatsuta-Hime is a minor wind goddess, one of many. She is distinguished by her unforgettable function. Every autumn, she weaves a vivid tapestry of orange, yellow, russet, crimson, and gold, and then she blows it all to pieces, making her the goddess of autumn leaves.

Taueret

For anyone who imagines that a goddess must be either beautiful or terrifying, there is something refreshing about the Egyptian goddess Taueret. In a destructive mood, she could turn into a lion-headed, dagger-wielding hippopotamus or even a crocodile. Most

of the time, she was depicted as a pot-bellied, sweet-faced hippo with sagging breasts. Nonetheless, she was a powerful goddess. As a sky goddess represented by the constellation Ursa Major, she assisted at the birth of the sun god and ruled the stars and planets. As a goddess of the underworld, she carried the dead into eternity. And as a fertility goddess and an aspect of the mother goddess Mut, she assisted women in labor and protected newborn babies. Not surprisingly, she inspired a large following. Pregnant women wore images of her on pendants around their necks, parents named their children after her, and graffiti artists of the Middle Kingdom invoked her at the temple of Karnak in Thebes.

*Taueret leaning on a protective amulet.
(Credit: Hannah Berman)*

She also had an interesting romantic history. According to Plutarch, she was once the concubine of the evil Seth, who murdered his brother Osiris. But when Seth tried to wrest the throne away from Horus, Taueret deserted him in favor of her husband Bes, a household god imported into Egypt from Nubia. He was a pop-eyed, bow-legged, lecherous dwarf associated with love, luck, marriage, music, and sweet dreams. Like his wife, he was wildly popular.

Tien-Mu

Every culture has weather gods. Thunder and lightning are normally the attributes of a storm god, like Zeus or Thor. But in Chinese mythology, lightning belongs to Tien-Mu, goddess of the North Star and benefactor of fortune tellers. The mother of the first nine rulers on earth, she is active during thunderstorms when she calmly manipulates two mirrors to create branching bolts of light. She is known as Mother Lightning.

Uke Mochi

Uke Mochi, the Japanese goddess of food, was married to Inari, the god of rice. One day the moon god Tsuki-yomi, brother of the sun goddess Amaterasu, dropped in for a visit. In an attempt to be hospitable, Uke Mochi threw up vast quantities of fish, seaweed, game, and boiled rice. Tsuki-yomi was so disgusted by the manner in which he had been served that he killed her. Herds of cattle and horses stampeded out of Uke Mochi's head. Rice, millet, and red beans spilled out of her eyes, ears, and nose. Wheat sprouted from her genitals, soy beans grew from her rectum, and even a mulberry tree crawling with silkworms sprang from her body.

Amaterasu, whose relationship with her brother was often strained, could hardly believe what he had done. Despite the magnificent harvest that issued from Uke Mochi's body, Amaterasu withdrew. The sky grew dark, the temperature dropped, and winter appeared for the first time. After several months she returned but she refused to see Tsuki-yomi again. And that is why, even today, they avoid each other. Amaterasu, goddess of the sun, shines only by day, while her brother Tsuki-yomi, god of the moon, illuminates the night.

The Valkyries

A thousand years ago, more or less, a Germanic soldier near Dublin had a bloody, spear-filled nightmare in which he saw a group of

The Valkyries.

women weaving on a loom made from men's entrails and weighed down in the corners with severed heads. He didn't need a soothsayer to tell him that this dream, which wakened him from sleep the night before a battle, was a bad omen. He knew that he had seen the Valkyries, "Choosers of the Slain," who appear before men when they are about to die in combat.

The Valkyries are goddesses of destiny, as the weaving imagery in the warrior's dream suggests. Like the Greek Moirae—Klotho, who spun the thread of life, Lachesis, who unraveled the thread, and Atropos, who cut it at the time of death—the Valkyries wield the power of life and death, though only in combat. During times of war, it was their function to determine which side would be victorious, to choose the warriors who would die, and to accompany them to Valhalla to await the final battle, Ragnarok. (Those who died of natural causes did not go to Valhalla but to the realm of the goddess Hel.) Fierce and implacable, the Valkyries could appear as wolves, ravens, crows, hawks, swans, or women, their preferred form. In their breastplates and helmets, they rode their white horses high above the plains of battle. The light glinting off their shields formed the aurora borealis.

Once the carnage was over, an amazing transformation took place. The Valkyries set their ferocity aside, retreated to Valhalla, stripped off their armor, put on white dresses, and became waitresses, serving horns of mead to the fallen warriors, who even in the afterlife continued to indulge themselves in games of combat. Helpful, subservient, and blond, they were the handmaidens (or companions or daughters) of Odin, and they did his bidding. In nineteenth-century artwork, they look hearty, buxom, and thoroughly operatic.

Like other goddesses of fate, the Valkyries existed in a group, often of nine (as in Richard Wagner's opera, *Die Walküre*) or thirteen. The most famous is Brunhilde (or Brynhild), who brought death to a warrior beloved by Odin. To punish her, Odin pricked her finger and put her to sleep, á la Sleeping Beauty, in a castle surrounded by a ring of fire. Not until someone dared to walk through the flames for her would she be awakened—and even then, she would never again possess the powers of Valkyrie.

Brunhilde slept for many years. At long last, the hero Sigurd (Siegfried) rescued her. Alas, they were star-crossed lovers. Thanks to a secret love potion and a complicated plot, Sigurd married someone else and Brunhilde, crazed by jealousy, arranged the murder of her beloved. When the foul deed was done and she was stricken with remorse, she mounted her horse and rode into the flames of the funeral pyre, where she died the death of a mortal woman, a scene that marks the end of Wagner's opera *Die Götterdämmerung*, The Twilight of the Gods.

White Buffalo Woman

The Oglala Sioux tell a story about two Indian scouts who noticed a blur on the northern horizon. At first, it was as indistinct as a puff of smoke but after a while, they could see that it was a long-haired woman in a white buckskin dress. One of the men wished desperately to sleep with her. The other realized that she was a sacred woman and counseled against it. He was wasting his words. The woman, who could read their thoughts, invited the lustful man to embrace her, and he didn't hesitate. As he stood face to face with her, a white cloud appeared out of nowhere and surrounded them. When the cloud blew away in the wind, the woman was standing there in her full glory, while the man had turned into a skeleton and worms were crawling on his bones.

White Buffalo Woman told the other scout to return to his tribe and tell them to erect a large teepee for her. When the teepee was finished, she handed the chief a pipe decorated with twelve eagle feathers and a drawing of a calf. She explained how to use the pipe to determine whether good times or bad times lay ahead, and she gave the people seven sacred ceremonies, including the vision quest, the sun dance, and the girls' puberty rites. Talking to the chief inside the teepee, she looked like a beautiful woman. But as she walked away from the teepee, she turned into a white buffalo, and everyone watched as she kicked up her hind legs and galloped to the horizon.

Xochiquetzal

After the great flood, only two beings survived: a nameless man and the Aztec goddess Xochiquetzal ("Flower Feather"). As the goddess of love and fertility, Xochiquetzal ate the forbidden fruit of the world tree and brought sexual pleasure into the world. Soon she became pregnant. Her offspring looked normal but they lacked the power of speech, and it wasn't until a dove gave them the gift of language that they were able to communicate. Sadly, each of her children received a different language, with results that still plague us today.

Xochiquetzal was also the mother of Quetzalcoatl, who was masturbating one day when his semen fell on a rock and turned into a bat. The bat careened into the sky, flew to Xochiquetzal, and tore a tiny piece of flesh from her genitals. That bit of flesh gave birth to all the flowers, including marigolds, her favorite. She is associated with weaving, magic, handicrafts, the family, the moon, and the underworld, which she visited with the god Tezcatlipoca, who kidnapped her from her lover.

Like other goddesses, she took revenge on those who thwarted her, as her encounter with the hermit Yappan revealed. He had decided to shun the pleasures of the flesh and devote himself to penitential acts. To prove his sincerity, he chose to live on top of a tall, cylindrical stone. The gods tortured him with various temptations but he held fast to his asceticism until the alluring Xochiquetzal arrived. She convinced him to come down from the rock and then to climb back up with her. When they reached the top of the pillar, he was unable to resist her advances. As a result of his failure to uphold his vows, his enemy Yaotl cut off his head, and the gods turned him into a scorpion. Now, instead of spending his time in contemplation on top of the stone, he scuttles throughout the dirt and skulks among the pebbles.

In the tenth century, people complained that Xochiquetzal, who once blanketed the earth in flowers and fruit, had withdrawn. To appease the goddess and assure continued fertility, an annual ritual arose known as the Feast of Flowers. Everyone adorned themselves and their houses with blossoms, and artisans displayed their wares in a festival of crafts. The event reached the climax when a young girl, chosen to impersonate the goddess by weaving beneath a "world tree," was sacrificed and flayed. Afterwards, a man put on her skin and sat at a loom, and the dancing began.

Yambe-Akka

Goddesses of the underworld are numerous and, most of the time, grand. Sometimes frightening (like Hecate or Hel), sometimes not (like Niamh, Oto-Hime, or the lovely Persephone), they are always powerful. Yambe-Akka, a goddess of the Scandinavian Lapps, is no exception. She rules the underworld, a dismal place located directly beneath the ordinary world where the dead, not entirely disembodied, walk on air. She requires the sacrifice of black cats, who were buried alive by her devotees, and she also has a servant, a diminutive man dressed entirely in blue whose function is to torture the deceased. Yet for all the horror that surrounds her, Yambe-Akka also possesses a touch of human vulnerability. For like many of the denizens of the underworld, Yambe-Akka is old, and her hands sometimes tremble. Whenever that happens, the earth shakes.

The Zorya

In Eastern Europe, the Zorya is a double or triple goddess. In her twin form, her task is to open the gates of the sky in the morning so that the sun can begin its daily passage and to close them at dusk, when its journey is through. In her triple form, she is the goddess of evening, the goddess of midnight, and the goddess of morning. Yet she is charged with only a single task: guarding a dog who is chained to the North Star, the only light in the heavens that appears in the same place every night (although, over eons, it too moves). Her vigilance is essential. For if the chain were to break and the dog ran free, the world would end. The Zorya's job is to make certain that never happens.

From the Annals of Mythology: The Legendary Mythologists

In the nineteenth century, mythology came alive. Archaeologists took mythology out of the airy realm of the purely literary and made it palpable by excavating, among other sites, Troy, Nineveh, and the Palace of Knossos, legendary home of the Minotaur. New myths appeared, including the *Gilgamesh Epic*, buried for over 2,400 years, and the *Popul Vuh*, the creation myth of the Quiché Maya of Guatemala, which was published for the first time in 1857. In addition, mythologists formulated some interesting ideas (such as the hero's journey) and devised a bewildering array of theories to explain the origin of mythology.

Three of the most engaging mythologists were Sanskrit scholar F. Max Müller (1823–1900), who used linguistics to prove that the vast majority of myths have something to do with the sun; Sir James George Frazer (1854–1941), whose 1890 opus, *The Golden Bough,* linked primitive mythology and ritual and introduced the concept of the dying-and-rising god to a large audience; and Jane Harrison (1850–1928), the first feminist mythologist. She applied Frazer's insights to the Greeks and came to deplore them utterly.

Max Müller and the Disease of Language

If you accept the theories of Max Müller, myth is basically one big misunderstanding. A German Sanskrit scholar who translated the *Rig Veda* and became a professor at Oxford, Müller based his theories on a widely accepted notion that stated that Sanskrit and most

European languages were derived from a primitive language brought to India by prehistoric invaders called Aryans. Müller believed that the Aryans revered nature and were anxious to communicate their thoughts about it.

Their efforts were stymied by a paucity of vocabulary. Limited to concrete nouns and root verbs, they were unable to express many ideas directly. Instead, clubbing their listeners with words Müller called "heavy and unwieldy," they personified physical processes and explained nature in ways that were largely metaphorical and focused on one topic: the sun. "Where we speak of the sun following the dawn, the ancient poets could only speak and think of the Sun loving and embracing the Dawn. What is with us a sunset, was to them the Sun growing old, decaying, or dying. Our sunrise was to them the Night giving birth to a beautiful child; and in the Spring they really saw the Sun or the sky embracing the earth with a warm embrace, and showering treasures into the lap of nature." These metaphors, which obscured meaning as much as they communicated it, required explanation and elaboration; myth provided just that. Thus myth was in essence "a disease of language."

When these primitive people swept out of Asia and into Europe, they brought their roundabout constructions with them, making the myths of the Greeks a devolution of the Aryan attempts to express their thoughts about the natural world. So no matter how "silly, savage, and senseless" a myth might seem (and Müller was appalled by the brutality and cannibalism of the Greeks, whose stories, he wrote, "would make the most savage of Red Indians creep and shudder"), the words, and the names in particular, if traced back to their etymological roots, would reveal the original meaning. Müller noted, for instance, that Athena is meaningless in Greek, but that in Sanskrit, *ahana* meant dawn; thus stories told about Athena must originally have been about sunrise. Using this method, all kinds of seemingly complex myths could be reduced to a solar analogy.

For perhaps half a century after the publication of his essay "Comparative Mythology" in 1856, anyone studying mythology had to grapple with Müller's theory, which saw every myth as an etymological screen behind which lurked a natural phenomenon. This idea stirred up enormous publicity and even stimulated variant theories, such as the idea that the thunderstorm, not the sun, is at the center of ancient myth. It also gained Müller a lifelong opponent in the form of Andrew Lang, a Scottish scholar best known today for his twelve fairy tale collections. Lang got the last word in when, having outlived Müller, he dismissed solar mythology in the celebrated 1911 edition of the *Encyclopedia Brittanica* as "destitute of evidence." Other scholars have called it untenable, distasteful, racist, elephantine, and obsessive, reducing mythology into "spirited chatter about the weather."

Müller was not unaware that many people thought his ideas ridiculous, and he struggled to defend himself. "What we call Noon, and Evening, and Night, what we call Spring and Winter, what we call year, and time, and Life, and Eternity—all this the ancient Aryans call Sun," he wrote. And yet wise people wonder and say, how curious that the ancient Aryans should have had so many solar myths. Why, every time we say 'Good Morning,' we commit a solar myth. Every poet who sings about 'the May driving the Winter from the field again' commits a solar myth. Every 'Christmas number' of our newspaper—ringing out the old year and ringing in the new—is brimful of solar myths. Be not afraid of solar myths. . . ."

Sir James George Frazer and The Golden Bough

The goddess Diana, to our minds, is barely distinguishable from the huntress Artemis, who was one among many in the pantheon of the Greeks. But there was another Diana. Long before Artemis came to Italy, the ancient Italians revered Diana as the great Mother Goddess, the supreme deity. Her honored priest, often a former slave, lived at her Roman sanctuary on the shores of Lake Nemi and was known as the King of the Wood. To obtain his position, he performed two tasks: he stole the "golden bough" (thought to be a branch of mistletoe clinging to a well-guarded tree) and he killed the previous occupant of the post in hand-to-hand combat. Afterwards, as the new king, he conducted his priestly functions but led an anxiety-filled existence, knowing that murder was the system of succession, and that no matter how vigilant he was, someday he too would be slain by another aspiring King of the Wood.

This barbarous ritual—never mind its questionable veracity—captured the attention of a shy Scottish anthropologist and classicist, Sir James George Frazer, and led him to write one of the most influential, unwieldy, and intriguing works of its day. Upon publication in 1890, *The Golden Bough: A Study in Magic and Religion* was a two-volume work but Frazer accumulated so much data about fertility rites, fire festivals, tree spirits, corn kings, scapegoats, dying-and-reviving gods, taboos, totems, and human sacrifice that it ripened into twelve volumes. When the first abridged edition appeared in 1922, it still ran to over eight hundred pages, and many abridgments followed (to this day). But Frazer never found his Maxwell Perkins, and the book itself, despite its dramatic, vigorous style and unending parade of weird and fascinating customs, remains an undigestible feast.

Diana of Ephesus. The many-breasted goddess was worshipped well into the Middle Ages, especially at her sanctuary in Ephesus, a Greek city on the coast of Asia Minor. The temple burned down for the first time in 356 BCE, on the night that Alexander the Great was born—not a surprising event, noted Cicero, since the goddess was undoubtedly assisting at the birth and hence unable to protect her shrine.

Frazer argued that the King of the Wood served a symbolic function. As a priest, he represented the spirit of vegetation and was the lover of the mighty Diana. His death, followed by his rebirth as the next King of the Wood, mirrored the cycles of nature: like grain, he died only to rise again. As a king, he represented society. Naturally, when he became weak or impaired, he had to be replaced. Slaying him saved him—and the society he symbolized—from withering old age and weakness. Resurrecting him assured the continued vitality of all. The system of murder, analyzed this way, was a symbolic attempt to ensure the beneficence of nature and to maintain the strength of the society.

Thus the ritual at Nemi, like many other bizarre customs and taboos, wasn't incomprehensible in the least. It had a distinct purpose. Moreover, it could be considered a form of science, a technology based on the principle of sympathetic magic, according to which like creates like. In the course of explaining this, Frazer delved into many hideously imaginative sacrificial rituals from around the world and examined Osiris, Tammuz, Adonis, Attis, and other dying-and-rising gods. Frazer showed that although the rites connected with these deities were dissimilar, their substance and symbolism were remarkably alike.

Frazer, whose leanings were distinctly anticlerical, didn't mention Jesus in his book. He didn't have to. The parallels between Jesus and other dying-and-rising gods were obvious, especially in the sweeping romantic last chapter, which ends as it began in the sacred grove. "The King of the Wood no longer stands sentinel over the Golden Bough," Frazer wrote. "But Nemi's woods are still green, and as the sunset fades above them in the west, there comes to us, borne on the swell of the wind, the sound of the church bells of Aricia ringing the Angelus. Ave Maria! Sweet and solemn they chime out from the distant town and die lingeringly away across the wide Campagnan marshes. Le roi est mort, vive le roi! Ave Maria!"

BAAL: A DYING-AND-RISING GOD FROM THE LAND OF CANAAN

Baal, god of storms and fertility, wished to be king of the gods but to do so he had to defeat his brothers, Yam, god of the sea, and Mot, the lord of death. With the help of his sister/consort, Anat, he easily conquered Yam. But afterwards he got so caught up in the process of building a house that he was inhospitable to Mot. Mot struck back, sneaking in through a newly installed window and summoning Baal to the underworld, where he ate mud and died.

Afterwards, everything on earth stopped growing and all the gods went into mourning. Anat, seeking revenge, journeyed to the underworld and found Mot. She chopped him up and scattered him everywhere. With death out of the way, Baal was revived. Life returned to earth. The fields blossomed.

The triumph was temporary, though, for death cannot be defeated. Mot returned like a figure in a horror movie and confronted Baal head-on. They fought fiercely, and Baal had to return to the underworld for a few month. Thus the agricultural cycles were established.

As a member of the myth-and-ritual school of Cambridge, Frazer believed that the two developed together, with the ritual representing a regular performed action and the myth providing a justification for that action (although myth could also arise to elucidate natural phenomena or as a distortion of historical events). Like other post-Darwinian thinkers, he believed that civilization evolved in stages. The first stage was magic, a world-view based on the supposition that events can be controlled. But magic inevitably disappoints, which leads to the second stage: religion, in which human beings acknowledge their powerlessness and appeal to higher beings for assistance. Eventually that too is rejected, and people turn to science, which Frazer, a committed rationalist, considered a "a golden key that opens many locks in the treasure of nature."

Although Frazer's book explores strange and thrilling customs from around the world, he led the narrow life of an academic, spending so much time reading that, according to an early biographer, "The facts of Frazer's life consist essentially of a list of books." He shunned publicity, but his wife Lilly Grove, an energetic widow whom he married in 1896, managed his career (and was given full credit for that by his friends). Frazer and his wife died in 1941 within hours of each other.

Today, Frazer is sometimes derided as an armchair anthropologist, and much about *The Golden Bough* has been discounted, including his evolutionary schema and many of his facts (including the story of the King of the Wood). Nonetheless, he made sense of primitive myths and rituals, explained the development of religion, and opened up an incredible mine of metaphor and image buried within the recesses of human history. In so doing, he inspired generations of anthropologists and scores of writers, including T. S. Eliot, James Joyce, William Butler Yeats, Ezra Pound, D. H. Lawrence, and Alfred Lord Tennyson, who listened to *The Golden Bough* read aloud while posing for a portrait. More than that, he shook the foundations of established belief, and not just within the academy.

Jane Harrison, another Cambridge ritualist and an acquaintance of Frazer (they took the same Hebrew class), received direct evidence of his influence in a conversation she once had with a local policeman. "I used to believe everything they told me," he confided. "But, thank God, I read *The Golden Bough,* and I've been a free-thinker ever since."

Jane E. Harrison

Of all the women who have made contributions to mythology, the most compelling is Jane Ellen Harrison, a flamboyant professor of classics who admitted to harboring "an intemperate antipathy to the Olympians" and looked instead to ancient rituals, "primitive and barbarous, even repulsive as they often are."

The youngest of three daughters, Jane was one month old when her mother died and her father's thirty-six-year-old sister Harriet moved in to care for the girls. Five years later, Auntie Harriet stunned everyone by leaving to get married. "My whole universe was deranged," Jane wrote sixty years later. Harriet hired a curly-haired governess to take her place. Within six months, as any reader of English novels might guess, the governess married the master of the house. Jane gained a stepmother about whom it was said that "the narrowness of her provincialism was only equaled by that of her Evangelicalism."

As was the custom of the day, Jane was educated at home by a series of governesses. When she was seventeen, her parents discovered that she was having secret meetings with a young curate whose ideas about Biblical translation excited her. She was banished to the home of distant relatives and sent to Cheltenham Ladies College, a school for Evangelicals where the rule of silence was so vigorously imposed that the girls weren't allowed to talk in their bedrooms. Jane excelled at her studies.

In 1874, she won a scholarship to Newnham College, which had recently opened its doors to women—an experiment so notable that it drew a series of visitors including Turgenev, Ruskin, and George Eliot, who visited Jane's room and admired her William Morris wallpa-

Jane Harrison playing the part of Alcestis in an 1877 production at Oxford University. (Reproduced by permission of the Principal and Fellows of Newnham College, Cambridge.)

pers. Jane pursued the classics and, after graduation, moved to London to study Greek art and archaeology. Gradually, her interest in mythology grew. She wrote a book, *Myths of the Odyssey,* began to lecture, and ended up back in Cambridge as a professor at Newnham College. A charismatic woman prone to fainting spells, she wore glittering shawls which would tumble from her shoulders at key moments in lectures, and she smoked and drank with enthusiasm. (Bertrand Russell wrote that she was "envied for her powers of enduring excess in whisky and cigarettes.") Students vied to sit at her table, and she always had a circle of people around her.

In 1888, she traveled to Greece, clambered over the ruins, and became convinced that mythology sprang from—and distorted—ritual. Though she criticized her fellow ritualist James Frazer ("The seductive simplicity of the 'Corn-mother' and the 'Tree-spirit,' and, worst of all, the ever-impending 'Totem,' is almost as perilous as the Old Sun and Moon snare," she wrote), she essentially applied his methods. Fueled by her interest in anthropology, she investigated ritual festivals, emphasized artistic representations over literature, and eventually came to reject virtually all the Greek gods in preference for the older spirits, the dieties of the earth referred to (sad to say) as chthonic.

The more she learned, the more the standard Greek pantheon struck her as artificial, superficial, and distinctly nonnuminous. She sought the primitive spirits, the daimons or year-spirits, who preceded the fine Olympian gods. And she found them.

Thus she began her 1903 masterpiece *Prolegomena to the Study of Greek Religion* with a discussion of an ancient festival of Zeus, a close reading of various artifacts associated with it, and the announcement that in those days Zeus was worshipped in the form of a snake. Everywhere she looked, she found evidence that "the beings worshipped were not rational, human, law-abiding gods, but vague, irrational, mainly malevolent . . . spirit-things, ghosts and bogeys and the like."

Her 1912 book *Themis,* influenced by the sociologist Émile Durkheim and the philosopher Henri Bergson, made these points: "that gods and religious ideas generally reflect the social activities of the worshipper; that the food-supply is of primary importance for religions; that the daimon precedes the full-blown god; that the Great Mother is prior to the masculine divinities." Although the book received a chilly reception, fifteen years later she reported with glee that "most of my old heresies that had seemed to my contemporaries so 'rash'" had been accepted "almost as postulates."

Jane Harrison drifted away from mythology during World War One, when many of the men who were her friends and colleagues became involved in the war effort, and she felt unmoored. A meeting with some Russian soldiers inspired her (perhaps because her father took many business trips to Russia in her childhood), and for the rest of her life she devoted herself to learning the Russian language. She died at age 78. (Virginia Woolf, who published Harrison's memoir, *Reminiscences of a Student's Life,* attended her dismal funeral and was appalled. The church was "only barely full of the dingiest people; cousins I fancy from the North, very drab: the only male relation afflicted with a bubbly chin, a stubbly beard, & goggly eyes," she wrote in her diary. "Distinguished people drag up such queer chains of family when they die.")

Yet throughout her life, Jane Harrison maintained intense attachments to interesting people, including two students who became, according to her biographer Sandra J. Peacock, her "spiritual daughters," and a series of men. "By what miracle I escaped marriage, I do not know, for all my life long I fell in love," she wrote. She rejected the proposal of the art historian D. S. MacColl (which did not prevent her from plummeting into depression in 1897 when he married someone else). In 1901, she got engaged to a man who died of appendicitis. She and the scholar Francis Cornford, an expert on Plato, became close friends; when he married in 1909, she was devastated, although she was twenty-four years his senior. Yet she wasn't a sad woman: she was an adventurous one (except, perhaps, sexually) and she participated in life. "Marriage, for a woman at least, hampers the two things that made life to me glorious—friendship and learning." Of those she had plenty.

THE GREEKS

Considering how many mythologies exist in this Tower of Babel world, it may seem odd that the tales of one small Mediterranean country continue to garner so much attention. After all, the myths of other cultures are equally saturated with drama and emotion, and many of those stories, because they are sometimes thoroughly unfamiliar, also offer the element of surprise.

Nonetheless, there are reasons, both good and bad, for this continued, millennia-long fascination with the goings-on of the Greeks. The best reason is that classical mythology has generated a profusion of great art and literature. Among the early writers who have preserved Greek myths for us, the following are irreplaceable:

- Hesiod and Homer. The earliest and most important sources, they wrote in the eighth century BCE;
- the fifth-century playwrights Aeschylus, Euripides, and Sophocles. Of the three hundred-odd plays they wrote, only thirty-three survive;
- Apollonius of Rhodes, the third-century BCE author of the *Argonautica*, which describes Jason's search for the golden fleece;

- two Romans writters born in the first century BCE: Virgil, the first-century BCE author of the *Aeneid,* and Ovid, author of *Metamorphoses* and the *Art of Love,* a popular guide to seduction which led to his exile from the eternal city;
- and an array of others including the fifth-century BCE poet Pindar; the first-century CE biographer Plutarch; the mythographer Apollodorus, whose handbook, *The Library,* written c. 140 BCE neatly summarizes the Greek myths; and two writters of the second century CE: the novelist Lucius Apulius, an initiate into the mysteries of Isis who invented the tale of Cupid and Psyche, and the peripatetic geographer Pausanias, whose ten-volume travelogue of Greece described sanctuaries, tombs, ruins, natural sites, and the historical and mythological stories surrounding them. "I am writing down these kinds of stories about the gods not because I accept them," he declared, "but I write them down all the same."

If literature was its only source, classical mythology would be a rich mine of story, glittering with variations of many tales. But there is more, for the myths of ancient Greece are lavishly embellished with art. The brilliant images carved in stone and painted on vases not only illustrate the ancient stories, they offer additional details—and sometimes, they provide the only version we have.

The Assembly of Gods. Zeus sits on his throne between Hera, who is swathed in draperies, and naked Aphrodite. Apollo, Athena, and a selection of muses are above.

In the nearly three thousand years that have passed since Homer and Hesiod turned the oral tradition into literature, writers and artists (particularly during the Renaissance) have ransacked classical mythology for characters, stories, and images. In addition, the dramatis personae of classical mythology have permeated our language and culture. On the island where I live, you can find Aphrodite Cleaners, Athena Swimwear, Artemis Design, the Apollo Theatre, Bacchus Optician (well, at least he's not a brain surgeon), Demeter Fragrances, the Hephaestus Works Company, Hercules Luggage, Hermes of Paris, Juno Shoes, Jupiter Video, Midas Muffler, the Poseidon Bakery, the Orpheus Chamber Orchestra—and much, much more. We use words such as cereal, atlas, or aphrodisiac without thinking about their mythological progenitors (Ceres, the Roman goddess of grain, Atlas, who held the world on his shoulders, and Aphrodite, the goddess of love). And everyone has an Achilles' heel, a hint of narcissism, maybe even an Oedipus complex.

In recent years, mythologies of other cultures have become increasingly familiar to us. Nevertheless, the tales of ancient Greece and Rome continue to provide inspiration. The 1990s gave us Woody Allen's *Mighty Aphrodite,* NBC's miniseries *The Odyssey: The Greatest Adventure of All Time,* with Isabella Rossellini as Athena and a sumo wrestler as the Cyclops; Derek Walcott's Nobel prize-winning epic poem *Omeros,* which brings *The Odyssey* to the West Indies; new translations of Homer by Robert Fagles and Ovid by Ted Hughes; experimental plays such as *Orestes: I Murdered My Mother* and a song cycle called *Saturn Returns.* ("Look at me," sings Icarus. "I'm going to be the stuff that myths are made of.") Greek mythology is so brimful of tragedy, comedy, and the truth of human personality that it continually attracts. It's as irresistible as the sirens' song.

Yet when you first stumble into it, it's not always welcoming, especially if you begin with the creation. Like a Cole Porter song that opens with a rarely heard, forgettable introduction before it modulates into a beloved tune, Greek mythology starts slowly, with dozens of abstract, personality-free deities who are impossible to keep straight. Chaos, Day, and Night come first. Next comes Gaia, the goddess of earth, followed by her son/lover Uranus; their children the Cyclopes, the hundred-handed Hekatonchires and the Titans; and at last, Zeus, Hera, and the gods of Mount Olympus.

The creation story of the Greeks is told on page 20. This section focuses on the Olympian gods. Deeply flawed, thoroughly human, and yet divine, they carry the timeless melody of Greek mythology. Here are their stories.

THE GREEKS AND THE ROMANS

The Romans absorbed the mythology of the Greeks, sometimes by direct borrowing and sometimes by conflating the names and stories of the Greek immortals with their own woodland spirits and lackluster deities until at last the Roman gods were congruent with the Greeks.

THE GREEKS	THE ROMANS
Aphrodite	Venus
Apollo	Apollo
Ares	Mars
Artemis	Diana
Athena	Minerva
Demeter	Ceres
Dionysus or Bacchus	Liber or Bacchus
Eros	Cupid or Amor
Hades or Plouton	Pluto or Dis Pater
Hephaestus	Vulcan
Hera	Juno
Heracles	Hercules
Hermes	Mercury
Hestia	Vesta
Kronos	Saturn
Leto	Latona
Pan	Faunus
Persephone	Proserpina
Poseidon	Neptune
Zeus	Jupiter or Jove

Zeus,
Lord of the Dark Storm Cloud

Zeus is so central to Greek mythology that you might expect him to be the locus of power right from the start, but this is not the case. Long before Zeus arrived on the scene, the denizens of ancient Greece worshipped goddesses such as Gaia and Hera. That began to change around 2,000 BCE (or so), when marauding tribesman from the north poured into Greece, bringing the horse, the Greek language, and a collection of divinities that included their sky god, Zeus. Just as the invaders conquered the locals, their gods van-

---

ZEUS, KING OF THE GODS

Domain: the sky, the weather, the law, the social order.

Characteristics: powerful, authoritarian, libidinous.

Parents: Rhea and Kronos.

Main Sanctuaries: Olympia and Dodona, where the oracle spoke through the rustling leaves of an oak tree.

Roman Name: Jove or Jupiter.

Lovers and Liaisons: Demeter, Eurynome, Ganymede, Leto, Maia, Mnemosyne, Themis, Thetis, and other immortals; Aegina, Alcmene, Antiope, Danaë, Europa, Io, Leda, Semele, and other mortals.

Wives: first Metis, then Hera.

Children: Apollo, Ares, Artemis, Athena, Dionysus, Eileithyia, Eris, Hebe, Hermes, Persephone, Polydeuces, the Seasons, the Fates, the Graces, and other immortals; Aeacus, Amphion, Amphitryon, Epaphus, Helen, Heracles, Minos, Perseus, Rhadamanthus, Sarpedon, and other mortals.

Animal: eagle.

Attributes: scepter, thunderbolt.

Best representation in post-classical art: Ingres' *Jupiter and Thetis.*

quished the indigenous deities. Zeus rose to the top. Gaia sank out of sight. And Hera was relegated in status until she was little more than the wife of Zeus.

Not surprisingly given the circumstances, Zeus was never the most beloved of divinities. Yet he became the very image of the Judeo-Christian God: bearded, broad-shouldered, and all-powerful, even when lounging on a puffy cloud. The Stoic philosopher Cleanthes called him "master of the universe," and Zeus acted accordingly. A tyrant as well as a bizarrely imaginative rapist, he strikes many people as an example of patriarchy gone mad. Yet he also reflects the grandiose (and universal) fantasy of obeying no limits and fulfilling every desire, no matter how taboo. As Sigmund Freud noted, "In myths the gods are granted the satisfaction of all the desires which human creatures have to renounce." Zeus's behavior may draw disapproving frowns. But without him Greek mythology as we know it would not exist.

His Childhood

Before Zeus was born, his father, the Titan Kronos, received an ominous prediction. He was told that, like his father Uranus, whom

he had castrated, he would be overthrown by one of his sons. To avoid this fate, he swallowed his children as soon as they were born. His wife Rhea, also a Titan, suffered from each loss. The sixth time she gave birth, desperate to save at least one child, she took action. She wrapped a stone in swaddling clothes and presented the bundle to her unsuspecting husband, who gulped it down whole. Then she gave the baby for safekeep-

The goat Amalthea suckles the infant Zeus.

ing to Amalthea, who was either a goat, a nymph, or a combination thereof. Thus the infant Zeus was saved.

Amalthea kept his whereabouts secret by hanging his cradle from the branch of a tree, where it was neither on earth, in heaven, nor on the sea, making it unfindable. To further protect the young god, she commissioned a group of spirits called the Curetes to surround the cradle. They clanked their swords and banged their bronze shields so vigorously that the cacophony hid the cries of the growing child. In this way, she kept him hidden and allowed him to reach adulthood. Amalthea was so important to Zeus that, after her death, he made an aegis (shield) out of her impenetrable hide, turned one of her horns into an overflowing cornucopia, and placed her among the stars as the constellation Capricornus.

The Clash of the Titans

Oracles in Greek mythology are sometimes misinterpreted but they are never wrong. So when Zeus grew up, he resolved, as the oracle had predicted, to overthrow his father and seize power. The first order of business was to free his brothers and sisters, swallowed so many years ago. He was assisted in this endeavor by his mother Rhea and his consort Metis, who told him about a drug which could be mixed with a special potion and given as an emetic. When Kronos drank this concoction, he grew so nauseous that he regurgitated the stone he had gulped down and spewed out all the children he had swallowed. Hestia, Demeter, Hera, Hades, and Poseidon, liberated at last, aligned themselves with Zeus.

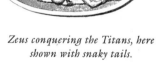

Zeus conquering the Titans, here shown with snaky tails.

With his children, the Olympians, banding together against him, Kronos and the Titans went to war. They were led by the formidable Atlas, while Zeus commanded the Olympians. Their battle, like the Trojan War, lasted ten years. The scales tipped in Zeus's direction when the one-eyed Cyclopes, the children of Gaia and Uranus, presented Zeus with his emblematic weapons, thunder and lightening. After that, Zeus hurled so many thunderbolts at the earth that the woods crackled and the land boiled. Yet the Titans held on—until Zeus received assistance from the hundred-handed Hekatonchires. They delivered the final blow, pummeling the Titans with such a barrage of stones that Kronos and his compatriots were driven beneath the earth into Tartarus and locked up in chains. Thus the prediction made so many years before had come true. Like his father before him, Kronos had been conquered by his son.

Triumphant, the Olympian gods (not the goddesses) drew lots for the spoils of war. Poseidon acquired the seas, Hades received the underworld, and Zeus won the sky. Having overthrown the old regime, Zeus became the unchallenged king of the gods.

A Stone at Delphi

The stone that Kronos swallowed and later regurgitated was more than a mythical construct. Hesiod says that Zeus placed that rock beneath Mount Parnassus as a monument to himself. The geographer Pausanias, writing about 150 years after the birth of Christ, claimed to have seen the actual object at Delphi. Using a scrupulously neutral tone to describe the stone's provenance ("There is an opinion that the stone was given to Kronos instead of his child. . . ."), he reported that the priests anointed it with oil every day and at festivals made it offerings of unspun wool. The story of the birth of Zeus was mythical; the object at Delphi was real.

Kronos devours his children in this drawing of an 1820 painting by Goya.

A Threat Overcome

A few enemies remained, notably Typhon, the largest monster ever born. He had a hundred snake heads sprouting from his shoulders, flames blazing from the eyes and, according to Hesiod, a different voice coming out of each mouth. Typhon could hiss like a snake, roar like a lion, bellow like a bull, yelp like a puppy, or speak the language of the gods. He was so terrifying that when he charged Mount Olympus, all the gods except Athena changed into animals and escaped to Egypt. Even Zeus turned into a ram and fled, but Athena shamed him and he returned with two weapons: his traditional thunderbolt and the sickle that his father, Kronos, had used to castrate Uranus. The weapons were insufficient. The many-headed Typhon wrested the sickle out of Zeus's hands and used it to slash the sinews of his limbs. Then he ripped them out of his body and hid them in a cave. Zeus could not move.

Fortunately, Hermes and his son Pan were able to help. Pan shouted, which shocked the monster and gave Hermes a chance to grab the sinews and sew them back into Zeus's body. Afterwards, Zeus scorched the monster's heads with lightning and buried him alive under Mount Aetna, where he continues to huff and puff.

His Authority

Like every great god, Zeus embodies contradictions. The god of thunder, lightning, power, and light (his name is derived from a Sanskrit root meaning "shine"), he was as majestic as the sky and as volatile as the weather. As Theocritis observed in the third century BCE, Zeus sometime shines brightly and sometimes rains.

As the ultimate leader, he was associated with military victory and the social order. It was his task to mediate quarrels and his decrees were absolute law. On the snowy slopes of Mount Olympus, he was treated accordingly. When Zeus entered the room, Homer tells us, the gods all stood.

Naturally, they eventually rebelled. The conspirators, led by Hera, Poseidon, and Athena, surprised Zeus as he was taking a nap and proceeded to wrap him in chains. Only the sea goddess Thetis came to Zeus's aid. She summoned Briareus, one of the Hekatonchires, who terrified the other gods so badly that they stopped what they were doing and Zeus wiggled free. As punishment, Zeus sentenced Poseidon and Apollo to work for a mortal. He also strung Hera up in midair with an anvil dangling from each ankle and an unbreakable chain wound around her wrists. In this way he survived the threat to his authority. Yet his authority was not total, for Fate was more powerful than he was, as the story of Sarpedon, his son with Europa, shows.

> *Zeus, great nameless all in all,*
> *if that name will gain his favour,*
> *I will call him Zeus.*
>
> —Aeschylus

Zeus Loses his Son

Of all the men in the world, Zeus loved his son Sarpedon the most, even though Sarpedon was mortal and therefore doomed to die. In one of the many astonishingly violent passages in *The Iliad,* Zeus watches as Sarpedon, fighting on the side of the Trojans, leaps from his chariot into the midst of battle, ready to attack. Knowing that his son is destined to die in this contest, Zeus longs to lift him up and set him down in the bucolic splendor of a distant land. Hera dissuades him on the grounds that he would infuriate the other gods, who might wish to save their own sons from the consequences of war. "None of the deathless gods will ever praise you," she contends. Zeus sheds many tears, but he also decides that Hera is right. So when the Greek warrior Patroclus hurls a bronze spear at Sarpedon, striking him "right where the midriff packs the pounding heart" and toppling him like a tree, Zeus does nothing. Dying, Sarpedon calls out to his friend Glaucus who watches as Patroclus wrenches the spear out of Sarpedon's body "and the midriff came out with it—so he dragged out both/the man's life breath and the weapon's point together."

The wounded Glaucus is appalled. "Our bravest man is dead, Sarpedon, Zeus's son," he laments. "Did Zeus stand by him? Not even his own son." Even in his grief, Zeus cannot alter the ways of Fate.

JUNG ON ZEUS

The gods have become diseases: Zeus no longer rules Olympus but rather the solar plexus, and produces curious specimens for the doctor's consulting room, or disorders the brains of politicians and journalists who unwittingly let loose psychic epidemics on the world.

The Amorous History of Zeus: Before Hera

"Love and war are the same thing," Miguel de Cervantes said. In the case of Zeus, that statement is literally true. Many mythologists have suggested that the unrelenting way in which Zeus rapes and seduces reflects a historical reality: the conquest of pre-Hellenic Mediterranean cults by Indo-European invaders, who subjugated the people and appropriated their gods. If this theory is correct, then each of Zeus's amorous pursuits represents a military or political triumph, which may explain why when Zeus was attracted to someone, no relationship was forbidden, no means of seduction was considered too extreme, and scruples were only for the weak.

Yet Zeus was not a thug. Blessed with a fertile imagination, the kind of access that only immortality can bring, and the ability to change shape at will, he was always in love. His affairs cut across the generations and it is largely due to him that the genealogical skein of Greek mythology is so tangled.

His first lover was the goddess Metis, who helped Zeus defeat Kronos and was celebrated for her wisdom. That relationship was doomed, for when she was pregnant an oracle predicted that she would have two children: first a girl whose intelligence and spirit would equal her father's and then a boy who would overthrow him. Zeus did the obvious thing: he eliminated the threat. Following the example of his father, Kronos, who had swallowed his children, Zeus went one step farther and swallowed the mother, who was already pregnant. When the time came for the child to be born, she could not emerge in the usual way. Instead, she sprang full-grown from Zeus's forehead, which is why Athena was always her father's favorite. Metis remained in Zeus's belly, where she could offer him counsel but could not become pregnant again. So Zeus's stratagem worked. Metis never had a son and Zeus was never overthrown.

Afterwards, Zeus was involved with a series of goddesses. Among them were:

- Themis, one of the Titans. She became the mother of two groups of sisters: the Horae or Seasons and the Moirae or Fates.
- Eurynome, a sea nymph. She gave birth to the three Graces: Aglaia, Euphrosyne, and Thalia.
- Demeter, one of Zeus's sisters. Her liaison with Zeus led to the birth of her beloved daughter Persephone.
- Mnemosyne, a fair-haired Titan. She spent nine nights with Zeus and gave birth to the nine Muses.
- and Leto, also a Titan. During a night with Zeus, she conceived Apollo and Artemis. She was still pregnant with them when Zeus fell in love with Hera, whom he beguiled through the use of his most persistent technique: disguise.

Love's Masquerade

Obsessive and unstoppable in his lust, Zeus overcame all sorts of resistance by taking advantage of his ability to change shape. His disguises were marked by variety and chutzpah. They included the following:

- a Cuckoo. Was Zeus a patriarchal god inflicted on a matriarchal tribe who worshipped Hera? That scenario would explain her initial reluctance, which Zeus cunningly overcame by appealing to her soft side. During a thunderstorm, he turned himself into a cuckoo so pitiful and bedraggled that Hera picked him up and held him to her breast to comfort him. That was when Zeus dropped the disguise and ravaged her. Despite that inauspicious beginning, their passion was so intense that, according to Homer, their wedding night lasted three hundred years. Afterwards Zeus returned to his freewheeling ways.
- a Serpent. When Zeus told his mother Rhea that he intended to marry Hera, Rhea suspected that marriage might not suit her lusty son and she counseled against it. This made him so angry that he threatened to molest her. To avoid that possibility she turned into a serpent. He followed her example and, in that guise, raped her.

- a Swan. Zeus fell in love with Leda, the queen of Sparta. When he mated with her in the shape of a swan, she conceived two children. That same night, however, she slept with her husband, Tyndareus, and conceived two more children. Ultimately she gave birth to four: Castor and Clytemnestra, the mortal progeny of the king, and Helen and Polydeuces (Pollus to the Romans), the undying offspring of a god.

  As often happens in mythology, there are other versions, particularly about Helen. According to one story, Zeus didn't mate with Leda but with the terrible goddess Nemesis, who laid a hyacinth-colored egg after their encounter and then ignored it. A shepherd saw what was going on and entrusted the egg to Leda, who took it home and hatched it. Or maybe Hermes picked up the egg and threw it between Leda's legs while she was sitting on a stool. Either way, Leda hatched the beautiful Helen and happily claimed her as her daughter.

- an Eagle, a Flame, an Ant. In his desire to mate with the nymph Aegina, Zeus turned into an eagle or a flame and carried her off to the island that now bears her name. Her father, the river-god Asopus, searched for her everywhere. At last Sisyphus, the king of Corinth, revealed her whereabouts, and Asopus tracked the lovers down. Zeus, unarmed, escaped by turning into a rock. Then he thought better of it, hurled a volley of thunderbolts at Asopus, and showered him with hot coals, with the result that, for years thereafter, lumps of coal were found in his (river) bed. Hera, angry at the infidelity, sent down a plague of darkness, famine, drought, and poisonous snakes. Many people died. At last Aegina's son appealed to Zeus and his prayers were answered. Rain fell. Darkness lifted. The serpents slithered away. And the ants he had seen

Taking the form of an eagle, Zeus abducts Ganymede, who became the cupbearer to the gods. From a mural by H.O. Walker (1843–1929) in the Library of Congress Jefferson Building. (Courtesy of the Library of Congress.)

in a dream carrying grains of corn to a sacred oak tree turned into men, replacing all those who had died. They were called Myrmidons from the Greek word for ant.

Either that or they were named for a king whose daughter was seduced by Zeus in the form of an ant.

- a Shower of Gold. When Acrisius, the king of Argos, consulted an oracle and was told he would be killed by his grandson, he could see only one way to protect himself: he locked his only daughter, Danaë, in a tower (or, alternatively, in an underground dungeon made of bronze). It

> . . . Leda by the swan was overpowered,
> And down on Danaë the ducats showered.
>
> —Heinrich Heine

was a strong defense, but against the force of the god, it was nothing. Zeus easily gained access by turning into a shower of gold that fell like rain onto Danaë's lap. Soon she gave birth to the hero Perseus who, after many adventures, accidentally killed his grandfather. Acrisius could not change his fate.

- a Bull. To entice the Phoenician princess Europa, the sister of Cadmus, Zeus turned into a snow-white bull. He was so gentle and appealing that she played with him, festooned his horns with wild flowers, and at last hoisted herself up on his back. That was what he was waiting for. He charged into the waves and carried her across the sea to Crete, where she gave birth to three sons: Minos and Rhadamanthys, who became judges in the underworld, and Sarpedon, Zeus's favorite son.

After Europa disappeared, Cadmus and his brothers looked for her relentlessly until Athena recommended that the search be called off. Cadmus went on to found the city of Thebes and to introduce the

Zeus abducts Europa in this sixteenth-century woodcut.

Phoenician alphabet to the Greeks, while Europa, who soon ceased to fascinate Zeus, married Asterius, the king of Crete, and lent her name to the continent.

In any case, that's the usual story. It's also possible that this famous tale is the conqueror's version and that originally, Europa was worshipped on Crete as the mother goddess.

- a Mortal Man. Zeus tricked Alcmene, the granddaughter of Perseus and Andromeda, into going to bed with him by seducing her in the shape of her husband Amphitryon, who was away at war. Zeus and Alcmene spent only a single night together, but Zeus enjoyed it so much that he lengthened that night into three, enough time to give Alcmene a detailed, first-person account of her husband's exploits in battle. Upon his return, Amphitryon launched into his story and was disappointed when his wife, having heard it all from Zeus, seemed impatient with the tale. Her reaction made Amphitryon so suspicious that he consulted the blind prophet Tiresias, who told him what had happened. Amphitryon was not amused. He could not forgive his wife's infidelity, and he decided to sacrifice her on a funeral pyre. His plans were well underway when, at the last moment, Zeus doused the flames and saved her life. Amphitryon relented.

> ### ANOTHER GOD WHO USED THIS TRICK
>
> The Egyptian sun god Ra used the same technique. He visited Reddedet, the wife of the high priest, in the shape of her husband and fathered the first three kings of the fifth dynasty. Afterwards, all the pharaohs spoke of themselves as Sons of Ra.

Alcmene's troubles were far from over. A vindictive Hera tripled the length of Alcmene's pregnancy, much as Zeus had extended their night of illicit love. She also sent her daughter Eileithyia, goddess of childbirth, to sit outside Alcmene's door with her limbs and fingers crossed. While

Eileithyia held that position, Alcmene could not give birth. For a long time, Eileithyia didn't move, and Alcmene suffered dreadfully—until suddenly a servant cried out that the babies had arrived. Astonished by the announcement, Eileithyia turned around to see what was going on and in so doing, uncrossed herself. At that instant, Alcmene delivered twin boys: Iphicles, the son of her mortal husband, and Herakles, the son of Zeus (who, according to some commentators, never mated with a mortal again). As for the well-meaning servant, the good deed did not go unpunished. Ovid reports that she was turned into a weasel.

- his Own True Self. Most of the disguises Zeus used were designed to make him less intimidating. On one occasion, though, he revealed his full magnificence as king of the universe. Disguised as a mortal, Zeus had been enjoying an affair with Semele, the daughter of Cadmus. But divinity cannot be hidden. When she asked him to reveal his true nature to her, he appeared before her in all his majesty, as bright as a blazing sun crowned with lightning. One glance, and she was consumed in flames.

Hera, Goddess of Marriage

If there is one character in all of Greek mythology who does not get a fair shake these days, it is surely Hera, who was widely and enthusiastically worshipped before Zeus was even a concept. Once a great goddess whose temples were the oldest and largest in Greece, she had three separate sanctuaries in Arcadia and three surnames, reflecting her rulership over the three major roles of a woman's life: maiden, wife, and widow.

After Zeus rode in with the conquering tribes and "married" Hera in the second millennium BCE, her image changed. Cow-eyed Hera, whose power extended over every phase of a woman's life, became a wife who never wavered in her commitment to her husband and yet could not close her eyes to his wandering ways. Motivated by jealousy, she turned mean-spirited and vindictive, not toward Zeus, whose power rendered him more or less immune, but toward her romantic rivals and the children who were born from those extracurricular unions. Due to her spiteful interference, Semele was incinerated; one of Aphrodite's children was born deformed; Io, whom Zeus turned into a heifer in order to fool his wife, was so tormented by a gadfly that she galloped over the entire world seeking relief from the itch; and Lamia lost all but one of her offspring—possibly because Hera forced her to eat them—and became a vampire with a sweet tooth for Greek children, many generations of whom

Hera or Juno. A nineteenth-century drawing of a Roman bust.

were threatened by their mothers with her imminent arrival. As Hera's image mutated from supreme goddess of women to resentful wife, she inspired less and less affection. The historian M. I. Finley described her as "the complete female . . . whom the Greeks feared a little and did not like at all."

Yet Hera's relationship with Zeus is far from loveless. Before they were married, Homer says, they used to hide from their parents and make love. In *The Iliad,* they continue to respond to each other. Once, they meander off together at the end of a feast, causing the other gods to break into fits of laughter. Another time, Hera, a supporter of the Greeks in the Trojan War, seduces Zeus, who backed the Trojans, in hopes of distracting him and thus obtaining a military advantage.

She put on her silver earrings, borrowed Aphrodite's magic girdle, a garment so seductive that no man could resist its wearer, and bribed Hypnos, the god of sleep, to close Zeus's eyes at the appropriate moment. All went according to plan. Zeus "caught his wife in his arms," Homer said, "and under them now the holy earth burst with fresh green grass,/crocus and hyacinth, clover soaked with dew, so thick and soft/it lifted their bodies off the hard, packed ground." Afterwards, Hypnos worked his magic and Zeus fell asleep. Meanwhile, the battle raged. Hera did her work well. She was not as subservient as she seemed.

HERA, QUEEN OF THE GODS

Domain: marriage and family.
Characteristics: jealous, vindictive, powerful.
Parents: Rhea and Kronos.
Main Sanctuaries: Argos, Samos, Olympus.
Roman name: Juno.
Lovers: none.
Spouse: Zeus.
Children: Ares, Eileithyia, Eris, Hebe, Hephaestus,
   Typhon.
Animal: the peacock.
Attributes: scepter and crown.
Best representation in post-classical art: Jacopo Titoretto's
   Origin of the Milky Way

Hera's Children

Hera's children, several of whom were conceived without the slightest contribution from Zeus (or any other male), didn't interest her, and her relationship with them was strained at best. The Greeks thought of her as the goddess of marriage, not motherhood. Nonetheless, she had half a dozen (or so) children. They were:

- the monster Typhon. Hera prayed to Gaia, struck the earth with her hand, and in that way conceived the largest monster ever born.
- Ares, the god of war. Homer says that his father was Zeus. Ovid, writing eight centuries later, disagreed. He reports that after Zeus gave birth to Athena from his forehead, the Roman goddess Flora touched Hera (or Juno) with a

flower, whereupon she became pregnant with the god of war—and also with . . .

- Eris, the goddess of strife (though she is more often said to be the daughter of Night).
- Hephaestus, the crippled god of fire and crafts. He too was the fruit of Hera's anger, conceived as an act of solitary retaliation against Zeus and tossed out of Olympus after he was born.
- Hebe, the goddess of youth. She was Hera's daughter by Zeus, unless one prefers the story that Hera conceived her by touching a lettuce. Originally cupbearer to the gods (meaning, she poured the nectar), Hebe was replaced by the beautiful boy Ganymede, Zeus's lover.
- Eileithyia, the goddess of childbirth. The daughter of Hera and Zeus, she could ease the pains of childbirth or she could prolong them, depending on her opinion of the mother.

Tiresias

What is sex like for the opposite gender? In ancient times only two people could confidently answer that question. One was the nymph Caenis who asked Poseidon to turn her into a man. He complied, and she became a famous warrior before being killed by a group of centaurs. But she was known for bellicosity, not sexuality, and is seldom mentioned in this context. The famous transsexual is Tiresias, whose adventures in gender began in the forest when he came upon two snakes copulating. He hit them with his staff and turned into a woman. For seven years, he was a highly successful prostitute. Then, once again he saw two serpents mating. He struck them with his staff and turned into a man again.

So when Hera and Zeus were arguing abut who received more pleasure from the act of love, they naturally thought Tiresias might know. Zeus was certain that women enjoyed the act more. Hera argued the other way, although she suspected that Zeus was right. So when Tiresias revealed that, as Zeus had suspected, women found greater enjoyment in sex—nine times as much—Hera was furious. In her anger at losing the argument, she struck Tiresias with blindness. In exchange for the loss of his eyesight, Zeus granted him the ability to foresee the future and a life seven generations long.

Tiresias became a celebrated prophet who revealed the terrible truth to Oedipus, foresaw the ascendancy of Dionysus, and described to Odysseus the entire course of his wanderings, up to and including his death. His powers were so extraordinary that he retained them even in the underworld, where Dante pictured him with his head turned around on his body, stuck in the eighth circle of hell with the astrologers.

Poseidon, God of the Sea-Blue Mane

Poseidon, brother of Zeus, ruled the seas. Resplendent in his flowing beard, handsome as only a Greek god can be, he is typically shown lounging in the waves, often in the company of fish, and holding his signature trident, an attribute that makes him instantly recognizable. No wonder artists love him.

Most of the time, though, Poseidon is petulant, angry, anything but loveable. His ill feelings first arose when he sat down with his brothers Zeus and Hades to draw lots and divide the world. Poseidon won dominion over the sea, a vast empire. But the empire of Zeus was vaster still, and Poseidon never got over his resentment. His rancor poisoned his interactions with both deities and mortals, including the Greek warrior Odysseus, who blinded his cannibalistic son, Polyphemus; Poseidon's malice fuels *The Odyssey*.

Easily provoked and altogether disagreeable, Poseidon was the god of earthquakes (Homer calls him the Earthshaker), the sovereign of the sudden squall, and he quarreled with everyone. Strangely enough, many of his disputes were over territory on land, where he was sure to fail. He competed with Athena for ownership of Athens, with Hera for the rulership of Argolis, with

Zeus over Aegina, and with Dionysus over Naxos. He lost each contest.

Another failure, this one with far-reaching consequences, took place when he conspired with Hera, Athena, and other Olympians to overthrow Zeus. When their coup failed, Zeus punished Poseidon (and Apollo) in a terrible way: he forced them to work for a mortal, King Laomedon of Troy.

A triton

To complete their sentence, Poseidon and Apollo built a fortifying wall around the city. But Laomedon refused to pay for this service. He even threatened to slice off their ears and sell them into slavery. In response, Apollo sent a plague to Troy and Poseidon dispatched a voracious sea monster.

The monster and intent on destroying the kingdom. Laomedon knew that the only way to stop it was to sacrifice his daughter, Hesione, and he prepared to do that. Luck was with her: Heracles rescued the girl and killed the monster, which only fueled Poseidon's anger. He became implacable in his animosity for all things Trojan—except the wall, of which he was rather proud.

Poseidon's wedding, always known as the Triumph of Amphitrite. In this nineteenth-century engraving, the god of the sea, shown with his trident and team of horses, gazes at Amphitrite beneath her canopy.

Despite his unpleasant demeanor, there is one charming story about him. A love story, it began on the island of Naxos, where Poseidon saw the sea nymph Amphitrite dancing with her fifty sisters. He was infatuated. But his advances were so clumsy that she ran from him and hid in the ocean's depths. Luckily, a dolphin volunteered to act as Poseidon's ambassador. He presented the sea god's case so engagingly that Amphitrite changed her mind and married him. Among their children: Triton, who was a man above and a fish below.

POSEIDON, EARTHSHAKER

Domain: the sea, earthquakes, horses.
Characteristics: wrathful.
Parents: Rhea and Kronos.
Roman Name: Neptune.
Lovers and Liaisons: Aethra, Alcyone, Celaeno, Demeter,
    Gaia, Halia, Libya, Medusa, Theophane, and others.
Wife: Amphitrite.
Children: Alcinous, Antaeus, Arion, Cercyon, Charybdis,
    Chrysaor, Despoena, Halirrhothiuss, Lamia, Pegasus,
    Polyphemus, Theseus, Triton, and others.
Animal: dolphin, fish, horses, bulls.
Attributes: trident
Best representation in post-classical art: Paolo Veronese's
    Mars and Neptune.

Poseidon Hippios,
Lord of Horses (and Other Animals)

On vase paintings, Poseidon frequently appears in the presence of
dolphins and fish. Yet his tie to creatures of the deep is minor compared to his connections with various quadrupeds, including the
ram, the bull, and the horse.

The ram is associated with Poseidon because he turned into one
during his pursuit of the nymph Theophane. As a result of that liaison, she gave birth to the ram with the golden fleece. His relationship to bulls was the usual one: they were sacrificed to him. Black
bulls in particular were herded into the sea in his honor.

His deepest animal tie was with the horse. Horses were sacrificed
to him (by drowning, among other methods); he gave horses as
gifts; and he invented horsemanship. Pausanias says that, after
Poseidon was born, Kronos wanted to swallow the baby but Rhea
fooled him by handing him a foal instead. Other commentators

report that Poseidon was the father of the first horse, which may have been conceived when the sea god fell asleep and inadvertently spilled his semen on a rock. Either that, or it trotted out of the earth when Poseidon struck his trident into the ground during his competition with Athena.

Poseidon even turned into a horse when he slept with the Gorgon Medusa, who was still a beauty in those days. Stupidly, she and Poseidon had their rendezvous in a temple of Athena, who punished Medusa for her effrontery by turning her hair into a coiling mass of snakes. Not long afterwards, Perseus sliced off her head with a golden sword. As her blood spurted into the sea, it gave birth to two offspring, the fruit of her encounter with Poseidon: the warrior Chrysaor, who became the father of many monsters, and the winged horse Pegasus.

A more disturbing story concerns Poseidon's sister Demeter. After Persephone was abducted, Demeter plunged into mourning. As she wandered around the world in search of her daughter, Poseidon began to lust after her. To avoid the insistent god, the grief-stricken mother turned into a mare and hid in the midst of a herd. Undeterred, Poseidon turned into a stallion and raped her. Demeter was furious. She soon gave birth to two children: a black-maned horse named Arion, who had the power of speech and right feet like those of a man, and a mysterious daughter called Despoena whose true, secret name could be spoken only within the Eleusinian Mysteries.

Scylla and Charybdis

Charybdis, Poseidon's daughter with Gaia, once stole a few cattle from Heracles and was punished when Zeus turned her into a whirlpool in the straits of Messina. Three times a day she gulped down huge quantities of water, and three times a day she spewed it out. She was so dangerous to passing ships that in *The Odyssey*, Circe warned Odysseus to avoid her. "Don't be there when the whirlpool swallows down—not even the earthquake god could save you from disaster," she said.

Avoiding disaster wasn't easy, though, for opposite Charybdis on the other side of the straits was her companion in metaphor, Scylla, once Poseidon's lover. When Amphitrite found out about their affair, she reacted in the time-honored mythological way—by seeking revenge.

While Scylla was bathing, Amphitrite tossed a handful of poisonous herbs into the water, which turned her beautiful rival into a monster with six dog heads, twelve dangling legs, and way too many teeth. After that, Scylla lurked in a dark cavern and was famous for snatching sailors off ships. So when Odysseus was preparing to navigate through the Straits of Messina, he had to decide whether to veer closer to the whirlpool, knowing that Charybdis could devour the ship, or risk an encounter with

Charybdis, shown here in a nineteenth-century rendition, was dangerous but Scylla, whom Homer called a "yelping horror," was even worse.

the many-headed Scylla. Ultimately he took Circe's advice. He slipped past the monstrous Charybdis, thereby shunning the whirlpool, and in the process lost six men to Scylla. When forced to decide between Scylla and Charybdis, there is no happy choice.

From the Annals of Mythology: Homer, Lawrence of Arabia, and the Homeric Question

Shakespeare's plays, it has been said, were written either by Shakespeare or by someone else with the same name. Scholars speak with even less certainty about the author of the *Iliad*, which traces the events of the last year of the Trojan war, and its sequel, the *Odyssey*, which follows the hero Odysseus on his ten-year voyage home after the war was over. The ancient Greeks thought that Homer was a blind poet, born on Chios, an island off the coast of Turkey, who wandered about singing his work at festivals and died on Ios, another island in the Aegean Sea. He was thought to have lived anywhere from the twelfth century BCE, when the Trojan War was fought, to the seventh century. The fifth-century historian Herodotus thought that Homer flourished around 850 BCE; modern historians believe that date is a century too soon.

The confusion about Homer's dates is nothing compared to the unresolved questions about his identity. Some scholars—the "separatists"—argue that the *Iliad* and the *Odyssey* were composed by two people in different locations and almost certainly in different generations (the novelist John Cowper Powys believed that the two epics may have been separated by as much as three or four centuries). Other scholars—the "unitarians"—are sure that both books were created by a single individual whose style changed with subject matter or with age (George Steiner suggested that Homer wrote the *Iliad* as a young man and the *Odyssey* as an old one). Still others believe that both books are pastiches of standard poems, epithets, motifs, and formulaic set pieces taken from oral tradition and woven together by a discerning editor. An Englishman writing in 1658 concluded that Homer was Jewish; a later thinker suggested that he was not only Jewish, he was King Solomon; in the eighteenth century, scholars embraced the idea that Homer was illiterate; Samuel Butler and, later, Robert Graves believed that Homer was a woman; and the debate, fueled by archaeology and literary analysis, continues.

As for the sort of person he was (assuming he was a single individual), the most stinging assessment comes from the English writer and translator T.E. Lawrence (1888–1935), who changed his name to T.E. Shaw but will be known eternally as Lawrence of Arabia. Lawrence, who led the Arabs in a war against the Turks and wrote *The Seven Pillars of Wisdom,* immersed himself in Greek literature even as a student. When the book designer Bruce Rogers asked him to translate the *Odyssey* in 1928, he jumped at the chance.

In his preface, he set forth his approach as a translator and gave his critique of the original. It was a decidedly mixed review. On the one hand, he found the *Odyssey* "neat, close-knit, artful, and various; as nearly word-perfect as midnight oil and pumice can effect . . . the oldest book worth reading for its story and the first novel of

Europe." On the other hand, he thought it limited in scope, complained that it was "never huge or terrible," and objected to the "tedious delay of the climax," the "thin and accidental characterization," and even the characters themselves: "the sly cattish wife, that cold-blooded egotist Odysseus, and the priggish son who yet met his master-prig in Menelaus."

As for Homer ("the poet of poets," according to Aristotle), Lawrence could not abide him. In a letter to Rogers, he bragged that "I have hunted wild boars and watched wild lions, sailed the Aegean (and sailed ships), bent bows, lived with pastoral peoples, woven textiles, built boats and killed many men." Having established his own credentials, he described the author of the *Odyssey* as "a bookworm, no longer young, living from home, a mainlander, city-bred and domestic. Married but not exclusively, a dog-lover, often hungry and thirsty, dark-haired. Fond of poetry, a great if uncritical reader of the

JOHN COWPER POWYS ON WHY HOMER IS GREAT

What has made Homer for three thousand years the greatest poet in the world is his naturalness. We love each other as in Homer. We hate each other as in Homer. We are perpetually being interfered with as in Homer by chance and fate and necessity, by invisible influences for good and by invisible influences for evil, and we see the unconquerable power that Homer calls keer leading our parents, leading our uncles and aunts, leading our grandparents to a particular death; and there do exist among us those who even feel this implacable destiny propelling themselves to a definite end. . . . None of the passionate defiances and challenges of Shakespeare's stage, nor any of the pandemoniacal eloquence of Milton's angels and arch-angels, nor the most contorted twists of Browning's tipsy piety with its belching outbursts of country-council optimism, really expresses, as we all well know, the actual experience of life which we poor mortals from childhood to manhood and womanhood have fled from or endured, have fought against or submitted to, ever since we were born. But Homer does express precisely this.

Iliad, with limited sensuous range but an exact eyesight which gave him all his pictures. A lover of old bric-a-brac, though as muddled an antiquary as Walter Scott." Lawrence contrasted his "infuriating male condescencion toward inglorious woman with his tender charity of head and heart for serving-men," noted that he is "all adrift when it comes to fighting, and had not seen deaths in battle," and finally washed his hands of him by calling him "very bookish, a house-bred man. His work smells of the literary coterie." The same might be said of Lawrence's translation, which is not generally among those most admired today. That honor belongs to, among others, E.V. and D.C.H. Rieu, Alexander Pope, Richard Lattimore, Robert Fitzgerald, Alan Mandelbaum, and Robert Fagles.

Demeter and Persephone

It's the most famous and ominous opening scene in Greek mythology: the young Persephone in a meadow with her friends innocently gathering a fragrant bouquet of roses, irises, violets, crocuses, hyacinths, and lilies. When she spied a narcissus plant, purposely placed there by Gaia, the goddess of earth, she could not resist its lure. Its one hundred yellow blooms were so lush and astonishing that, according to the Homeric Hymn, "all wide heaven above, and the whole earth below, and the swell of the salt sea laughed." Persephone reached out to pluck one of the blossoms—and the world cracked open.

Ceres or Demeter. A sixteenth-century woodcut by Jost Ammons.

Out of the earth, galloping towards her in a golden chariot pulled by dark blue horses, thundered Hades, the lord of the underworld, who had fallen in love with her. As he rode past, he grabbed her and pulled her into the chariot. Persephone screamed in protest. No one—not even the olive trees—came to her aid.

Only her mother, Demeter, the goddess of grain (Ceres to the Romans), heard her cries. For nine days and nights Demeter searched for her daughter. Holding aloft burning torches, she looked continuously, neither eating nor drinking nor stopping to bathe. Her grief was so deep that the earth mourned with her. Nothing bloomed. Not a seed sprouted. And no one—not even the birds, usually such helpful messengers—had any information for her.

On the morning of the tenth day, the goddess Hecate, who lived in the underworld, approached the grieving mother and told her that she too had heard Persephone's wails. However, because she had been inside her cave, she had not actually observed the abduction. So she and Demeter paid a visit to Helios, the god of the sun, who saw everything with his single eye. He told Demeter that Persephone had been abducted and raped by Hades with the permission of Zeus, Demeter's brother and Persephone's father. Not that this bothered Helios. Upon reflection, he decided that Demeter's grief and anger were excessive. Hades would make an excellent husband, he said, and he rode off, leaving Demeter unconsoled and unconsolable.

> **DEMETER, GODDESS OF THE HARVEST**
>
> Domain: grain, agriculture, fertility, motherhood, loss.
> Characteristics: persistent, bountiful, maternal.
> Parents: Rhea and Kronos.
> Main Sanctuary: Eleusis.
> Roman Name: Ceres.
> Lovers and Liaisons: Zeus, Poseidon, Iasion.
> Children: Persephone (or Kore); Philomelus, who invented the chariot; Parius; Ploutus; Arion; and Despoena.
> Attributes: stalks of grain, snakes, torch, crown.
> Best representation in post-classical art: Lord Frederic Leighton's *Return of Persephone*.

Still determined to find Persephone, Demeter disguised herself as a mortal and continued her search. One day, while sitting near a well and looking as gray and gnarled as an olive tree, she fell into conversation with the four daughters of Celeus, the king of Eleusis. She told them her name was Doso and that pirates had brought her, against her wishes, from Crete. (There was a touch of truth in this, for Demeter is thought to have

Demeter holding sheaves of grain, her primary attribute, in a drawing of a terra-cotta relief. (Credit: Hannah Berman)

reached the Greek mainland from Crete.) Afraid that they would sell her as a slave, she escaped when they disembarked for a meal. Now she was hoping to secure a position as a servant who might care for a newborn, make the master's bed, or teach a woman her household tasks. The four girls told her that their own mother, Metaneira, had just given birth to a son and might be in need of a nurse.

So Demeter went home with them. At the house of Celeus, she held a veil over her face and waiting to meet Metaneira, who suspected right away that her visitor might be a goddess. As she stood there, Demeter's sadness seeped into the atmosphere like ink dropped into water. At last Iambe, Metaneira's slave, coaxed a smile from her with a barrage of quips and jokes, and the mood brightened. Metaneira offered a glass of red wine. The goddess asked instead for some barley water flavored with mint leaves, which she received. An agreement was reached, and Demeter became the nurse for Metaneira's baby.

Under Demeter's care, the child, named Demophoön or Triptolemus, flourished. Unbeknownst to everyone else in the household, she fed him ambrosia, and every night she held him in the fire, hoping to bestow upon him immortality and eternal youth, just as the Egyptian goddess Isis had done when she was working as a nursemaid. Unfortunately, Metaneira saw Demeter roasting the baby and screamed in anguish, causing Demeter to drop the boy. Her disguise ruined, she revealed her true identity in a flash of light which lit the entire house. The baby could no longer become immortal, she said, but since he had slept in the arms of the goddess, honor would be his. She also instructed the people to build a temple in her honor at Eleusis. This marked the beginning of the Eleusinian Mysteries, one of the great religions of ancient Greece.

Yet even after the temple was built, Demeter mourned. The fields fell fallow, the trees grew bare, and famine threatened humankind. Zeus realized he had to do something. He called Iris, the rainbow goddess, and asked her to tell Demeter to rejoin the company of the gods in Olympus. Demeter refused: Until she saw her daughter again, she would shun the other deities and nothing would grow. Angrily, she remained in the temple in Eleusis and held to her decision.

Her resolve paid off. Zeus called in Hermes and instructed him to bring back Persephone. When Hermes ventured into the underworld and told her the news, Persephone leaped up in pleasure, for she longed to see her mother. Hades, who loved Persephone, pretended to comply with Zeus's wishes, but just as she was about to leave, he fed her a single juicy pomegranate seed. Or perhaps, as Ovid claims, Persephone split open the fruit herself and ate seven seeds.

Persephone and Hermes climbed into a chariot and left the underworld. They drove over the sea and across rivers, through grassy fields and over mountain passes, and at last they came to a halt in front of the temple in Eleusis.

PERSEPHONE, GODDESS OF THE UNDERWORLD

Domain: death and the underworld
Characteristics: young and gentle.
Parents: Demeter and Zeus.
Main Sanctuary: Eleusis.
Other Names: Kore ("maiden" or "girl" in ancient Greek); Proserpina (to the Romans)
Lovers and Liaisons: Zeus, Hermes.
Spouse: Hades
Attributes: Pomegranate, stalks of grain, crown.
Best representations in post-classical art: Niccolò dell'Abbate's *Abduction of Proserpine*, Dante Gabriel Rossetti's *Proserpine*.

Persephone jumped out of the chariot and ran into her mother's arms. Demeter was overjoyed to see her daughter. Yet she felt a wave of trepidation. She knew that if Persephone had consumed anything in the underworld, even a single morsel, she would have to return. So she asked Persephone if she had eaten. According to the Homeric Hymn, Persephone admitted the truth. Ovid, writing six or seven centuries later, said that Persephone lied to her mother, claiming that she had eaten nothing. Her ruse failed. Ascalaphus, the son of the River Acheron, had secretly observed her in Hades. He revealed the truth (and was turned into a screech owl for his trouble).

Either way, the pomegranate made all the difference. Persephone was forced to return to Hades

from *The Pomegranate*
The only legend I have ever loved is
The story of a daughter lost in hell
And found and rescued there.
Love and blackmail are the gist of it.
Ceres and Persephone the names.
And the best thing about the legend is
I can enter it anywhere. And have.

—Eavan Boland

for a third of every year, causing her mother to mourn and the earth to become barren. After that, she was allowed to emerge from the underworld, whereupon Demeter's joy would cause the earth to bloom once more. In this way the cycle of the seasons was established along with the pattern of birth, death and resurrection.

HECATE'S FALL:
FROM GLORIOUS GODDESS TO HANDMAIDEN IN HELL

The goddess of magic, witchcraft, and sorcery, Hecate was a triple deity: a moon goddess in heaven, a huntress on earth, and a mother goddess welcomed wherever women gave birth. Known for her ability to confer honor, riches, victory, and fame, she was so ancient that, according to Hesiod, Zeus revered her above all other deities. Over time, her image became less benevolent and her importance ebbed.

Several stories account for her fall from grace. Perhaps she stole a pot of rouge from Hera and ended up in the underworld. Or maybe the gods threw her into the Acheron after she helped a woman give birth, and the river carried her to Hades. As a goddess of the underworld, she became Persephone's attendant and degenerated into a terrifying spook.

Hecate haunts cemeteries, crime scenes, and crossroads, where her devotees—especially numerous in Rome during the fourth century BCE—petitioned her with small three-faced statues called Hecataea and sacrifices of dogs, honey, and black female lambs. She was said to wander about on moonless nights accompanied by a pack of infernal hounds and the restless spirits of those who were murdered or buried without appropriate rites. As Persephone's representative, she was the queen of ghosts and ghouls, the patron of witches, and the conjurer of nightmares. She was also the goddess called upon by King Lear at the pivotal moment when, "By the sacred radiance of the sun,/The mysteries of Hecate, and the night," he commits his single worst mistake and renounces his loving daughter, Cordelia.

The Eleusinian Mysteries

Mystery religions, with their secret ceremonies and complex initiations, were widely accepted in ancient Greece, and none more so than the Eleusinian mysteries, which revolved around the myth of Demeter and Persephone. The cult was so popular that in 480 BCE, Herodotus estimated that roughly 30,000 people had participated in its rites. Here's what that involved:

- Who could join: anyone, including women and slaves. The only exceptions: barbarians and murderers (although Heracles, who murdered his family, was allowed in).
- What did you have to do? In February, bathe in the Illisos River, sacrifice an animal (most likely a pig, which then would be roasted and consumed), and learn about Persephone's marriage to Hades. In September, bathe in the sea, sacrifice a sow, offer a libation to Dionysus. If you're being initiated, fast for nine days just as Demeter fasted after Persephone was abducted; break the fast by drinking barley water flavored with pennyroyal or mint; wear special garments; put myrtle in your hair. Participate in a procession from Athens to Eleusis, one purpose of which is to return certain sacred objects to the sanctuary at Eleusis (from which they had been removed a few days earlier). En route, shout obscenities in recognition of Iambe, whose joking made Demeter smile. In Eleusis, sit in the darkened hall of initiation with thousands of other believers. See the sudden blaze of the fire. Listen to the song of the hierophant. View the sacred objects (whatever they may have been). Rejoice at the birth of a divine child, born to Persephone, the goddess of death.
- Who was that child? He had several names, including Triptolemus, Iasion, Eleuthereos the Liberator, and Dionysus. In ritual, he was eaten. His flesh was bread, his blood was wine.
- What was the purpose? To live in joy, to die with hope, and to have a better time in the hereafter.

Demeter's Son Ploutus

Demeter and Persephone, known as the Two Goddesses, are so strongly linked that it's a surprise to learn that Demeter had other children. It shouldn't be, though, because in Greek mythology even a single sexual encounter had consequences—and Demeter had a lusty side.

At the wedding of Cadmus and Harmonia, for instance, Demeter met the titan Iasion and was captivated. They wandered into a field that had been ploughed three times and made love. When they returned, Zeus grabbed his thunderbolt and killed Iasion on the spot.

Afterwards, Demeter gave birth to Ploutus, whose name means "riches" in Greek. According to Aristophanes, who wrote a play about him, Ploutus grew up to be a kindly god who traveled over land and sea, making some people wealthy and leaving others in perpetual poverty. To make sure that riches continued to be distributed without regard to merit, Zeus blinded him. That's why the wicked may accumulate a fortune while the worthy remain poor. In Aristophanes' *Plutus,* this randomness so disturbs the main character that he brings Plutus to the temple of Asclepius to have his vision restored. Unfortunately, once the wealth is redistributed in an equitable manner, the balance of nature is overturned and people stop sacrificing to the gods. Things reach such a sorry pass that the silver-tongued Hermes, who relied upon those sacrifices to fill his needs, is reduced to looking for a job.

Although Ploutus doesn't figure in the story of Demeter and Persephone, he was worshipped at Eleusis and eventually conflated with Hades, whose name was considered so dreadful that people hesitated to utter it. Instead, they called the lord of the underworld Plouton, signifying that he commanded the riches buried in the earth, including the gold, silver, precious gems and dead bodies hidden underground. In Latin, the god of the underworld is known as Pluto or Dis Pater, which is also derived from the word for "rich."

Hades:
Lord of the Dead, Land of the Dead

Hades was a figure of dread, and his sunless domain was loathsome even to the gods. Yet he was a weakling, none too bright, and so lacking in courage that when war broke out among the immortals, Hades cringed in fear. Even while wearing his cherished helmet of invisibility, he left the infernal regions only rarely. Three times, he was motivated by lust: Once he ran off in pursuit of the nymph Minthe, who turned into a mint plant; once he chased after Leuce, who became a white poplar; and once he abducted Persephone. On another occasion, after Heracles wounded him in the shoulder, he was in such agony that he made his way to Mount Olympus, where he was treated with pain-killing drugs. The rest of the time, Hades stayed home and ruled over his subterranean domain, which came to be known by his name. (Similarly, the Norse realm of the dead was known by the name of its ruler, the goddess Hel.)

HADES,
GOD OF THE UNDERWORLD

Domain: the underworld, death, hidden riches.
Characteristics: grim, relentless, frightening, weak.
Parents: Rhea and Kronos.
Roman Name: Pluto or Dis Pater.
Lovers and Liaisons: Leuce, Minthe.
Spouse: Persephone.
Animal: Cerberus, the infernal dog.
Attributes: scepter, cornucopia, crown.
Best representations in post-classical art: Agostino Carracci's *Pluto* (1592), Niccolò dell'Abbate's *Abduction of Proserpine*.

Hades was a hilly place, dotted with lakes, strewn with groves of trees, and cross-hatched with rivers, including the Styx, the river of hate, the Acheron, the river of woe, and the Lethe, the river of oblivion, whose water caused one to forget the events of one's entire life. (The Chinese equivalent was the broth of oblivion, the beverage of choice for souls who are exiting hell on their way to new lives.) In Hesiod's day, Hades featured two regions of darkness, Erebus and Tartarus, which

Hades, from Gustave Doré's 1861 illustrations for Dante's Inferno.

held an abyss so like a black hole that anyone sucked into it would fall unencumbered for an entire year. A few centuries later, the underworld expanded into three main sections: Erebus for the bad people, the Elysian Fields and Isles of the Blessed for the good people, and for everyone else, the Fields of Asphodel, where souls wander about among sickly looking flowers in a dark miasma of gloom.

Tucked among these dreadful scenes was the single most human feature of Hades: the furniture-filled palace of its king and queen. Although Persephone came to the underworld unwillingly, she and Hades were bound by love, and it was there that she established a permanent residence. For despite the fact that Persephone theoretically spends time both in the underworld and in the land of the living, other mythological characters invariably find her in the underworld, eternally receiving visitors in the realm of the dead.

TREES IN HELL

The trees in Hades—black poplars, white cypresses, and weeping willows—may sound dramatic but they pale in comparison to Zaqqum, the fetid tree which separates the fires of the Islamic underworld from the wonders of Paradise. Its flowers are the heads of demons, and its fruit, once swallowed, turns to molten metal in the stomach.

Residents of Hades

Getting to Hades wasn't difficult. Hermes accompanied dead souls to the banks of the River Styx, and Charon ferried them across for a fee. (Paupers buried without a coin under their tongues had to wait a hundred years before crossing over.) Inside the infernal regions, the dog-headed, snake-haired furies, who drove mortals mad on earth, tortured the dead; three judges arbitrated any disputes that might arise; and the three-headed watchdog Cerberus did his best to made sure that no one escaped. And yet, most of the dead don't have it so bad. Though they lack energy and have to spend eternity wandering around mindlessly in a depressing place, that's the extent of the torture.

Cerberus

The misery of it all is nonetheless indisputable. As Achilles tells Odysseus in *The Odyssey,* he would rather be a slave on earth than king of the dead. Still, compared to the sadistic, vividly imagined terrors we know from, say, Hieronymous Bosch or Dante's *Inferno,* Hades doesn't sound so terrible—except for the unlucky few. Consider what happened to these poor sinners:

- Tityus the giant. He tried to rape Leto while she was conducting a ritual in a grove of trees. Her children Apollo and Artemis heard her scream, let loose a flurry of arrows, and killed Tityus, who descended into the underworld. Given the frequency of rape among the gods, it's surprising that this particular crime would demand an

THE JUDGES OF HADES

- Aeacus, son of Zeus and Aegina. Aeacus was such a superb athlete that his brothers killed him out of jealousy;

- Rhadamanthys, son of Zeus and Europa. Before he died, he was the king of Crete;

- and his brother, Minos, who ruled Crete before being scalded to death in his bath by his former employee, Daedalus. In the underworld he presided over the most troublesome cases.

eternity of punishment. But Leto was a goddess. So Tityus was stretched on a rack and pegged to the ground over a nine-acre area, with two vultures pecking away at his liver for all eternity. (Prometheus suffered from the same liver-devouring ordeal but was eventually rescued.)

- Tantalus. Once beloved by the gods, he was invited to join them at their table for nectar and ambrosia but he abused the privilege by sharing these delicacies with his gross, mortal friends. Worse, he served the gods a stew cooked from the limbs of his own son, Pelops. Except for the grief-stricken Demeter, who was so numb and oblivious that she took a bite out of the shoulder, the deities at this grisly feast saw what was going on and refused to eat. For his culinary crimes, Tantalus received his just desserts. Exiled to Tartarus, he stands chin-deep in water while branches heavy with ripe pears, pomegranates, apples, figs, and olives dangle above his head. Yet whenever he tries to drink, the waters recede, and whenever he reaches out to pick a fruit, the wind blows it just beyond his reach. Thus he is thirsty, hungry, and forever tantalized, a word derived from his name.

- Ixion, king of the Lapiths. Instead of paying the bride price for his wife, Dia, he set a trap for his father-in-law which caused him to stumble into a pit filled with hot coals, where he died. Thus Ixion, the Greek equivalent of Cain, became the first mortal to murder a relative. He made a more serious mistake when he became enamored of Hera. After she told Zeus that Ixion had tried to seduce her, Zeus set a trap by creating a cloud that was identical to Hera in every respect. Ixion was fooled. He mated with the cloud (which later gave birth to Centaurus, the ancestor of the race of centaurs) and was punished for his audacity by being bound on a wheel of fire which revolves for all eternity in the underworld.

- the Danaids, the fifty daughters of King Danaus. They were to marry the fifty sons of his brother Aegyptus, thus ending a long-standing quarrel between the two. However, Danaus didn't trust his brother. Fearing for his daughters, he gave them each a dagger along with instructions to kill their husbands in bed. The next morning, forty-nine of the husbands were dead. Only one daughter, Hypermestra, fell in love with her husband and failed to murder him. Though she was put on trial for her disobedience, the gods intervened and she was acquitted. As for her sisters, their punishment was postponed. First they remarried, pairing up with the winners of a foot race arranged by their father. When they died, they were condemned to an eternity of frustration in the underworld, where they each had to carry water in a jar pierced like a sieve.

- Sisyphus. Although his punishment is well known, his full story is seldom told. His crime, not violent in the least, is so ordinary, so human, that it seems barely a crime at all. It comes down to this: he didn't want to die.

  One day Sisyphus saw Zeus seducing the nymph Aegina. Instead of keeping quiet about the tryst, he told Aegina's father, the river god Asopus, who chased Zeus so relentlessly that eventually the great god grabbed a thunderbolt and killed him. Afterwards, still angry at Sisyphus, Zeus turned to his brother Hades for help. Hades captured Sisyphus and was about to drag him away in chains when Sisyphus outsmarted the god via a trick that was surely old even then: he convinced Hades to demonstrate on himself exactly how those handcuffs worked. Afterwards, Sisyphus locked him up in a dungeon—and created a universal disaster. With the lord of the netherworld in chains, no one could die, not even a man who had been beheaded or dismembered. Violent Ares, god of war, stepped in, freeing Hades and killing Sisyphus—once and for all, one would have thought. Yet even in death Sisyphus was crafty. Having told his wife Merope (who later became one of the Pleiades) not to bury his body, he then turned around and complained about this omission to Persephone, queen of the underworld. He argued that the letter of the law had not been followed and that he shouldn't have been allowed to cross the River Styx. In fact, he suggested, Persephone should let him go back to the land of the living to arrange his own funeral. He vowed to return, and Persephone, no smarter than her spouse, let him go. After a while, Hades and Persephone realized that Sisyphus had no intention of keeping his promise. Finally

Hades had to drag him back to the underworld, where the judges of the dead devised a way to keep him in line: they ordered him to roll an enormous boulder repeatedly up a hill, keeping him permanently occupied. Every time he pushes the stone to the summit, gravity does its work, the stone rolls back down, and Sisyphus has to trudge downhill and start all over again.

ALBERT CAMUS ON SISYPHUS

If this myth is tragic, that is because its hero is conscious. Where would his torture be, indeed, if at every step the hope of succeeding upheld him? The workman of today works every day in his life at the same tasks, and this fate is no less absurd. But it is tragic only at the rare moments when it becomes conscious. Sisyphus, proletarian of the gods, powerless and rebellious, knows the whole extent of his wretched condition: it is what he thinks of during his descent. The lucidity that was to constitute his torture at the same time crowns his victory. There is no fate that cannot be surmounted by scorn.

Another Greek Afterlife: Plato and the Myth of Er

In the last book of *The Republic*, Plato relates the story of a man named Er who died in battle, or so everyone thought. His seemingly lifeless body was already on the funeral pyre when he awoke from what can only be called an after-death experience. He reported that he had traveled to a way station in the realm of the dead. Not only did he see newly deceased souls ascending or descending to their due rewards, he also listened to more experienced souls, dead a thousand years, exchange stories about their afterlives. The virtuous souls described holidays in heaven, while the dusty souls from below complained about a miserable millennium. Er learned that, after being punished ten times over for every sin they had committed, they were allowed to leave the underworld and ascend to earth, where one of two things might happen. If they heard a gigantic roar, their punishments were not over: this happened to especially evil people such as Ardiaeus, a tyrant who had killed his parents and older brother. Er watched as he was flayed and dragged through banks of thorns.

Returning souls who were greeted by silence were more fortunate, for they were permitted to choose new lives. There were animal lives and human lives, public lives and private lives, the lives of tyrants and saints, the strong and the weak, the famous and the infamous, the exceptional and the ordinary. These lives were laid out like so much merchandise, and everyone had to pick one in an order determined by the casting of lots. The challenge for those who chose first was to select wisely; the challenge for the others was to avoid being discouraged for "even for the one who comes last, there lies a life that is desirable and not evil, if he chooses intelligently and lives it unflinchingly."

Er saw that those who had spent a thousand years being punished mulled their choices over warily, while those who had enjoyed a millennium of bliss tended to be unreflective. One soul, for instance, had lived a virtuous life, but his virtue was only a habit created by dwelling in a city with a strong constitution. The good behavior was not backed up with wisdom—with the result that the soul greedily picked the life of a tyrant and only later noticed that one of the evils

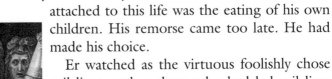

attached to this life was the eating of his own children. His remorse came too late. He had made his choice.

Er watched as the virtuous foolishly chose evil lives, and as those who had led evil lives settled upon good ones. Many souls even chose the life of an animal. Orpheus wanted to be a swan, the musician Thamyras, who fell in love with Hyacinthus and was therefore considered the first homosexual, picked the life of a nightingale, the Trojan warrior Ajax, who fell upon his sword in his previous life, elected the life of a lion, and Agamemnon, who sacrificed his daughter and was killed by his wife, chose

The Three Fates, from a drawing by Michaelangelo.

to be an eagle. All of them had suffered so grievously that they wished to avoid mankind entirely. The last to select a new life was none other than Odysseus, who happily chose to be an ordinary man.

Once the returning souls made their decisions, the three Fates (or Moirae) confirmed their choices and gave them each a daimon or spirit to accompany them through life. At the banks of the Lethe, all the souls had to drink (although some drank too enthusiastically and forgot everything they had learned). Then they slept. In the middle of the night, an earthquake jolted them awake and sent them hurtling like shooting stars towards birth. That's when Er woke up, just in time to climb off the funeral pyre and tell this story.

Hestia and the Vestal Virgins

The myth of Hestia is a tale of paradox. She was the youngest and the oldest, the first and the last, the least visible and the most central. As the first child of Rhea and Kronos, she was the first to be swallowed whole by her father and the last to emerge when Kronos regurgitated all his children. Thus she was both the oldest, because she was born first, and the youngest, because she was the last to emerge into the world. Mild-mannered and shy, she is the Olympian divinity with the least hold on our imaginations. The reason is simple: there are hardly any stories about her.

> *Conceive of Vesta as naught but the living flame.*
>
> —Ovid

She remained aloof from love. Although Apollo and Poseidon both lusted after her, she refused to wed and was clear in her decision to remain a virgin. She succeeded in this, although Ovid reports that on one occasion Priapus, the supraphallic misbegotten child of Aphrodite, tried to violate her. Fortunately, the braying of an ass alerted her and the rape never occurred.

Outside of the story of her birth, that's the main myth about

Hestia; indeed, it's the only one about her, unless you count the time when the other Olympians rebelled against Zeus but Hestia didn't join them. Unlike other virgin goddesses such as Athena and Artemis, she participated neither in war nor in the hunt nor in the general ruckus of life on Olympus. No wonder Homer never mentions her. She is notable for her absence in literature and her near-invisibility in art. Other than a few vases and some coins in which the goddess appears veiled, there are no visual representations of her. Ovid was surprised to learn that even at her temple, there were no images of her, and Pausanias noticed the same phenomenon. "If you go by to the sanctuary of Hestia," he wrote, "you find no statue, only an altar where they sacrifice to her." Unlike other Greek and Roman deities, she existed in a narrative vacuum, without personality, image, or anecdote.

Yet her position was central—literally. In private homes and public buildings, her designated spot was the center, where a perpetual flame was kept burning in her honor. She was the guardian of the hearth, the hearth itself, and the fire that burned upon it; she was the pile of burning coals that at Delphi represented the center of the world; she was the perpetual flame that burned on every hearth, making her a goddess of fire and an earth goddess, as the roundness of her shrines indicated. The first part of every sacrifice always went to her, and every banquet began and ended with the offering of sweet wine to Hestia. Thus she was worshipped in every home and on every public occasion. Nonetheless, when the Parthenon was built in the fifth century BCE, she was not pictured among the deities of Olympus. Dionysus appears there instead: the theory is that Hestia resigned in his favor.

Her Roman equivalent, Vesta, was more important. As the guardian of the city, she was accorded a round temple (its ruins are still impressive) in the Roman Forum, where her priestesses, known as the Vestal Virgins, were entrusted with several talismanic objects including the famous Palladium, the wooden statue of Pallas Athena thrown down to earth by Jupiter himself. The priestesses, who numbered first four and later six, were chosen from among members of the Roman aristocracy when they were between six and ten years old. They served a term of thirty years, and if they so chose, could remain in the temple for the rest of their lives. Honored on all state occasions, they were viewed with such admiration that when they walked about, an official preceded them carrying a bundle of wooden rods surrounding an ax, a traditional symbol of authority called a fasces (and admired many centuries later by Mussolini's Fascists, who took it as their symbol). Their power was so great that if a condemned man happened to meet one of them, he would receive a reprieve.

In exchange, their major duty was to make certain that the flame burned continuously. If it flickered out, the virgins were whipped. To rekindle the fire, they had to generate a spark by rubbing a borer against a piece of lucky wood and then they had to carry that newborn flame back to the temple in a bronze sieve.

On March 1, the first day of the new year, the flame was ritually relit. On June 9, the festival known as the Vestalia began. During that week, the sanctuary, normally closed to the public, was opened to married women. The local asses, whose labor powered the mills, were given a day off, as were their owners, the bakers, who festooned the animals with violets and small loaves or cakes in recognition of the assistance they gave the goddess when she was threatened by Priapus. On June 15, the temple was cleaned, and after that, life returned to normal for the Vestal Virgins.

In addition to being keepers of the flame and performing related tasks (such as making a certain salt cake used in festivals), the Vestals, as they were called, had one eternal duty: chastity. Penalties for losing their virginity were severe. Initially, they were whipped to death. This punishment was later refined so that a Vestal who broke the taboo against sexuality would be whipped—but not fatally—and buried alive in a small underground chamber built especially for the purpose and furnished with a few supplies and a bed on which to die. Once the priestess was inside this tomb, it would be covered up with dirt—and that was that. Over the course of approximately a thousand years, about twenty Vestal Virgins were condemned to death in this way.

Two mythological figures, however, may have escaped the fate of the erring virgins. One was able to prove her chastity by carrying water in a sieve. The other, named Ilia or Rhea Silvia, was the most famous Vestal Virgin of all. Her career was compromised when Mars, the god of war, took a fancy to her. She remained in the sanctuary until she gave birth to her children, Romulus and Remus, but she didn't live to tell the tale. One account says that her parents insisted that she suffer the prescribed punishment, whereupon she was buried alive and the babies were abandoned. The other report, told by Horace, indicates that she was thrown into the River Tiber, where she became the wife of the river god.

HESTIA,
GODDESS OF THE HEARTH

Domain: the home.
Characteristics: retiring, independent, serene, chaste.
Parents: Rhea and Kronos.
Main Sanctuary: Rome.
Roman Name: Vesta
Lovers and Liaisons: none.
Animal: ass.
Attributes: the eternal flame.
Best representation in post-classical art: none.

Golden Aphrodite

The Greeks and Romans gave their deities dozens of epithets or honorary last names which link them with geographical locations, identify their divine functions, or allude to their personal qualities. Aphrodite's epithets are especially telling. As a goddess of sensual love and the ultimate sex symbol, she was called Aphrodite Phillomeides, lover of laughter, and Aphrodite Phillomedes, lover of genitals. Sappho knew her as Aphrodite Peitho, goddess of Persuasion. She was also called Aphrodite Ambologera, who postpones old age, and Aphrodite Androphonos, destroyer of men, not to mention Aphrodite Nympha, Aphrodite Porne, and Aphrodite Kallipygos, of the Beautiful Buttocks.

Aphrodite and Ares

She was born, Hesiod tells us, in the white foam (*aphros* in Greek) which surged around the severed genitals of the sky god Uranus after Kronos tossed them into the sea. For some time after her birth, the goddess floated in the water (and was therefore known as Aphrodite Euploia, goddess of Good Sailing). Eventually she visited Cythera and the island of Cyprus, where she left the sea behind. In the twelfth century BCE, a temple was dedicated to her there. Over two millennia later that same spot became a shrine to the Virgin Mary.

> *like a wind*
> *crashing down*
> *among oak tree*
> *love shattered*
> *my mind.*
>
> —Sappho

Homer, Euripides, and Apollodorus tell another story about Aphrodite's birth. According to them, Aphrodite was conceived like the rest of us, through the force of physical attraction—in this case, between Zeus and the earth goddess Dione (a figure so lacking in distinction that even her name is merely a linguistic variant of Zeus's). All agree that Desire, known as Eros, was her companion from birth. Her powers, Hesiod says, included flirtation, seduction, and love, as well as "fond murmuring of girls, and smiles, and tricks,/And sweet delight, and friendliness, and charm." Within the world of romance, she was irresistible. On the few occasions when she ventured beyond that sphere—when she entered battle, for instance, or tried to do a little weaving—her efforts were a failure.

One of her first lovers was Nerites, who captured Aphrodite's attention while she was still living in the sea. The only son of Nereus, the old man of the sea, he refused to accompany her to Olympus. She begged him to go, even offering him a pair of wings. He declined. She gave the wings to Eros instead and turned Nerites into a cockle which lives in a shell buried among the underwater reefs of the Mediterranean.

Another lover was the Argonaut Butes. Among all the members of Jason's crew, he alone was seduced by the Sirens. While the others listened to Orpheus or tried to stop up their ears, Butes jumped overboard. That was the kind of action that Aphrodite could respect. She rescued him and spirited him away to Sicily, where she gave birth to their son, Eryx.

Poseidon, Hermes, Dionysus, and even Zeus were also her lovers, as were Hephaestus, whom she married, bellicose Ares, whom she adored, and Adonis and Anchises, whose stories follow.

APHRODITE, GODDESS OF LOVE

Domain: love, beauty, and fertility.
Characteristics: beautiful and bewitching.
Parents: Uranus, or Zeus and Dione.
Main Sanctuaries: Cypress, Cythera, and Corinth.
Roman Name: Venus.
Lovers and Liaisons: Adonis, Anchises, Ares, Butes, Hermes, and others.
Spouse: Hephaestus.
Children: Aeneas, Eros, Eryx, Harmonia, Hermaphroditus, Priapus.
Animal: doves and sparrows.
Attributes: magic girdle, scepter.
Best representations in post-classical art: Botticelli's *Birth of Venus,* Bronzino's *Allegory with Venus and Cupid,* and many more.

Anchises

Except for Athena, Artemis, and Hestia, the three virgin goddesses of Olympus, no one—neither gods nor humans nor birds nor animals—was immune to the wiles of Aphrodite. She repeatedly humiliated the other deities by causing them to fall in love with mortals. Finally Zeus decided to punish her. He did it in the most obvious way.

One day on the slopes of Mt. Ida, Aphrodite noticed Anchises, a Trojan prince, tending his cattle. She fell in love on the spot. Determined to seduce the beautiful mortal, she went to her temple, rubbed herself with ambrosial oil, and headed for the hut where Anchises lived. Wolves, lions, bears, and panthers followed in her wake. Nonetheless, she appeared before him in the guise of a mortal girl. The moment he saw her, he was filled with desire—and hesitation. She was so luminous that he was certain she must be a grace, a nymph, or possibly even a goddess. But which one? To cover all the possibilities, he greeted her (according to a Homeric

Hymn) with a litany of names, calling her "Artemis or Leto or golden Aphrodite, or well-born Themis or gleaming-eyed Athena . . ." Aphrodite assured him that he was wrong, that she was mortal. To convince him, she invented a biography. It began with her father ("Otreus, who rules over all Phrygia . . . perhaps you have heard of him") and ended with a story about how Hermes told her she was fated to marry none other than Anchises, to whom she would bear "splendid children." She suggested to Anchises that he introduce her to his family and send a messenger to Phrygia to announce the happy news to her parents, who she was certain would send back many gifts, including gold.

Poor Anchises, the most mortal of men, fell right into her trap. He argued that if they were going to get married anyway, it was pointless to postpone the inevitable. Why restrain themselves? Pretending he had convinced her, Aphrodite shyly climbed into bed and allowed him to remove her ornaments, flowers, and clothing. Then they made love, a goddess and a mortal man.

Afterwards she revealed herself as divine. Filled with fear, for he knew that mortal men who sleep with goddesses are often weakened by the encounter, he begged her to keep him from harm.

Once again, she assured him that no harm would come to him. All he had to do was the one thing that was impossible: he had to keep quiet about the encounter. If he were immortal, she said, she would proudly claim him as her husband, but since "soon you will be enveloped by pitiless old age," she wasn't interested. She told him that when their son, not yet born, was five years old, she would bring him to Anchises. She warned him that if anyone asked who the mother was, he was to say she was the daughter of a wood nymph, "beautiful as a flower." If he revealed the truth, Zeus would hurl his thunderbolt at him.

For a long time, by human reckoning, Anchises kept the secret. But one day in a drunken state he bragged that he had slept with the goddess of love. He was punished immediately, although there is some dispute as to whether he was struck by lightning and crippled or blinded by bees. Either of those misfortunes might explain why at the end of the Trojan War, when the city was in flames, he had to be carried to safety by none other than his loyal son, Aeneas, the only one of Aphrodite's children to inspire maternal feelings in her. Although Aeneas had been injured, he left the burning city with his father on his shoulders. The two of them wandered about until they reached the western tip of Sicily, where Anchises died. Afterwards, according to Virgil, Aeneas visited Anchises in the underworld and had many descendants, including Romulus, Remus, and Julius Caesar. Thus Aeneas, a minor figure to the Greeks even if he was the child of Aphrodite, is a founding father of Roman mythology.

Adonis

Handsome Adonis had a noble heritage that included an Olympian god, a handful of mortals, and an ivory statue. It was carved by Pygmalion, who loved it so much that he touched it constantly, bought it gifts, and tucked it into bed with feather pillows cradling its head. At last he prayed to the goddess of love that his creation be made mortal and his prayers were answered. The ivory grew warm and soft, the veins throbbed with life, and when Pygmalion kissed it, the statue opened her eyes and saw her lover.

Not long afterwards, their daughter Paphos was born. In time, Paphos slept with Poseidon and had a son, Cinyras, who settled down with Cenchreis and had a daughter named Myrrha (or Smyrna). For one reason or another, Aphrodite did not love Myrrha. It may have been because Myrrha's mother bragged that her daughter was more beautiful than the goddess of love. Maybe Myrrha secretly thought her hair was lovelier than Aphrodite's. Or perhaps Myrrha failed to worship the goddess in the proper way. In any case, Aphrodite decided to punish Myrrha by causing her to become hopelessly infatuated with her father.

The lovestruck Myrrha was on the verge of suicide when she confided the source of her desperation to her old nurse, who saw a solution. Taking advantage of a festival in honor of Demeter during which men were encouraged to shun their wives and make love with other women, the nurse convinced Cinyras to go to bed with a young woman who did not want her identity revealed. Flattered, he went along with this arrangement, and for twelve (or nine) nights in a row Myrrha and her father slept together. At last his curiosity won out and he brought a lamp into the room. When he saw his daughter in his bed, Cinyras was so horrified that he wanted to kill her. To escape his wrath, Myrrha ran into the forest with her father fast in pursuit. Just as he was about to catch up with her, she begged the gods for help and was transformed into a myrrh tree.

Ten months later, a wild boar tore into the tree with its tusks and out popped a baby: the beautiful Adonis (whose name derives from the Semitic *adon* or lord). The moment she saw him, Aphrodite fell in love.

Because he was still an infant, she placed him in a chest and gave him to Persephone to raise. Persephone's reaction mirrored Aphrodite's. As soon as she saw him, she was overcome by his beauty.

THE GARDENS OF ADONIS

Like other gods, Adonis was honored with an annual festival. Called the Adonia, it was celebrated in the hottest part of the summer with carousing (Adonis was associated with wanton sexuality) and mourning (in recognition of his early death). In Athens, courtesans planted fennel, lettuce, and other fast-growing seeds in baskets and clay pots. Placed on rooftops for maximum sun, these miniature gardens were watered to sprout quickly and wither soon, thus symbolizing the short life and untimely death of Adonis as well as, some scholars suggest, the cycle of vegetation.

Yet not everyone agrees that Adonis is a vegetation god. Classics professor Marcel Detienne, for instance, notes that, like those little gardens, Adonis is immature and superficial. He was born from a myrrh tree, a spice associated with seduction, and died in a field of lettuce, which was believed to cause impotence. He possesses physical beauty but nothing more, and his gardens are decorative at best. Thus, rather than being the spirit of vegetation, Adonis is the god of seduction—a meaning entirely in line with what we mean when we describe an attractive man as an Adonis.

Both goddesses wanted him, and they asked Zeus to mediate. He passed the problem on to Calliope, muse of epic poetry. She decreed that for a third of the year, Adonis would live with Persephone in the underworld; for another third of the year he would stay with Aphrodite; and for the remainder of the year, he could go where he wished, freed from the demands of either goddess. Thus Adonis, like other vegetation deities whose return coincides with the growth of crops, ended up spending part of the year in the underworld and part of the year on earth.

This solution sounded equitable but was not a success, for once Aphrodite donned her magic girdle, Adonis couldn't tear himself away. He stayed with her for two thirds of the year, twice as long as directed. Persephone complained to Ares, Aphrodite's hot-tempered lover. He was so angry that he turned into a boar and gored his handsome rival. When Aphrodite heard her beloved's dying groans, she flew to his side but he was dead on a field of lettuce. In memory of her beloved, she turned the blood flowing from his wounds into the red anemone.

The Judgment of Paris

Thetis was a sea goddess who was so lovely that both Zeus and Poseidon lusted after her. But before either could consummate the union, Prometheus, who could foresee the future, announced that Thetis was destined to give birth to a son who would be stronger than his father. Zeus and Poseidon, neither of whom could abide a threat to their power, lost interest immediately. To protect the other immortals, Zeus arranged a marriage between Thetis and a mortal man named Peleus. All the gods and goddesses attended the wedding, including Eris, the goddess of strife, who brought a golden apple carved with the words "for the most beautiful." When she tossed it onto the table, three goddesses stepped forward to claim the prize: Aphrodite, Athena, and Hera.

To settle the dispute, they went to Zeus. Because he was the husband of Hera and the father of Athena, he disqualified himself as a judge and suggested that they consult Paris, the handsomest man alive. So the three goddesses, accompanied by Hermes, journeyed to Mount Ida, where Paris was tending his sheep, and turned the decision over to him.

It wasn't an easy call and Paris had to do some thinking, which gave the goddesses plenty of time to bribe him. Hera offered him the riches of the earth and promised to make him ruler over Asia. Athena promised wisdom and victory in all battles. And golden Aphrodite tempted him with the love of Helen, the most beautiful woman on earth. Naturally, Paris gave the apple to her.

> *I had a dream I was Helen of Troy*
> *In looks, age and circumstance,*
> *But otherwise I was myself. . . .*
>
> —Stevie Smith

The consequences were far-reaching. Helen left her husband Menelaus and ran away with Paris to Troy, which caused Menelaus and his brother Agamemnon to attack that city; and soon the Trojan War was being waged in earnest. During that long conflict, Aphrodite sided with the Trojans while Athena and Hera, feeling snubbed, allied themselves with the Greeks. Their greatest warrior, Achilles, was the son of Peleus and Thetis, at whose wedding the troubles began—and the victim, ultimately, of Paris, who killed him with an arrow in his vulnerable heel.

The Punishments of Aphrodite

Like other Olympian deities, Aphrodite was quick to anger and creative in retribution. If she felt personally slighted, if her sacred rites were ignored, or if someone poached on her territory, she retaliated, sometimes with the harshest of punishments. Thus when Glaucus refused to allow his mares to breed, thereby insulting the very concept of love, she drove his horses into such a fury that they ate him alive.

And when Calliope decreed that Adonis should spend part of the year with Aphrodite and part with Persephone, Aphrodite was so offended that she hadn't received full custody that she caused the women of Thrace to fall in love with Calliope's adored son, Orpheus—and in their frenzy to tear him apart.

In Aphrodite's world, love was always the answer, and the punishment usually fit the crime. Those who offended her risked being afflicted with some terrible disorder of amour including obsessive love, violent love, unrequited love, lost love, and taboo love.

Thus when Poseidon's sons wouldn't let Aphrodite land on the island of Rhodes, she made them so lusty and violent that they raped their mother Halia, who leaped into the sea.

Hippolytus, the son of Theseus, also incurred the wrath of Aphrodite. He offended her by erecting a temple to the virgin goddess Artemis and, by implication, pledging celibacy. What could be more offensive than that? Aphrodite fought back by filling his stepmother, Phaedra, with desire for him. After that, all Aphrodite had to do was to sit back and watch events unfold. (See page 313.) They ended, needless to say, with the death of Hippolytus.

Finally, there was rosy-fingered Eos, the goddess of Dawn. She was married to Astraeus and had many wonderful children including Boreas, the cold north wind, Notus, the south wind, Zephyr, who blows in from the west, and all the stars in the sky. For the most part, she was faithful to Astraeus but on one occasion she yielded to temptation and went to bed with Ares, Aphrodite's lover. Aphrodite punished her with the curse of infatuation. After that, Eos couldn't quiet her mind; she was constantly obsessed with one young man or another. She yearned for Cephalos, who was devoted to his wife, and the giant Orion, who was killed by Artemis. Her best-known lover was the mortal Tithonus, whom she took to Ethiopia. Eos loved him so much that she asked Zeus to grant him the gift of immortality. Zeus complied, and for several years, all was well. Eos and Tithonus even had two sons who became the kings of Ethiopia and Arabia. But Eos (like the Sibyl of Cumae) made a crucial mistake: she neglected to ask Zeus for perpetual youth in addition to immortality. Soon grey hairs were sprouting from Tithonus's head and Eos withdrew from his bed. A little while later, Hesiod tells us, "loathsome old age pressed full upon him," so she shut him away in a room and closed the doors, leaving him to babble endlessly. Thanks to Aphrodite, only young men would do for Eos, and none of them stayed around for long.

Aphrodite's Children

As befits a fertility goddess, Aphrodite had many children. Some are minor players but the most famous are unforgettable. In addition to the Roman hero Aeneas, they are Eros, Priapus and Hermaphroditus, icons of sex and desire, the natural progeny of the goddess of love.

Eros

> *"We are the only love gods."*
> —William Shakespeare

Winged Eros, better known as Cupid, was Aphrodite's constant companion. Before the fifth century BCE, he was depicted as a winged adolescent, but he got younger and younger until eventually he became a laughing baby, ready to let his arrows fly. Theories as to his parentage abound. He was said to be the child of Chaos, or Gaia, or the rainbow goddess Iris, who gave birth to him after she coupled with the west wind. The most popular theory was that of the poet Simonides (556–468 BCE), who suggested that Eros was the son of Aphrodite and Ares. As the spirit of love, Eros plays a part in many stories but is seldom a major character. One exception: the love story of Cupid and Psyche, written by Lucius Apulius in his second-century novel, *The Golden Ass*. (See page 136.)

Priapus

Priapus was the son of Aphrodite but his misshapen appearance was entirely Hera's fault. She was so jealous of Aphrodite's beauty, or so aggravated by her promiscuity, that she touched her abdomen while she was pregnant and caused her son to be born with an enormous tongue, a round belly, and an oversized, ever-erect phallus. Aphrodite was so unnerved by this that she refused to raise him, and Priapus was brought up by shepherds.

Despite his conspicuous sexuality, Priapus was not a successful seducer (although he did teach Ares, the god of war, how to dance). When he pursued the nymph Lotis, she fled and turned into the lotus tree, and when he tried to violate Hestia (in her Roman incarnation as Vesta), he was interrupted by a loudly braying ass. Outside of his remarkable member, his best known symbol was the ass, which was sacrificed to him. His most important function, besides providing merriment for all, was as a god of gardens, where his easily recognizable statue was placed, scarecrowlike, to ward off the evil eye.

Hermaphroditus

Although Aphrodite wasn't especially attracted to Hermes, she agreed to go to bed with him in exchange for her sandal, which had been stolen by Zeus's eagle and given to Hermes for precisely this purpose. As a result of that one night, Aphrodite gave birth to Hermaphroditus, her other sexually distinguished child. When Hermaphroditus was fifteen, he left the mountains where he was raised and began to travel. One day he stopped at a pool of clear water that was home to the water nymph Salmacis. She was so shy that, alone of all the naiads, she was unknown to the huntress Diana. Yet when

The union of Aphrodite and Hermes produced Hermaphroditus, the two-headed figure in this alchemical drawing. Michael Maier, 1618.

Salmacis saw Aphrodite's beautiful son, she lost her reserve and self-absorption and began demanding kisses. Blushing, Hermaphroditus threatened to leave. She backed off and hid, whereupon Hermaphroditus, thinking she was gone, stripped off his clothes and dove into the pool. She jumped in after him and wrapped herself around his body "like the ivy encircling tall tree trunks, or the squid which holds fast the prey." Ovid wrote. Hermaphroditus fought as best he could but she prayed to the gods that the two of them would never be separated— and her prayers were answered. Their bodies melded together, becoming a single form, neither male nor female but both at the same time. When Hermaphroditus saw what had happened, he prayed to the gods that from then on any man who entered the pool would become impotent. And this vindictive prayer was answered too.

Apollo, God of Light

Zeus is a dictator, Hermes is a liar, Hades is weak, Poseidon is resentful, Ares is belligerent, Hephaestus is a complainer, and wild Dionysus is a drunk. But Phoebus ("bright") Apollo, the god of light, music, poetry, healing, and divination, is gifted, controlled, and omniscient: "The God of life," Lord Byron called him, "The Sun in human limbs array'd." Herodotus says he knew "how many grains of sand there are, and the dimensions of the earth," and Sophocles reported that he could see the future in the ashes of a dying fire. Some scholars have suggested, based on etymology and certain inconsistencies within the myth, that Apollo may originally have been Asian or Nordic, not Greek at all. Yet beautiful blond Apollo, second only to Zeus, is the epitome of what we mean by the phrase "Greek god."

Apollo

The Birth of Apollo

Before Apollo was born, an oracle predicted that the goddess Leto, pregnant with twins, would bear unruly, mighty children, including a son whose power would be second only to that of his father, Zeus. When Hera heard that, she ordered the monster Python to pursue Leto unceasingly and she forbade Leto to give birth anywhere on earth where the sun shone.

When her time to give birth arrived, Leto was in trouble. Like Mary and Joseph, she had to search for a place to give birth. No place would accept her. At last she stumbled upon the island of Ortygia, which was floating beneath the surface of the water and hence was not exactly on the earth. As soon as she set foot on it, the island heaved upwards, breaking through the surface of the water, and

Apollo and Artemis, crowned by the sun and the moon, join forces to kill the Python. Michael Maier, 1618.

Poseidon encircled it with a curtain of waves to shield it from the sun. Leto, having met the terms of Hera's edict, gave birth to Artemis. Leto and Artemis then traveled to the neighboring island of Delos, where Leto tried for nine days to give birth to the other twin. Hera kept it from happening by making certain that Eileithyia, the goddess of childbirth, knew nothing about the situation. At length the other goddesses intervened. They gave wind-footed Iris, the rainbow goddess, a golden necklace which they hoped would induce Eileithyia to help. Their bribe paid off. As soon as the two goddesses arrived back in Delos, perhaps in the form of two turtle doves, Leto threw her arms around a palm tree, kneeled on the soft ground, and gave birth to Apollo. Even as a child, his beauty, skill with lyre and bow, and inability to tell a lie were notable, and he was indeed second only to Zeus.

APOLLO, GOD OF LIGHT

Domain: music, poetry, medicine, prophecy, archery, light.
Characteristics: logical, objective, vengeful.
Parents: Leto and Zeus.
Main Sanctuaries: Delos, Delphi.
Roman Name: Apollo
Lovers, Liaisons, and Objects of Desire: Calliope, Cassandra, Cyparissus, Cyrene, Daphne, Dryope, Hecuba, Hyacinthus, Koronis, Marpessa, Ocyrrhoe, Stilbe, Thalia, Urania, and others.
Spouse: none.
Children: Amphissus, Aristaeus, Asclepius, Linus, and others.
Animal: snakes, deer.
Attributes: stringed instruments, bow and arrows, the tripod.
Best representations in post-classical art: Giambattista Tiepolo's *Death of Hyacinth,* Nicolas Poussin's *Apollo and Daphne,* Bernini's *Apollo and Daphne.*

The Delphic Oracle

Zeus sent two eagles to opposite ends of the earth and instructed them to fly towards the middle. The spot where they met at the center was called the omphalos, the navel of the world. It was also the location of the Delphic Oracle, where anyone could ask a question of Apollo and receive an answer.

There seems to have been no doubt, either in antiquity or today, that before Apollo took it over, the Delphic Oracle belonged to Gaia. Pindar thought that Apollo conquered it by force, and many modern commentators agree that the Apollo's coup represents a real historical takeover.

The mythological conquest took place three or four days after Apollo's birth, when he went in search of the Python that had harassed his mother while she was pregnant. After tracking it down on the slopes of Mount Parnassus, where it was guarding Gaia's oracle, he trapped it, killed it, and left it to rot in the sun. In that way, he wrested control of the oracle from the goddess.

Afterwards, in honor of the slaying of the Python, Apollo gained the epithet "Pythian." His priestess was known as the Pythia and the area also became known as

> *Everyone stands here*
> *And listens. Listens.*
> *Everyone stands here alone.*
>
> *I tell you the gods are still alive*
> *And they are not consoling.*
>
> *I have not spoken of this*
> *For three years,*
> *But my ears still boom.*
>
> —from "At Delphi" by May Sarton

Pytho, meaning "I rot." ("Putrefy" comes from the same root.) There, in the shadow of Mount Parnassus, the ancients swore sacred oaths, held religious festivals, sought advice, and freed the occasional slave.

Originally, Plutarch says, people could consult the oracle only once a year. Demand was so great that by the sixth century BCE, the oracle was open for business every month (though Apollo was not in residence during the winter, when he journeyed north to the land of the Hyperboreans. During his absence, the vacancy was filled, in a roundabout way, by Dionysus). Those who wished to consult the oracle needed to make elaborate preparations. They bathed in a certain spring, made offerings of special cakes, and sacrificed animals. Only then could they approach the priestess of Apollo, the Pythia. At various times either a young virgin or a woman over fifty, she would take a ritual bath, drink from a sacred stream, and do whatever was necessary to enter a trance state. It was long thought that she inhaled an intoxicating mist that wafted up from the river gorge, but that idea has been debunked. If the Pythia received a chemical assist, no one knows what it was.

We do know that the priestess, crowned with laurel, sat on a tripod (essentially a cauldron balanced on a three-legged stand), went into a trance, and spoke her mind. The priests then turned her sacred utterings into verse. Unlike other forms of divination which depended upon the interpretation of external signs such as the movement of birds or the disemboweled entrails of an animal, the oracle at Delphi relied on words alone.

Although poetic vagueness even now is often a hallmark of professional prognostication, the Delphic Oracle could be both specific and clear, as the written-in-stone archaeological record reveals. It contains oracular statements that are downright pedestrian, covering topics such as the sacrifice of an ox to Apollo, the construction of altars, and all manner of military and political advice. Literature tells us that the Delphic Oracle pre-

"KNOW THYSELF" "NOTHING IN EXCESS" "E"

These mottoes, carved in stone on the temple of Apollo at Delphi, were recognized throughout the classical world. "Know thyself" was a reminder of hubris and human limitations. "Nothing in Excess" was a cautionary reminder of how to live (even if it does bring to mind the epitaph of comedian Ernie Kovacs: "Nothing in Moderation."). As for "E," its message remains a mystery, although Plutarch, a citizen of Delphi, believed that it meant "Thou Art" in Greek and thus expressed the eternal existence of the soul.

Other sayings, less celebrated and less appealing, were also inscribed at Delphi. Among them: Fear authority. Keep women under rule. Curb thy spirit.

dicted the terrible fate of Oedipus and, on another occasion, pronounced Socrates the wisest man on earth. (The great philosopher felt compelled to check the accuracy of that statement by talking to other people, who proved to be fools, thus verifying the oracle.)

Yet the Delphic Oracle could also be obscure and enigmatic, which may be why Apollo was occasionally known as Loxias, "the ambiguous one." During the Persian Wars, for example, confusion arose among the Athenians when the oracle instructed them to protect themselves with a "wooden wall." Was the oracle referring to the wall of the city, which once surrounded the Acropolis? Or was it referring to the Athenian fleet of wooden ships? After arguments on each side, the Athenians acted in a thoroughly nonmystical way: they took a vote. The majority decided to reinforce the fleet, which was the right thing to do. In a naval battle not long after, the fleet of Xerxes attacked and the Athenians destroyed it.

It was easy to misinterpret the oracle's pronouncements or to hear what you wanted to hear. That's what happened to King Croesus, who once aspired to be the happiest man alive. In an incident described by Herodotus, he asked the Delphic Oracle what would happen if he attacked the Persians. He was told that he would destroy a mighty empire. Heartened by this response, Croesus went to war. But the empire he destroyed was his own.

The Mouse God and His Son

Early in the *Iliad,* in response to a heartfelt prayer from an old priest, Apollo decimates the Greek forces by attacking mules, dogs, and men. His weapon: the plague.

Afterwards, Apollo became known as Smintheus, the Mouse God, after the animal associated with the arrival of the plague. In the strange way that these things work, Apollo also became associated with victory over the plague and the return to health. Yet Apollo's skills as a healer were nothing compared to those of his son, Asclepius, the son of Koronis.

Koronis was already pregnant with Apollo's child when she became obsessed with someone else, a circumstance Pindar remarked upon around 472 BCE. "She was in love with what was not there; it has happened to many," he wrote. "Hunting impossibilities on the wings of ineffectual hopes," she went to bed with a stranger.

When Apollo found out, he killed her. As she lay dying, Koronis pulled the fatal arrow out of her white body and scolded Apollo, telling him that he should have waited until she had given birth: now, two lives would be lost instead of one. Flooded with remorse, Apollo implored the fates, poured perfume over her body, and tried to bring her back to life, to no avail. Just as her body was consigned to the funeral pyre, Apollo remembered the child and stepped into the fire. The flames parted. Apollo reached into the womb of the dead Koronis and tore out his son, Asclepius.

As often happened with the Greek gods, he gave the child to someone else to raise: in this case, the centaur Chiron, an expert in the healing arts. Asclepius learned what magical incantations to make, how to mix healing portions, what salves to use on injured limbs, and how to perform surgery with a knife. As a physician he was extraordinarily skilled.

"But even genius is tied to profit," Pindar wrote. One day Asclepius was offered gold to bring a man back from the dead. He accepted the offer and revived the man. Hades, lord of the dead, saw this as a threat to his authority. He complained to Zeus, who loosed his fatal thunderbolt and killed both doctor and patient.

The children of Asclepius continued in the tradition of their father. Among them were his sons Machaon and Podalirius, surgeons who died in the Trojan War; his daughter Hygeia, goddess of health and hygiene; and his elusive daughter Panacea, still sought by one and all.

Two Musical Competitions

I. Marsyas versus Apollo

Hermes, a precocious child, invented the lyre on the day he was born and gave it to Apollo, who quickly became its master. As the god of music (though far from the only one to play a musical instrument), Apollo was vain about his skill. The satyr Marsyas learned that the hard way.

It all started with Athena, who made a double flute from the bones of a stag. Although the melodies and harmonies she coaxed out of this instrument were sweet, Hera and Aphrodite laughed at her efforts, and Athena wondered why. One day while she was playing, she chanced to see her reflection in the water, and the reason became obvious. Her cheeks were so puffed out with the effort of playing that she looked absurd. She threw the flute to the ground and cursed anyone who might pick it up.

Along came Marsyas. He picked it up and started to blow, and the music that flowed out sounded divine. At least that's what the people in Phrygia thought. They doubted that even Apollo, the god of music, could make such gorgeous sounds, and they said as much. Marsyas failed to disagree.

So Apollo suggested a contest. He would strum his lyre, Marsyas would play the flute, and the muses, Apollo's companions from childhood, would judge who was the more musical. The winner could then punish the loser in any way he chose. Marsyas assented to the conditions, and the contest began. Both played beautifully until Apollo turned his lyre upside down and, continuing to play, challenged Marsyas to do the same. Naturally this couldn't be done with a flute, and so by unanimous agreement, Apollo won.

He decided upon a severe punishment. Marsyas was hung on a pine tree and his skin was torn from his body until, as Ovid tells us, blood was everywhere and it was possible to see his throbbing entrails and lungs. The satyrs mourned. The nymphs and shepherds couldn't stop crying. After a while, the whole countryside was awash in tears and even the earth joined in, for water gushed out of the ground and flowed to the sea, forming the clear waters of the Marsyas River in Asia Minor.

II. Pan versus Apollo

On another occasion, Pan boasted that his expertise on the pipes surpassed Apollo's on the lyre. He unwillingly entered a competition with Apollo, this time with the mountain Tmolus as judge and an audience that included, as chance would have it, King Midas, who still suffered from the same lack of sense that had caused him to ask for the golden touch.

Pan began noodling on his pipes, and his tunes were charming in a rustic sort of way. Then Apollo showed up in his long purple robes and his golden curls wreathed with laurel, and even before he plucked the strings on his bejeweled lyre, says Ovid, he stood like a true musician. When he played, his melodies were so enchanting that almost everyone acknowledged that Apollo was the superior player.

Not King Midas, though. Ever since the episode of the golden touch, when even the food he put in his mouth turned to metal, Midas had shunned the trappings of wealth in preference for country things. Thus he preferred the simple airs of the pipe to the sophisticated melodies Apollo plucked on the lyre, and he wasn't smart enough to keep his opinion to himself. He announced boldly that the pipes of Pan were superior to Apollo's celestial sounds.

Apollo had no patience for the mortal's idiocy. To punish Midas for his failure to hear, he lengthened his ears, lined them with rough grey hairs, and made them twitch. Midas hid these humiliating appendages beneath a purple turban. Only his barber knew the secret, and although he promised to remain silent, he needed to tell someone. So he dug a hole in the ground, whispered his secret into it, and filled the hole with earth. But as everyone knows, a secret, once told, cannot be confined. Reeds sprouted up in that spot and a year later, they were so tall that whenever a south wind blew, they shifted and rustled and murmured the truth, and soon the whole world knew that King Midas had the ears of an ass.

The Loves of Apollo

Unlike the other gods, Apollo was never lucky in love, despite his extraordinary beauty. Instead, he committed many rapes and used his ability to change shape to manipulative advantage. These are some of the women who rejected him:

- the mortal girl Dryope. She attracted Apollo's interest when he saw her playing with some tree nymphs. Knowing that his usual efforts at seduction were ineffectual, he changed into a turtle. When she picked it up and held it in her arms, he turned into a snake, twisted and curled around her body, and raped her as her friends, the tree nymphs, ran away and scattered.

Soon after this encounter, Dryope married someone else and gave birth to Amphissus, Apollo's son. When Amphissus was still an infant, Dryope took him to a myrtle grove where she paused to pick a few deep purple blossoms from a tree. To her horror, the tree began to bleed. She tried to run away and found that her feet were rooted to the ground. She felt bark climbing up her thighs, her hair turning into leaves, and her arms becoming branches. Just before the bark crept over her lips and eyes, her husband and father arrived in time to take the baby and hear her dying speech. Moments later, the transformation was complete.

> *Not that I want to be a god or a hero. Just to change into a tree, grow for ages, not hurt anyone.*
>
> —Czeslaw Milosz

- Daphne, whose sister Stilbe already had two or three children by the god. Apollo chased Daphne into the valley of Tempe and was about to overwhelm her when she cried out to Gaia and was miraculously transported to Crete, leaving in her place a laurel tree. Or perhaps Daphne prayed to her father, the River Peneius, and was transformed into a laurel tree. Bernini's startling statue in Rome depicts this metamorphosis.
- Ocyrrhoe, another daughter of a river god. To escape his advances, she sailed away in a boat. Apollo turned the ship's skipper into a fish and the vessel itself to stone, which undoubtedly sank.
- Cassandra, the clairvoyant daughter of King Priam and Hecuba. According to one story, she gained her psychic ability when she and her brother spent a night in a temple of Apollo. As they slept, snakes wound around their bodies and licked their ears, bestowing upon them the ability to foretell the future.

Aeschylus tells a better tale. He writes that Apollo, once again trying to seduce an unwilling mortal, gave her the ability to prophesy. Nonetheless, when he took her in his arms, she pushed him away. Apollo felt betrayed. Knowing that the boon could not be revoked, he spit into her mouth, adding a terrible rider to his original gift: She would always foresee the future but no one would believe her. She warned the Trojans not to haul that wooden horse through the gates of the city; they ignored her and were defeated when the horse proved to be packed with Greek soldiers. She predicted the death of Agamemnon, the overthrow of his family, even her own death. Everything she said came true, and no one ever believed her.

- Marpessa, a mortal women who captured the heart of the Argonaut Idas. Had Marpessa's father not been in the habit of beheading his daughter's suitors, Idas might simply have asked for her hand. Instead, he abducted her in a winged chariot, only to discover that he still had to contend with Apollo, who was also lusting after Marpessa and was prepared to fight. To avoid this confrontation, Zeus told Marpessa to make her own decision.

She chose wisely. Fearing that Apollo, a deathless god, would lose interest in her as she aged, she picked Idas, a mortal like herself, and hence, she reasoned, less likely to desert her. As it turned out, though, Idas was killed in a quarrel and her daughter, Cleopatra, committed suicide. In the end Marpessa was alone anyway and so unhappy that she killed herself. She learned that it doesn't matter how sensibly you try to outwit destiny. You can't avoid your fate.

APOLLO'S AMOROUS CATASTROPHES

Apollo's relationships with men, while fewer, were no less troubled. He loved and lost two men:

- Cyparissus, who accidentally slew Apollo's stag and was turned into a cypress tree.
- Hyacinthus, a Spartan. Apollo threw a discus which, misdirected by the jealous west wind, smashed into the young man's head and killed him. As Hyacinthus died, his blood formed the flower which bears his name. Some say that the marks on its blue petals spell out the syllables Ai Ai, the grief-stricken sounds that Apollo made when he saw that his beloved friend was dead.

The Sibyl of Cumae

The most influential woman to reject Apollo was one of his priest-esses, the Sibyl of Cumae. In his attempt to seduce her, he offered her anything she wanted. She leaned down, filled her hands with sand, and asked to be granted one year of life for every grain of sand. Apollo assented, but he saw a point of negotiation, for she had neglected to ask for perpetual youth to accompany her long life. He would give her this too, he promised—in exchange for her virginity. She declined the offer.

As the generations passed, she aged, becoming withered and frail. Fearing that one day only her voice would remain, she repeated a constant complaint: "I want to die. I want to die." A thousand years passed before she got her wish. By then, she resembled a cicada and was kept in a small cage in the Temple of Apollo, or in a bottle hung from the ceiling of a cave, or even in a jar—perhaps the very one shown to Pausanias when he visited Cumae, a little north of Naples.

This story resembles that of Eos and her lover Tithonus, who was granted immortality without eternal youth (see page 186). How-ever, Tithonus was a figure of myth while the Sibyl of Cumae lives in the shadowy region where history and myth overlap. Many women, known as sibyls, were recognized for their ability make prophesies. Some of them wandered about at will while others were associated with a particular location. Cumae, the site of a cave which was rumored to be the entrance to the underworld, was the home of the most famous seer of the ancient world.

The prophesies made there, generally in an ecstatic frenzy, actually existed. Written in Greek hexameter on palm leaves, they came into the possession of the Roman government when the Sibyl of Cumae sold them to Tarquinius Superbus (543–510 BCE), the last of the seven kings of Rome, and one of the bloodiest. She offered him nine volumes of her collected prophesies, and she named her price. He refused to pay. Perhaps he hoped to bargain. But as she had demon-strated in myth when she refused Apollo's offer of eternal youth in exchange for her virginity, she wasn't one to negotiate. Once he said no, she burned six of the volumes. Then she offered Tarquinius the remaining three, for the same price. This time, he paid.

Collections of Sibylline prophesies, which were filled with historical references and predictions, could be found in a number of locations.

In Rome they were kept in the temple of Jupiter, where temple priests at the direction of the Senate consulted them regularly, somewhat in the manner of the *I Ching.* Under the direction of various Sibylline oracles, a temple to Apollo was constructed in 433 BCE, cults were created in honor of Ceres and Asclepius, and a ritual involving human sacrifice was performed in 216 BCE. After a fire destroyed the Sibylline Books in 83 BCE, they were reconstituted from other collections and

THE NINE MUSES

At Delphi and other spots of worship in the ancient world, the Muses were said to be three in number. Over the centuries, that figure grew and finally it was agreed that they were nine. Born after their mother Mnemosyne (Memory) spent nine nights with Zeus, they were beauties with blond or violet tresses (depending upon whether Hesiod or Pindar is the source). They could see into the future, and they loved the pleasures of

Apollo, resembling George Washington, and the Muses. Engraving by physician and philosopher Robert Fludd (1574–1637).

feasting and song. Since Apollo was the god of music, poetry, and the arts, it was natural that the muses became his companions and in some cases his lovers. The muses were:

Calliope	epic poetry
Clio	history
Erato	the lyre
Euterpe	the flute
Melpomene	tragedy
Polyhymnia	hymns and pantomime
Terpsichore	dance
Thalia	comedy
Urania	astronomy

reinstalled in the temple of Apollo, where they remained until the temple was sacked around 408 CE by a Roman general. By then, their time had passed. They hadn't been consulted for forty-five years.

Unlike other figures, the Sibyl of Cumae was not confined to the mythological realm of the Greeks. Instead, she became a sort of honorary Old Testament prophet and has frequently been pictured in Christian art. Her prophesies were incorporated into the body of Jewish and then Christian literature, and that material evolved. As late as the seventh century, Jewish writers were making additions to the Sibylline Books, and Christians continued to do so throughout the Middle Ages. By the sixteenth century, when eight of the books were published with the stamp of Christian interpretation upon them, the Sibyl of Cumae was famous for having predicted the coming of Christ. Her image can be seen in glorious color on the ceiling of the Sistine Chapel.

Apollo and Helios, Gods of the Sun

Although we associate Apollo with the sun, that classification was not part of his identity until the fifth century BCE, when members of the cult of Orpheus began referring to the sun as Apollo. The earlier sun god was Helios, brother of the Moon (Selene) and the Dawn (Eos).

Every day, Helios rode his golden chariot across the vault of heaven, starting in the east and completing the journey in the west. At night, he slept in a winged golden cup (a gift from Hephaestus) while his chariot and horses waited for dawn in Ethiopia. Or else he spent the night in a golden boat sailing from west to east along the ocean stream that was thought to encircle the earth. By morning he was back on the job. He didn't miss a day. Consequently, when Zeus apportioned all the places on earth to the immortals, only Helios, who was driving his chariot across the sky, received nothing. As recompense, he requested any new lands that might appear. Zeus agreed, giving him the island of Rhodes, which was just rising out of the sea.

On Rhodes, festivals, games, and sacrifices were dedicated to Helios, and every year, a chariot drawn by four horses was driven into the sea in his honor. He was also glorified with the Colossus of Rhodes, a 105-foot bronze statue erected in 284 BCE. It towered above the harbor for sixty-six years until it was felled by an earthquake.

As the sun god, Helios was charged with the march of time and he performed responsibly. Once, however, when Helios saw the newborn Athena, freshly sprung from the head of Zeus, he was so stunned that he pulled his chariot to a stop and stared. Thus time stood still. Fortunately, no damage occurred.

Another time, famous because Homer tells the tale in the opening lines of the *Odyssey*, Helios was so angry at the shipmates of Odysseus, who had stolen his snow-white cattle, that he withheld a single day of the lives from them: the day of their homecoming. Thus they were fated to wander forever.

The most serious problem Helios ever faced concerned his son Phaëthon, who asked his father to prove his love (and paternity) by promising him anything he requested. This was always a setup in Greek mythology. Helios nevertheless agreed. To his horror, Phaëthon asked to drive the chariot of the sun across the sky. Knowing that his son was unprepared for this arduous task, Helios tried to dissuade him. But Phaëthon insisted, and Helios was forced to comply. He placed the blazing rays on the boy's head and told him everything he could about how to handle the horses.

As soon as Phaëthon took the reins, he lost control, just as Helios had feared. The horses went wild, first climbing so high that the earth froze, then skimming so low that the Ethiopians turned deep brown and Libya became a parched desert. Zeus had to step in. He hurled his thunderbolt at Phaëthon, who plunged to his death in the Eridanus River. His grieving sisters collapsed alongside its banks and became poplar trees, and their tears turned to amber.

In art, Helios was pictured in his chariot, often with a halo of bright rays. In myth, he had a single round eye with which he could see everything, making him an important source of information for the other immortals. Helios caught Aphrodite and Ares in the act and reported their liaison to the cuckolded Hephaestus. He also told Demeter that her daughter Persephone had been kidnapped. But he knew nothing of the future: that ability belonged to Apollo, the sun god in post-classical art whose swan-drawn chariot, a gift from Zeus, mirrors the horse-drawn chariot of fire which Helios piloted across the sky each day.

Artemis: Wild Thing

The untamed patron saint of girlhood, the mistress of wild animals, and the goddess of the hunt, Artemis (Diana to the Romans) lived outdoors with her attendants, tracking animals and bathing in mountain streams. Typically shown with her bow and arrow and her hunting dogs, she was the goddess of the moon, associated with times of change in the lives of women and in particular with the two biggest transitions of all: childbirth, which transformed the girl into the woman, and death, which she brought about painlessly with a volley of arrows.

Yet Artemis is a youthful goddess and one of the few about whom childhood stories are told. When she was nine days old, she

Artemis, crowned by a tiny crescent moon, rides a stag in this sixteenth-century woodcut.

helped her mother give birth to her brother Apollo. At age three, she climbed on her father Zeus's knee and asked for many gifts, chief of which was perpetual virginity. According to Callimachus, a poet of the fourth century BCE, she also requested "as many names as my brother Apollo; a bow and arrow like his; the office of bringing light; a saffron hunting tunic with a red hem reaching to my knees; sixty young ocean nymphs, all of the same age, as my maids of honor; . . . all the mountains in the world;

and lastly, any city you care to choose for me, but one will be enough." Charmed, Zeus gave her thirty cities.

Artemis chose her attendants, all of whom were nine years old, in Crete. She also visited the one-eyed Cyclopes, who forged Zeus's thunderbolts and from whom she received her essential attributes: a silver bow and a quiverful of arrows. According to Callimachus, the first two arrows that left her bow struck trees, the third hit an animal, and the fourth slammed into a city of unjust men.

In Neolithic times, Artemis was so fierce that men were sacrificed to her. In time, her image softened (in the *Iliad*, she even bursts into tears in one scene). But as one might expect from the goddess of the hunt, her harshness never entirely disappeared.

ARTEMIS, GODDESS OF THE MOON

Domain: the hunt, the moon, wild animals, transitions in the lives of women.
Characteristics: independent, nature-loving, ruthless, chaste.
Parents: Leto and Zeus.
Main Sanctuary: Ephesus.
Lovers and Liaisons: none.
Animal: deer, bear.
Attributes: bow and arrow, crescent moon.
Best representations in post-classical art: School of Fountain-bleu's *Diana the Huntress,* Titian's *Death of Actaeon,* Boucher's *Diana in Her Bath.*

Niobe's Children

Niobe was a fortunate woman with a fatal flaw: she lacked humility. She boasted repeatedly that she had twelve splendid children whereas the goddess Leto, mother of Artemis and Apollo, had only two. Even while attending Leto's festival in Thebes, Niobe continued to brag. Finally Apollo and Artemis, enraged for their mother's sake, decided to show Niobe just what Leto's two children could do. They grabbed their bows and arrows and between them slaughtered all twelve of Niobe's offspring. Apollo shot the boys while Artemis killed the girls.

For nine days, Niobe wept. On the tenth day, the funeral was held and life reasserted itself. Even Niobe, Homer tells us, "worn to the bone with weeping, turned her thoughts to food."

Yet some sorrows cannot be overcome. After the funeral, her husband Amphion, unable to bear the loss, committed suicide, and Niobe asked Zeus to turn her to stone. He mercifully complied. In the second century CE, Pausanias saw this very stone while climbing a mountain in Asia Minor. "Niobe from up close is a rock and a stream, and nothing like a woman either grieving or otherwise," he wrote. "But if you go further off you seem to see a woman downcast and in tears."

The Death of Actaeon

Actaeon was hunting one day with his dogs. Around noon, when the shadows were short, he wandered off through dense groves of pine and cypress until he came to a clear mountain stream where Artemis happened to be bathing. One innocent, accidental glimpse of the god

dess sealed his fate. Artemis, fearful that he might tell others what he had seen, sprinkled water over him, and the metamorphosis began. Horns sprouted from his head, his neck lengthened, and his hands and feet thickened into hooves. Within moments, Actaeon turned into a spotted stag. His hounds picked up the scent and chased him over the hills and rocky cliffs. He called out repeatedly, but his beloved dogs did not recognize his voice. When he was exhausted and could run no more, they tore him to pieces.

To emphasize the personal horror of it all, Ovid names and describes over thirty of those hounds. Shakespeare, as usual, used the story most effectively. In *Twelfth Night*, the Duke describes his reaction when he first saw Olivia:

> *That instant was I turn'd into a hart,*
> *And my desires, like fell and cruel hounds,*
> *E'er since pursue me.*

The Death of Orion

As the goddess of the chase, Artemis loved to wander through the forests, often with Poseidon's gigantic son Orion, a hunter as skilled as herself. Apollo noticed that Artemis and Orion were spending a lot of time together, and it worried him. Orion was the handsomest man on earth and Apollo feared that his sister, who had vowed to remain a virgin, would succumb to his charms. Apollo decided to save her from this fate.

One day he saw Orion swimming in the ocean, possibly on his way to Delos. When the great hunter was so far away that his head looked like a dark spot bobbing on the waves, Apollo pointed it out to Artemis and told her it was a man named Candaon who had attacked one of her priestesses. Artemis, unaware that Candaon was one of Orion's nicknames, drew her bow and arrow and, with fault-less aim, shot her beloved friend through the head.

When she discovered what she had done, she pleaded with Apollo's son Asclepius to bring Orion back to life. Zeus wouldn't hear of it. So Artemis placed Orion in the heavens, where the majestic constellation even now dominates the night sky.

No great myth goes unchallenged, though, and there are several other explanations for the death of Orion and for his position on the celestial sphere. One is that he made the fatal mistake of bragging that no animal could possibly kill him. In response, Artemis—or Hera or Gaia—sent in the scorpion, which brought the giant down with a single sting.

There was a lesson to be learned in that. To remind everyone of the folly of hubris, Zeus set the lowly scorpion in the heavens, but as far from Orion as possible. Now the constellation Scorpius rises as Orion sets, and the two are always a maximum distance apart.

The Bears of Artemis

Artemis is the goddess of all wild animals, but her most totemic creature is the bear. It appears most notably in a story about her attendant Callisto. As a priestess of Artemis, Callisto was naturally required to be chaste. Unfortunately, she caught the eye of Zeus and he violated her. Callisto kept her secret for as long as she could. Then one day, as the goddess and her retinue undressed by a stream, the truth was revealed: Callisto was pregnant, irrefutable proof that she had failed to uphold the rites of Artemis. Questions of guilt or innocence aside, she had to be punished. So after she gave birth to a child named Arcas (the Greek word for bear), she was changed into a bear.

After that, Callisto lived in the woods, where one day she unexpectedly came upon her son. She recognized him immediately and lumbered towards him on all fours. But she was a bear, and Arcas was a boy, and his terror was so great that he pulled an arrow out of his quiver and prepared to shoot. At that moment, Zeus took pity. He grabbed the boy, changed him into a bear, and hurled both mother and son into the sky, where they were transformed into the constellations Ursa Major and Ursa Minor.

Another time, a wild bear stumbled into the shrine of Artemis in Athens. After her attendants tamed it, the bear became a major attraction—until a little girl mocked the animal and it scratched her face. In retaliation, her brothers killed the bear. Soon a plague swept through Attica.

An oracle was consulted. It replied that to end the plague, the Athenians must agree to perform a ceremony known as the arkteia, the ritual of the bear. The citizens so voted, and the ritual became part of the festival of Artemis.

The arkteia was essentially an initiation, especially in Brauron, one of the twelve townships of the Athenian state. Performed by girls between the ages of five and ten who were known as "arktoi" or female bears, the arkteia was a rite of passage in which the girls, wearing saffron-colored robes, placed toys, dolls, and locks of their hair on an altar to Artemis. In addition, they each sacrificed a goat. Then, having symbolically left childhood behind, they were ready to move on to the next stage of life, when Artemis would no longer be their primary goddess. Instead, Callimachus wrote, they "acquired a taste for the talents of frivolous Aphrodite."

Yet Artemis was also a goddess of fertility and childbirth, and someday she would reappear in the lives of the girls. When that happened, it wasn't necessarily good news, for Zeus gave Artemis the right to inflict pain during labor and, should she so desire, to kill women in childbirth—or indeed, at any time at all. Thus the sudden death of a woman was always ascribed to Artemis, and the young girls in the arkteia who were her attendants might someday become her victims.

Lunar Goddesses

Like other goddesses, Artemis is often included in a triumvirate of divinities who reflect the phases of the moon. The virgin Artemis symbolized the new moon and the young girl; gorgeous Selene, sister of the sun god Helios, signified the full moon and the woman at the height of her sexual powers; and the crone Hecate, the goddess of witchcraft, represented the waning moon and the process of aging. Hecate spent most of her time in the underworld as an attendant to Persephone, but Selene rode across the heavens in a chariot drawn by a pair of winged, snow-white horses (or—better yet—cows). Her lovers included Zeus, Pan, and Endymion, whom she visited during the dark of the moon, when Hecate reigned supreme. During those few days at the end of the lunar cycle, Selene went to Mount Latmos to be near him. To more fully enjoy his beauty, she begged Zeus to grant him eternal youth and to let him drift into eternal slumber. Zeus granted both requests. Endymion became immortal and unconscious, and Selene went on to have fifty children by him.

Moon Gods

In the thirteenth century, Genghis Khan claimed to be the descendant of a woman who had been inseminated by the moon—which goes to show that the moon is not always perceived as female. Here is a sampling of lunar gods:

- Chandraprabha, a moon god from India. He was born after his mother swallowed the moon.
- Gidja, the Australian lord of dreams, sex, and the moon.
- Khonsu, a young Egyptian moon god famed for his healing abilities.

- Periboriwa, a Venezuelan moon spirit. When his blood splattered on the earth, the drops turned into men.
- Rona, a Maori god. He went to the moon to look for his missing wife but when he arrived, he and the moon started to fight. The battle continues to this day. As Rona and the moon struggle, the moon wanes, growing progressively smaller; as they heal from their wounds, the moon waxes.
- Sin, the Sumerian moon god, known as Asinmbabbar during the new moon, Sin during the crescent phase, and Nanna, a bull with a blue beard, when the moon was full. During the last three days of the lunar month, when Sin descended into the underworld, death, storms, and other difficulties plagued the earth. Three days later, he reappeared. Thus, like Inanna, who also spent three days in the underworld, Sin was a dying-and-rising god. He was celebrated at the ziggurat of Ur (which itself was named after the moon god Hur).
- Tarqeq (or Igaluk), the Inuit god of the moon. A hunter, he is also the god of all animals valued for their meat or fur.
- Ticciztecatl, the Aztec god of the moon.
- Thoth, the ibis-headed Egyptian god of knowledge, writing, magic, measurement, and the moon.
- Tsuki-yomi, the Japanese god of the moon, brother of the sun goddess, Amaterasu.

Atlanta and the Calydonian Boar Hunt

Oeneus, the king of Calydon, once sacrificed several oxen to the other gods but forgot to make an offering to Artemis. "It slipped his mind/or he failed to care," wrote Homer, "but what a fatal error!" To punish him, Artemis sent a bristling boar with enormous tusks into Calydon. It trampled his crops, attacked his cattle, gored his workers, and terrified the populace. Desperate for assistance, Oeneus promised the tusk and pelt to anyone who killed the boar.

Warriors and hunters arrived from all over Greece. Among them were Theseus, Jason, Nestor, who fought at Troy, Meleager, the son of Oeneus, and one woman, Atalanta.

Abandoned at birth because her parents wanted a boy, Atalanta was saved by Artemis, who sent a bear to suckle her. She grew up to be brave, adventurous, and skilled with the bow and arrow. Nonetheless, some of the men who came to hunt for the Calydonian boar objected to her presence. Only Meleager insisted that she be included, for although he was married (to a woman named Cleopatra), Atalanta had bewitched him.

After much wrangling, the hunt began, and it was a bloody. The boar gored several men, castrated and disemboweled one, and drove Nestor up a tree. Jason hurled his javelin at the animal and missed. Another hunter grazed its shoulder with his spear, but the beast lumbered off. Then one of Atalanta's arrows struck the boar behind the ear. It stumbled. Moments later, Meleager speared the boar and down it went.

Meleager presented the prize to Atalanta because she had made the first direct hit. His uncles, who had joined the hunt, found this insulting. In the melee that followed, Meleager killed them.

When Meleager's mother, Althaea, heard that her son had killed her brothers, she wanted to kill him—and she knew just how to do it. She recalled that, seven days after Meleager's birth, the Fates had appeared before her. They pointed to a smoldering log on the fire and announced that when it turned to embers, her son's life would end. At the time, Althaea leaped up, doused the log with water, and hid it. Now she retrieved the log, grown dry with age, and angrily tossed it into the flames. Before she could reconsider, the fire turned the log to ashes and Meleager died. Althaea hung herself, the widowed Cleopatra followed suit, and the mourners at Meleager's funeral turned into small birds known by the Greeks as meleagrides.

Atalanta Gets Married

Like Artemis, Atalanta did not want to wed, despite her father's pleas. She stubbornly refused to marry anyone except a man who could outrun her. Since she was the swiftest runner on earth, this was impossible. So Hippomenes, who was enchanted by her, relied on something more powerful than speed: strategy. Before the race, he consulted the wily Aphrodite, who gave him three golden apples. During the competition, Hippomenes tossed them one by one in front of his beloved. And one by one, she stooped to pick them up. With each delay, he spurted ahead until he crossed the finish line before her, winning the race and Atalanta's hand.

If this seems like a pretty fable, consider the analysis of the nineteenth-century jurist J. J. Bachofen, author of *Mother Right*. Atalanta, he pointed out, was seduced not by love but by the golden apples. She sacrifices victory and freedom for material objects. In exchange, her mate is forced to set aside the quest for sensual satisfaction and aim instead at "the production of golden fruit." Thus swift-footed Atalanta, once an independent pre-Hellenic goddess, ultimately became a wife, and a gold-digging one at that.

Naturally, they did not live happily ever after. Hippomenes forgot to thank Aphrodite, who reacted by turning both Atalanta and Hippomenes into lions, a crueler fate than it seems, since it was thought that lions could mate only with leopards—not with each other.

FROM *ATALANTA IN CALYDON*

Come with bows bent and with emptiness of quivers,
*   Maiden most perfect, lady of light,*
With a noise of winds and many rivers,
*   With a clamor of waters, and with might;*
Bind on thy sandals, O thou most fleet,
Over the splendor and speed of thy feet . . .

—Algernon Charles Swinburne

Gray-Eyed Athena: A Motherless Child

In these days of postfeminist glory, with women in the military, in outer space, on the basketball court, and on the Supreme Court,

(Credit: Hannah Berman)

one might think that Athena, warrior goddess of wisdom, would be celebrated. Instead, with her logical mind and slightly masculine demeanor, she inspires discomfort. At the root of this ambivalence is the central story about Athena: her birth.

ATHENA, GODDESS OF WISDOM

Domain: wisdom, weaving, war, civilization.
Characteristics: wise, chaste, independent, rational, helpful to heroes.
Parents: Metis and Zeus.
Main Sanctuaries: Athens.
Animal: owl.
Attributes: helmet; armor; shield or aegis with the head of the Medusa; a small figure of Nike, goddess of victory.
Best representation in post-classical art: Jacopo Tintoretto's *Minerva and Arachne*.

Athena's Birth

Athena sprang from the forehead of Zeus after Hephaestus cracked it open with an ax. Michael Maier, 1618.

Before Zeus married Hera, he consorted with Metis, who was known for her good judgment. But he got scared when his parents warned him that Metis would give birth to two children, one of whom would pose a serious threat to him. The first child would be a daughter (and hence nothing to worry about). The second, a son, was fated to be more powerful than Zeus himself.

To eliminate that unthinkable possibility, Zeus followed the example of his father, who devoured his children, and did him one better by swallowing Metis, who was already pregnant. A few months later, Zeus was strolling alongside a lake when he developed an excruciating headache. His pain was so intense that Hephastus (or one of the other divinities) took an ax and split Zeus's forehead. Out sprang Athena, fully grown, spear in hand, clad in golden armor, and shrieking.

Athena, the independent virgin, became his adored favorite. She had no relationship whatsoever with Metis. Rather, she thought of herself as the offspring of Zeus, the ultimate motherless child. "No mother gave me birth," she announces in *The Eumenides* by Aeschylus. "I honor the male, in all things but marriage./Yes, with all my heart I am my Father's child."

ARE WOMEN NECESSARY?

Mythology has its own rules, and one of them is that anyone can have a baby. Being female is not a prerequisite, as Apollo explains in *The Eumenides* by Aeschylus. His hypothesis is that man produces the seed (*sperma* in Greek) and donates it to the woman, whose function is strictly custodial. Anyone, theoretically, could do her job, while only the man can perform the godlike task of creating life. "The father can father forth without a mother," Apollo asserts. As proof, he points to Athena, born from her father's forehead, clear evidence that women are irrelevant even in childbirth.

Athena and Her City

Athena and Poseidon both wanted Athens as the center of their cults, so the gods held a contest. To illustrate the benefits she could confer upon the city, Athena presented the inhabitants with a simple olive tree. Poseidon thrust his trident into the Acropolis, and a salt water spring gushed up out of the stone. Because both gifts were worthy, the immortals took a vote to decide upon a winner. The goddesses chose Athena, while the gods cast their ballots for Poseidon—with the exception of Zeus, who abstained in an effort to maintain neutrality. As a result, Athena won.

Poseidon did not deal with defeat gracefully. He retaliated with his usual weapon: a flood. When the rain showed no sign of abating, the citizens of Athens realized that they had to calm him down. They did so by denying the women of the city the right to vote and by ruling that men were no longer permitted to keep their mother's names. Thus Athena's supposed victory was ultimately a Pyrrhic one.

Pallas Athene

Preferring not to raise his own daughter, Zeus placed the young Athena in the custody of Poseidon's son Triton, a sea god with a human face, a fish's tail, and a daughter of his own named Pallas. The two became best friends, playing together constantly. But Athena was a goddess with divine protection, and Pallas was just a girl. One day they were quarreling when Zeus happened to glance their way just as Pallas was about to smack Athena. He grabbed his protective aegis, a shield made of goatskin, and held it between the friends. Startled, Pallas paused, giving Athena the opportunity to lunge forward and strike. To Athena's horror, Pallas died on the spot. To acknowledge her fallen friend, Athena took her name and was afterwards known as Pallas Athene.

To further honor her friend, Athena carved an olive-wood statue of her that came to be known as the Palladium. The statue made its way from the mists of Olympus to the material world when the mythical Ilos, pacing out the boundaries for the city of Troy (also known as Ilium), asked Zeus for a sign that he was doing the right thing. Zeus responded by throwing

HOW PALLAS ATHENE GOT HER NAME: A WEIRDER VERSION

The twelfth-century scholar John Tzetzes had a different theory. He held that Pallas was actually Athena's father. When he tried to rape her, she flayed him, afterwards taking his name, his wings, and his skin, which she used to make her famous aegis.

down the sacred statue, which was somehow no longer a statue of Pallas but of his daughter, Pallas Athene. During the Trojan War, it was housed in the citadel in Troy (although Athena herself was on the side of the Greeks). Its mere presence protected the city. And indeed, after Odysseus and Diomedes stole it, the city was sacked.

The statue did not disappear. Instead, like fragments of the true cross, it turned up in Argos, in Sparta, in Athens, and in Rome, where it was installed in the Temple of Vesta and credited with saving the city from the Gauls in 390 BCE. Belief in the sanctity of this object was so strong that when the Temple of Vesta caught fire in 241 BCE, the Palladium was rescued by the pontifex maximus, the head priest, who lost his sight in the process.

Arachne

Like other deities, Athena demanded recognition for her accomplishments and was angered if her supremacy was questioned. The unfortunate Arachne, who came from an area known for the beauty of its deep purple dye, did just that when she challenged Athena to a weaving competition. Out of kindness, Athena disguised herself as an old woman and counseled Arachne to reconsider. Convinced that she could triumph, Arachne dismissed the warning. So the contest commenced. Athena designed a complicated tapestry picturing all the gods and their attributes, with special emphasis on the olive tree which won her the city of Athens. To complete the design, Athena wove into each corner a cautionary scene depicting a mortal who was transformed into something else—a mountain, a bird, the steps of a temple—for having displeased the gods.

Arachne turning into a spider, from Gustave Doré's 1868 illustrations for Dante's Purgatorio.

Arachne wove a montage that vividly depicted the trickery of the gods in their many love affairs. Zeus was there as a bull, a swan, a satyr, a flame, a spotted snake, and other disguises he used to trick the unwary. Poseidon was disguised as a bull, a ram, a river god, a horse, a dolphin, and a bird. And so it went. Arachne was creating a masterpiece. But watching her weave made Athena furious, in part because the pictures implicitly criticized the gods, and in part because the execution of these scenes was flawless. So she snatched Arachne's tapestry away from her, tore it to pieces, and proceeded to beat her terrified competitor with a boxwood shuttle she grabbed from the spinning wheel. Arachne was so frightened that she made a noose and tried to hang herself.

Athena wasn't about to allow such a simple death. She sprinkled Arachne with a poisonous juice and watched as the mortal turned into a spider or arachnid. In that shape she continues to weave.

Erichthonius

Although Athena liked men, she took no erotic interest in them. Hephaestus, however, didn't know that. So when Poseidon, who resented Athena for winning the city of Athens, told Hephaestus that the goddess was longing for him to make love to her (and rough love at that), he believed it. Naturally, he was thrilled when she visited him in his workshop to discuss a new set of armor, and wasted no time in attacking her. She was repelled. She pushed him away but he was so excited that he ejaculated on her leg. In disgust, she grabbed a handful of wool, wiped off the semen, and threw it on the ground.

That was enough to impregnate Gaia, the goddess of the earth, who gave birth to a son named Erichthonius. Gaia presented him to Athena, who tucked him into a covered basket and handed him over to the three daughters of the Athenian king Cecrops, who was half man and half snake. Herse, Pandrosus, and Aglaurus were instructed not to look inside the box, but that sort of prohibition, as anyone who has read about Bluebeard knows, only guarantees that the forbidden action will occur. Inevitably, the sisters, no longer able to contain their curiosity, peeked inside the basket and saw a baby whose lower body was a serpent's tail. The sight so appalled them (although given the nature of their father, it's hard to see why) that they went mad and jumped to their deaths from the Acropolis.

A white crow reported the bad new to Athena, who was so upset that she turned the crow black. Afterwards, she kept Erichthonius closely guarded, either inside her temple or within her aegis, until he was grown. As king of Athens, he established a cult in her honor.

What Athena Wore:
The Aegis and Other Garments

Golden Aphrodite, the goddess of beauty and seduction, might be expected to possess a wardrobe of alluring clothing. In fact, she is the goddess of undress, known for only a single garment: her irresistible girdle or sash. Athena, on the other hand, can be recognized solely by her outfit. In the ancient world, it was Athena's wardrobe, not Aphrodite's, which received the most attention in literature, art, and ritual.

Armored from birth with helmet, spear, and shield, she wore one emblematic garment: the aegis, a shield or cloak made from the skin of the goat Amalthea who raised Zeus. He too wore an aegis, though his was a simple piece of attire. In contrast, the aegis that Athena tossed over her shoulder was worthy of Hollywood at its finest. Homer says that it was trimmed with a hundred golden tassels. Sculptors and vase painters show it fringed with snakes and adorned with the serpent-haired head of Medusa, the sight of which could turn men to stone.

Dresses and embroidered robes were also associated with the goddess's festival, an annual event celebrated with special fervor every fourth year, on Athena's birthday. Like other festivals, the Panathenaea included sacrifices, a procession, torch races, athletic games, and the recitation of

Athena and her owl. Note the head of Medusa on Athena's garment (Credit: Hannah Berman)

epic poetry, an event later replaced (at the urging of Pericles) by musical contests. Prize winners received large amphorae of olive oil decorated with pictures of Athena brandishing her spear.

Also at this festival, Athena—or her statue, the Palladium—received a new woolen robe called the *peplos*. Preparations began nine months ahead of time, when a group of girls, daughters of the aristocracy, gathered around a loom to weave the brightly colored garment, which was covered with scenes of Athena in battle. On the last day of the festival, the dress was taken to the statue.

It was an honor to participate in making the peplos, but the job grew daunting over time because the Palladium changed. It was a human-sized wooden carving until 456 BCE, when the brilliant sculptor Phidias completed a thirty-three-foot high bronze statue of Athena which stood on the Acropolis. Eighteen years later, in 438 BCE, he finished a still more spectacular piece: the Athena Parthenos, a gold and ivory statue which showed Athena in a tunic and aegis, holding a tiny Nike in one hand and a spear in the other. By her side was a serpent (one of her symbols) and a shield on which Phidias carved portraits of himself and Pericles, an impiety for which he was eventually imprisoned. The statue, which was housed within the newly completed Parthenon, was about thirty-eight feet high. As the central object of Athena worship, it required a wardrobe that was colossal. The Athenians provided it. After weaving a peplos the size of a sail, they displayed it on the mast of a model ship which was mounted on a cart and wheeled through the city like a parade float.

In May, ten months after the Panathenaea, Athenians held a festival organized around a related task—washing the goddess and the dress—and celebrated in memory of Aglaurus, who leaped to her death when she saw the child Athena had hidden in the basket. After her suicide, her mourners refused to wash their clothes for an entire year. The festival, a women-only event known as the Plynteria, celebrates the occasion when mourning was over and the clothes were finally washed. Participants undressed the statue, carried the garments and the statue to the sea, scrubbed them, and brought them back to the temple by torchlight. This ritual was easily enacted when the statue was wooden and life-sized, but the evidence nonetheless suggests that the ceremony continued even after Phidias made his gigantic statue. However, by 408 BCE, thirty years after the completion of the Athena Parthenos, Athenians came to think of the festival as unlucky (or unprofitable) for on that day the goddess was involved in the drudgery of the laundry and could not attend to the concerns of mortals. To protect their interests, business frequently closed.

Athena: Now and Then

Athena is famous for her unnatural birth from the forehead of Zeus. Yet she predates him. In the Minoan civilization of Crete and other Bronze Age sites, she was a protector of the city, worshipped as a goddess of architecture, weaving, arts and crafts. When Minoan culture faded, largely due to a volcano eruption around 1470 BCE and a Mycenean invasion, her character became more militaristic and her heritage was altered. Thus she became Zeus's daughter.

In that guise, she was worshipped throughout Greece and, in particular, at the Parthenon (from the Greek word for virgin). Fully armed at birth and well protected, with her body hidden behind her shield and her cloak adorned with the head of the Medusa, she was wise, compassionate, cool-headed, strategic (the cunning idea of the Trojan horse was hers), and arguably the most powerful among the goddesses.

Unfortunately, she inhabits a world that is military, political, and patriarchal. And therein lies the problem. Brilliant, asexual, and so male-identified that she even appears to Odysseus, her favorite mortal, in the guise of a man, Athena subverts stereotype and in the process makes people deeply uncomfortable.

In many recent books that identify psychological types with mythological figures, virtually any woman of accomplishment is described as "an Athena woman"—and it's seldom a compliment. For although the lists of such women invariably include such remarkable people as Rosa Luxembourg, Simone de Beauvoir, and Simone Weil, the descriptions sound negative. Athena women, it is suggested, are politically astute, efficient, successful, and sexless, the kind of woman one doesn't want to be. Often depicted as rational, undemonstrative, and in one book so emotionless that even widowhood doesn't upset her (she "knows her life expectancy is longer than a man's"), the typical "Athena woman" is described as unbalanced, out of touch with her body, intellectually alive but emotionally clueless, logical rather than intuitive, living solely for her work or "in her head"—like one of those career-driven spinsters in old movies who needs to take off her glasses, loosen her hair, and reveal herself for the Hollywood beauty that she is.

So Athena's light has dimmed. She loses points for being male-identified and for her military bearing. She doesn't even get credit for her intellect. Indeed, Jane Harrison dismissed the story of Athena's birth as "a dark, desperate effort to make *thought* the basis of being and reality."

Nonetheless, some people still love the goddess with the clear, incisive mind and the willingness to help a hero. "Let not our hearts break before the beauty of Pallas Athené. No; she makes all things possible for us," wrote the poet H.D. "The human mind to-day pleads for all; nothing is misplaced that in the end may be illuminated by the inner fire of abstract understanding."

Ares and Mars, Gods of War

Although we perceive Ares, the Greek god of war, and Mars, his Roman counterpart, as equivalent, they did not receive equal treatment. The Romans admired Mars, whereas the Greeks considered Ares rude, crude, brutish, and maniacal. Despite his many followers, Ares never inspired the kind of devotion that the other deities could claim. Even the gods held him in contempt. Except for Aphrodite, who carried on a steamy affair with him, they neither loved nor respected him. Zeus, his father in some accounts, was contemptuous of him, and even Hera felt no love for her bloodthirsty son. Stories about him clearly show why.

Ares, god of war. Above his head is the astrological symbol for the planet Mars.

He was a whiner who envied cool-headed Athena, his opposite, because Zeus adored her. In the *Iliad,* he grumbles about this obvious favoritism. His complaints do him no good. Athena mocks him and with Zeus's approval hurls a jagged boulder against his neck, nearly killing him.

Neither strong nor savvy, he was easily overcome. Once, for instance, the twin giants Ephialtes and Otus bound Ares in chains and stuffed him inside a bronze jar. He remained there for thirteen months, growing weaker by the day. Finally, Eriboea, the stepmother of the handsome giants, discovered the prank and told Hermes, who rescued him.

Ares fought enthusiastically but without courage or restraint. Hot-tempered and violent, he lacked strategy, making him the god of war—not the god of victory. (That honor belonged to Nike, whose miniature image accompanies statues of Athena.) Nor did he exhibit even the limited virtues of machismo, for he was frequently injured (by Athena and Heracles, among others) and he had no tolerance for pain. After Diomedes smashed his hipbone in the midst of battle, he sprawled on the ground and, according to Homer, "bellowed with a sound as great as nine thousand men make, or ten thousand." Zeus called him the most hateful god on Olympus and healed his wounds grudgingly, and only out of paternal duty.

The other gods and goddesses disliked him so much that they even tried him for murder—a strange thing, considering the regularity of that crime among the Olympians. Nor was this particular murder even close to the most egregious. It seems that Ares' daughter Alcippe had been raped by Halirrhothiuss, one of Poseidon's sons. When Ares found out, he killed the young man on the spot, and Poseidon took him to court. But no one saw the crime occur, and Ares was acquitted.

Things were different in Rome, where Ares melded with an ancient Italian agricultural god named Mars and enjoyed a reputation second only to Jupiter himself. The more militaristic Roman society became, the more his stature grew. He was considered the father of Romulus and Remus and many temples were dedicated to him. Every spring and fall festivals were held in his honor replete with war dances performed by a dozen priests, sacred trumpets, and sacrifices of all sorts. One ceremony, performed on the Ides of October in hopes of achieving military victory, was a two-horse chariot race in which the horse on the right-hand side of the winning team was sacrificed. In the mightiness that was Rome, the martial god was fully respected and lavishly acknowledged.

ARES, GOD OF WAR

Domain: war and strife.
Characteristics: aggressive, tempestuous.
Parents: Hera and Zeus.
Main Sanctuaries: Thrace and points north; Rome.
Roman Name: Mars
Lovers and Liaisons: Aerope, Aglaurus, Aphrodite, Rhea Silvia, and others, including the war goddess Bellona, sometimes said to be his sister. Bellonian rites included human sacrifice.
Children: Aeropus, Alcippe, Deimos, Harmonia, Hippolyta, Phobos, Romulus and Remus, and others.
Attributes: weapons and armor.
Best representation in post-classical art: Diego Velasquez's *Mars*.

Romulus and Remus

Life isn't fair, and neither is mythology. When Rhea Silvia was a vestal virgin, Mars raped her, and she became pregnant with twins. Although rape wasn't perceived as a crime, becoming pregnant when you were supposed to be a virgin was. Consequently she was either imprisoned or drowned, and her children, Romulus and Remus, were taken away. They too were supposed to be drowned. Instead, like Moses, they were set adrift in a basket. It came ashore on the banks of the Tiber under a fig tree, where a she-wolf suckled them. As often happens in myths about heroes, the boys were raised by foster parents: a herdsman named Faustulus and his wife, Acca Larentia.

When Romulus and Remus were grown, they wanted to found a city. But they argued about location, and in the course of the quarrel, Romulus killed his brother. After the city—Rome—was built, many men came to live there, including exiles and fugitives to whom Romulus offered asylum. Women were notable for their absence. To fill the vacancy, Romulus invited the neighboring people, the Sabines, to a religious festival. Upon their arrival, the Romans raped the women and war broke out. The women, who somehow aligned themselves with the Romans, threw themselves between the opposing factions, and brought the fighting to a halt.

Ultimately Romulus went the way of tyrants. After many battles, Plutarch reports, he "forsook his popular behavior for kingly arrogance, odious to the people." He dressed in scarlet and purple, gave audiences while reclining on a couch, and surrounded himself with a gang of thugs who carried leather thongs and were happy to bind up anyone he so designated. Romulus died under mysterious circumstances. Some say he disappeared into a thundercloud while reviewing his troops during a solar eclipse. Others say that the Senators chopped him up in the Temple of Vulcan and left, with each Senator secretly carrying a small piece of the body out with him. After his death, in 715 BCE, a friend of his, one Julius Proculus, announced that he had seen Romulus on the road, "looking taller and comelier than ever, dressed in shining and flaming armor." Romulus, son of Mars, told Proculus that

Romulus and Remus. (Credit: Hannah Berman)

the gods took him to heaven, where he became a god known as Quirinus. "Farewell," he said. "And tell the Romans, that, by the exercise of temperance and fortitude, they shall attain the height of human power."

Hephaestus, the Crippled Smith

The oddest of the gods and in some ways the most human, Hephaestus, the god of fire, was rejected by his mother, laughed at by the other gods, and loved insufficiently even by his wife for the most basic and terrible of reasons: he was physically flawed.

His mother, Hera, conceived Hephaestus (and Ares) as an act of vengeance against Zeus, who had given birth to Athena from his own forehead (although in other accounts, Hephaestus was born first). After giving birth to Hephaestus, Hera saw that things hadn't worked out as she had hoped. For while Athena was superior in every way, second only to Zeus, Hephaestus was lame and dwarfish, with shrunken legs and feet turned back to front. Hera was so ashamed that she threw him off Mount Olympus.

He splashed into the sea, where the goddess Thetis and the sea nymph Eurynome rescued him. For nine years he lived with them in secret, mastering the craft for which he was famous. In a vaulted cave hidden in the ocean depths, he forged bronze and learned to make exquisite brooches, opulent necklaces, richly detailed armor, and chains as fine as gossamer.

Still, even after nine years, Hephaestus could not let go of his anger at his mother. Eventually he sought his revenge by sending her a present: a golden throne so ingeniously crafted that, once Hera sat down, she was inextricably caught in a net of invisible, unbreakable cords. Despite the pleas of Ares and other gods, Hephaestus was adamant in his refusal to free her. Finally Dionysus got Hephaestus drunk and brought him back to the Olympus, a procession often illustrated on Greek vases. Hephaestus released Hera and in exchange asked to marry the lovely Aphrodite. Permission was granted.

In the *Iliad,* Homer tells another story. In his version, Hephaestus was born without defects. He loved his mother above all and was always willing to protect her, even if it meant risking the wrath of Zeus. One time, Zeus was so angry at Hera that he tied her hands behind her with a golden chain, dangled a metal anvil from each of her feet, and suspended her in the middle of the sky. Although the other gods objected, Zeus refused to release her, and they didn't dare oppose him. Only Hephaestus valiantly ignored the king of the gods and tried to free his mother. He paid for his disobedience. Zeus grabbed his foot and hurled him over the ramparts, out of Olympus, and down towards earth.

The fall was a long one. He tumbled through the atmosphere for an entire day, from morning to evening, and at last he crashed into the island of Lemnos. Hephaestus was badly injured from the fall, and even though the local people nursed him tenderly, he never fully recovered and even afterwards was lame. Thus, as the scholar Timothy Gantz has pointed out, "either Hephaestus is lame because he is thrown out of Olympos, or he is thrown out of Olympos because he is lame."

Either way, he eventually made his way back to the heavenly realm of the gods, where he established a home and created many beautiful and ingenious objects, one of which enabled him to reveal the infidelity of his wife.

HEPHAESTUS, THE DIVINE SMITH

Domain: artisans, craftsmanship, fire, the forge.
Characteristics: industrious, cunning, lame, resentful, artistic.
Parents: Hera and Zeus.
Roman Name: Vulcan.
Lovers and Liaisons: Cabeiro, Aetna, and others.
Spouse: Aphrodite, Charis, Aglaia.
Children: Cacus, Erichthonius, Periphetes, and others.
Animal: mule.
Attributes: metal tools.
Best representations in art: François Boucher's *Venus in the Forge of Vulcan*, Diego Velasquez's *The Forge of Vulcan*.

The Tale of a Cuckold

The marriage between the lovely Aphrodite and Hephaestus, the limping god, was not destined to be a happy one, for marriage did not stop the goddess of love from continuing her amorous activities. Word of this finally came to Hephaestus from Helios, the Sun, who saw everything with his one enormous eye. He told Hephaestus that Aphrodite was sleeping with his brother Ares, the god of war, by whom she had several children. Devastated by the news, the previously unsuspecting Hephaestus headed straight to his workshop determined to catch Aphrodite and Ares in the act. He covered the bed with a fine metal mesh and attached lengths of invisible chain to the overhead rafters. It was an ingenious contraption, a masterpiece of craft and calculation.

Hephaestus told his wife that he was going to Lemnos. At the first possible moment, Ares and Aphrodite climbed into bed and were instantly captured by the golden net. Helios reported the news to Hephaestus, who returned home in anguish. In one of Homer's many heart-wrenching scenes, Hephaestus reveals his sadness and humiliation, which he blames on his parents. Aphrodite loves Ares, he says in *The Odyssey*, "because he is handsome, and goes sound on his feet, while I am/misshapen from birth, and for this I hold no other responsible/but my own father and mother, and I wish they never had got me."

The other gods, watching the lovers in their illicit bed, could not stop laughing. Apollo asked Hermes if he'd be willing to sleep next to Aphrodite; Hermes asserted that he would like nothing better. Poseidon, pretending to be unaffected by the sight of the golden goddess tangled up in chains, bargained with Hephaestus over the damages that Ares would pay and promised to cover the debt should Ares renege. Hephaestus was forced to accept the settlement.

Despite this painful experience, Hephaestus was destined for happiness. After his marriage to Aphrodite fell apart, he married either Charis or Aglaia, the youngest Grace. Hephaestus built her a house of bronze and filled it with beautiful objects and labor-saving devices including twenty three-legged wheeled stools capable of moving around on their own and his most spectacular invention: a group of intelligent, strong attendants—Stepford robots—who were coated in gold but otherwise looked exactly like real live women.

> *now Ugly was the husband of*
> *(as happens every now and then*
> *upon a merely human plane)*
> *someone completely beautiful;*
> *and Beautiful, who (truth to sing)*
> *could never quite tell right from wrong,*
> *took brother Fearless by the eyes*
> *and did the deed of joy with him*
>
> —e.e. cummings

The Masterpieces of Hephaestus

When Hephaestus was working, plumes of smoke and ash would curl into the sky from his underground forge, which was hidden in a volcano. With the help of his one-eyed assistants, the Cyclopes, he could make anything, and Greek mythology is filled with objects of his devise. He crafted Harmonia's necklace, a silver-studded chair for Thetis, gold and silver guard dogs for the Palace of Alcinous (which Odysseus visited), and many other magnificent objects. But which single piece could be called his masterpiece? It depends on whom you ask.

Homer's choice was the shield which Hephaestus made for Achilles, the son of Thetis. She begged him to make it even though she knew that her son was fated to die young. In making the shield, an object so intricately detailed that Homer spends four pages describing it, Hephaestus reveals the full extent of his artistry, for Achilles' shield represented nothing less than the known universe. There were valleys, meadows, vineyards, and two cities. The relatively peaceful city was filled with weddings, festivals, dancers, musicians, and two men who were quarreling in the marketplace about a murder. The other city was at war, with Ares and Pallas Athene in attendance and the bloody slaughter well underway. Elsewhere on the shield, harvesters, ploughmen, reapers, and sheaf-binders performed the labor of the countryside, heralds arranged a feast beneath an oak tree, and all manner of ordinary human activities were going on. The shield, with its five layers of metal, was busier than a Brueghel painting and grander, for in addition to scenes of everyday life, it depicted the earth, the sea, the sun, the moon, and all the stars in the sky, including the Pleiades, the Hyades, Orion, and the great Bear, Ursa Major.

Hesiod wrote a poem about a similar object, the shield of Heracles. But he was more interested in something that Hephaestus made of earth and water. Shaped like a girl with the face of a goddess, that creation was Pandora, whom Hesiod considered the ruination of mankind. Even more impressive was her golden crown, which Hephaestus made to please Zeus. It showed his skill to advantage, for it was covered with miraculously realistic monsters, "and beauty in abundance shown from it."

Several centuries later, Aeschylus weighed in with a dreadful third opinion. In *Prometheus Bound,* he describes what Hephaestus does after Zeus commands him to nail Prometheus to a rock for the crime of giving fire to mankind. Against his will, Hephaestus completes the dreadful task. As Strength and Violence watch (Strength engages in conversation; Violence does not), Hephaestus wraps Prometheus's wrists in bands of iron and rivets them to the rock,

MYTHS OF SMITHS

"The workers of the world unite under the banner of Hephaestus," writes the psychoanalyst Murray Stein. That's because, among the gods and goddesses of Olympus, Hephaestus is the only one who works. Similar figures appear in other mythologies too. Among them are:

- a Celtic troika of craft gods: Luchta the wright, Creidhne the metalworker, and Goibhnu, the divine smith and god of the underworld, who forged invincible weapons and brewed a beer which conveyed immortality to all who partook of it;
- Gu, the West African god born in the shape of a sharp blade projecting from a stone. He was sent to earth by his father for the explicit purpose of helping humanity;
- Koshar-wa-Hasis, the Canaanite smith who made a pair of clubs which Baal used to pummel Yam, the god of the sea;
- Ndomadyrir, the divine blacksmith of the Banbara people of Mali. He separated things and differentiated between them, thereby completing the process of creation;
- Nommo, the Dogon blacksmith who stole glowing embers and iron from the sun and brought them to earth;
- Ogun, the Yoruban patron of smiths and surgeons, who dropped to earth when it was still a primordial marsh and put the finishing touches on all of creation, including human beings;
- Regin, the Norse smith, who killed his father for his treasure and crafted the sword which brought about his own doom;
- Tvastr, the Indian smith who forged the weapons the great god Indra used in his battle with Vrtra.
- Wayland, the northern European smith who made the sword Beowulf used to kill the monster Grendel;
- and Vulcan, the Roman fire god who became identified with Hephaestrus. His feast day was celebrated on August 23, in the heat of summer, when the Romans celebrated his association with volcanoes by frying fish alive.

shackles his legs and nails them to the rock, girds his ribs with metal bands and drives "the unrelenting fang of the adamantine wedge" through his chest. Throughout, he is miserable. "I hate my craft, I hate the skill of my own hands," he says. Yet once the Limping God is safely off stage, Strength gazes with satisfaction at the completed work and pronounces it "this blacksmith's masterpiece."

The great traveler Pausanias, writing in the second century, knew all about these so-called masterpieces and wasn't impressed. He saw no reason to believe that the fabulous creations ascribed to Hephaestus, either in poetry or conversation, ever existed. The exception was a staff which Hephaestus crafted for Zeus. It made its way to Agamemnon and then, Pausanias believed, to Agamemnon's daughter, Elektra, who brought it to Phokis, where the people worshipped it. "It has no public temple," he wrote, "but the priest in each year keeps the staff in his house. Sacrifices are offered every day, and it has a table full of every kind of meat and sweet-cake." That simple staff, neither fancy nor terrible, was entirely real.

Prometheus, Champion of Humankind

He stole fire from the gods and presented it to mortals, saved the human race when Zeus decided to annihilate it, and is sometimes said to have created the first human beings in the image of the gods. Although he could see into the future, he denied us that ability, thereby giving us hope by making it impossible for us to foresee our deaths. For these and other reasons, Prometheus was acknowledged as the champion of humankind.

The Sacrifice

In ancient times, an animal who was to be sacrificed to the gods might on certain occasions be completely burned. This event, known as a holocaust, could represent a serious loss to the community. So more commonly, the animal was divided between the gods and the humans. Prometheus was involved in just such a sacrifice. After the ox was dismembered, Prometheus put the various parts into two piles equal in size but not in quality. One pile consisted of all the delicious meat topped with the unappetizing stomach of the ox. The other pile looked more appealing, for it was covered with glistening fat, a delightful sight to the ancient Greeks (who were also partial to the look of fat rubbed into hair). But the fat hid an assortment of inedible bones. Having apportioned the ox in this way, Prometheus asked Zeus to chose his share.

Zeus wasn't as dumb as Prometheus thought and he was not deceived. Nonetheless, he chose the fat-covered bones, with the happy result that ever since, the edible meat of a sacrifice has gone to mankind and the bones have been placed on the altars of the gods. But to assert his authority and to retaliate for the trick, Zeus deprived humanity of fire. We could have the meat; we just couldn't cook it.

Prometheus did not accept his defeat. He slipped into the underground forge of Hephaestus and stole "the flowery splendour" of fire (the phrase is from Aeschylus). Or he grabbed a burning chunk of fire from the chariot of the sun, hid it in a stalk of a fennel, and snuck it out of Olympus. Either way, he presented humanity with the gift of fire. Zeus was infuriated.

THIEVES OF FIRE

Certain motifs are so ubiquitous that they support the idea that humanity shares a collective unconscious. Consider these stories:

- the Bushmen of Africa report that the praying mantis stole fire from the ostrich;
- the Hawaiians say that the trickster Maui stole fire from the goddess Mahui-ike, who lived in the underworld and hid the secret of combustion in her fingernails;
- the Maidu Indians of California maintain that Mouse stole a flame from Thunder and brought it to mankind hidden inside a flute;
- and the ancient Greeks assert that Prometheus stole fire from the gods, tucked it into the hollow of a dried stalk of fennel, and presented it to mankind.

Zeus Strikes Back

Angry that mortals now had something which should have belonged only to the gods, Zeus devised a scheme to punish both Prometheus and the human race. He asked the master craftsman Hephaestus to take earth and water and sculpt the likeness of a lovely girl. Hephaestus constructed a figure that was marvelous in its beauty. According to Hesiod, who may have invented this story, Athena breathed life into her and clothed her in a belt, a silver dress, and a grassy wreath; Aphrodite invested her with charm and desire; and Hermes gave her the ability to lie persuasively. Then Pandora ("all gifts") was given a jug which held within it all the troubles of mankind. The trap was set.

Zeus knew that Prometheus, whose name means "forethought," would be too wise to accept this gift from the gods. The same could not be said for his brother Epimetheus, whose name means "afterthought." Prometheus warned Epimetheus not to accept any gifts. He was wasting his words. When Hermes showed up with Pandora, whose many talents included, in the immortal words of Hesiod, "sly manners and the morals of a bitch," Epimetheus welcomed her. Not long afterward, she opened her jar. Pain, evil, diseases, misery, and woes of all kinds flew out like a swarm of insects and spread to every corner of the globe. Only one creature remained inside, stopped by the heavy lid: Hope.

In later versions of the story, Hope occasionally flutters out of the jar. For instance, in Nathaniel Hawthorne's 1851 tale "The Paradise of Children" (from *A Wonder Book,* his first volume of bowdlerized myths), Hope knocks on the sides of the box and convinces Epimetheus and the sobbing Pandora to set her free, thereby compensating humanity for their troubles and holding forth the promise of "an infinite bliss hereafter."

Hesiod, a bitter misogynist who called Pandora the progenitor of the "deadly female race and tribe of wives," had no such dream.

Prometheus Is Punished

Having punished humanity for possessing fire, Zeus turned his attention to Prometheus. He ordered Hephaestus to bind him hand and foot to a rocky crag in the Caucasus, and then he split the rock with his thunderbolt, leaving Prometheus entombed within. After "a long age" had passed, he brought Prometheus back to the mountainside, where every single night a vicious eagle pecked at his liver, and every day, while the sun scorched his skin, the liver grew whole again. For centuries, Prometheus was tortured in this way.

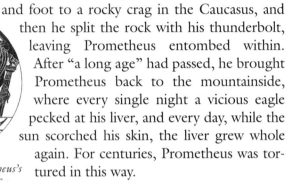

An eagle pecks at Prometheus's liver in this drawing of a sixth-century kylix.

Fortunately, Prometheus was in a position to bargain, for he had something Zeus wanted. Both Prometheus and Zeus knew that there was a goddess whose son was fated to overthrow his father. This was a matter of concern to Zeus, whose habit it was to mate with as many goddesses and mortal women as possible. But only Prometheus, who could foresee the future, knew the identity of the goddess in question. After Prometheus finally agreed to reveal her name (she was the beautiful sea nymph Thetis), Zeus's son Heracles showed up, shot the eagle, and loosened the chains. Prometheus was free.

He gained his immortality in an unusual way. By mistake, Heracles shot an arrow that struck the centaur Chiron in the knee. The wound was so painful that Chiron begged to die even though he was immortal. Zeus listened to his pleas and finally agreed to let Chiron bestow his immortality on someone else. So Chiron descended gratefully to Hades, and Prometheus received eternal life.

Hermes, Lord of Rascals, Prince of Thieves

The First Lyre

The busiest day of Hermes' hyperactive and eternal life was the first. The son of Zeus and the shy goddess Maia, who was one of the Pleiades, he was born at dawn on the fourth day of the month. Later that morning, he left Maia's cave to look for Apollo's cattle, which he intended to steal. As he stepped out of the dark cave and into the sunlit landscape outside, he noticed a tortoise with a spangled shell waddling through the tall grass. He considered this such a fine omen that he burst out laughing, and, according to the author of the Homeric Hymn, offered to bring the turtle inside to protect it from spells and witchcraft. Then he hacked off its limbs with an iron knife and by noon was strumming a lyre fashioned from the animal's shell. His discovery, stumbled over by chance, led the ancient Greeks to call any lucky find or unexpected windfall a gift of Hermes.

Hermes, with his caduceus, winged helmet, and sandals.

Hermes Becomes an Olympian God

Hungry for meat, Hermes traveled north to Pieira, where Apollo kept his herds. He fashioned a pair of sandals out of myrtle and tamarisk twigs and bound them to his feet, leaves and all. Then he isolated fifty head of cattle from the rest of the herd and drove them backwards down the mountain. This maneuver left a trail of strange tracks in the dirt, for the cows all seemed to be heading uphill while Hermes's own footprints were erased by the twigs and leaves that dangled from his sandals and obscured his tracks as he walked. The only flaw in the plan was that an old man working in a vineyard saw him driving the cattle downhill. Hermes advised him to forget what he had seen, and he led the cattle south to Arcadia.

There he gathered wood and built a fire. As the flames leapt up, he corralled the animals into a cave, wrestled two horned cows to the ground, and sacrificed them. After spreading their skins over two rocks, he roasted the meat and divided it into twelve equal portions. Then he burned the hooves and the heads and tossed his leafy sandals into the river. At dawn he returned to Maia's cave, sneaking in so quietly that even the dogs didn't bark. He climbed into his cradle with his lyre, wrapped himself in his swaddling clothes, gazed at the dim, shadowy interior, and announced to Maia that he didn't intend to live like this any longer. He wanted to dwell among the immortals. He wanted to be a god.

Meanwhile, Apollo met the old man in the vineyard and asked if he had seen his cattle. After a moment of obfuscation, the old man admitted that he had seen a herd of cattle driven by a child, indeed by an infant, who zigzagged from side to side and kept the cows gazing at him even as they shuffled backwards. Upon hearing this, Apollo realized at once that the thief must be a child of Zeus. And soon he found the peculiar tracks. It didn't take long before he made his way to Maia's cave.

Inside the cave, Apollo demanded that Hermes, who was snuggled in his blankets, tell him where his cattle were. Hermes argued that he was a baby with tender feet, and hence it was unlikely that he could have committed the crimes of which he was being accused. Apollo laughed, lifted the little liar out of his cradle, and announced that he would forevermore be known as the prince of thieves. At that precise moment, Hermes farted and sneezed but he would not confess to the crime. Finally, at Hermes' suggestion, they agreed to appeal to Zeus for a decision.

They found their father at home on the snow-capped peak of Mount Olympus. Apollo presented his case, and the eloquent Hermes presented his, assuring Zeus that he was so honest that he did not know how to lie. The absurdity so pleased Zeus that he laughed out loud—and ordered Hermes to point to the spot where he had hidden the cattle. When Apollo noticed two familiar-looking cow skins spread over the rocks, Hermes could not deny the evidence. He admitted that he had sacrificed cows and added, in his own defense, that he had also divided the meat into twelve portions, one for each of the gods. When Apollo protested that there were only eleven gods, Hermes announced that from now on, there were twelve, for he himself must henceforth be included among the Olympians. Zeus assented, and the trickster Hermes became a god.

To patch up the differences between himself and Apollo, Hermes pulled out his lyre and sang. Apollo was transfixed. He struck a deal: he would forgive the theft if Hermes would give him the lyre and the ability to play. Hermes agreed and the two became fast friends. Later on, Hermes tried to exchange the shepherd's pipe, also called the pipes of Pan, for Apollo's skills of divination. Apollo was unwilling to trade. But he gave Hermes the golden caduceus with its intertwined serpents and he recommended that he study with three beelike sisters called the Thriae, experts in the art of prophecy through the use of pebbles.

Hermes promised Zeus that he would never lie, even if he could not vow to tell the whole truth, and thus he became the god of communication, commerce, literature, journalism, oratory, travel, sleep, dreams, advertising, public relations, and all forms of duplicity. Zeus granted him dominion over lions, boars, dogs, herds, and "birds of good omen." He assigned him various other duties, gave him many magical objects including winged sandals, and appointed him as messenger of the gods and guide to Hades.

HERMES, MESSENGER OF THE GODS

Domain: speech, commerce, literature, travel, borders.
Characteristics: swift-footed, eloquent, duplicitous.
Parents: Maia and Zeus.
Roman Name: Mercury
Lovers and Liaisons: Aphrodite, Dryope, Hecate, Persephone, and others.
Children: Cephalus, Hermaphroditus, Pan, and others.
Attributes: winged hat, winged sandals, caduceus.
Best representations in post-classical art: Peter Paul Rubens's *Mercury and Argus*, Corregio's *Venus and Mercury and Cupid*.

Hermes, Io, and the Herms

In Greek mythology, there is no such thing as omnipotence. Every deity, including the great Zeus, occasionally needed help. On more than one occasion, Hermes was able to provide it—though in one instance, he was punished for his efforts.

The problem was that Zeus was once again in love, this time with Io, the daughter of the river god Inachus. Naturally, he didn't want Hera to know, so when she questioned him about it, he denied all interest and to prove it, he turned Io into a snow-white heifer. Unconvinced, Hera insisted that he give the cow to her, and Zeus complied, which did nothing to quiet Hera's suspicions. To make sure that Zeus wouldn't sneak around while she was gone, Hera asked the all-seeing Argus to guard the cow. The monster, who had four eyes according to Aeschylus and one hundred according to Ovid, tethered Io to an olive tree and kept a vigilant watch over her. Io might have languished there forever except that Zeus petitioned Hermes for assistance.

If there was one talent Hermes had above all others, it was the ability to beguile. He soothed Argus with the musical pipes and regaled him with stories. After a while, Argus grew sleepy. One eye fluttered shut, and then another, and when every one of his eyes was closed, Hermes killed the monster, untied Io, and set her free. This benefited Io hardly at all, for when Hera saw what had happened, she sent a gadfly to torment Io. It pursued her relentlessly and she could not shake it. The itch became so unbearable that, in a frenzied attempt to escape, she galloped over the entire world. She ran through Europe, Asia Minor, India, Arabia, and Ethiopia. Finally she came to Egypt, where Zeus changed her back into a human. There she gave birth to a son named Epaphus, who was conceived by a touch, and a daughter named Libya. The Ionic Sea is named in her honor.

As for Hermes, the other gods put him on trial for killing the Argus (whose eyes Hera placed in the tail feathers of her sacred bird, the peacock). After the case had been presented, he stood awaiting a verdict as each immortal tossed a voting-pebble at his feet. When he was finally acquitted, he was standing in the midst of a stone heap—in Greek, herma. Scholars are in near-total agreement that this word is the source of Hermes' name, although the myth—at least the part about the trial—was created long after the association of Hermes with stone heaps had been established.

In Homer's time, stone heaps or cairns were used as markers along the road and at crossroads. By the fifth century BCE, these rock piles had evolved into rectangular pillars called herms which were sculpted with heads and male sexual organs, fully erect. Herms were used as markers in places that paralleled Hermes' duties. Because he was a god of travel, herms appeared along the road, where they were his altars. Because he was the god of borders, herms were used as property markers to indicate the dimensions of an estate. And because Hermes was a psychopomp who accompanied dead souls to the underworld, herms were used to emphasize those points of entrance and transition. We use them even now: they are grave markers.

But why, one might ask, were the herms so aggressively erotic? Although we don't think of Hermes as especially sexual, he was a fertility god, responsible for the well-being of the animals under his domain. He had many dalliances but, because he lived on the boundary, he was perceived as bisexual and is sometimes said to have invented the art of masturbation. (Robert Graves suggests that his rapid growth on the day he was born represents "Homer's playful obscenity.") In any case, he bequeathed his heritage to three strangely sexed offspring: Hermaphroditus (whose story is told on page 188), the god Priapus who, like the herms, was perpetually erect (see page 187), and the woodland god Pan.

Hermes Trismegistus

Of all the Olympian gods, Hermes had the most interesting post-Hellenic career. While other immortals were slowly relegated to the worlds of art, literature and civic sculpture, Hermes was reinvented, given an expanded persona with its own genealogy, accomplishments, and historical reality. All this happened because in the fifth century BCE Herodotus identified Hermes, the Greek messenger of the gods, with Thoth, the Egyptian scribe and god of writing. Gradually the two gods adhered to each other. The identification became official in 196 BCE when the priests of Rosetta decreed that Thoth and Hermes were one and the same. After that, distinctions between Thoth, Hermes, and Mercury (the Roman version of Hermes) blurred, and the names Hermes and Thoth melded together to produce a new and amazing figure: Hermes Trismegistus, whose literary output was to figure not only in Hellenistic philosophy and religion but also in medieval alchemy, magic, and astrology.

The creation of this new figure was born in the Egyptian language, which indicated Thoth's superiority with a troika of repeated syllables: either *aa aa ur* or *paa paa paa*. When this phrase was attached to Hermes and translated into Greek, it emerged as *megistos kai megistos theos, megas Hermes*—greatest and greatest god, great Hermes. The essential meaning of that bulky phrase was simply "three times great" or Trismegistus. Such was the derivation of the word.

Over time, another explanation for the title arose. Perhaps instead of being three times great, Hermes existed in triplicate. Beginning in the third century BCE, various Hermes were identified. In the first century BCE, the Roman orator Cicero distinguished five different Mercurys, including one who was the father of Pan, a mysterious one who was "the son of the Nile, whose name may not be spoken by the Egyptians," and one who killed Argus, gave the Egyptians the art of writing, and was known as Thoth.

This game continued into the Middle Ages, when Hermes was identified with the devil and various Biblical characters. In 1144, Robert of Chester, in the preface of a book on alchemy, identified three ancient philosophers named Hermes. "The first was Enoch, whose names were also Hermes and Mercury. The second was Noah, also called Hermes and Mercury. The third was the Hermes who ruled Egypt after the Deluge and long occupied that throne. Our predecessors called him Triplex . . . ," he wrote. "It was this Hermes who after the Deluge was the founder of all the arts and disciplines, both liberal and mechanical."

By the Renaissance, various commentators placed Abraham, Zoroaster, Moses, the Brahmins, the Druids, David, Orpheus, Pythagoras, Plato, and the Sibyls on the Hermetic family tree. In the seventeenth century, on the theory that "Thoth" was very like "Theut," which was virtually the same as "Teutonic," one scholar did his best to prove that Hermes must be the original German, the ancestor of an entire people. And in the eighteenth century, an alchemist tried to link Hermes Trimegistus with Saint Joseph.

Supporting all this was a body of literature, a sizable collection of papyrus manuscripts, codices, and scrolls showing a blend of Greek, Jewish, Biblical, Egyptian, Gnostic, and other influences, all supposedly written by Hermes Trismegistus. The writings include a set of Platonic dialogues which described the creation and the soul's journey through the celestial spheres; fragments focusing on theology, philosophy, alchemy, astrology, and magic; and a Latin text called the *Asclepius*. A passage in that work explains that some men have the power to invite certain spirits to dwell within the statues of gods and thus, in a sense, to make gods. In the fifth century of our era, Saint Augustine, convinced that Hermes Trimegistus predated the philosophers of ancient Greece, deplored this passage because Hermes failed to invoke the name of Christ.

These manuscripts were though to be unimaginably old. The theory was that they were incised on clay tablets before the great flood, stored in Egypt, and only later copied onto papyrus. In fact, as was demonstrated in 1614, most of this literature was written in Alexandria during the first three centuries or so of our era, and a few sections were not written until the twelfth century (and in some cases not published until the twentieth).

During the Middle Ages, Arabic alchemists were partial to Hermetica and especially to a section of the *Book of the Secret of Creation* known as the Emerald Tablet. Written as late as 750 CE, it is known for its beginning: "All that is above is like all that is below, all that is below is like all that is above . . ." This summarizes the idea behind Hermetic literature, which finds allegories to human experience in mythology, astrology, and alchemy. The basic axiom of all forms of occultism—as above, so below—comes directly from Hermes Trismegistus.

Despite this vogue, many Hermetic writings disappeared during the Medieval period, and interest waned. It was revived in the Renaissance when a monk discovered a set of fifteen Hermetic treatises. He gave them to the Florentine ruler Cosimo de' Medici, who asked Marsilio Ficino to translate them into Latin. Ficino's manuscript was published in 1471, and by the end of the next century it had gone through sixteen editions. It created a Renaissance fad for Hermes Trismegistus, who was depicted on the floor of the Sienna cathedral, in the frescoes of an apartment in the Vatican (in company with Isis and Moses), and in the pages of manuscripts. Often labeled simply "Hermes," this Hermes is not the quicksilver god of the Greeks with his caduceus and winged sandals. In the art of the Renaissance, he is old (and wise), bearded, robed, sometimes turbaned, and often shown holding an armillary sphere which suggests his connection with astrology and his understanding that the world above mirrors the world below. He is, in short, Hermes Trismegistus, another Hermes altogether.

The Great God Pan

Hermes once worked in Arcadia tending curly-fleeced sheep for a mortal just because he was fond of his daughter. Their alliance (a "merry marriage," in the words of the Homeric Hymn) produced one son. Unfortunately, no sooner did his mother catch sight of her

Pan, 1744.

baby than she screamed and fled, for the child had a full beard and the legs, ears, and horns of a goat.

Hermes, on the other hand, was filled with joy at the sight of him. He proudly carried the child to Mount Olympus, where all the other gods (and Dionysus in particular) were likewise entranced. They called him Pan, from the Greek word for all, because he delighted them all.

Pan, the god of flocks and fields, holds a peculiar position in the annals of mythology. He was unknown to Homer and Hesiod, and stories about him are relatively few. Yet his image—part god, part goat, splendid and shaggy-haired, horned, hooved, and lusty—has a continuing hold on the imagination. That's because his true function has little to do with husbandry and everything to do with two uncontrollable feelings—sexuality and the sudden, irrational fear that bears his name: panic.

A lazy god, Pan spent his days sleeping and was said to get angry and foul-tempered if awakened unexpectedly, especially around noon. He inhabited mountains, caves, pastures, and woodland spots so isolated and serene that the softest, most innocent rustle in the underbrush might scare a person and cause the pulse to race.

Pan's heritage is uncertain. In addition to Hermes and the mortal's daughter, his parents may have been Zeus and Callisto, or Kronos and Rhea, or Uranus and Gaia, or a shepherd and a nanny-goat. One post-Homeric story reports that Pan's mother was Penelope, the loyal wife of Odysseus—except that in this version of the tale, Penelope, rather than rejecting her suitors, sleeps with each of them and afterwards gives birth to Pan.

Pan's lustiness was well-known. The moon goddess Selene became his lover after he covered himself with the skins of white rams. And the nymph Echo (back when she still had a body) became the mother of his daughters Iynx and Iambe, who was famous for her dirty jokes. However, not all the nymphs were impressed by Pan's insistent ways. Pitys, for instance, preferred to become a pine tree rather than submit to him. (Pan wears a crown of pine in her honor.) Syrinx, a wood nymph, felt similarly disinclined. A follower of Artemis, she ran away from Pan to the shores of the Ladon River. Just as he caught up with her, she turned into a patch of hollow reeds. The wind rustling through them made such an enticing sound that Pan chopped them down, tied reeds of varying lengths together with wax, and created the musical instrument known as the pan pipe or syrinx.

Pan's cult was centered in Arcadia, an isolated region where his statue was ritually whipped when the animals failed to give birth. He became an official god—not an Olympian, but a god nonetheless—in 490 BCE, when Pheidippides raced to Sparta during the battle of Marathon. On the way, Pan stopped him and complained that despite all his help in their war against the Persians, the Athenians persisted in ignoring him. Pheidippides conveyed the message, and after defeating the Persians, the Athenians began to worship at Pan's shrine.

Over five centuries later, around the time of the crucifixion, another incident occurred. According to Plutarch (who wrote about it decades later), a disembodied voice boomed out the name of a man at sea and instructed him to proclaim that "the great god Pan is dead." It has been suggested that the sailor misheard a lamentation for the god Tammuz, whose death was ritually mourned each year. Nonetheless, commentators came to associate this cry with the demise of paganism and the rise of Christianity.

Pan was not forgotten. His image was incorporated into Christianity as Satan, who also has the legs of a goat, cloven feet, and

FROM "PATERNOSTER TO PAN"

. . . Our Pan, which art on earth
because the universe might take fright,
hallowed be thy name
for all that it signifies . . .

You are always violently alive;
with your wild impulsiveness,
shake your celestial horns in the sky,
sink your goat's feet in the earth.

Give us rhythm and measure
through the love of your song;
and through the love of your flute, give us
this day our daily love.

—Rubén Darío

horns. He reemerged in something like his Arcadian form in 1787, when a new translation of the Orphic Hymn to Pan brought him to life once again as a god of the woodlands. In the nineteenth century, a new generation of self-conscious worshippers arose. Among the admirers of his wild, bucolic ways were Shelley, Byron, and Henry David Thoreau, who wrote "Pan is not dead, as was rumored. No god ever dies."

But as James Hillman has pointed out, they can be repressed—for a while. "Pan still lives, and not merely in the literary imagination. He lives in the repressed which returns, in the psychopathologies of instinct." He can and will reappear at any time, in dreams, in nightmares, in erotic fixations, and in panic attacks. He never died and he never will.

Echo and Narcissus

The nymph Echo was loquacious in the extreme. She once helped Zeus by waylaying Hera with a torrent of words, a cascade so unstoppable that even the great goddess was unable to wiggle out of the encounter. When she finally escaped, Hera discovered that while Echo was chattering, Zeus had been cavorting with the nymphs. To punish Echo, Hera took away her ability to initiate a conversation or say anything original. She could only wait for someone else to start talking and then echo the last words that had been spoken.

So when Echo fell in love with Narcissus, she had to wait for him to speak. It wasn't easy. Narcissus was so beautiful that everyone, male and female alike, desired him, and so detached that other people were afraid to approach him. Echo was besotted. Fueled by her infatuation, she followed him everywhere, though she stayed out of his view. At last he sensed her presence and cried out (in Ovid's words), "Come here, and let us meet!" She could only repeat his words, so she exclaimed, "Let us meet!" and rushed to embrace him.

> *To love oneself is the beginning of a life-long romance.*
>
> —Oscar Wilde

Alas, he recoiled. The rejection was so terrible that Echo never recovered. She faded away until only her voice remained.

Narcissus got the fate he deserved, for he too fell in love with someone who was unavailable. While wandering in the woods, he stopped to drink at a crystalline pool and for the first time saw a clear reflection of himself. It was love at first sight but his desires, like those of Echo, were unrequited. When he tried to embrace his beloved, he plunged his arms into the water and the image he adored disappeared in the ripples. Unable to tear himself away, he finally took a dagger and killed himself. His soul went to the underworld (where he became transfixed by his reflection in the waters of the River Styx). His legacy remained in the form of a flower and a psychiatric diagnosis, both of which bear his name.

"Wind-footed" Iris, Goddess of the Rainbow

Before Hermes was born, the winged goddess Iris was the messenger of the gods and Hera's special assistant, patiently waiting by her throne to draw a bath or run an errand. Like Hermes, she carried a caduceus and wore winged sandals, and when she did the gods' bidding, she moved so swiftly that she left a rainbow shimmering in her wake. Although never the central player, she played a role in many dramas, including the following:

- she rescued her sisters, the Harpies, when they were about to be murdered by the sons of the North Wind.
- she helped Aphrodite when she was wounded in battle.
- she told the mortal Peleus that Zeus wanted him to marry the goddess Thetis.
- she informed King Menelaus that his wife, Helen, had run away with his houseguest Paris.
- she came to the aid of the heartbroken Dido when, deserted by Aeneas, she fell upon her sword. Hera sent Iris to end her anguish and help her die.

Although Iris and Hermes both acted as messenger of the gods, there was one crucial difference between them. Whereas Hermes was a master of distortion, Iris was associated with truth. So when the Olympians wished to take an oath, a process which required that they swear by the water of the River Styx, fleet-footed Iris would fly to the underworld and fill a golden ewer with sacred water. Only then could the immortal take a pledge.

Truth was something the gods took seriously—and woe to those who lied. For an entire year, the guilty deity would be denied the pleasures of eating, drinking, speaking, and even breathing. When the year was done, the ban against breathing was lifted but for nine years the errant immortal was not allowed to attend the gatherings of the gods, festive or otherwise.

Iris, goddess of the rainbow.

Death and the Rainbow

In the Biblical story of Noah, the rainbow is a sign of hope, symbolizing God's promise not to destroy the world by water. Even so, the evanescent arc inevitably recalls the stormy weather and threats of destruction that preceded it. Which may be why stories about the rainbow are often about death.

Take this story from the Amazon. A black jaguar married a woman, impregnated her, and killed her. After her body was cut open, her son leaped out of the womb and could not stop crying. No one knew what to do. The people tried ignoring him but he continued to weep. The animals tried to distract him by amusing him but he was inconsolable. Finally the owl sat down and had a serious talk with him. When the owl told him the circumstances of his birth, the boy quieted down and thought about ways to avenge his mother. He began by killing all the jaguars. Then he floated into the sky and as he ascended, he turned into the rainbow. Along the way, he decided that since the people had ignored his cries, he should shorten their lives. Ever since then, people have been mortal and the rainbow has been a symbol of death.

RAINBOW THREADS

Shall gods be said to thump the clouds
When clouds are cursed by thunder,
Be said to weep when weather howls?
Shall rainbows be their tunics' colour?

—Dylan Thomas

What could be prettier than the sight of the rainbow arching above the earth on a soggy afternoon? In mythology, the rainbow often functions as a decorative device, making frequent appearances in descriptions of clothing. To wit:

- the Egyptian goddess Isis wore seven diaphanous veils, one for each color of the spectrum;
- the Greek goddess Iris flew across the sky clad in rainbow hues;
- the Norse goddess Freya wore the rainbow as a necklace;
- and the sun god of the Siberian Samoyeds used the multi-colored band to trim the hem of his greatcoat.

Dionysus, God of Joy

We run with the good of laughter;
Labour is joy and weariness is sweet,
And our song resounds to Bacchus!
—Euripides

Zeus adored Semele, the daughter of Cadmus and Harmonia, and he promised to deny her nothing. But because Semele was mortal, he dared not reveal himself to her as he really was. Instead, he disguised himself during their assignations as a human being. Semele knew she was being deceived and it bothered her. Who was he, really? An elderly neighbor, jealous Hera in disguise, persuaded her to find out. Ask him to display his true form, she said. Semele was six months pregnant by then. Her pregnancy had been so joyous that every time she heard a flute she was overcome by the urge to dance. Nonetheless, the seed that Hera planted in her mind took root. She begged Zeus to reveal himself.

He didn't want to grant her request but, having promised her anything she asked, he had no choice. He appeared before her in all his blazing radiance, a sight that was more than mortal eyes could bear. Semele perished on the spot.

Dionysus. (Credit: Hannah Berman)

When Zeus saw that she was dead, he snatched the baby from her womb and sewed it up inside his own thigh. Three months later, he removed the stitches and Dionysus was born again. Zeus crowned the child with a wreath of serpents and took him to Mount Olympus, where despite being the son of a mortal, he became an Olympian god, the last to join that select society. Thus the god Dionysus, ripped from the womb of Semele and the thigh of Zeus, came to be known as "twice-born."

Afterwards, a vengeful Hera intended to fling Dionysus out of heaven (as she had thrown out Hephaestus). To mollify her, Zeus molded a piece of the ether that encircles the earth into the shape of a baby and gave it to her. The trick worked. As Hera busied herself with the ether baby, Zeus handed the actual infant to Hermes, who took him to Semele's sister, Ino, who agreed to raise the child.

To protect him, Ino and her husband, Athamas, dressed him as a girl. That flimsy camouflage was a failure (for one thing, Dionysus had horns), and the story ends, as many Dionysian tales do, in disaster. Once she discovered the young god's whereabouts, Hera drove Athamas and Ino mad. In his delirium, Athamas mistook one of his sons for a stag and killed him with an arrow, while Ino, equally deranged, dropped another son into a kettle of boiling water. She came to her senses immediately, plucked him from the water, and leaped into the sea with the scalded child. He became a helpful sea spirit, and she was transformed into Leucothea, the white goddess. Dionysus was transported to Mount Nysa, where the nymphs finished raising him.

Or perhaps he reached Mount Nysa via a different route. Dionysus is sometimes said to be the child not of Semele but of Persephone, who mated with Zeus when he took the shape of a serpent and gave

DIONYSUS, GOD OF WINE

Domain: wine, ecstasy, appetite, vegetation.
Characteristics: licentious, immoderate, joyful.
Parents: Semele and Zeus.
Roman Name: Bacchus
Lovers and Liaisons: Althaea, Erigone, and others.
Spouse: Ariadne.
Children: Oenopion and others.
Animals: leopard, panther, bull, goat.
Attributes: a leafy crown, ivy and grape vines, cymbals, tambourines, and the thyrsus, a vine-wrapped wand made from a reed or a stalk of fennel and topped with a pinecone.
Best representations in post-classical art: Leonardo da Vinci's *Bacchus*, Caravaggio's *The Young Bacchus*, Titian's *Bacchus and Ariadne*.

birth to a baby called Dionysus Zagreus, a name that may represent the fusion of Dionysus with another god. His first act after birth was to climb onto the throne of Zeus and grab the lightning, a sure sign of the power that would be his. When Hera heard this, she called upon the Titans to destroy him. They smeared their faces with white chalk and, while Dionysus was innocently playing with his toys and looking at his reflection in a mirror, snuck up on him and tore his body into seven parts. They threw the parts into a cauldron, boiled them, roasted them over a fire, and ate them. But a god cannot be consumed. A god is immortal. Soon he returned to life. Since then, Dionysus has been associated with resurrection and the hereafter.

Finally, Zeus turned him into a goat as a way to protect him and gave him to the nymphs. They raised him in a sweet-smelling cave on Mount Nysa, where Dionysus brought forth his greatest gift: wine.

RECIPE FOR RESURRECTION

How was Dionysus resurrected? Here are four possibilities:
- He may have been reconstituted from the steam that wafted up from his roasting parts . . .
- or pieced together by Demeter or Rhea . . .
- or maybe Athena gave his heart to Zeus, who ground it up, mixed it into a drink, and served it to Semele. She swallowed the solution and conceived the child all over again . . .
- or perhaps Zeus swallowed the heart and gave birth to Dionysus himself.

The Invention and Spread of Wine

Dionysus had a beloved friend named Ampelos who fell from the branch of an elm tree while trying to reach a bunch of grapes and died. Or else he was gored to death by a bull. Either way, Dionysus was so distressed that he cried. When his tears splashed on the body of his friend (whose name means vine in Greek), it gave forth wine. The joy-giving Dionysian beverage was born in sorrow.

The first person to make wine also discovered its dark side. This happened during the reign of King Pandion, when Dionysus came to Athens to proselytize on behalf of the Bacchic mysteries. Although many Athenians treated Dionysus poorly, Icarius was hospitable, and his daughter Erigone, who went to bed with Dionysus, was even more so. As a token of gratitude, Dionysus taught Icarius how to make wine and presented him with several goatskin bags filled with the beverage, which Icarius happily shared with some shepherds. It made them feel warm, relaxed, and companionable. They began to laugh uproariously. After a while, though, they started to feel woozy, and soon they were seeing double and throwing up. Icarius, they thought, was trying to poison them. In their drunken frenzy, they killed him and buried him beneath a pine tree.

Erigone looked for her father everywhere. She never would have found him had it not been for her dog, Maera. Grabbing Erigone's robe in his teeth, he tugged her over to the pine tree and unearthed the corpse. When she saw her father's body, Erigone hanged herself from a branch of the tree. Afterwards, an epidemic of copycat suicides afflicted the young women of Athens, who one after another hanged themselves from trees. Only when the shepherds who killed Icarius were brought to justice did the plague of hanging disappear.

Once the secret of making wine was known, Dionysus disseminated it widely, and his worship spread. When he met people who were receptive to him, he rewarded them generously. If they resisted him, he punished them. King Oeneus, the ruler of Calydon, was so hospitable that when Dionysus slept with his wife, Althaea, he politely looked the other way. Dionysus graciously responded with the gift of a vine. On the other hand, the king of Damascus made the mistake of uprooting grapevines which Dionysus had planted. He was skinned alive.

A less dreadful fate came to a group of pirates. They saw Dionysus in a purple robe by the shore and, thinking he was the wealthy son of a king, decided to capture him. It wasn't as easy as they expected, for when they tried to tie him up, the knots would not hold and the ropes unraveled. The helmsman realized that this must be a god, though he wasn't sure which one, and he recommended setting him free. The other pirates dismissed his suggestion and set sail.

When wind filled the sails, Dionysus revealed himself. Fragrant wine poured over the ship; the air quivered with the sound of flutes; dark ivy, thick with flowers and berries, twined about the mast; and a vine festooned with heavy clusters of grapes snaked across the tops of the sails. The pirates decided they had made a mistake. But it was too late. Dionysus changed into a bear and a lion, both at the same time, and he pounced upon the head pirate. The others were so terrified that they jumped into the sea and turned into dolphins. Only the helmsman, who had recognized his divinity if not his precise identity, was saved.

All told, Dionysus traveled as far east as India. Everywhere he went, the previous intoxicant of choice—primitive beers made of barley and other grains—faded in popularity, and the fruit of the vine was joyously welcomed.

DIONYSUS KEEPS HIS WORD

Mythology regularly posits mutually exclusive options. One story has it that Dionysus, as the son of Persephone, was raised in Hades. Another says that, as the son of Semele, he was so unacquainted with the underworld that when he planned to go there to rescue his mother, he had to ask directions. A man named Prosymnus offered to give him the information if Dionysus promised to have sex with him. Dionysus readily agreed.

The man's directions were excellent. Dionysus descended into Hades as instructed, found Semele, brought her back to Mount Olympus, and returned to earth to honor the agreement. Unfortunately, Prosymnus was dead and buried. This, of course, was no excuse for breaking a contract. So Dionysus took a long piece of fig wood, whittled it into the shape of a phallus, and stuck one end into the grave. Then he sat down on the carved portion, thereby sodomizing himself and fulfilling the bargain.

The Rites of Dionysus

Of course, all gods are other, since they are other than mortal,
but some are more other than others.

—Wendy Doniger O'Flaherty

Dionysus, the horned god of wine and altered states of consciousness, was wild and paradoxical. At once young and old, human and
animal, heterosexual and homosexual, he was the god of license and
intoxication, mania and madness, death and resurrection, mob rule
and personal salvation.

His identity was unclear, his origins uncertain. Tacitus and
Plutarch believed that Dionysus was originally the god of the Jews,
Heraclitus stated unequivocally that "Hades and Dionysus . . .
are one and the same," and the Eleusinian mysteries celebrated
Dionysus as a savior and divine child. For centuries, commentators
assumed Dionysus to be an upstart god from Thrace or Phrygia.
Now, thanks to linguistic and anthropological evidence, his worship on Crete can be traced to the fifteenth century BCE, making
him an intrinsic part of Greek mythology and religion—not a new-
comer at all.

His popularity was immense, for unlike the other Olympians,
Dionysus was the child of a mortal. As such, he knew what mortals
long for. He offered joy and release, and his rites (which Pindar
and Euripides likened to those of the Great Mother goddess in

Phrygia) were, well, Dionysian. In addition to drinking, worshippers engaged in erotic activities (including sexual initiation), carried giant phalluses in long
processions, and made gory sacrifices in which animals (originally humans?) representing the living
god were torn asunder and eaten raw. Dancing,
riotous singing, and mime were also part of the Dionysian revels,
which ultimately led to the creation of the drama. As E. R. Dodds
writes, Dionysus is "the God who . . . enables you for a short
period of time to stop being yourself." Hence he is also the god of
acting.

More Tales of Dismemberment

No matter where you look in the literature of Dionysus, you find dismemberment. Sometimes that fate befell his enemies; sometimes his worshippers went mad and tore to pieces those whom they loved the most; and even Dionysus himself was torn apart by the Titans. In ritual, the followers of Dionysus ripped apart small animals, which they devoured raw, the implication being that they were consuming the body and blood of the god himself. In myth, the sacrificial victim usually died in the same violent way. Here are a few of their stories:

Dionysus traveled with a merry retinue of nymphs, satyrs, centaurs, and Maenads or Bacchae, his female followers who were prone to frenzied fits of ecstasy and abandon. The Maenads frightened people, so when Dionysus and his followers arrived in Thrace, King Lycurgus rushed at them with a cattle prod, threw many of the satyrs and Maenads into prison, and scared Dionysus so badly that he leaped into the sea.

Needless to say, Lycurgus paid for his transgression. Homer says that Zeus blinded him. Apollodorus reports that Dionysus made the king hallucinate so badly that he took an axe and chopped away at what he thought was a vine. When he came to his senses, he saw that he had hacked off the hands and feet of his son Dryas, thereby killing him. Soon Thrace became barren and dry. After months of famine, Dionysus declared through an oracle that this scourge would continue until Lycurgus was put to death. The Edonians promptly tied their king's hands and feet to four different horses, and Lycurgus was drawn and quartered.

Many women were attracted to the Dionysian orgies (which were so threatening to the powers that be that in 186 BCE, the Roman Senate suppressed the Bacchanalia and killed thousands of women). But Alcithoë, Luecippe, and Arsippe, the daughters of King Minyas, weren't tempted by the Bacchic revels, and Dionysus could not change their minds. He turned into a girl and gently tried to convince them to put aside their reservations and participate. Then he turned into a lion, a bull, and a panther, and tried to scare them into joining. They continued to resist the Dionysian call. Finally he gave up his disguises, reverted to his usual methods, and drove them insane. In their addled state, they decided to sacrifice Leucippe's son. They tore the child to pieces and ate him raw. Afterwards, when they recognized at last that Dionysus was a god, he transformed them into owls or bats.

The fate of the unlucky King Pentheus, who denied the divinity of Dionysus and paid the ultimate price, is described in Euripides' play *The Bacchae*. The action begins in Thebes, where Dionysus runs around disguised as a mortal, enticing young girls and proclaiming the worship of Dionysus. Soon the women of Thebes abandon their looms in favor of dancing in the woods and cavorting with lecherous men.

Pentheus declares that he will decapitate this unruly stranger and capture the women, among whom number his mother Agauë and her sisters Ino and Autonoë. The blind prophet Teiresias tries to dissuade him by arguing the importance of Dionysian ecstasy: "Pentheus, pay heed to my words," he says. "You rely/On force: but it is not force that governs human affairs." Unconvinced, Pentheus tries to tie up Dionysus. In his delusional state he ties up a bull instead.

Word comes that the women, led by his mother and aunts, are running wild in the woods, where they have nursed wolf cubs and gazelles, caused milk to flow from the earth, and literally torn a heifer to pieces with their bare hands. Dionysus convinces Pentheus to watch these astounding rituals and, to avoid being detected, to do so while wearing women's clothing. His disguise is soon discovered. The women punish him for his deception in the Dionysian way: by tearing him to pieces. In a final irony, it is his mother, foaming at the mouth, her eyes rolling in her head, who wrenches the head from his body.

The Greek writer Strabo (64 BCE to 24 CE) wrote a forty-seven-volume history of the world. Had those books survived, he surely would have been recognized as a historian. But since only his seventeen-volume geography survived, he is famed as a geographer. Fortunately, even in his scientific explorations he described the ways of the people. Here is part of his report about a small island in the Atlantic near the mouth of the Loire:

> The woman of the Samnitae inhabit it. They are possessed by Dionysus and propitiate the god with initiations and other sacred rites; and no man may land on the island, but the women themselves sail out from it and have intercourse with men and then return. It is their custom once a year to remove the roof from their temple and to roof it again the same day before sunset, each woman carrying part of the burden; but the woman whose load falls from her is torn to pieces by the others, and they carry the pieces around the temple crying out "euoi," and do not cease until their madness passes away; and it always happens that someone pushes against the woman who is destined to suffer this fate.

King Midas

Greek mythology is filled with stories of people who got what they wished for and suffered the consequences. None is more famous than King Midas. When he was born, a cavalcade of ants traipsed into his cradle and each one placed a grain of wheat between his baby lips. Those who observed this miracle predicted that riches would materialize for this child. And indeed, in all of history, no one has ever been more skilled at the creation of wealth than Midas. Yet in the end he lost it all.

The story begins with the former tutor of Dionysus, pot-bellied Silenus, who drank too much and passed out in the rose gardens for which Midas was famous. When the gardeners found him, they festooned him with chains of flowers and paraded him mockingly in front of the king. Although Silenus had the legs, ears, and tail of a horse, Midas saw no reason to laugh. He was kind and hospitable. Indeed, he felt privileged. For despite his appearance, Silenus was so wise that Plato compared him to Socrates. Midas honored him with ten days and nights of celebrations, during which time Silenus entertained his host with stories of other lands and imparted a piece of wisdom for which he is still known. It is most fortunate never to be born at all, he told Midas, but barring that, it is best to die early.

On the eleventh day, Midas and Silenus paid a visit to Dionysus, who had the ability to grant virtually anything, especially if it concerned the sense of touch. One time, for instance, he blessed three sisters known as the Winegrowers with the ability to transform anything they touched into another substance simply by invoking his name. One sister could turn anything into oil; a second sister could turn anything into corn; and a third, whose name was Oeno, could turn anything into wine. Out of gratitude to Midas, Dionysus offered him whatever he wanted.

So Midas made his famous wish. He asked that everything he touched be turned to gold, and Dionysus uneasily granted his request. At first Midas was delighted. When he snapped a twig off a low-growing oak tree, it turned to gold. He touched a stone, a clod of earth, an apple, and the pillars on either side of his doorway, and each turned to glittering gold. When he washed his hands, even the water turned to gold and, as Ovid says, "his hopes soared beyond the limits of his imagination."

As soon as he tried to eat, he brushed up against those limits. Bread and meat became gold in his hands, and when he tried to swallow a mixture of wine and water, it turned to molten metal in his mouth. Some say (Ovid not among them) that even this was not enough to show Midas the error of his ways, that it was only when he touched his young daughter, thus turning her into a golden statue, that he truly understood the problem. So he prayed for relief to Dionysus, who told him to go to the source of the Pactolus River and immerse himself in the waters. Midas dove into the spring and thus cleansed himself of the golden touch, which flowed from him into the river with the result that even in Ovid's day, many generations later, the soil around that area glistened with flakes of gold.

Later on, having strayed into a neighboring kingdom, Midas was adopted by the Phyrgian King Gordius (who is best known for having tied the Gordian knot, which Alexander the Great slashed centuries later). When Gordius died, Midas became king of Phrygia. By then, he had learned the lesson of the golden touch and had renounced the trappings of wealth in preference for simple rustic ways.

But much as he might change his style, he could not change his mind, which remained as foolish as ever. That story is told on page 195.

Dionysus and Orpheus

Every religion generates its own Martin Luther. The religion of Dionysus was no exception. In the sixth century, a rival sect arose which was inspired by Orpheus, a follower who strayed from the Dionysian path. There was only one way to do that: by sobering up. While the followers of Dionysus, primarily women, frolicked in the woods seeking elation and abandon, the devotees of Orpheus, mostly men, went the other way, becoming restrained and puritanical. They believed that the body was a prison, that one's behavior in life determined one's fate after death, and that a virtuous life was celibate, vegetarian, and alcohol-free. Following such a life, a soul would gain entrance to the Elysian Fields. After three virtuous (Orphic) lives, one could step off the wheel entirely and became part of the divine ether, at which point one was no longer mortal but godlike.

In contrast, a sinful life resulted in punishment—and sin included both lapses in the here-and-now and transgressions from the past, chief of which was the murder of Dionysus by the Titans. In the rites of Orphic initiation, devotees reexperienced this original sin by dabbing themselves with white clay—the very stuff the Titans smeared over their faces when they ambushed the baby Dionysus—

and devouring raw flesh (something the members of this no-meat religion presumably never did again). Orphic religion featured ceremonial cleansings, wineless rituals and, in the opinion of many Athenians, an overabundance of self-righteous priggery.

Nevertheless, it attracted adherents for twelve centuries. A body of literature grew up around it, all supposedly written by Orpheus or by his son or disciple Musaios. Whether Orpheus was a real person (as Pausanias thought) or an imaginary one (as Aristotle believed), his output was enormous. It included poems, spells, songs, incantations, a manual titled *Thuepolikon: How to Make Bloodless Offerings* (honey-soaked cakes were a good choice), and that perennial staple of anti-Dionysian fervor, the diet book. Such a volume may seem as peripheral to Orphism as pope T-shirts are to Christianity, but it was actually quite central. For although the Orphics believed in the power of renunciation, it was not their goal to transcend the flesh. Instead, they tried to perfect the body and to heal themselves. Ultimately, writes the French scholar Marcel Detienne, they sought "one goal and one goal only: health." The only way to do that was to withdraw from the world of experience.

Writing in 1903, the great Jane Harrison described the distinction between the worshippers of Dionysus and those of Orpheus:

> Those to whom wine brings no inspiration, no moments of sudden illumination, of wider and deeper insight, of larger human charity and understanding, find it hard to realize what to others of other temperament is so natural, so elemental, so beautiful—the constant shift from physical to spiritual that is of the essence of the religion of Dionysus. But there are those also, and they are saintly souls, who know it all to the full, know the exhilaration of wine, know what it is to be drunken with the physical beauty of a flower or a sunset, with the sensuous imagery of words, with the strong wine of a new idea, with the magic of another's personality, yet having known, turn away with steadfast eyes. . . . Such have their inward ecstasy of the ascetic, but they revel with another Lord, and he is Orpheus.

Orpheus and Eurydice

Orpheus was a follower of Dionysus and a musician of unsurpassed skill. When he played his lyre, the trees and rocks gathered around him to dance, and when he sang, he could compete with the Sirens, whom the Argonauts were able to resist only because Orpheus was on board with them. Shortly after the voyage of the Argo, he married Eurydice, a tree nymph. He did not forget to invite Hymen, the Greek god of weddings, to the festivities. Nonetheless, disaster struck. As Eurydice wandered in the meadow with a band of naiads, a snake bit her on the ankle and she died on the spot. Although Orpheus wept profusely, his grief didn't fade. He decided to bring her back.

To do so, he ventured into the underworld, where his ethereal playing bewitched Charon the ferryman, Cerberus the dog, Hades, and Persephone, queen of the underworld. He begged them to allow Eurydice to return and he promised that, at the end of a normal lifespan, she would return to the unverworld, like every other mortal. Alternatively, he offered to stay in the underworld to be near her. As he made this statement, he strummed on the lyre. The sounds mesmerized everyone. Tantalus forgot about the dangling fruit and turned his ear to the music. Sisyphus stopped pushing the boulder uphill and sat down to listen. Even the Furies cried for the first time ever. All that love and music brought hell to a stop. So Hades and Persephone gave in. Eurydice, they said, could follow Orpheus out of the underworld. There was one proviso: until they were safely back on earth, he must not look back.

Eurydice appeared. Still fragile on account of her injured ankle, she emerged from among the newly arrived ghosts and, with Orpheus in the lead, began the tortuous trip back. Uphill through darkness and gloom they traveled, and throughout that long journey, Orpheus looked straight ahead and concentrated on where he was going. Yet he was so anxious that when he was just a step or two away from the land of the living, he glanced back. Before his eyes, Eurydice faded into mist and slipped into eternity.

What happened next? Several commentators report that Zeus blasted Orpheus with a thunderbolt. Pausanias suggests that

Orpheus committed suicide right then and there. Ovid writes that Orpheus tried to follow Eurydice to the underworld. This time Charon refused to ferry him across, even though Orpheus sat by the banks of the river for seven days and wept. Three years passed: three times, the sun "reached the watery sign of Pisces." During this period, many women were attracted to this best of all possible musicians. Orpheus rejected them all. The truth was, his inclinations had changed, and he now preferred the company of young boys. According to Ovid, this was a custom which Orpheus introduced to the people of Thrace.

He switched his allegiance in another way as well. Once, Orpheus had worshipped Dionysus. Now, he served as a priest in a temple of Apollo and ignored the Maenads. Feeling scorned, they grew angry.

EURYDICE'S STORY: RILKE'S VERSION

Male or female, we all identify with Orpheus. He is the one who feels overwhelmed by grief, caves in to temptation, and is his own undoing. More importantly, he is the one who is alive. But what about Eurydice?

Hers is the journey to death and forgetting. In "Orpheus. Eurydice. Hermes," Ranier Maria Rilke, a less optimistic fellow than Ovid, tells the story from her point of view. As the poem opens, Orpheus is in the underworld with his wife trudging behind him, accompanied by Hermes. Orpheus cannot hear their footsteps, and his attention is divided, "for while his sight raced ahead like a dog . . . his hearing lagged behind like a smell." Straining to hear them, he can barely contain his desire to look back.

Eurydice is oblivious. Although she is following him, she is not thinking of him. She feels complete, composed, brimming with her own death like "a fruit filled with sweetness and night." Orpheus is the one who's wrought up and impatient. At last he glances behind him, condemning Eurydice to an eternity in the underworld. Eurydice barely notices. She no longer even knows who he is. The tragedy, in Rilke's view, is only for the living. The dead don't care.

The results were predictable. Howling, playing flutes, and shaking tambourines, the frenzied women pelted him with stones, branches, and clods of dirt, and finally with the hoes and rakes which the farmers had dropped in terror. Using these implements, the women quickly dispatched Orpheus by tearing off his limbs and ripping his head from his body.

Trees bent their branches in mourning, the birds were disconsolate, and the rocks sobbed. Orpheus's head and his lyre were washed into the river, where the strings of the lyre made doleful sounds while the head spoke, sang, or at the very least murmured sadly. When it washed up on shore, a snake bit it and Orpheus died. His head was buried on the island of Lesbos. It was said that the nightingales who rested on his tomb sang more sweetly than they did anywhere else.

His shade descended to the underworld, where he took Eurydice in his arms and, according to Ovid, was united with her for eternity. Plato, who had reincarnation on his mind, imagined a different ending. In *The Republic,* he writes that when it was time for Orpheus to choose a new life, he acted out of hatred for women, who had killed him, and picked the life of a swan.

From the Annals of Mythology: Ovid

Homer is immortal. Hesiod is essential. But Ovid, wonderful Ovid, fades in and out of fashion like high-heeled mules, a style he would have appreciated. Born Publius Ovidius Naso on March 20, 43 BCE, he grew up in a prosperous family in "watery Sulmo" some 90 miles east of Rome. He and his brother, one year older to the day, studied rhetoric and grammar and were expected to become lawyers or politicians. It was not to be. His brother died at age twenty ("and then I lost a part of

Ovidius Naso was the man.
—Shakespeare,
Love's Labours Lost, IV.ii

myself"). Ovid took "the first step up the governmental ladder," but was so gifted that even when he decided to follow his father's advice and give up writing poetry, "a poem, spontaneously, would shape itself to metre—/ whatever I tried to write turned into verse." He was still in his twenties, with one of his three marriages behind him, when he gave up a possible career in the Senate in favor of the literary life.

The quintessential sophisticate, Ovid was friendly with a circle of poets that included Horace ('that metrical wizard"), Tibullus, Propertius, and Macer, the author of didactic poems on birds, snake bites, and herbal cures. He was also welcomed into the smart set of Roman society, where he enjoyed himself immensely and established a reputation as a poet.

His first book, *Amores (The Loves)*, was a ribald, witty chronicle of his love affair with a young woman (or a composite of several women) he named Corinna. ("So, that husband of yours is going to be at the party—/Well, I hope he chokes.") He followed it up with *Heroides (Heroines)*, a collection of letters between mythological heroines and their lovers, Helen and Paris being one such couple, and several other works on the topic of love and seduction: *Medicamina Faciei (Cosmetics, or The Art of Beauty)*, a four-page fragment that begins, "Listen and learn, dear girls, how to improve your appearance . . ."; *Ars Amatoria (The Art of Love)*, a clever, cynical manual for lovers, adulterous and otherwise; and *Remedia Amoris (Remedies for Love)*, still the book to read when you've been dumped. These worldly-wise poems, with their lively, confessional style and pithy mythological examples, were wildly popular with the Romans. However, with the last volume, he exhausted the topic and was forced to turn elsewhere. Mythology was the natural choice. He wrote a highly praised play about Medea, now lost; *Fasti (Feasts)*, a book about the festivals of the Roman year; and his masterpiece, *Metamorphoses*.

Metamorphoses is a compendium of about 250 stories, some of which are swiftly summarized and some of which receive the full narrative treatment. Although these stories lack a central character, they share a common motif: transformation. Within its pages, humans interact with gods, generally to their disadvantage. Arachne becomes a spider, Niobe turns to stone, Callisto and Arcas are transformed into constellations, and so on. Written in a style that is deft, sympathetic, often comic, and grounded in a deep understanding of human nature, *Metamorphoses* covers virtually all of classical mythology. True, some stories are more effective than others. That's to be expected in a narrative that begins with Chaos, which was transformed into the ordered universe, proceeds chronologically through the stories of the gods and heroes, and concludes with the death of Julius Caesar (the year before Ovid was born), his transformation into a star, and the ascendancy of the emperor Augustus. Ovid was more than generous in his praise of Augustus. It didn't help. In 8 CE just as *Metamorphoses* was on the verge of publication, the emperor banished Ovid to Tomis, a half-barbarian outpost of the Roman empire, located over eight hundred miles away on the coast of the Black Sea.

To this day, it is unclear exactly what Ovid did to deserve such a punishment. He himself, slightly coy on the matter, claimed it was "an indiscretion," not a crime. In *Tristia*, a poem written from exile, he explains that he saw something he shouldn't have seen and failed to report it. ("Why did I see what I saw? Why render my eyes guilty?/ . . . Actaeon never intended to see Diana naked,/but still was torn to bits by his own hounds.") He may have gotten into trouble for not reporting what he saw. Or he may have been indirectly involved in an affair being conducted by the granddaughter of Augustus who, like her mother before her, was banished for adultery. Whatever Ovid's mistake may have been, Augustus, a family values traditionalist, took the opportunity to banish the urbane author of *Ars Amatoria* for encouraging licentious behavior. Ovid complained that his accuser failed to distinguish between his literary persona and his actual person, between his "flirtatious Muse" and his "respectable life-style." "It's not/as though *I* were the only composer of erotic verses," he wrote, "yet I, and I alone have paid the price/for producing such things."

Ovid left Rome feeling "like a corpse minus the funeral." Exile was a blow from which he never recovered. His devoted wife stayed behind, managing his property and campaigning for his release. (It's possible that she may have joined him after a few years, but if so, he doesn't mention it in his poems or letters.) In Tomis, Ovid learned the local language (Getic), composed poems in it, and found kindness and even recognition among the inhabitants (although he also angered them by talking incessantly about how much he hated the place). His friends back in Rome were supportive but his long-distance efforts to mobilize them to help him came to naught. Eventually he gave up. ("Why did I ever hope to obtain more lenient treatment?/Could I so misjudge my fate?") He died in exile.

As he hoped and frequently expressed, his name lived on. After his death in 17 CE, his popularity remained. But by the end of the first century, both literary critics and Christians were expressing disapproval. For several centuries, Ovid's fortunes, like those of the empire, declined and fell. Serious Virgil was revered. Frivolous Ovidius, teller of bawdy tales and dispenser of explicit sexual advice, was not, although people never stopped reading him. During the twelfth to fourteenth centuries, the age of courtly love, Ovid came into his own, far outranking Homer in popularity. His books were translated into other languages and he was so widely read that his influence can be traced in everyone from Dante and Chaucer to Shakespeare. In addition, fresh interpretations further broadened his appeal. For instance, an anonymous fourteenth-century French poet composed *Ovide Moralisé,* which viewed Ovid's tales as Christian allegory. Thus Apollo killing the Python at Delphi was merely another way of talking about Christ battling with the devil, and Ovid wasn't really a pagan poet at all: he just looked like one.

The first English translation of *Metamorphoses* appeared in 1480. (A recent translation by Ted Hughes was published in 1997.) Arthur Golding's verse translation, published in 1567, was used by both Shakespeare and Ezra Pound, who considered it "the most beautiful book in the language." And in 1626, George Sandys, treasurer of the Virginia Company, penned an English translation—the first major book of verse to be written in America.

In the world of art, Ovid's influence surpasses any other writer of myth. Throughout the Renaissance and beyond, painters and sculptors in need of inspiration dug into *Metamorphoses.* Among them were Titian, Guido Reni, Nicholas Poussin, Velazquez, and Peter Paul Rubens, arguably the most astute artist of myth. Not long before his death in 1640, he accepted a commission to illustrate the book. Forty-five oil sketches survive, along with dozens of Rubens's earlier paintings which accurately depict the ancient tales.

The vogue for Ovid continued in the eighteenth century but in the nineteenth century his books were bowdlerized and his influence waned. As one critic wrote in 1934, "Ovid died for at least the third time in the nineteenth century and was buried under mountains of disparaging comment to make a throne for Virgil." It's true that unlike Virgil and Homer, Ovid doesn't write heroic epics; that he follows Homer and Hesiod by seven or eight centuries, making him a compiler rather than a primary source (even though in some cases his version of a myth is the earliest one we have); and that he shows a woeful lack of gravitas. Nonetheless, Ovid sparkles. His ability to tell a story with wit, brevity, passion, insight, and descriptive grace assures that he will always be in print (or the electronic equivalent). Like certain fashions which, however impractical, never completely disappear—like platform shoes or stiletto heels or bright white sneakers—Ovid is too much fun to go out of style for long.

> *My spirit is moved to sing of shapes changed into new bodies. Gods, inspire my undertaking (for you have changed it too), and accompany my song—finespun, continuous—from the beginning of the world to my own day.*
>
> —*Metamorphoses* 1.1–3, translated by Sara Mack

HEROES

Thirteen Ways of Looking at a Hero

Now, as in antiquity, heroes appear in many guises. Whether illustrious or unknown, they take daring risks, probe the unknown, combat evil, overcome their weaknesses, conquer terrible opponents, go on quests for fabulous objects or forbidden knowledge, and boldly accomplish feats beyond the reach of lesser mortals. Though a list of contemporary heroes might include saints and scientists, athletes and explorers, symbols of resistance, icons of art and literature, and—it goes without saying—brave souls of every age and gender, mythological heroes are above all warriors, even if they never set foot near a battlefield. By using their skills to advantage, they defy their opponents, no matter how terrible, fight for what is their due (generally, the crown), and implicitly encourage the rest of us to push beyond the drabness of the everyday into a life that glows with meaning.

The heroes described in this section have been chosen not because they are better, braver, or more admirable than other figures, but because the stories of their lives reveal prototypical patterns of heroism. One of those patterns, I regret to report, is male-ness. Not that there aren't heroines aplenty in the world of myth and legend: see Part II for stories about heroic goddesses. It's just that, while fairy tales and folklore are teeming with heroic girls, most epic heroes are male.

Like Theseus, who slays the Minotaur but abandons his wife (and inadvertently causes his father's death), these heroes are superhu-man figures with all too human flaws. Mythology is flexible enough to allow its heroes to make appalling slip-ups without endangering their status. Contemporary heroes face a tougher standard. Once they are revealed to have human failings, they tumble off the pedestal of heroism—which is one reason why the most inspiring heroes come from days gone by. Seldom do they walk among us, for the living, who are in constant danger of tarnishing their reputa-tions, if only by growing old, cannot compete with the glamorous dead, be they historical figures or mythological ones.

To have a hero, real or imaginary, is to nourish the dream of a larger self. Over the course of the last three thousand years or so, heroes have been worshipped, loved, honored, and analyzed in a variety of ways. A few of the those analyses—thirteen, to be pre-cise—are presented in the pages that follow.

1. The Valet's Hero

The one-eyed general Antigonus I (382–301 BCE), sometimes known as Cyclops, was an astute politician and a formidable military man. After the death of his commander, Alexander the Great, he seized control of Syria, Mesopotamia, and Asia Minor and entertained hopes of rebuilding the empire. In Athens, where he was crowned king, he was considered a divine savior. Yet he retained a sense of humility, and when an admirer described him as "the Son of the Sun," he had the grace to remark, "My valet is not aware of this." So Antigonus, killed in battle at the age of eighty-one, was perhaps the first to ponder the concept that "No man is a hero to his valet."

The phrase itself was coined in the seventeenth century and expli-cated in the nineteenth by Thomas Carlyle (1795–1881). A propo-nent of the Great Man theory of history, Carlyle regarded most human beings as pathetic slugs in dire need of leadership, which he believed was provided by nobler specimens or heroes whose actions, like lightning, sparkled the fuel that drove the engine of history. While these heroes were often seriously flawed, Carlyle found solace in the fact that other human beings revered them.

Nonetheless, he observed that hero worship often flowed to the wrong person, for a simple reason: the valet is a dunce, unable to distinguish between real heroes and pretenders. "The Valet," Carlyle lamented, "does not know a Hero when he sees him!"

The English humorist G. K. Chesterton (1874–1936) had another take. He insisted that the essential point, which Carlyle missed, was "not that no man is a hero to his valet. The ultimate psychological truth . . . is that no man is a hero to himself."

2. Hero Worship in Antiquity

In antiquity, a hero or heroine did not need to be a moral exemplar. Great courage, bold acts, deep suffering, and extraordinary abilities were required; virtue was not. Heroes included warriors like Achilles; tragic figures like Oedipus; adventurers like Odysseus who sallied forth on picaresque quests; nameless functionaries like the Hero Physician and Hero Garland-Bearer of Athens; founders like Cadmus; protectors like Theseus; and heralds of culture like Prometheus, who stole fire from the gods (and still ranks, according to one commentator, as "the hero of the official Western ideology of progress and dominance through technology"). These demigods were not just figures of myth: they were worshipped. People prayed to them for assistance, wept over their demise, offered them libations and blood sacrifices, and feasted in their honor.

Hero worship became so widespread that when Draco, remembered today for his great affection for the death penalty, codified the laws of Athen in 621 BCE, he insisted that heroes be accorded rites that were equivalent in solemnity to those of the immortals but quite opposite in style. Thus whereas Divinities were worshipped by day, heroes and heroines were honored by night. The altars of the gods were elevated; those of the heroes were built low to the ground. Even sacrifices varied in crucial respects, for the creatures sacrificed to the gods were killed facing heaven, while the animals, preferably black, who were slain at the tombs of heroes were killed with their faces pointing down, signifying the fact that heroes, dead by definition, resided in the earth.

Though some heroes were the offspring of mortals and gods, literally a race apart, the ancients also worshipped real people such as the poet Sappho, the Spartan general Brasidas, and the athlete Philippos of Kroton, famed for his good looks. Because these men were human, they understood suffering. Yet their remarkable talents marked them as divine. Thus, like saints, ancestor figures, and mythological heroes, these real-life heroes could act as intermediaries between gods and human beings.

3. Heroines in Antiquity

About three hundred years after Homer and Hesiod wrote about the heroes, the word for heroine appeared in literature for the first time. That long gap indicates the secondary position in which they were held. Though heroines were also worshipped at temples and shrines, the pivotal events of their lives centered on marriage and childbirth, and their lives reflect the adage that anatomy is destiny. Rather than battling monsters or pursuing shimmering ideals, they appear in tragedies as rejected wives or loves like Medea and Phaedra, grieving daughters like Electra, or victims like Iphigenia, who was sacrificed by her father for the good of the country. Like Christian saints, classical heroines are often martyred to a greater cause.

Yet there were exceptions. Not all heroines were defined by the men in their lives. The ancients also revered Amazons, sibyls, priestesses, and athletes, heroines who were famed for their own aptitudes. Though these heroines were more numerous than we might imagine, they were still outnumbered six to one by male heroes. The Greeks—and not only the Greeks—reserved their most exciting adventures for the men, a bias that continues today at a movie theater near you.

4. Emerson's Hero

On January 24, 1838, Ralph Waldo Emerson gave a lecture at the Masonic Temple in Boston in which he explained what it meant to be a hero. He believed that heroism comprises confidence, persistence, boldness, pride, humor, and hilarity, as well as a distinct lack of regard for personal safety, public opinion, or even the greater good. In Emerson's opinion, heroism is the ultimate expression of individuality.

Yet the hero is never bogged down in personal concerns or

inconsequential matters such as health and wealth (both of which Emerson considered "the foil, the butt and merriment of heroism"). Instead, the hero takes up arms against evil. Looking to society for neither guidance nor approval, the hero acts in accord with his instincts. He trusts himself entirely, for "heroism feels and never reasons, and therefore is always right." This might sound like a recipe for zealotry or criminal behavior, but it is not, for the hero values virtue above all else, though he is not a prig. Undeterred by philosophy, religion, or the desire for fancy food or physical comfort, the hero "advances to his own music" yet benefits us all. As an example, Emerson pointed to the Reverend Elijah P. Lovejoy, who died a martyr's death in 1837 while defending his right to publish an abolitionist newspaper. Emerson observed that such people, though rare, tend to appear in troubled times.

> *The hero is not fed on sweets;*
> *Daily his own heart he eats.*
>
> —Ralph Waldo Emerson

Emerson gave plenty of advice about how to model oneself after these superior people. He suggested confronting fears by taking those actions which are the most frightening. He encouraged truthfulness, temperance, and generosity, and he suggested that even unpleasant aspects of life such as abstinence, debt, solitude, and unpopularity, were tonic for the soul, as was a nodding familiarity with disease, denunciation, and violent death. Above all, he believed in optimism and the power of intention. Exhorting his readers to resolve to be great, he noted that "a hero is no braver than an ordinary man, but he is brave five minutes longer." And he encouraged them to ignore the expectations of others. "Be true to your own act," he said, "and congratulate yourself if you have done something strange and extravagant, and broken the monotony of a decorous age."

5. Carlyle's Hero

Emerson believed in the spiritual potential of every human being, and thus he saw heroism as a goal toward which anyone might strive. Thomas Carlyle (1795–1881), Emerson's friend, had little regard for most people. He thought of heroes as visionaries and geniuses whose talents, wisdom, sincerity and originality contrast with the stupidity, small-mindedness, and laziness of the contemptible masses. These extraordinary individuals appear in every age. However, as Carlyle remarked in a series of lectures in 1840, the heroic style that excites one age may be outmoded in the next. In the dawn of history, heroes inspired wonder and were perceived as gods. As the eons rolled on, people stopped viewing heroes as divine and came to see them as prophets who were merely touched by divinity, like Muhammad. After that, the hero continued to devolve, appearing as a poet, like Shakespeare, or as a priest, like Luther.

In Carlyle's view, these heroic forms—the god, the prophet, the poet, and the priest—belonged to the past. In the modern age, heroes were more likely to appear in one of two forms: as men of letters, like Rousseau, or as military or political leaders, like Napoleon. Carlyle had no love for Napoleon. He considered him an inferior sort who "trampled on the world, holding it tyrannously down," slipped into "vacuity," and died, astonished and heartbroken, on an isolated rock. Yet he changed the world. Carlyle called him, with all due irony, "our last great man."

6. E. B. Tylor's Hero

In 1871, English anthropologist Edward Burnet Tylor (1832–1917) turned his back on the hero's personal traits and focused instead on the events that happen to him. Tylor observed that in many myths, the action follows a predictable three-part sequence: being abandoned at birth, being rescued by a human or animal, and finally becoming a national hero, like Romulus. Although Tylor did not interpret his model in a symbol way, he argued that the frequent appearances of this plot, too numerous to be coincidental, suggested "the evident regularity of law." In this way he planted a seed that blossomed into the idea of the hero's journey.

7. Von Hahn's Hero

The Austrian scholar Johann Georg von Hahn expanded Tylor's scenario into a sixteen-point template of the life of an "Aryan" hero. (That loaded word, lacking the taint it later acquired, referred to the nomadic tribes who spread Indo-European languages throughout Asia Minor, Mesopotamia, and India). In Von Hahn's pattern, the hero was the high-spirited son (never the daughter) of a princess and a god. Abandoned at birth because his father was afraid of being overthrown, he was saved by animals and raised by shepherds, after which he went abroad, returned in triumph, killed his enemies, freed his mother, murdered his younger brother, founded a city, and died in an extraordinary way.

THE LIFE OF A HERO
FROM *THE HERO* BY LORD RAGLAN

1. The hero's mother is a royal virgin;
2. His father is a king, and
3. Often a near relative of his mother, but
4. The circumstances of his conception are unusual, and
5. He is also reputed to be the son of a god.
6. At birth an attempt is made, usually by his father or his maternal grandfather, to kill him, but
7. He is spirited away, and
8. Reared by foster-parents in a far country.
9. We are told nothing of his childhood, but
10. On reaching manhood he returns or goes to his future kingdom.
11. After a victory over the king and/or a giant, dragon, or wild beast,
12. He marries a princess, often the daughter of his predecessor, and
13. Becomes king.
14. For a time he reigns uneventfully, and
15. Prescribes laws, but
16. Later he loses favour with the gods and/or his subjects, and
17. He is driven from the throne and city, after which
18. He meets with a mysterious death,
19. Often at the top of a hill.
20. His children, if any, do not succeed him.
21. His body is not buried, but nevertheless
22. He has one or more holy sepulchres.

8. Raglan's Hero

The plot-summary approach reached its apex in 1936 when Fitzroy Richard Somerset, known as Lord Raglan, identified twenty-two components in the life of a hero. These incidents had nothing to do with psychology; instead, they echoed, albeit dimly, the rites of passage of prehistoric kings. When Raglan stacked up twenty-one heroes, all male, against the twenty-two benchmark elements in his scale, not one merited a perfect score. However, Oedipus and Moses got 21 points, Theseus earned 20, King Arthur won 19, Romulus and Perseus were awarded 18, and Heracles earned 17 points. In 1976 Alan Dundes applied Raglan's formula to the life of Jesus and awarded him 17, the same number as Heracles.

9. Otto Rank's Hero

The psychoanalyst Otto Rank was one of the first to make the hero a universal figure whose biography symbolically paralleled our own. Taking a Freudian approach (although he would later break with the master), Rank focused on the birth of the hero and interpreted heroic myths as wish-fulfillment fantasies created from the point of view of a child. As he saw it, the Oedipal component in these fantasies explained why the virgin birth is such a widespread motif: it negates the possibility that the mother ever had sex. It also explained why the mythological father, having been told that his son will endanger his life, abandons him to die (generally in the water, as in the cases of Perseus, Oedipus, and Moses). Although the child is fortuitously rescued, often by animals, the hero's anger remains. Eventually he kills his father (or retaliates in some other fashion) and receives the acknowledgment due him. What's at work here, Rank asserts, is simple projection: the child, not wishing to admit to murderous thoughts against his father, imagines that his father wishes to kill him, a belief which enables him to rebel guilt-free. Rank's hero has the needs of a child.

Rank found the myths less than ennobling. Hero myths, he wrote, were important to neurotics, psychotics, and criminals. As an example, he pointed to the anarchist who, never having gotten over his childish resentments, literally tries to kill the king.

10. Sigmund Freud's Hero

Sigmund Freud had a lifelong love of antiquity, and his office reflected it. A bronze figurine of Athena, a bust of Osiris, and other statuettes adorned his desk like so many votive images, and his collection overflowed to the walls and shelves. He described the myths accompanying these figures as "the age-long dreams of young humanity," and he frequently referred to mythological characters, at least one of whom—Oedipus, the errant son—will forever be linked with his name. But in truth Freud's fascination with dreams and collectible art objects exceeded his interest in myth.

Nonetheless, he pondered its implications. He believed that myth represents "the step by which the individual emerges from group psychology," and he agreed with Rank that the hero's tale mirrors the history of a growing child. He pointed out that the two families that exist in many myths—the noble family which gives birth to the hero and the humble, anonymous family which raises him—represent the all-powerful family of babyhood and the flawed, imperfect family that soon replaces it in the child's increasingly critical perception. Thus the two families are actually "one and the same and are only differentiated chronologically." The central action of the myth occurs when the hero, like Zeus or Kronos, revolts against the

SIGMUND FREUD ON OEDIPUS

His fate moves us only because it might have been our own, because the oracle laid upon us before our birth the very curse which rested upon him. It may be that we are all destined to direct out first sexual impulses toward our mothers, and our first impulses of hatred and resistance toward our fathers; our dreams convince us that we were. King Oedipus, who slew his father Laius and wedded his mother Jocasta, is nothing more or less than a wish-fulfillment.

father and the status quo. "A hero is someone who has had the courage to rebel against his father and has in the end victoriously overcome him," Freud wrote. Whether the father appears in the myth as a man or a monster, the hero must, by definition, slay him.

11. The Jungian Hero

More steeped in mythology than Freud, Carl Jung found in it the remnants of humanity's earliest experiences as well as a collection of recurring motifs and archetypes that he believed roam around in the collective unconscious like zombies in a horror film: even when you think they're dead and buried, they might pop up at any moment. Among these archetypes are such familiar figures as the mother, the trickster, the child, the wise old man, and the hero, "a powerful man or god-man who vanquishes evil in the form of dragons, serpents, monsters, demons, and so on, and who liberates his people from destruction and death."

Unlike the Freudian hero, who rebels against the family, the Jungian hero is a pilgrim on the path toward becoming conscious, developing a unique personality, and achieving what Jung called individuation. Jung saw that endeavor as a quest during which the hero must combat his destructive impulses and overcome his fears without either regressing or inflating his ego. Most people aren't up to it. Fortunately, religion, art, and dreams provide invaluable images, as do heroic sagas, both ancient (*The Odyssey*) and modern (*Alice's Adventures in Wonderland*). These epic tales offer an ego-strengthening boost of identification and exhilaration.

Within those myths, as in a dream, every element represents an aspect of the self. "Even the cross, or whatever other heavy burden the hero carries, is *himself*," Jung declared. The most important symbol is the dragon, which every hero must slay. To Freud, that monster represented the father; to Jung, it signified the unconscious, the rejected portion of the self known as the shadow, or the Terrible Mother, an archetype which incorporates the unconscious. The battle against the dragon, even when it is seemingly successful, is never really complete. It continues to be played out through relationships, for part of the hero's task is to integrate the female aspects of self with the male aspects, the yin with the yang.

Jung's disciple Erich Neumann (1905–1960) suggested that the hero establishes his identity in five major episodes: a miraculous birth; the slaying of a monster which represents nature, the unconscious, and the mother, all of which threaten to engulf him; the slaying of the father, which represents patriarchy; the acquisition of a treasure or the rescue of a captive; and the transformation of the hero, who may turn into a star or be welcomed into the company of the gods.

Though the hero is almost always male, females appear at pivotal moments to provide assistance and to pair up with the hero. Nonetheless, the mythological duo rarely lives happily ever after, for heroes tend to bungle their relationships by choosing poorly, mistreating the woman, and undermining their own efforts. These catastrophic relationships, Jungians suggest, represent the hero's failure. For regardless of whether the female represents an external figure or an aspect of self, the hero who does not come to terms with the feminine never completes the journey.

12. Wallace Stevens's Hero

The poet Wallace Stevens (1879–1955) had a famous double career. He studied at Harvard, toiled briefly and unhappily at the *New York Herald Tribune,* graduated from law school, married, became a father, and in 1916 went to work for the Hartford Accident and Indemnity Company, where he remained until his death. *Harmonium,* his first volume of poems, sold fewer than a hundred copies when it was published in 1923, but his reputation rose steadily. In the last year of his life, Stevens won both the National Book Award (for the second time) and the Pulitzer prize for poetry. Yet some of his colleagues in the insurance business never knew that his greatest triumphs were literary.

Though Stevens was rumored to have converted to Catholicism on his deathbed, throughout his life he found a more reliable source of solace and inspiration in the imagination. He considered it the ultimate human facility, equivalent to, and therefore capable of replacing, God. But if God was replaceable, the idea of the hero was not. "Unless we believe in the hero, what is there/To believe?" he wrote. In Stevens's conception, the hero was an ideal and an abstraction. Nothing so small as a symbol of self or a role model, the hero was never a specific person. As he wrote in his journal, "No man is a hero to anyone that knows him." Even acknowledged heroes, the great liberators who are honored with marble statues in civic gardens, only hint at the ideals and concept of heroism.

Heroism, he believed, is a way of living without self-consciousness, without doubt, without paralysis. In the life of the hero, intention and action are one because the hero, unlike the rest of us, is not of two minds about anything. His purity makes him splendid, distant, and cold, like "winter's iciest core, a north star." At the same time, the hero has an ordinary aspect ("Make him of mud,/for every day"). Stevens felt that two types of human beings hint at his existence: the poet, "the ten-foot poet among inchlings," who traffics in the imagination, and the common man. In the midst of World War Two, Stevens wrote, "The common man is the common hero./The common hero is the hero." In that statement, he captured the spirit of the age.

13. Joseph Campbell's Hero

Among Jung's many followers, the most influential has surely been Joseph Campbell (who, proving that Freud wasn't wrong when he spoke about killing the father, denied he was a Jungian). In his 1949 opus, *The Hero with a Thousand Faces,* Campbell used myths from around the world to trace the hero's prototypical adventure, a story so universal that, taking a term from James Joyce, he called it a "monomyth." Throughout his life, he pursued that idea, finding similarities and parallels in virtually every mythology. The underlying unity of all mythologies was his great theme, and the role of the hero was its leitmotif. In his view, the challenge facing the individual is to discover the unrecognized parts of the personality by taking what he called the hero's journey. To undertake that journey, the hero must withdraw from the external, everyday world and enter the raw wilderness of the psyche. Myth—virtually any myth—provides the map to that territory.

The hero's journey begins with a call to adventure, perhaps through an event that occurs as if by chance. Although our hero—Campbell was ambivalent as to whether the hero could be female—may initially resist the call, eventually he must respond. To do so means stepping into the unknown. Soon he is in deep trouble, like Jonah in the whale. His task is to escape from that dark place. This episode, which Campbell called "the Belly of the Whale," represents the shedding of the old self and the emergence of the new.

Next, the hero finds himself trudging along the Road of Trials. He confronts his enemies, slays the dragon, travels to the underworld, and achieves a sacred union with the goddess, a triumphant act which symbolizes love, self-knowledge, and the integration of the masculine and feminine aspects of the self. Afterwards, he receives a boon. Jason retrieves the Golden Fleece; Psyche finds love and equality; and the African hero Mwindo receives compassion, knowledge, and a set of laws to live by.

> *We do not like some things and the hero doesn't;*
>   *deviating head-stones,*
>   *and uncertainty;*
>   *going where one does not wish*
>   *to go; suffering and not*
>   *saying so; standing and listening where something*
>   *is hiding. The hero shrinks*
> *as what it is flies out on muffled wings . . .*
>
> —Marianne Moore, "The Hero"

Along the way, the hero faces opposition, is occasionally blocked, and is sometimes unwilling to take a step (because, as George Bernard Shaw pointed out, "You cannot be a hero without being a coward"). Yet he forges ahead and in the end, like Odysseus reuniting with Penelope, achieves his goal and returns to ordinary life.

In the great myths, the adventures are external, even when they involve such metaphorical spelunkings as the voyage into the underworld. In the experiences of average human beings, Campbell asserts, the hero's journey provides a handy allegory for a life or a chapter thereof. Whether the journey begins voluntarily or under duress (as is more likely), the hero must confront danger, grapple with loss, exile, uncertainty and stupidity, venture into the labyrinth, underworld, cave or lion's den and, ideally, do it with panache.

Like any good metaphor, the hero's journey resists simplification, and there is hardly a myth in existence that conforms to every aspect of the pattern. Yet Campbell was convinced not only of the utility of the concept but also of its miraculous ability to heal. As the scholar Robert A. Segal has pointed out, Carl Jung saw therapy and mythology as complementary, whereas for Campbell, mythology was so illuminating that it eliminated the need for therapy.

After the publication of *The Hero with a Thousand Faces,* Campbell's fame grew. By the 1980s, he was appearing with such emblematic figures as Robert Bly and the Grateful Dead, and "the hero's journey" had become a common phrase, overheard in coffee shops, discussed in screen-writing seminars, glimpsed in the names of gift shops in New York and bicycle shops in New Delhi, and invoked in therapy sessions from coast to coast. His celebrity went stratospheric in 1987, the year of his death (on Halloween), when a series of PBS interviews with Bill Moyers assured his iconic status. Yet despite his wide-ranging erudition, his many awards, his years as a professor at Sarah Lawrence, and his ability to charm, scholars of mythology don't seem to like him.

They have accused Campbell of shoddy scholarship, fuzzy thinking, and—in the words of the mythologist Wendy Doniger—turning the great myths of all time "into easy-listening religion, Muzak mythology." He has been criticized for hopping from one hero to another, for focusing on the similarities between stories and ignoring the differences, for not being sufficiently knowledgeable about languages, for devoting too little attention to Greece and Rome, for being sexist, racist, anti-Catholic, anti-Indian, and anti-Semitic. (It's hard to say whether this last criticism, oft repeated, was deserved, but there's no doubt that he was tone deaf. He spoke disparagingly of the Old Testament God and asserted that whereas Mohammed, Jesus, and Buddha were universal heroes with "a message for the entire world," Moses, like Tezcatlipoca, was merely a tribal hero with a localized message: the Ten Commandments, presumably.)

Nonetheless, Campbell's popularity was immense. As he grew more celebrated and assumed the role of sage, he became increasingly convinced that mythology can teach us how to navigate through times of crisis and, more broadly, how to live. Though a scholar and an academic, he didn't put his faith in intellectual analysis. "Myths don't count if they're just hitting your rational faculties— they have to hit the heart," he said. "You have to absorb them and adjust to them and make them your life." He saw mythology as entirely relevant, a subject to be embraced with passion, and he brought it alive for others. As he famously wrote in *The Hero with a Thousand Faces*, "The latest incarnation of Oedipus, the continued romance of Beauty and the Beast, stand this afternoon on the corner of Forty-second Street and Fifth Avenue, waiting for the traffic light to change." In that recognition lies the secret of his success.

Gilgamesh

A hero is mortal, and therein lies the problem. Human beings, no matter how extraordinary, must sooner or later tangle with the prospect of death, which is why the round trip to the underworld is one of the set pieces of mythology. Yet in most of those stories, fear of death goes unmentioned. The hero descends into the underworld for love, like Orpheus; on a lark, like Theseus; for advice, like Odysseus (who meets his mother's spirit in the House of Death and tries three times to embrace her). Only Gilgamesh, the oldest hero and the most intensely human, goes in search of immortality and for the most basic reason: he is afraid to die. His attempt to conquer his fears (and to share immortality with others) makes him a hero for the ages.

Gilgamesh and a lion from an eighth-century BCE relief.

Gilgamesh was a real Sumerian king who lived in Uruk around 2,600 BCE and was celebrated for surrounding the city with a spectacular, copper-colored wall. His story, embellished into myth, was known throughout the Mesopotamian world. In the seventh century BCE, an Assyrian translation, written in cuneiform script, was stored in the library of Assurbanipal in Nineveh. When that city was decimated in 612 BCE, the library was buried and the story of Gilgamesh gradually vanished from human memory. It reappeared in 1853, when archaeologists unearthed the clay tablets among the ruins of the library. The first English translation was published in 1928.

Gilgamesh and Enkidu

The son of the goddess Ninsun and the king/god Lugalbanda, Gilgamesh was two-thirds god and one-third man. A beautiful man with a perfect body, he was also a tyrant who insisted on his right to sleep with all the local virgins. The people complained to Anu, the god of Uruk, who turned to Aruru, the mother of the gods, and asked her to create a rival for Gilgamesh.

Aruru dipped her hands in water, pinched off a glob of clay, and threw it into the distant country. When it landed, it turned into a wild man named Enkidu, "offspring of silence." Covered with long, matted hair, Enkidu ate with the gazelles, drank with the cattle at the watering hole, and knew nothing of civilization—until a priestess, "a wanton from the temple of love," spent a week with him. After that, the tablets tell us, he thought like a man, the taint of civilization was upon him, and the animals bolted away from him.

Not long afterwards, Enkidu and Gilgamesh met and fought. Gilgamesh triumphed, Enkidu acceded to his superiority, and the two became best friends. They talked about everything. One night Gilgamesh had a dream in which Enlil, the father of the gods, decreed his fate. When he told his friend about it, Enkidu had a ready interpretation. He said it meant that Gilgamesh had been given kingship, not eternal life. "Everlasting life is not your destiny," Enkidu said, and he began to cry. Gilgamesh decided that, under the circumstances, he'd better do something to assure that his name would be known to future generations.

With that in mind, Gilgamesh and Enkidu killed the monster Humbaba. Afterward, the goddess Ishtar wanted to marry Gilgamesh. When he rejected her, pointing out that all her previous lovers had come to a wretched end, she was insulted. Seeking revenge, she sent the Bull of Heaven to destroy Gilgamesh.

The bull was so powerful that on his first snort fissures opened in the earth and a hundred young men fell down dead. On his second snort, cracks crisscrossed the land and two hundred men died. On the third snort, Enkidu literally seized the bull by the horns. The bull spat in his face and lashed him with its tail, but Enkidu held on and Gilgamesh thrust his sword between the neck and the horns. When the bull was dead, they cut out its heart and presented it to Shamash, the god of the sun. Gilgamesh took the horns himself, and there were feasts throughout the city.

That night, Enkidu had a nightmare in which the gods decreed that because Enkidu and Gilgamesh had killed Humbaba and the Bull of Heaven, one of them must die. Enkidu knew that he would be the one.

Weeping, he cursed everyone who had brought him to this state, including the priestess who had civilized him. Shamash came to her defense, arguing that she had taught him many things and given him Gilgamesh as a companion. Enkidu took back the curses and blessed the woman instead.

Soon he began to feel ill, and the nightmares continued. In his sleep, he encountered a bird-man with the legs of a lion, the talons of an eagle, and the face of a vampire. The bird-man led him into the underworld, a place of total darkness where everyone ate dust and clay. "We must treasure the dream whatever the terror," Gilgamesh told him. He knew that the signs were ominous.

For twelve days Enkidu lay sick in bed, denied the death of a warrior. "Happy is the man who falls in battle," he said, "for I must die in shame." When he finally died, Gilgamesh wept for seven days and nights and commanded that a statue of gold and lapis lazuli be made of Enkidu. Then he began to wander in the wilderness.

The Search for Immortality

Grieving and afraid of death, Gilgamesh came to the twin-peaked mountain Mashu, which was guarded by Scorpion men. He told them that he wished to question Utnapishtim, another Sumerian king, who had survived the primordial flood and was the only man ever to be granted eternal life.

No one else, the Scorpion men said, had ever attempted such a feat. To reach Utnapishtim, Gilgamesh would have to walk through a pitch-dark tunnel that burrowed for twelve leagues (about thirty-six miles) beneath the mountain. Without hesitation, Gilgamesh stepped into the tunnel. After striding for nine leagues through darkness, he felt the north wind brush across his face and he saw the light of dawn seep into the tunnel. By the time he traveled the full twelve leagues, the sun shone brightly.

Emerging from the tunnel, he found a garden dripping with leaves of lapis lazuli and blossoms of hematite, agate, carnelian, and pearls. As he strolled through this paradise, Shamash called out, "You will never find the life for which you are searching." Gilgamesh was undeterred.

The Woman of the Vine and the Ferryman

In the garden, Gilgamesh met a young woman named Siduri, a winemaker who was sitting with a golden bowl in her lap and a veil draped over her head. She noticed his forbidding demeanor and moved to bar the gate but Gilgamesh stopped it with his foot and told her his story. He was afraid of death, he said, because of what happened to Enkidu, and so he was seeking eternal life.

Echoing the sentiments of Enkidu and Shamash, she repeated that his search was futile, for the gods reserved immortality for themselves. Instead of worrying about death, she told him, he should enjoy life. "Fill your belly with good things; day and night, night and day, dance and be merry, feast and rejoice. Let your clothes be fresh, bathe yourself in water, cherish the little child that holds your hand, and make your wife happy in your embrace; for this too is the lot of man."

Not content with that advice, Gilgamesh said that he still wanted to talk to Utnapishtim, who lived across the waters of death. Siduri instructed him to go see the ferryman, Urshanabi.

Gilgamesh found Urshanabi in the woods fashioning the prow of the boat amidst his sacred stones. Rather than trying to present his case, Gilgamesh grabbed his axe and dagger, attacked the ship, and shattered the stones. Urshanabi advised him that he had done his cause serious damage, for now they couldn't sail across the sea. To get across, he said, Gilgamesh would have to chop down 120 trees, prepare 120 long poles, and use them one by one to push the ship across the water, being careful not to get his hands wet. Gilgamesh did as he was told. When he had used all the poles, he held his arms up for a mast and used his discarded clothing as sails. And so he crossed the waters of death and came face to face with Utnapishtim.

Utnapishtim's Test

Although Utnapishtim was immortal, his message was the same as everyone else's. He said that the judges of the dead and the mother of destinies allotted everyone their fate but did not disclose the day of death. He also suggested that if Gilgamesh really wanted to be immortal, he should practice. Start by spurning sleep, he said. Test yourself by staying awake for six days and seven nights. Yet even as he spoke, Gilgamesh grew tired, and "a mist of sleep like soft wool teased from the fleece drifted over him."

Utnapishtim knew that, upon awakening, Gilgamesh would pretend that he hadn't slept. So he told his wife to bake a loaf of bread every day. After a week, Utnapishtim woke him up. As predicted, Gilgamesh put on a good show. But the circumstantial evidence at his side—seven loaves of bread, which ranged from fresh and soft to stale and rock hard—spoke the truth. Despite being two-thirds god, Gilgamesh was so mortal that he couldn't stave off sleep, let alone death.

The Old Men Are Young Again

Utnapishtim told Gilgamesh to wash up, discard the skins he was wearing, and put on a set of new clothes which magically would look fresh until his journey was over. Just as he was about to depart, Utnapishtim's wife suggested that he give Gilgamesh something else to take back with him. So Utnapishtim revealed a secret. He told him about a thorny underwater plant which could restore youth.

Gilgamesh tied two stones to his feet, jumped into the water, and sank to the bottom. On the ocean floor, he found what he was looking for, cut the ropes which held the stones to his feet, and floated up, plant in hand. He named it "The Old Men Are Young Again" and planned to share it with all the old men of Uruk. But when he stopped at a well to bathe, a serpent slithered out of the water and snatched the plant away. The snake shed its skin and regained its youth while Gilgamesh, despite all his efforts, had nothing. Several days later, he arrived empty-handed in Uruk, where he had this story engraved on stone tablets.

A powerful king who won many battles, Gilgamesh had a wife, a concubine, a son, and many servants, including musicians and a jester. When he died, tearful laments swept across the city, and the people made offerings to the gods. But Gilgamesh, who sought the secret of immortality, was dead in his tomb. Everlasting life was not his destiny.

Perseus and the Medusa: The Hero's Task

The prototypical hero's journey begins before birth and features at least one defining challenge. Gilgamesh found the watercress of youth; Moses received the Ten Commandments; and Perseus sliced off the head of the Medusa, the single most memorable image in all of Greek mythology.

Before Perseus was conceived, an oracle told his grandfather, Acrisius, that one day his grandson, not yet born, would kill him. Hoping to avoid his fate, Acrisius imprisoned his daughter Danaë in a tower. But Zeus slipped into the tower in the form of a shower of gold and soon she was pregnant. After the baby was born, Acrisius locked Danaë and her son into a wooden trunk and threw it into the sea. It washed ashore on the island of Seriphos, where Perseus and his mother were rescued by a man named Dictys ("net" in Greek).

Dictys was kind to Perseus and his mother. But when Perseus grew up, King Polydectes, the brother of Dictys, announced that he wished to marry Danaë, despite her distaste for the idea. When

Perseus leaped to his mother's defense, Polydectes mockingly made him an offer: if Perseus presented him with the head of the Medusa, a virtually impossible task, he would accept Danaë's refusal. So the adventure began.

Medusa was one of three sisters known as the Gorgons. Once a beautiful woman, she made the mistake of sleeping with Poseidon in Athena's temple. Athena, a virgin goddess, reacted angrily. She turned Medusa into a monster with a mass of coiling serpents for hair and a gaze so lethal that it could turn men to stone. To glance at Medusa, however fleetingly, meant death.

Although it wasn't easy to find the Medusa, Perseus, like other heroes, had the gods on his side. They directed him to the mountain of Atlas, where he asked the three weird sisters called the Graiae to direct him to Medusa's lair. The Griaea, who possessed only a single tooth and a single eye among them, refused to divulge the whereabouts of the Gorgons. Perseus had to do something. So as they passed the eye back and forth, he grabbed it. Without their eye, they were helpless. Soon Perseus had the information he needed.

The gods also helped him with gifts. Hermes gave him a sword and a pair of winged sandals, Hades loaned him a cap of invisibility, the Graces donated a magic bag or wallet, and Athena gave him a polished shield and told him to use it as a mirror. This last item was fundamental, for it enabled Perseus to approach Medusa without looking directly at her.

The Head of Medusa as shown on a Roman cameo.

While gazing at her reflection in the shield, he sliced off her head with his sickle and popped it into the bag. As the blood spurted from her neck, it gave birth to two sons of Poseidon: a warrior named Chrysaor and the winged horse Pegasus. Perseus mounted Pegasus and headed back to Seriphos.

On the way, he chanced to see a beautiful young woman chained to a rock. It was Andromeda, whose parents, Cepheus and Cassiopeia, had been forced to sacrifice her to the sea monster Cetus. Once again, a glance was enough. Perseus fell in love on the spot. He pulled Medusa's snaky head from the magic bag and brandished it in front of the sea monster, thereby petrifying it. Then he released Andromeda and married her.

When he returned to Seriphos, he continued to use Medusa's head. He confronted King Polydectes, waved the head in front of him, and turned him to stone. Perseus also used the head on one other occasion: he showed it to Atlas, who was exhausted from holding up the heavens. Atlas gaped at it for only a moment but that was sufficient. His body turned to stone and became the mountain that bears his name. Finally Perseus gave the head of the Medusa to Athena, who affixed it to her shield.

With Andromeda by his side, Perseus became ruler of Tiryns and the founder of Mycenae. But he could not avoid his fate any more than his grandfather could. One day, while participating in a discus-throwing contest, he lost control of the discus, which spun into the stands and fractured the foot of Acrisius, thereby killing him. The prophecy was fulfilled.

On the Medusa

Of the many people who have explored the meaning of the Medusa, none deserve more attention than Sigmund Freud, who recognized immediately that anything that could turn men to stone had sexual implications. However, those implications were confusing at best. Writing in 1922, he suggested that Medusa's head represents the genitals of the mother, the terrifying sight of which proves to little boys that some people don't have a penis; thus, fear of the Medusa represents fear of castration. Paradoxically, the Medusa's snaky locks also "represent the penis, the absence of which is the cause of the horror." Thus the image, which symbolizes both the presence and the absence of the penis, is at once frightening and reassuring, accounting, perhaps, for its perennial allure.

Jungians see the Medusa (and the Minotaur) as a shadow projection, a dark image of the despised portion of the self. In life, that rejected aspect of the self must be incorporated into consciousness. Perseus, however, has no intention of doing that. When he decapitates the Medusa, he pops the horrifying head into his magic bag, which functions as a symbol of repression. Even so, he can't forget about it and he uses the head repeatedly. Finally he gets rid of it entirely by giving it to Athena. She turns it into a public statement, affixing it to her shield as a symbol of protection, wrath, and the underside of the self.

Ultimately, according to the philosopher Jacques Derrida, it is even more than that. The Medusa, he writes, is that core element of the self without which there is no self. The act of confronting the Medusa, however petrifying, makes a person whole. To gaze at the Medusa and to be transformed by the experience is the hero's task, the task of a lifetime. "How can one be Medusa to oneself?" Derrida asks. "One has to understand the he is not himself before being Medusa to himself. He occurs to himself since the Medusa. To be oneself is to-be-Medusa'd . . ."

MAY SARTON ON MEDUSA

. . . I turn your face around! It is my face.
That frozen rage is what I must explore—
Oh secret, self-enclosed, and ravaged place!
This is the gift I thank Medusa for.

—from "The Muse as Medusa"

Heracles

Once worshipped as a savior, Heracles had godlike strength, a violent temper, exuberant appetites (he was partial to roasted meat and barley cakes), and the full range of human emotions, including remorse, compassion, despair, self-criticism, and love. He suffered greatly but his deeds of derring-do made him the most important of the Greek heroes.

What motivated him? All credit goes to Hera, whose enmity toward Heracles did not exhaust itself until after his death. Many scholars believe that in the primordial past, Heracles, whose name means "Hera's glory," was her mate. Yet in the picaresque adventures that have come down to us, she hounds him continually.

Heracles's mother was Alcmene, who unknowingly mated with Zeus when he appeared in her bedroom disguised as her husband, Amphitryon. After Heracles was born, Zeus (or Athena) tricked Hera into nursing him. A mouthful of mother's milk gave Heracles his godlike powers, but he sucked so hard on Hera's breast that she pushed him away and her milk spurted across the sky, creating the Milky Way (an event depicted in paintings by Tintoretto and Rubens).

As Heracles grew, he was tutored in archery, chariot-driving, the military arts, literature, astronomy, philosophy, and music, which in a roundabout way caused him to commit his first murder. One day, his music teacher Eumolpus, who instructed him on the lyre, was unavailable and a replacement was required. Heracles's literature tutor, Linus, volunteered for the job. Like every substitute teacher, he encountered resistance. Heracles was so defiant that Linus hit him, whereupon Heracles bashed him with the lyre and killed him. He was tried for murder and acquitted on the grounds of self-defense. Nonetheless, Amphitryon decided that this boy was trouble. He sent him to a cattle ranch near Thebes, where he remained until he was eighteen years old. Hera bided her time.

In Thebes, Heracles met Thespius, who encouraged Heracles to sleep with his fifty daughters, an event which took place either over a fifty-night period or, as Pausanias tells it, in a single amazing night. In exchange, Heracles killed a lion.

He also got involved in a dispute between Erginus, king of the Minyans, and King Creon of Thebes, who owed Erginus, as tribute, a hundred head of cattle. On the way to collecting the cattle, the emissaries of Erginus ran into Heracles and scornfully told him that Erginus could also have demanded the ears, nose, and hands of all the men of Thebes. Heracles, never one to negotiate, cut off the ears, noses, and hands of the envoys, strung them around their necks, and sent them home.

In the battle that ensued, Heracles helped the Thebans defeat the Minyans. In gratitude, Creon offered Heracles his daughter Megara in marriage. The happy couple soon had three sons.

Then one day, Hera struck. Out of nowhere, Heracles went dizzyingly mad. He grabbed his weapons and let fly a volley of arrows. In a matter of minutes, his sons were dead, along with a few of his nephews, and, some say, his wife Megara.

The Labors of Heracles

Heracles fell into dark despair. To purify himself, he went to the Delphic Oracle, where he was told to serve King Eurystheus of Tiryns as a slave for twelve years. During this period of atonement, Eurystheus ordered him to perform a series of tasks known as the twelve labors. Mythology being what it is, there is disagreement as to precisely what those labors were. Most commentators accept the following episodes:

1. The Nemean Lion

Hera sent a lion to Nemea for the express purpose of attacking Heracles. Its impenetrable hide made it invulnerable to arrows. Heracles killed it using his bare hands and his olive-wood club. After he skinned it and draped the fur over his shoulders as a cloak, the pelt became his most recognizable artistic attribute. When he returned to Tiryns and threw it on the floor in front of Eurystheus, the king was so frightened that he vaulted into a bronze jar.

As for the lion, it became the constellation Leo, one of the most easily recognized formations in the sky.

2. The Hydra of Lerna

A many-headed poisonous snake with the body of a hound, the Hydra was the sister of the infernal dog Cerberus, and it almost defeated Heracles. Each time he sliced off one of its heads, another one popped up from the bloody stump. Heracles was making no progress, and after Hera sent a giant crab to nip at its heels, the battle became even more daunting. Fortunately, Heracles's nephew Iolaus showed up with a brilliant plan: Using a red-hot brand, he kept the Hydra's heads from growing back by cauterizing every cut. When the Hydra was nothing but a mass of stumps, with its one immortal head buried deep beneath a rock, Heracles dipped his arrows into the animal's poisonous blood, rendering any wounds they might create incurable.

In recognition of their efforts, Hera raised the Hydra and the crab into the sky. The Hydra became the biggest constellation in the sky. Cancer the Crab, which failed to prevent Heracles from killing the Hydra, became one of the faintest.

3. The Cerynitian Hind

Capturing this golden-antlered deer wasn't difficult. but it was sacred to Artemis and tracking it down was a challenge. Heracles pursued it for an entire year. He finally cornered it up north, in the land of the Hyperboreans, where he simply trapped the animal in a net.

4. The Erymanthian Boar

Once again, capturing the boar wasn't difficult, despite the creature's size; Heracles drove it into a snowdrift and caught it in his net. The real problem, for which he was to pay later on, developed while he was tracking the boar. He stopped to share some wine with the centaur Pholus, but the scent attracted the other centaurs and they ended up in a drunken brawl. During the fighting, Heracles killed several of them with his poisonous arrows, including his friend Pholus, who dropped an arrow on his foot and succumbed to the venom. The centaur Nessus escaped—with dire consequences.

Between 1841 and 1843, Honoré Daumier published a series of lithographs that presented the ancients, both mythological and historical, as no more noble than the French politicians he habitually mocked. In this lithograph, a stout, middle-aged Heracles ("un héros superbe") pauses as he cleans out the Augean stables.

5. The Augean Stables

Heracles was given a single day in which to clean the immense stables of King Augeas, the son of Helios, the sun god—a seemingly impossible task. In one of his more spectacular solutions, he accomplished it by punching holes in the sides of the stable and diverting the river Alpheus so that it flowed right through the stables, cleaning them overnight.

6. The Stymphalian Birds

The Arcadians who lived near Lake Stymphalian had been plagued by vicious birds. Their droppings were lethal to crops; their metal-tipped feathers, whether spiraling through the air or lying on the ground, were a hazard; and worst of all, they devoured both animals and people. Heracles got rid of them easily. He shook a bronze rattle so hard that the trees trembled and the birds fluttered out of their nests and into the sky. Heracles shot some of them with his poison arrows and scared the rest away.

7. The Cretan Bull

The Cretan bull was not just any animal. Its white coat was so beautiful that Pasiphaë, the wife of King Minos, fell in love with it and mated with it. Thus the Cretan bull became the father of the Minotaur. Heracles captured it alive, showed it to Eurystheus, and released it.

8. The Mares of Diomedes

Diomedes, king of the Bistonians, had four vicious horses which he kept in chains and fed with human flesh. Heracles tried to drive these horses into the sea, but the Bistonians attacked him. In the melee that followed, Heracles killed Diomedes and fed him to his own horses, which calmed them down considerably and enabled Heracles to herd them back to King Eurystheus. Later, while grazing on Mount Olympus, the horses were devoured by wild animals.

9. The Amazon's Girdle

Eurystheus loved his daughter Admete so much that he asked Heracles to bring her the girdle (or sash) of Hippolyta, queen of the

Amazons. Heracles gathered many companions, including his friend Theseus, and sailed off to the land of the Amazons. Hera, who expected the Amazons to resist, hoped that Heracles would fail to obtain the garment. To her surprise, when Heracles asked Hippolyta for it, the Amazon queen was happy to oblige. The ease of the exchange made Hera so angry that she turned into an Amazon herself and provoked the others into a furious attack on Heracles. Certain that Hippolyta had betrayed him, Heracles, ever the hothead, killed her.

Many adventures later, Heracles presented the girdle to Eurystheus, who didn't give it to his daughter after all. Instead, he brought it as an offering to Hera's temple at Argos.

10. The Cattle of Geryon

Eursystheus demanded that Heracles round up the cattle of the three-headed monster Geryon, who lived with a giant herdsman and a two-headed dog on an island so far west that it was close to Spain and Hades. To get there Heracles went first to Libya, where he found the heat so oppressive that he aimed a few arrows at Helios, the sun god. Surprisingly, this worked to his advantage. To reward Heracles for his courage, Helios lent him the golden bowl in which he sailed every night on his journey beneath the Ocean. Heracles climbed into the bowl, spun past the Straits of Gibraltar, and reached the island where Geryon guarded his flock. After clubbing the two-headed dog and the herdsman to death, Heracles finished Geryon off with his bow and arrows and drove the cattle into the bowl.

On the trip back to Tiryns, he had many adventures. He was robbed by Echidna, a serpent-tailed woman; afterwards, according to Herodotus, he dallied with her long enough to have three sons. He established his own cult, built a road along the coast, swam to Sicily in pursuit of a bull, and killed the king of that island in a wrestling match. He was just about ready to deliver the cattle of Geryon to King Ehyrstheus when Hera sent down a gadfly which caused the animals to scatter in all directions. Heracles chased after the cattle, corralled them, and presented them to Eurystheus, who sacrificed them to Hera.

11. The Golden Apples of the Hesperides

A wedding gift from Gaia to Zeus and Hera, the golden apples of the Hesperides grew on a magical tree in the garden of the gods, where they were guarded by a dragon and three nymphs called the Hesperides. After Eurystheus ordered Heracles to bring him these fruits, our hero took the advice of Prometheus and sought help from Atlas, the father of the Hesperides.

Atlas was happy to help. He said that, if Heracles would hold up the sky while he was gone, he would go to the garden and retrieve the apples from his daughters. Heracles agreed, and Atlas handed over the heavy burden. When he returned with the apples in hand, Atlas realized that he didn't want to carry the heavens on his shoulders

Atlas holds up the sky in this eighteenth-century engraving.

any more. He announced that he would bring the apples to Eurystheus, and Heracles would just have to continue holding up the sky. Heracles, smarter than Atlas, reluctantly assented. But he wondered if Atlas, as a favor, might assume the burden for just a moment so that Heracles could put some padding around his head. Atlas fell for the trick and took back the sky. Heracles brought the apples to Eurystheus. The king presented them to Athena, who spirited them back to the garden of the gods from whence they came.

12. The Descent to the Underworld

The last labor was the most challenging, for this time Heracles had to descend into Hades. His assignment: to steal the three-headed guard dog Cerberus, whose duty was to make sure that no one escaped from the underworld.

To gain entrance to the underworld, Heracles was initiated into the Eleusinian Mysteries, making him the only known murderer to receive the rites of Persephone. Accompanied by Athena and Hermes, he crossed the River Styx and proceeded to fight with the lord of death himself. Strangely, Hades wasn't a formidable opponent. Heracles wounded him so grievously that Hades had to leave the underworld and go to Olympus in search of a cure. In his weakened state, Hades promised that, if Heracles could catch the infernal canine without using a weapon, he could borrow him.

But first, Heracles freed Theseus, who had spent several years stuck to a chair in the underworld. He also fell into conversation with Meleager, whose untimely death (see page 209) made Heracles so sad that for the only time in his life, he cried. His feelings were so strong that he offered to marry Meleager's young sister, Deianira. Then he turned his attention to Cerberus, tied him up and dragged him out of the underworld. Thus Heracles completed his service to Eurystheus.

After accomplishing these tasks, Heracles divorced Megara (assuming he hadn't killed her earlier) and married Deianira. But his troubles weren't over. On the journey back to Tiryns, they had to cross the River Evenus. There they encountered the centaur Nessus, who had escaped the melee that broke out during Heracles' attempt to capture the Erymanthian Boar. Nessus carried Deianira across the water and when they reached the other side, he tried to rape her. When Heracles realized what was happening, he drew one of his poisoned arrows and shot the centaur. As he lay dying, Nessus whispered to Deianira that by collecting his blood, she could prevent Heracles from loving another woman. Deianira gratefully wiped up the blood and put it away for safekeeping.

The centaur Nessus.

In time, Heracles abandoned Deianira and went off in pursuit of Iole. Yet even after he won an archery contest, Iole's father refused to let the match take place. So Heracles returned to Deianira. Not long afterwards, Iole's brother Iphitus came to Tiryns in search of his lost cattle. In a fit of anger, Heracles threw him off the thick stone walls surrounding the city. This was such a gratuitous act that Heracles felt he needed to purify himself. He asked Neleus, the king

of Pylos, for help. Neleus refused, whereupon Heracles killed eleven of his twelve
sons, including one who took the form of
a bee.

Next, he sought advice from the Delphic Oracle. Even on that sacred site, his
out-of-control behavior continued to get
him in trouble. He tried to steal the holy
tripod and might have succeeded except
that Apollo wrestled with him and Zeus
threw down one of his thunderbolts.
When he spoke with the Oracle, the

Heracles, raising his club, wres-
tles with Apollo for the tripod.
(Credit: Hannah Berman.)

priestess instructed him to spend another year in servitude, this time
to Omphale, the queen of Lydia. She became his lover and also
switched clothes with him, donning his lion-skin while he wore
women's clothes and was forced to do women's work.

At the end of the year Heracles returned home, calmer but
no wiser than before, his interest in Iole undiminished. In despair,
Deianira remembered the blood she had been saving for just
such an occasion. She took a robe which Heracles was planning
to wear during a ritual sacrifice and dipped it into the blood.
Heracles put it on and stood by the fire where the meat was roasting. As the heat of the fire warmed the blood-soaked robe, his skin
began to burn. Soon the pain was so agonizing that Heracles
beseeched the others to build his funeral pyre. Then he leaped
into the flames and died. Grief-stricken and remorseful, Deianira
stabbed herself.

And so Heracles ascended to snowy Mount Olympus, where he
and Hera patched up their differences. He married Hebe, Hera's
daughter, and was awarded with eternal life in the company of the
gods. So was he a god or
was he a hero? Even the
ancients weren't sure—
especially on the island of
Kos, where worshippers
of Heracles honored him
twice: once in the evening

> *Let Hercules himself do what he may,*
> *The cat will mew and dog will have*
> *his day.*
>
> —William Shakespeare, *Hamlet*

with a sheep, the usual sacrifice accorded a hero, and again the next
morning with a bull, an offering fit for a god.

Heracles Helps Out: Another Round Trip to the Underworld

King Admetus was young, but the fates had almost finished spinning the thread of his life. Unlike most people in that sad position, he had reason to believe that he might be able to circumvent fate and change the time of his death. His hopes dated back to his wedding day, which Artemis had almost ruined by filling his marriage bed with a mass of snakes. Horrified, Admetus realized that he had failed to perform the proper rituals and he conducted the ceremonies posthaste. Artemis forgave him and, to make up for the snakes, she promised that he could delay the moment of his death under one condition: he had to find someone else to take his place.

It wasn't as easy as he had imagined. When Admetus was summoned to Hades, he discovered that not even his aged parents would agree to die before their time. Only one person stepped forward: his devoted wife Alcestis, who took poison and died.

That night, who should drop by but Heracles, in need of a place to stay. Reluctant to tell the great hero what had transpired, Admetus allowed Heracles to believe that the household was grieving for a stranger. Heracles was embarrassed when the learned the truth, because he had failed to note the king's deep state of mourning and hence abused the hospitality of a friend. To atone for his mistake, he traveled to the sunless palace of Persephone, wrestled with Death, and, against all expectations, succeeded in returning to the land of the living with Alcestis.

Jean-Paul Sartre found nothing to admire in this tale of a self-sacrificing woman devoted to a man who wouldn't even admit that he was in mourning for her. He saw it as we might—as the story of an unreasonable husband and an abused wife. "If I wrote on this theme as an illustration of the husband-wife relationship," he wrote, "my version would imply the whole story of female emancipation."

Jason and the Golden Fleece

There are times when all children feel unrecognized, alienated, and alone. Heroes don't have to wonder why, like Oedipus, Moses, and Harry Potter, they are often raised by strangers. But sooner or later, they must claim their birthright. For Jason, who was sent away at birth and educated by the centaur Chiron, that moment arrived when he was twenty years old and decided to return to Iolcus, where his father Aeson was king. Or so he had been told.

Along the way, Jason encountered an old woman—Hera in disguise—and carried her across a river, losing a sandal in the process but gaining the assistance of the goddess. In Iolcus, he dis-

BACKSTORY: THE GOLDEN FLEECE

King Athamas of Boetia married several times. His first wife was Nephele. His second wife was Ino, who contrived to get rid of her stepchildren, Phrixus and Helle. First she ruined the harvest by roasting the seeds, as a result of which the grain didn't sprout and famine swept across the region. Then, when Athamas sent a representative to Delphi in search of advice, Ino bribed the messenger to falsify the report. Arthamas was told that the gods wished him to sacrifice his son, Phrixus.

Like Abraham and Agamemnon, who also agreed to sacrifice their children, Athamas prepared to follow the will of the gods. Just as he was about to cut his son's throat, Nephele swept down from the sky, scooped up both her children, and planted them on a golden ram she had received from Hermes. The ram soared into the sky. When it flew over the straits where Europe meets Asia Minor, Helle lost her grip and tumbled into the water. The Hellespont was named in her honor. Phrixus held on, landing in Colchis on the edge of the Black Sea. He sacrificed the ram to Zeus and gave its fleece to King Aeetes, who nailed it to an oak tree in a sacred grove. There it remained, guarded by a dragon that never slept, until Jason retrieved it.

covered that his uncle Pelias had overthrown his father. Pelias wore the crown nervously, though, for he had visited the Delphic Oracle and been warned to beware of a man with one shoe. When Jason showed up partially shod and demanded to be king, Pelias knew that his demise was certain. To postpone the inevitable, he promised to grant Jason the throne in exchange for the Golden Fleece. Jason set about making preparations. He obtained a ship, the fifty-oared Argo, and assembled a crew. Though reports naming the Argonauts vary, sooner or later virtually every Greek hero made the list.

The Women of Lemnos

The Argo's first stop was Lemnos, an island once populated by women who had foolishly ignored the rites of Aphrodite. To punish them, she made them exude a stench so foul that the men turned away in disgust and took up with the women of neighboring Thrace. Scorned, the Lemnian women murdered all the males on the island. Only one escaped—King Thoas, whose loyal daughter Hypsipyle stuffed him into a trunk and sent him off to sea.

Fortunately, by the time Jason arrived on the island, the stench

ANOTHER MALODOROUS EVENT ON LEMNOS

Philoctetes was a famous warrior and expert marksman. During the Trojan War, he sailed with the Greeks but before they reached Troy he was bitten by a poisonous snake. The wound festered and refused to heal. It stank so badly that his shipmates abandoned him on Lemnos. For ten years he lived there in isolation and pain, feeding himself by shooting birds with the bow and arrow of Heracles, which he had inherited from his father and which never missed its mark. Meanwhile, the war was raging. When a prophet revealed that the Greeks would never defeat the Trojans without Philoctetes and his irreproachable weapon, Odysseus and Neoptolemus rescued him and took him to Troy, where Machaon, the son of Asclepius, healed him at last.

had evaporated, and the Argonauts had a fine time with the Lemnian women. When they sailed off a year later, even Jason left behind two sons, the children of Hypsipyle.

The Doliones

Things worked out less happily in Cyzicus, where Jason and his men enjoyed the hospitality of the Doliones and their king, also named Cyzicus. Trouble came on the night they sailed away, when an ill wind blew them off course into a port they did not recognize. The local residents, thinking they had been invaded, attacked, and the Argonauts fought back. In the morning, the terrible truth was revealed. The wind had blown the ship back to Cyzicus, and the Argonauts had been battling their friends, the Doliones. King Cyzicus was among those who fell. The Argonauts mourned him before they sailed on.

Phineus and the Harpies

Soon afterwards, they encountered the blind soothsayer Phineus. Once again an offensive odor enters the story, this time in the form of the Harpies, who had faces like women and bodies like birds. Whenever Phineus tried to eat, the Harpies defecated on his food, and even when they flew off, they left a revolting aroma in their wake. As a result, Phineus was starving. Fortunately for him, the Argonauts were able to help. In exchange for a glimpse of the future, Zetes and Calais, sons of the North Wind, drove one of the Harpies to the Tigris River and another to an island in the Ionian Sea. They would have attacked the others too, except that Iris, goddess of the rainbow, intervened on behalf of her sisters and promised that they would never torment Phineus again.

The Clashing Rocks

At the Black Sea, the Argonauts reached the Clashing Rocks, which clapped together so fiercely that even the birds had a hard time flying between them. Phineus told them that, before they attempted the passage, they should let a dove fly between the mammoth boulders. If it was crushed, they must turn back. If the bird slipped through, they should set sail at once, while the rocks were on the rebound.

The Argonauts followed these instructions precisely. They released a bird, which successfully flew between the boulders, although it lost a few tail feathers when the rocks collided. As the rocks drew apart, the Argo slipped through safely, though a few timbers in the stern were clipped. Afterwards, the Clashing Rocks were rendered immobile and other ships no longer had to contend with them.

The Golden Fleece

In Colchis, Jason faced his greatest challenge. Aeetes promised to give him the Golden Fleece if he could yoke together two fire-breathing bulls, plow a field with them, and sow the dragon's teeth, which Aeetes had received from Athena. These were difficult tasks, and Jason didn't feel up to it. At the suggestion of the Argonauts, Jason sought out a priestess of Hecate who knew how to concoct magical drugs.

Their meeting was fated. Thanks to Eros, that young woman, the golden-eyed granddaughter of the Sun, took one look at Jason and fell in love. She was filled with desire—and despair. For much as she wished to help him, she was also the king's daughter. Her conscience was in an uproar.

She soon cast aside her hesitation. Misjudging her as kind and gentle, Jason enthusiastically accepted her help. So Jason and Medea came together.

With her knowledge of herbs and potions, she mixed a magical ointment to rub over his body and his weapons. It strengthened and protected him, enabling him to harness the oxen without being burned by the flames they exhaled. He plowed the field and scattered the dragon's teeth. To his surprise, soldiers, bristling with spears and shields, began to pop up all over the field. Medea told him to follow the example of Cadmus (who sowed the other half of the same dragon's teeth) by heaving a large stone into their midst. Not knowing where it came from, the sown men attacked each other. Jason joined the fracas. Wielding a sickle, he cut them down like a farmer harvesting his crops. The furrows of the field ran red.

Afterwards, he confronted the dragon who was guarding the Golden Fleece. There are several versions of that encounter. In the fifth century BCE, an artist named Douris painted a red-figured vase, now in the collection of the Vatican, which showed Jason being regurgitated from inside that monster. How he got to that dark place we don't know.

Apollonius of Rhodes, writing in the third century BCE, tells a less dramatic tale. According to him, Medea hypnotized the three-tongued dragon and sprinkled soporific drugs in its eyes while Jason hung back, terrified. When it fell asleep, Jason picked up the Golden Fleece and, with Medea, returned to the Argo.

As the happy couple sailed away, King Aeetes boarded a ship and pursued them, hoping to regain his prize possession. And now Medea shows what she is made of. Apollonius says that before embarking she lured her brother Apsyrtus to a temple and averted her eyes while Jason killed him and cut off his extremities. According to an older tradition, Medea killed and dismembered Apsyrtus herself. Then she stood on the deck and, with Aeetes in pursuit, tossed the pieces overboard. As each piece splashed into the water, Aeetes felt compelled to retrieve it, which slowed his ship down considerably. Soon the Argo was far, far away.

Adventure Reruns

Certain obstacles are so intrinsic to the human condition that the Greeks couldn't let them go after a single encounter. On the trip back to Iolcus, Jason faced several hazards that also bedeviled Odysseus:

- Both heroes visited the sorceress Circe, Medea's aunt. She purified Jason and Medea and absolved them of the murder of Apsyrtus. She also turned Odysseus' men into pigs. But when Odysseus, protected by an herb, threatened her, she turned them back into human beings. She and Odysseus lived together for a year.
- Both heroes sailed past the island of the Sirens, who bewitched sailors with their song and then devoured them. To escape their lure, Odysseus ordered his men to block their ears with wax, to bind him to the mast, and to ignore his pleas to be untied while the Sirens were within earshot. Jason and the Argonauts had an easier time because Orpheus was on board. His song was so sweet that everyone listened to him instead of the Sirens.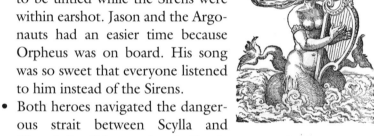
- Both heroes navigated the dangerous strait between Scylla and Charybdis. Odysseus lost half a dozen men in the passage. Jason—a later hero—was more successful, making it through without sacrificing a single Argonaut.

The Return to Iolcus

Back in Iolcus at last, Jason discovered that, despite his promises, Pelias was unwilling to abdicate. Medea had a solution. She befriended his daughters and convinced them that she knew the secret of rejuvenation. To prove it, she cut up an old ram and boiled the pieces in a cauldron. When she sprinkled in a handful of magic herbs, a feisty young lamb leaped out of the pot. The daughters, convinced by this phony demonstration, dismembered their father and threw the pieces into the cauldron. This time, Medea refused to provide herbs. No matter how furiously they stirred the pot, the old man did not come back to life. Nevertheless, Medea had made a tactical error, for although Jason became king, popular sentiment ran against them. Jason and Medea were driven out of the city.

Jason and Medea

They settled in Corinth and had two children. But after a while, as Euripides explains in his play *Medea,* Jason's interest in Medea waned and he decided to marry Glauce, which was more than Medea could bear. Unable to contain her rage, Medea took an embroidered robe and a golden coronet, objects she had inherited from her grandfather, the Sun, and infused them with poison. Then she wrapped them as gifts and told her two small sons to deliver them to Glauce. As Glauce put them on, a ring of flames flickered out of the coronet and the poison in the robe seeped onto her skin and ate her flesh. Horrified, her father, King Creon, ran to her and held her in his arms, whereupon he was infected with the same poison. Father and daughter died together.

> *. . . Let no one think of me*
> *As humble or weak or passive; let them understand*
> *I am of a different kind: dangerous to my enemies,*
> *Loyal to my friends. To such a life glory belongs.*
> —Euripides, *Medea*

After that Medea commits the act for which she is famous and which she had been contemplating throughout Euripides' play. "Oh my heart, don't, don't do it!" she cries. "Oh, miserable heart,/Let them be!" Her wrath overcomes her better instincts, and she kills her own children to break Jason's heart. She is not the only mythological character to do such a thing—but she is far and away the most conscious.

A Flawed Hero

In many ways, Jason seems as much a victim as a hero. He retrieves the Golden Fleece, thanks to Medea, but fails to kill the dragon. He reigns as king so briefly that the quest seems pointless. And his career in Corinth is a disaster. He marries Medea because it is expedient, divorces her when he finds advantage elsewhere, and justifies himself with the most banal of excuses. As a hero, he cannot compete either with the members of his crew such as Heracles and Orpheus or, more importantly, with his wife. Once Medea comes onstage, her personality is so vigorous, her passion and anger so undiluted, that Jason falters in comparison.

Norman Mailer once complained to an interviewer that "I've been waiting to become the hero of my own life in order to write it. I have never become the hero of my own life." That was Jason's problem. He was never the hero of his own life: Medea was.

Parents Who Kill

Greek mythology is rife with infanticide. Agamemnon sacrificed his daughter Iphigeneia in hopes of getting a better wind; Heracles killed his entire family; Agave tore off her son's head; Tantalus chopped up his son and served him in a stew; and Aedon, Niobe's sister was so jealous of her sister's children that she decided to kill one of them. Instead, she accidentally murdered her own son.

Procne, daughter of the King of Athens, also killed her son. But in her case, it was no accident. Procne's troubles began when she married Tereus, the king of Thrace, in a ceremony so inauspicious that the Furies were in attendance. Procne had a son named Itys but after a few years in Thrace, she missed her sister Philomela so badly that she begged Tereus to bring her back for a visit. He agreed and left for Athens. During the return trip, he became so obsessed with Philomela that he raped her. To insure her silence, he cut out her tongue and imprisoned her in the woods.

Alone and unable to speak (or write), Philomela nonetheless found a way to communicate her distress. She wove a rich tapestry illustrating her tale and sent it to Procne, who understood immediately and freed her. Then the aggrieved sisters banded together to punish Tereus. Procne stabbed her son, chopped him up, cooked the pieces, and served the roasted flesh to Tereus. When the king realized that he had eaten his son, he grabbed a sword and ran after the sisters. The chase was so furious that Philomela turned into a nightingale, Procne changed into a swallow, and Tereus, angry and sickened, became a hawk.

Tales of the Cauldron

Medea failed to rejuvenate Pelias with her magic cauldron only because she purposely withheld the necessary ingredients. Still, even on her best day, she was only able to restore youth to the elderly. The cauldrons of Celtic mythology, on the other hand, could provide an inexhaustible supply of food and bring the dead to life.

The Dagda's Cauldron

Wise, invincible, and thoroughly uncouth, the potbellied Dagda was the father god, the lord of magic, knowledge, and druidism, and the chief of the Tuatha De Danann, the last race of gods to rule over Ireland. He wore a falstaffian tunic that was a little too short and he carried a magic club so huge that it was fitted with wheels and had to be dragged behind him. One end of it could kill and the other end could bring people back from the dead, giving the Dagda the powers of life and death. He also owned two magical pigs that could be roasted on one day and reborn on the next, and he possessed an all-you-can-eat cauldron, a symbol of abundance and generosity.

But there's such a thing as too much, as the Dagda learned one November first, a sacred day in the Celtic calendar. On that day, the Dagda, who was also a fertility god, ritually made love with a goddess. Usually, he coupled with the formidable Morrigan, goddess of war. On one occasion, he mated with the Mother goddess Boann, who became the River Boyne. Although she was married to someone else, she realized after they made love that she had become pregnant. Because their liaison had to be secret, Dagda and Boann cast a spell that caused the sun to stand still for nine months. Thus their child, Oenghus, the god of love, was born on the same day on which he was conceived.

Another time, the Dagda utterly failed in his duty. During a truce in the battle with the Fomorians, his enemies made him eat a porridge consisting of eighty gallons each of milk, meal, bacon, goats, sheep, and pigs. They cooked it in an enormous cauldron, poured it into a hole in the ground, and ordered him on pain of death to consume the entire meal. The Dagda easily downed the whole mess, scraping up the last few bites with his fingers. He was humiliated nonetheless, for afterwards his belly was so distended that he was unable to make love.

Brân's Cauldron

Another cauldron appears in a story about the Welsh heroine Branwen and her brothers, the hot-blooded Efnisien and the giant Bendigeidfran who was known as Brân the Blessed. Branwen was engaged to Matholwch, the king of Ireland. When he came to Harlech, the court in North Wales where Branwen lived, Efnisien was so upset that he snuck into a stable where Matholwch's horses were housed and cut off their lips, ears, and tails. To forestall hostilities, Brân replaced the horses and gave Matholwch his most prized possession: a magic cauldron which Brân had received from an enormous red-headed man who emerged from a lake carrying the cauldron on his back and accompanied by a woman who was even larger. This cauldron was prized for its ability to bring fallen warriors back to life. Corpses tossed into the cauldron at night were as good as new in the morning in every respect but one: they were unable to speak.

This generous gift calmed Matholwch, and he and Branwen settled into their home in Ireland, where she gave birth to son named Gwerm. But Matholwch made her toil in the kitchen and boxed her ears on a regular basis, and the people began to complain that the cauldron was inadequate compensation for the insult Matholwch had received from Efnisien. Fearing for her life, Branwen tied a message to the leg of a starling and trained it to fly to Wales. Thus her brothers learned about her plight.

Brân responded immediately. He waded across the sea shoulder-to-shoulder with his ships and engaged Matholwch in battle. After a fierce struggle, Matholwch was deposed. Branwen's son Gwerm would have claimed his place as king except that during the festivities, Efnisien threw Gwerm into the fire. Fighting broke out.

At first, the Irish were victorious, for every night they stuffed their dead into the cauldron, and every morning, their forces were replenished by rejuvenated, silent soldiers. Then Efnisien pretended to be dead and allowed himself to be tossed into the cauldron. He stretched it, cracked it, and caused it to burst, depriving his enemies of their greatest weapon. Thanks to his heroism, the Welsh won, though only seven heroes survived (along with five pregnant Irish women). Among the injured was Brân, who was fatally wounded with a poison spear. Knowing that his time was short, Brân ordered his men to decapitate him, to take his living head to London, and to bury it facing France.

Getting to London took time. First they traveled to Harlech, where they feasted merrily for seven years, listening to the three birds of Rhiannon and chatting with the head. Then they proceeded on to Gwales, where they found a spacious hall with three doors. Two of the doors were open; the third door was shut, and they were forbidden to use it. For eighty mirthful years, they lingered there, entertaining the head. But as everyone knows, a door which must remain shut must be opened. One of the seven heroes decided to find out what would happen if he opened the door.

What happened was this: consciousness returned. The men became aware of how much time had passed, of everything evil they had ever done and everything sad that had ever happened to them. Sorrow washed over them like a wave and they remembered their promise to the head. They took it to the White Mount of London and buried it. As long as it was buried there, no foreigner from across the channel would ever invade.

Theseus

Even compared to other heroes, Theseus, the hero of Athens, had more than his share of adventures. The son of the god Poseidon or the mortal Aegeus, he was brought up in Troezen by his mother Aethra. When he was sixteen, she revealed that after he was conceived, Aegeus, who was king of Athens, had buried a sword and a pair of sandals in the earth, covered them with a heavy rock, and told Aethra that, when her son was strong enough to move the rock and claim his inheritance, he should come to Athens.

Theseus was a slight, redheaded boy. Nevertheless, when he was sixteen, he pushed that stone aside and, like King Arthur, lifted up the sword that was meant for only him. Then he set off for Athens, choosing not the short, direct route over the Aegean, but the longer, more dangerous overland route. At almost every stop, he encountered a villain and hoisted him on his own petard. The most famous was Procrustes, who was known for offering strangers the hospitality of a bed and then fitting them to it by lopping off part of their anatomy if they were too tall or stretching them on the rack if they were too short. Theseus tied Procrustes to his own bed and sliced off his head. When he arrived in Athens, he had dispatched half a dozen such scoundrels, always in the manner that they richly deserved.

Theseus, balancing on the hands of a Triton, reaches out to Amphitrite, who is holding a wreath with which to crown him. Athena stands between them.

Theseus in Athens

Nonetheless, Theseus did not receive the welcome in Athens that he had anticipated. The Athenians mocked his feminine appearance, and Aegeus did not recognize Theseus as his son. Worse, Theseus had to content with the sorceress Medea, who fled Corinth after killing her children and married Aegeus. She recognized Theseus immediately. Intent on protecting the inheritance of her own son, she convinced Aegeus to send Theseus to capture the bull of Marathon. It was a dangerous mission but to her frustration, Theseus succeeded in the task. This time, Medea decided to kill him with a noxious herb harvested from the flecks of foam that the dog Cerberus shook from his mouths. After inviting Theseus to a feast, ostensibly to celebrate his victory over the bull, she poisoned the wine with a few drops of the deadly substance.

Before the wine was poured, Aegeus noticed the stranger carving his meat with an ivory-hilted sword. The sword looked familiar, and he realized with a start that it was the one he had buried under a rock so many years before. Suddenly he understood what Medea was up to. He knocked the wine to the floor and embraced his son.

With Medea's plan foiled, Theseus was ready to embark on his greatest adventure.

Theseus and the Minotaur

For several years, the people of Athens had been forced to pay a terrible tribute to King Minos of Crete. His son had been killed by a group of Athenians. As retribution, Minos demanded that fourteen youths, seven boys and seven girls, be sent to him every year (or every nine years) and sacrificed to the Minotaur, a monster, half man and half bull, who was imprisoned within a labyrinth. Two times, fourteen

THE BIRTH OF THE MINOTAUR

Before Theseus was born, Zeus took the shape of a bull, abducted Europa, and galloped across the sea with her to Crete. She had three sons, one of whom was King Minos. When he grew up, he petitioned Poseidon for a sign of his favor. It was granted in magnificent fashion when a white bull clambered out of the sea. Awestruck by the animal, Minos let it live, thus neglecting the number one rule for petitioning the gods: don't forget the sacrifice.

The Minotaur, from a fifth-century BCE amphora.

Punishment was swift and strange. The king's wife, Pasiphaë, developed an unnatural obsession with the bull. She would not rest until she fulfilled her desire, a feat she accomplished through the skill of the craftsman Daedalus. He built a hollow, wooden cow so capacious that Pasiphaë was able to climb into it and so seductive that the bull was inspired to mate with it. Soon Pasiphaë gave birth to the Minotaur, who had the body of a man and the head of a bull. To keep the monster out of sight, Daedalus designed a labyrinth so complicated that no one could find the way out. The Minotaur was imprisoned inside.

young Athenians boarded a black-sailed ship and set out for Crete. The third time, Theseus volunteered to stop the carnage.

He said good-bye to his father and promised that, upon his return, he would hoist a white sail to signal his success. He traveled across the sea with the other youths. In Crete, he won several athletic contests  and caught the eye of Ariadne, one of the daughters of Minos. She gave him the secret to navigating the labyrinth: a ball of string. Following her instructions, Theseus tied the string to a post at the entrance to the labyrinth and rolled it in front of him. It guided him silently to the sleeping Minotaur, which he killed using either a sword, a club, or his bare hands. Then he followed the thread back to the entrance.

Afterwards, he and Ariadne sailed to the island of Naxos (or Dia) and he married her out of gratitude. But in truth, he felt little affection for her. So while she was sleeping, he boarded the ship and headed for Athens.

Alas, in his excitement Theseus forgot to hoist the white sail. As the ship drew within sight of the Acropolis, King Aegeus, who stood on the rocky heights watching for his son, saw the black sails and assumed the worst. He jumped to his death in the sea below, which since that time has been known as the Aegean.

With Aegeus dead, Theseus became king. He abolished monarchy, minted the first coins, unified the communities of Attica into a sovereign state, and established a democracy (an event said to have occurred around 1400 BCE).

As for Ariadne, her story is a matter of conjecture. Some say that after Theseus abandoned her, she died, brought down by the arrows of Artemis. Others say that she lost no time and married Dionysus. He made her immortal and gave her as a wedding present a glittering crown, which can be seen even now in the summer sky as the constellation Corona Borealis.

Daedalus, Icarus, and Minos

Next to Hephaestus, Daedalus was the most ingenious craftsman in Greek mythology. His designs included the labyrinth, from which no one could escape, and the wooden cow which permitted Pasiphaë to mate with the bull. When King Minos realized that Daedalus was partially responsible for the birth of the Minotaur, he imprisoned the craftsman and his son Icarus inside the giant maze. It didn't take long for Daedalus to devise a method of escape. Using wax and feathers, he fashioned two sets of wings for himself and his son. According to Ovid, he kissed his son and tearfully told him exactly where to fly: halfway between the sun and the water, no higher and no lower. But Icarus was a dreamer. He ignored those warnings. He flew too close to the sun. The wax melted and he plunged into the sea.

Daedalus continued on to Sicily, where he took up residence in the household of the king. Meanwhile, Minos was searching for him by asking everyone he met to pass a thread through a chambered nautilus shell. When he finally ran across Daedalus, the craftsman could not resist the challenge. He drilled a small hole in the shell, smeared it with honey, tied a gossamer thread to the body of an ant, and placed the ant at the entrance of the shell. Drawn by the honey, the ant navigated its way through the miniature labyrinth of the shell, dragging the thread behind it. When he reached the honey, the shell was threaded.

Minos knew that the only person clever enough to devise such a method was Daedalus, the master of the labyrinth. Minos told his daughters that he intended to capture the craftsman, but his daughters revealed the plan, and the ever-inventive Daedalus struck first. He hooked up a pipe and, while Minos was bathing, sent a cascade of boiling water or scalding hot pitch into the bath, thus killing his former employer.

On Labyrinths

This is what happens when you hurry through a maze: the faster you go, the worse you are entangled.

—Seneca

There is something about a labyrinth that attracts lovers of analogy. Over the centuries, they have likened the journey through the labyrinth to virtually every mysterious or circuitous process you care to name including birth, flirtation, sex, politics, psychoanalysis, and life itself. In the thirteenth century (as now), spiritual analogies were in vogue, and labyrinths were thought to offer sacred images of the pilgrimage to Jerusalem, the life of Jesus, the descent into sin, or the ascent to heavenly glory. In the fourteenth century, Boccaccio used the phrase "labyrinth of love" and that concept gained immediate recognition. By the seventeenth century, a craze for outdoor labyrinths that represented the hide-and-seek of seduction spread across Europe. In the twentieth century, the labyrinth became a literary device, appearing in the work of Kafka, Borges, and Umberto Eco, among others, as an image of doubt, futility, confusion, secrecy, bureaucracy, and urban despair. (The labyrinth, after all, was built as a prison.) On the other hand, Joseph Campbell and his followers see it as an image representing the hero's journey, while contemporary pilgrims have found that the byways of the labyrinth can act as an aid to meditation. As an image, the labyrinth is flexible enough to represent all kinds of processes, both positive and negative.

Yet while meanings are legion, styles are not. Whether they are made of stone, turf, or manicured hedges, there are only two sorts of labyrinths. In the first kind, called unicursal, a single path coils around and around until it reaches the center. This kind of labyrinth looks convoluted but its route, as relentless as a freeway without an exit, leads in one direction only. It offers no choices and permits no mistakes. Like the labyrinth on the floor of the Cathedral at Chartres (or the one modeled after it at San Francisco's Grace Cathedral), it is a symbol of inevitability. Before the sixteenth century, these error-proof labyrinths were the only kind depicted in art.

The other kind of labyrinth, called multicursal, is an elaborate, devious puzzle, suffused with the threat of getting permanently trapped. The labyrinth that Daedalus built was presumably of this kind, designed with so many cul-de-sacs, retracings, and meandering pathways that, according to Ovid, Daedalus himself had trouble finding his way back out.

A pilgrim, assisted by God or an angel, navigates a labyrinth in this engraving from 1627.

Theseus in the Underworld

Many mythological characters visit the underworld, but Theseus was one of the few to bring along a companion. He came with his

friend Pirithous, who had a serious crush on Persephone, the queen of the underworld. Since Theseus owed his friend a favor, he agreed to help him abduct Persephone. But once they arrived in Hades, they sat on the chair of forgetfulness and their plans floated away like mist. For four years, surrounded by furies and hissing serpents, they perched on that infernal sofa, which merged with their flesh until they were unable to move. At last mighty Heracles arrived and ripped Theseus bodily

Theseus at the wedding of Pirithous, king of the Lapiths. A battle broke out when the centaurs tried to rape the bride. Theseus, shown clubbing a centaur, fought on behalf of the Lapiths.

from the chair, which resulted in the unfortunate loss of part of his anatomy. (In Celtic mythology Conán the Bald suffered a similar injury when he was stuck to the floor in the Otherworld and had to be torn away.) Pirithous had a sadder fare. Even Heracles was unable to wrench him away from the hellish furniture, and he remains there still.

Theseus and Phaedra

The union between Theseus and Ariadne was not our hero's only failed relationship. He also married Ariadne's sister, Phaedra. Several years later, Phaedra became infatuated with a handsome young man named Hippolytus. He was the fruit of a brief liaison between Theseus and Hipployta, the queen of the Amazons, and he felt loyal to his father. So when Phaedra revealed the depth of her longing, he rebuffed her. In response, she unleashed the forces of catastrophe.

She tied a rope around her neck and hanged herself, not forgetting to leave behind an accusatory letter claiming that Hippolytus had raped her. Theseus read it and believed it. He banished Hippolytus from the city. But the thought of his son raping his wife festered in his mind, and exile seemed an inadequate punishment. So he called upon Poseidon, who had once given him the emblematic gift of fairy tales: three magic wishes. Theseus wished that Hippolytus would die, and his wish was granted. Naturally, a bull was involved. As Hippolytus drove his chariot along the shore, a bull galloped out of the waves and frightened his horses, who dragged him to his death.

Theseus, like many heroes, died in a manner that seems humiliatingly inconsequential. He was kicked over a cliff on the island of Scyros. Though his death was little noted at the time, his reputation grew and he became a demigod. At the Battle of Marathon in 490 BCE, soldiers saw his spirit leading the troops. Afterwards, his bones were reinterred in Athens and his tomb became a sanctuary for slaves, poor people, and the oppressed.

BUT WHAT DOES IT MEAN?

In order to be spared, one must say "yes" to the Minotaur.
—Albert Camus

I am the Minotaur.
—Pablo Picasso

"Every myth is a condensation of human drama," writes Gaston Bachelard. "That is why every myth can so easily be used as a symbol for an actual dramatic situation." The myth of Theseus and the Minotaur is especially amenable to analysis. Over the centuries, it has been seen in a startling diversity of ways.

Literalists, always among us, have diminished the story by offering sensible substitutions for its fantastic elements. Chief among these is Servius, a grammarian of the fifth century CE, who suggested that the bull from the sea was a scribe named Taurus, that Pasiphaë cavorted with him not from within a wooden cow but (yawn) inside a wooden house, and that the Minotaur was not a fanciful, impossible creature but a set of twins, one fathered by King Minos and one by the busy scribe.

Aristotle understood the story as a political drama in which the Minotaur represents tyranny and Theseus symbolizes democracy.

Fourteenth-century Christians viewed the Minotaur as the embodiment of sinfulness, Theseus as Christ, and the entire myth as a spiritual parable. The Benedictine prior Pierre Bersuire explained that Pasiphaë was the lascivious soul, the bull with which she coupled was the devil, the ball of string represented divinity, and Ariadne was a symbol of human nature. However, this analysis failed to account for the inconvenient fact that Theseus abandoned Ariadne. An anonymous French poet resolved the difficulty by suggesting that if Theseus was Christ, then Ariadne must have been abandoned for cause, in which case she clearly symbolized the Jews.

Today, Jungian analysts see Theseus as the hero, Ariadne as the hero's feminine side or anima, and the Minotaur, once an image of sin, as the hidden part of the self, the shadow that lurks in the labyrinth of the unconscious. The hero's challenge is to acknowledge that component of the self, for only by doing so can he lead a full, creative life. Theseus provides a cautionary example because he fails at this task. By killing the Minotaur and leaving it there, within the labyrinth, and again by abandoning Ariadne, he dooms himself. The disasters that follow—the suicides of his father and his wife Phaedra, the loss of his son, even his own peculiar paralysis in the underworld—are inevitable.

Krishna

Heracles was widely worshipped as a hero and as a god. But the religion of the ancient Greeks is no longer living, and perhaps for that reason, we think of him only as a Disneyfied hero, not as a god. Krishna also became a god, but since Hinduism is entirely alive, the divine identification has stuck.

Nevertheless, Krishna's life followed the traditional heroic pattern. Conceived in an unusual way (Vishnu planted a hair in his mother's womb), he was abandoned at birth for the usual reason—his father had been frightened by a prophecy—and raised by peasants. A mischievous child and lusty adolescent, he slew a many-headed serpent, entered the belly of a demon, went to war, and died, as

Vishnu as a fish. heroes must, in an unusual way.

Yet he was also a god, for Krishna was one of the incarnations of the four-armed, blue-skinned Vishnu, who returns to earth in a different form whenever it is necessary to save the human race. Krishna was the eighth such avatar.

Vishnu as a boar.

THE INCARNATIONS OF VISHNU

Vishnu the Preserver, god of a thousand names, lived many lives and can claim many identities. Ten are especially important, for they mark the occasions when he appeared on earth to save the human race. Here are the ten incarnations of Vishnu, given in their usual, non-chronological order (because what is time, if not an illusion?):

1. Matsya the Fish, who saved mankind from the great flood;
2. Kurma, a tortoise who helped the gods obtain soma, the elixir of immortality;
3. Varaha, a boar who created the earth;
4. Narasimha, a man-lion who killed a demon;
5. Vamana, a dwarf who sent the demons to hell and created the world from his body;
6. Rama-with-an-Ax, who beheaded his mother and killed every member of the warrior class;
7. Rama, the hero of the epic *Ramayana;*
8. Krishna;
9. Buddha;
10. Kalki, the avatar of the future.

Krishna's Exploits

Before Krishna was born, an oracle told his uncle, evil King Kansa, that he would be murdered by his sister Davaki's eighth child. To protect himself, Kansa decided to kill her children. His plans were foiled by the gods, who outmaneuvered him in a manner too complicated to explain (suffice it to say that it involved multiple incarnations, faked miscarriages, and various late-pregnancy embryos transferred to the wombs of other goddesses). Krishna was saved.

King Kansa, no fool, realized he had been outwitted. He sent the demon Putana ("Stinking") to nurse the newborn avatar and to poison him with her milk. Instead, Krishna killed her by sucking the life out of her body. Like Heracles, his powers were extraordinary even in infancy.

Gods and heroes often have no childhood at all. Krishna is an exception to that general rule, for his childhood escapades are many. Brought up as a herdsman in the simple home of Yashoda and Nanda, he danced, played the flute, and stole butter, which he sometimes gave to the monkeys. He loved to play pranks and occasionally misbehaved so egregiously that Yashoda, who did not know he was divine, felt obliged to punish him. One time, she heard that Krishna had been eating dirt. Although he denied it, she asked him to open his mouth and she gazed inside. To her surprise, she saw everything that existed including heaven and earth, the constellations of the zodiac, the distant reaches of outer space, time, nature, and even her own small village, with herself in it. She realized that Krishna, whose dark blue skin was the color of night, was divine.

As a young man, Krishna was known for his amorousness and his irresistibility to the opposite sex. At night, when he played his flute, he resembled the Pied Piper, except that rather than attracting children, the melodious sounds of his flute had a magnetic pull on the local wives. When the gopis, or milkmaids, were bathing in a river, he stole their clothes, thereby providing a happy subject for many generations of artists. He returned them when the young women, still naked, approached him individually and bowed before him, their hands on their heads. He was willing to satisfy one and all, but his favorite partners, both incarnations of Lakshmi, were Rukmini and the golden-skinned Radha, who longed for him in his absence, it is said, much as human beings in the midst of their fragmented, stressful lives yearn for spiritual wholeness.

He also performed many good deeds. Once, when Indra sent a terrible rainstorm, Krishna lifted up Mount Govardhana like a giant umbrella and let everyone huddle underneath. Another time, he battled the serpent Kaliya, whose oily secretions had polluted the River Kalinda. When Krishna approached the serpent, it caught him in its grip, spit venom into his eyes, and licked his face with one of its repulsive tongues. The serpent could not kill the god, though. Nimble Krishna moved this way and that, exhausting him utterly. When Kaliya loosened his grip, Krishna danced on each of its many heads. One by one, he smashed the cobra's hoods and banished him to the ocean.

> **KRISHNA SPEAKS**
>
> *I am the taste of living waters and the light of the sun and the moon. I am OM, the sacred word of the Vedas, sound in silence, heroism in men . . . I am the Father of this universe, and even the source of the Father. I am the Mother of this universe, and the Creator of all. . . . I am the Way.*
> —from the *Bhagavad Gita*

Still, like any hero Krishna had to face death. One day, as he was sitting in the lotus position, a hunter named Jaras or "Old Age" wandered past in pursuit of an antelope. Glancing at the clearing where Krishna was resting, he saw the soles of Krishna's feet looking as luminous as the ears of an antelope, and he shot an arrow at him. It pierced the sole of Krishna's foot, which was his Achilles's heel, the one vulnerable spot on his body, and Krishna died.

The Last Incarnation of Vishnu, and the Next

Hinduism, which dates back 3,500 years, did not greet the rise of Buddhism with enthusiasm. To account for its popularity, Hindu commentators suggested that Vishnu incarnated as the Buddha for the purpose of misleading demons. A text composed around 450 CE suggests that Buddha—that is, Vishnu—turned demons into freethinkers and seduced them off the path of righteousness, which enabled the gods to destroy them. Thus Buddha benefited mankind, not because he illuminated the path to enlightenment or addressed the causes of suffering but because he fooled the demons through his specious philosophy and thus led them away from Hinduism and into destruction.

Buddha, born around 556 BCE, was the ninth incarnation of Vishnu. Since then, Vishnu has not sent a major avatar, but one is waiting in the wings. At the end of the evil Kali Yuga, which is the present age, Kalki will ride in on (or as) a white horse, ready to destroy barbarians and heretics, Buddhists included. His arrival will end the Kali Yuga and start the cycle of time anew. The people who remain will be transformed, and their offspring will return to the Krita Age in which everybody meditates regularly, accepts their dharma, and knows their place.

Blue

Among the many deities around the world who are described as entirely or partially blue, Krishna is the most well-known. Others include:

- Poseidon, described by Homer as "God of the sea-blue mane" and the "god with the blue-black hair;"
- the Sumerian moon god Nanna, a bull with a beautiful blue beard;
- Cailleach Bheur, the blue-faced goddess of winter, a Scottish deity whose reign was brought to an end every spring by the goddess Brigid;
- the blue-skinned Egyptian god Amun, who wears two feathers on his head and is consequently known as the "Master of the Headband;"
- Huitzilopochtli, the Aztec god of war, who was born painted blue;
- the mischievous Brazilian devil Curupira, who is distinguished by his unusual feet and his blue teeth. One time a hunter, using trickery, got the Curupira to kill itself. A month later, he returned to the scene of the crime to get the teeth. The moment he touched them, the Curupira came back to life;
- the Navajo Blue God. In the beginning, existence was like a tower with five floors. On the first story, where the world was red, people lived in the form of bats and insects. To

punish them for committing adultery, the gods sent an enormous flood. Fortunately, a blue head emerged from the sky and showed the people the way to the second story, where the world was blue and the people were turned into swallows. Twenty-four nights later, adultery once again forced them upwards, to the third story, where the world was yellow and the inhabitants were grasshoppers. When the predictable occurred, the people climbed to the fourth story, the world of all colors, where the Pueblo Indians cultivated pumpkins and maize. Four gods ruled over this world: White Body, Black Body, Yellow Body, and Blue Body. Together, they created First Man and First Woman, who ended up here on earth, which is the fifth story.

HINDU MYTHOLOGY: THE MAJOR SOURCES

The monumental mythology of Hinduism is supported by an impressive body of literature. It includes:

- The *Rig Veda,* a collection of 1028 hymns composed between 1550 and 1200 BCE.

- The *Mahabharata.* Compiled between 300 B.C.E. and C.E. 300 by the mythical sage Vyasa, this Sanskrit epic, focusing on the issue of right conduct, is seven times as long as the *Iliad* and the *Odyssey* combined.

- The *Ramayana* (Romance of Rama). Written between 200 BCE and 200 CE by the poet Valmiki, this epic recounts the adventures of Rama, his wife Sita, and Ravana the demon king.

- The *Bhagavad Gita.* A sacred Hindu text included in the *Mahabarata* about 100 CE. In it, Prince Arjuna is riddled with doubts about participating in a war. Krishna convinces him to go ahead and instructs him on the paths to spiritual enlightenment.

- The *Puranas.* A collection of manuscripts containing ancient legends, beliefs, and practices composed between 400 and 1000 CE. The major deities in these texts are Brahma, Vishnu, and Shiva.

Mwindo: Little-one-just-born-he-walked

Like the Persian prophet Zarathustra, the African hero Mwindo came into this world laughing. His superiority was immediately evident, for he could walk and talk at birth; his name for himself was "Little-one-just-born-he-walked."

Nevertheless, he did not have the blessing of his father, Shemwindo, chief of Tubondo. Before Mwindo's birth, Shemwindo instructed his seven wives to give birth only to daughters. The wives did their best to comply. They became pregnant at the same time and six of them succeeded in giving birth to girls—all on the same day. But Shemwindo's favorite wife, Nyamwindo, remained pregnant longer than the others, and when she finally went into labor, the infant did not come out of her body in the usual way. Instead, the baby emerged from her palm (or the tip of her middle finger) with an ax in one hand, a ceremonial conga or switch in the other, and a bag containing a magic rope slung over his shoulder. Worse yet, he was a boy.

After a cricket told Shemwindo the news, he tried to kill his son. He hurled six spears into the birth hut and when they struck the ground without injuring anyone, he ordered the child to be buried alive beneath heaps of plantains and dirt. That night, a light as bright as the sun shone out of the grave, and the baby crawled out.

SOURCES

The epic of Mwindo, a myth told by the Nyanga people in the Democratic Republic of Congo (formerly Zaire), has been performed for hundreds of years within the oral tradition. Recorded in 1956 and published in 1971, the story is a complicated saga, truncated here by necessity. A complete version involves other chiefs and gods, a helpful hawk, a long snake, two hunting dogs, dozens of baboons, a Pygmy, a dragon's daughter, Mwindo's many wives, and more. A performance of the entire epic takes a full twelve days.

Shemwindo was so upset that he stuffed his son into a wooden drum and dropped it into the middle of a large, stagnant lake. When the drum bobbed to the surface, everyone could hear the imprisoned child singing a plaintive tune to his father. Shemwindo knew that he was in trouble.

Mwindo Meets His Aunt

Unlike Moses, Perseus, and other heroes who were left in the water, Mwindo did not simply drift ashore. Instead, after singing his farewell aria, he plunged into the deepest part of the water and followed the underwater current upstream until he arrived at the spot where his aunt Iyangura lived with her husband Mukti. As soon as she heard that her nephew was imprisoned inside the drum, she freed him from it. Mukti, a water serpent who was also lord of the unfathomable depths, was not happy to hear that. Using every weapon and trick at his command, he tried to capture the little hero. Mwindo dried up the water in the pool where Mukti lived, killed his henchman Kasiyembe by setting his head on fire, and thoroughly eluded his uncle.

Iyangura loved her nephew but she begged him to be compassionate, and Mwindo took her advice. Waving his magic conga, he restored the waters and brought Kasiyembe back to life. Afterwards, he told his good-hearted aunt that he was leaving for Tubondo in hopes of encountering his father face to face. She insisted on accompanying him and they departed together.

Into the Underworld

Mwindo easily conquered Tubondo. The animals, the palm trees, and even the salt supported him. So did Nkuba, the master of lightning, who hurled seven bolts of lightning at the town and burned it to the ground. Only one person escaped the flames: Shemwindo.

He yanked a fern up by the roots, wiggled into the little hole in the earth that was left behind, and plunged into the underworld. Mwindo followed. He handed his aunt one end of his magical rope and told her that if it went slack, she could assume that he was dead. Then he found the fern, slipped into the hole in the ground, and followed his father into the underworld.

There he encountered Kahindo, daughter of Muisa, the king of the underworld. She was also the goddess of good luck but you wouldn't know it to look at her, for her body was covered with lesions. Mwindo cleaned her sores and healed her. In exchange, she coached him on how to act in the underworld (an essential tip: decline all food and drink, including banana beer) and she put in a good word with her father. Muisa promised to help him find Shemwindo. But first, he demanded that Mwindo perform a few tasks, including planting and harvesting an entire grove of banana trees.

Like other heroes beset with seemingly impossible challenges, Mwindo received help from an unlikely source: his iron tools. With their help, he completed the job in a single day. Muisa was not happy. Rather than completing his part of the bargain, he attacked. He ordered his special belt to lash out at Mwindo. The little hero struck back with his magic conga.

The belt literally beat Mwindo into the ground and the magic conga was equally tough. The fight was so vicious that at various times, both adversaries were separated from their internal organs. However, Mwindo had the upper hand. He killed Muisa not once but twice. The first time, at Kahindo's urging, Mwindo acted compassionately, using his magic conga to bring Muisa back to life. The battle resumed. Once again, Mwindo killed his adversary. This time, he decided to let the underworld lord languish while he went in search of his father.

He found him staying with another god who suggested that Mwindo gamble for the right to be united with his father. Mwindo accepted the challenge. He was on the verge of losing everything when he bet his magic conga and his luck turned. All the winnings were his. In addition, he received help from a sparrow who led him to his father. When he confronted his father at last, Shemwindo realized that he had been defeated.

Father and son forgave each other. The father agreed to share his power with his son. Mwindo restored Muisa to life and became chief of Tubondo. But the story doesn't end there, for Mwindo made a terrible mistake.

Mwindo and the Dragon

One day Mwindo developed an irresistible craving for wild pig. Unable to stop thinking about the taste, he ordered several hunters to kill a pig. They tracked one down and slaughtered it, but while they were working, a seven-headed dragon with seven eyes appeared out of nowhere and swallowed them whole. To save the hunters, Mwindo killed the dragon, Kirimu. Then his men took their knives and sliced into its body. To their surprise, the hunters jumped out of the dragon's belly. Afterwards, Mwindo and his men prepared to barbecue the dragon. They piled the meat on the fire and watched as the dragon's seven eyes swelled up and exploded in a fine spray. With each droplet that splashed onto the ground, a human being— a supporter of Mwindo— was born.

Nevertheless, a problem remained. For unlike the Minotaur, the Medusa, and other monsters slaughtered by other heroes, Kirimu had a friend: Nkuba, the master of lightning. He was so distressed at the dragon's death that he forced Mwindo to say farewell to the earth and spend a year in the heavens.

Mwindo Is Purified

Just as Apollo cleansed himself after killing the Python, Mwindo purified himself in the celestial realm, where he wandered around for a year, unprotected from the forces of nature. It wasn't easy. Rain pummeled him, Moon burned his hair, Sun made him thirsty, and Star lectured him on his inadequacies, of which arrogance and pride were uppermost. These gods told him the right way to live and cautioned him against breaking any of their commandments, including the prohibition against killing animals.

When Mwindo was allowed to return after his year in exile, he was a changed man. He gathered his people together and told them how to live harmoniously. Among other rules, they were to cultivate a variety of crops, to dwell in beautiful homes and villages, to avoid arguments, and to shun adultery. In addition, he told them to be compassionate and to accept one another, no matter what the differences between them might be. This was a radical change. Before Mwindo was born, his father decreed that his daughters were to be allowed to live while his sons must die. Under Mwindo's rulership, pronouncements favoring one group of people over another were no longer permitted, and all people, even those who were invalids, were considered equally worthy.

Nyamitondo: A Sister's Story

In African mythology, heroes are male but they live in a world populated by powerful women who support them, fortify them, and take heroic actions on their own. One such female is Mwindo's sister Nyamitondo. She was married to Nkuba, the master of lightning, who lived in the sky and taught her, among other skills, how to cultivate bananas. When she descended to earth for a visit, she passed her expertise on to Mwindo, who used it to his advantage in the underworld.

During that same visit, she and Mwindo stumbled across an egg. They carefully placed it into a hen's nest to be hatched, and soon a bird emerged. It grew so big that it gobbled up chickens and goats—and it continued to grow. Mwindo and Nyamitondo wanted to protect the community but they didn't know what to do. So they climbed into heaven via a hollow tree and discussed the problem with Nkuba, who gave them weapons.

Upon their descent to earth, they discovered that the bird had devoured all the people of the village and yet it was still hungry. The moment it saw Nyamitondo, it swallowed her too. Fortunately, like any hero, she had her weapons ready. She cut her way out of the bird's stomach, killing the bird, freeing all the residents of the town who had been swallowed, and becoming, at least in this version, the liberator of the people.

Cú Chulainn

The Celtic hero Cú Chulainn may have actually lived during the first century CE. He passed into myth in *The Cattle Raid of Cooley* (*Táin Bó Cuailange*), an epic tale about the struggle between the forces of Ulster in northern Ireland and Connaught in the west. First committed to print around the seventh or eighth century (although we know it from twelfth-century versions, the earlier manuscripts having been destroyed by Scandinavian invaders), *The Cattle Raid of Cooley* has been called the Irish *Iliad*. Cú Chulainn is its Achilles.

Although his exploits in war were remarkable, what distinguishes Cú Chulainn is his childhood. Unlike those heroes who drop out of sight after birth and reemerge, like Jesus or Hercules, only when they're old enough to be interesting, Cú Chulainn had a childhood filled with incident. By the time he was five, he had fully established himself as a hero—violent, dominant, loyal, and clever.

The Birth of Cú Chulainn

Cú Chulainn's birth was surrounded by mystery and uncertainty. His mother (or foster mother) was Dechtire, who was known for little else; his father was either King Conchobar of Ulster, who was Dechtire's father or brother; the sun god Lugh; or a mortal named Suataimh. And the circumstances of his birth were so complicated that, according to one story, Cú Chulainn was born three times.

Before he was born, a flock of birds descended upon the land and consumed everything in sight. Like other elements of Celtic mythology, they behaved in mathematically precise ways, flying in nine groups of twenty each, with each pair linked by a silver chain. Dechtire and Conchobar went out to chase the birds. In the course of their journey, they took shelter with a couple who were awaiting the birth of a baby.

That night, the woman went into labor and gave birth to a boy. Outside, a mare delivered two foals, the Gray of Macha and the

Black of Saingliu, which ultimately became Cú Chulainn's steeds. In the morning, the house, the birds, and everything else disappeared. Only the baby and the two foals remained. Dechtire and Conchobar took the child and returned to Emain Macha, the capital of Ulster, to raise it. But to her great sorrow, the baby died. Dechtire went into mourning. Then one day while she was sipping from a copper vessel, a tiny creature, hitherto invisible, jumped into her mouth.

Shortly afterwards, Lugh appeared in her dream. He was the father of the child who died, he told her, and he would be the father of the child she would bear, whose name would be Setanta. Dechtire realized that she was pregnant. Soon everyone else in Ulster knew it too. They suspected that the person responsible must be her father, Conchobar, who was prone to drunkenness and bad behavior. To squash the rumors, Conchobar married her off to a man named Suataimh. Nevertheless, Dechtire was so ashamed that she induced a miscarriage.

Then she got pregnant again. Conchobar could have been responsible, but the same might be said of Lugh or Suataimh. It's even possible that the baby was conceived when his mother swallowed a fly. In any event, Dechtire had a baby boy whom she named Setanta.

Cú Chulainn Earns His Name

Five years later, a smith named Culann invited Conchobar to a feast. Before he left Ulster to attend this event, Conchobar noticed a group of boys playing ball on the palace grounds. On one side of the green, one hundred fifty boys—three times fifty—were trying to throw their balls into a hole; on the other side, Setanta, acting as goalie, would deflect them. Not one ball entered the hole. When it was Setanta's turn to throw balls into the hole, he hit the mark one hundred fifty times.

Conchobar was so impressed that he asked the boy to accompany him. Setanta promised to follow when he was done playing. Conchobar suggested that he wait, lest the boy get lost. Setanta assured him that he would have no difficulty tracking the king's horses and chariots.

So Conchobar rode ahead. When he reached Culann's home, the

smith asked if anyone else might be arriving. No, said Conchobar, for he had forgotten about the boy. In that case, said Culann, he would unleash his bloodhound, who guarded his estate. Culann and Conchobar went inside, leaving the savage dog to patrol the premises.

Soon the boy appeared, carrying his toys. He tossed his toy javelin and shield onto the lawn, and the bloodhound started to growl. Now, this was not an ordinary dog. He was as muscular as a hundred other dogs combined and he wanted to devour the boy. To protect himself, Setanta hurled his last toy, a child's ball, at the dog. It ripped through the air, into the dog's mouth, and through his body, exiting in the back and dragging the dog's guts with it. Setanta picked up the dog by the hind legs, smashed it against a stone, and broke it into pieces.

Culann was not happy. Without the hound, he explained, he would have no livelihood, for the dog guarded his land. The boy promised to find a puppy from the same line and to raise him as a substitute. Until then, he promised to guard Culann's estate himself. And that is how Setanta, the guardian of his people, came to be named Cú Chulainn, the Hound (*cú*) of Culann.

Cú Chulainn the Warrior

When Cú Chulainn was small, he heard Cathbad the Druid say that anyone who took up arms for the first time on that day would be guaranteed the warrior's dream: a short life and an eternity of fame, the very fate that befell Achilles. Inspired, Cú Chulainn put aside his toys and asked Conchobar for real weapons. Conchobar gave him one set of weapons after another—fifteen in all—but none could withstand his strength. Only one sword, shield, and chariot proved sturdy enough for the boy: the king's own.

With those weapons in hand, Cú Chulainn and his charioteer drove off in search of adventure. As they drove, Cú Chulainn noted the name and location of every fort. At one, he encountered three men, the sons of Nechtan, who had killed many warriors of Ulster.

Seeing that Cú Chulainn was only a child, they spoke threateningly to him. In return, he cut off their heads.

That was the beginning of an impressive career in carnage. Cú Chulainn trained for battle under the auspices of the warrior queen Scathach, who gave him a magical barbed spear known as the Gae Bolga and taught him to vault over castle ramparts like a salmon leaping over the waves. He also had a magical chariot complete with a charioteer who knew the secret of invisibility.

But his real secret weapon was his appearance. Normally, Cú Chulainn had seven fingers on each hand, seven toes on each foot, and seven pupils in each eye. His cheeks were red, blue, yellow, and green. He wore jewels in his tricolored hair, and his chest gleamed with a hundred golden ornaments. In the frenzy of battle, he changed shape so bizarrely that he was known as "the warped one." His muscles swelled and his body twisted in its skin until his calves and backside faced forward and his feet and knees turned backwards. Flames shot out of his mouth, light radiated from his head, and his hair stood on end with each individual hair topped by a drop of blood or a tiny flash of fire. From the crown of his head, a jet of black blood gushed into the air like the mast of a ship. When he was most enraged, one eye receded into his skull while the other popped out on a single optical stalk. His bellicosity knew no bounds.

The problem was that after such a display, he needed to calm down. It wasn't easy. Words didn't help. At last Conchobar hit upon a method. He asked the women of Ulster to parade naked in front of Cú Chulainn (just as the gopis paraded naked in front of Krishna) and he lowered him into a barrel of icy water. When the barrel burst from the heat of his body, Cú Chulainn dove into a second barrel. The water bubbled and steamed, but the hero was cooling off and the barrel held its shape. Finally, he plunged into a third barrel. The cold water grew tepid and he returned to his normal shape.

Macha's Curse

Macha, one of many Celtic goddesses of war, had three incarnations and three husbands. In her first life she was married to Nemed, the leader of the third mythical invasion of Ireland. In her next life, she was a warrior who was killed with her husband by Balor of the Evil Eye, the Celtic Medusa. Finally, she was married to a widower from Ulster named Crunnchu. One day at a festival, he boasted that his wife could run faster than the king's horses. Angered by the insult, the king gave her a choice: either she agreed to race against his steeds or Crunnchu would be killed.

The king didn't care that Macha was nine months pregnant. He wouldn't back down. So Macha entered the race. The horses took off in a blur of hooves and dust, and Macha stretched herself to the limit and outran them all. As she crossed the finish line, she collapsed, gave birth to twins, and died—but not before putting a curse on all the men of Ulster.

Macha's curse was this: for nine times nine generations, whenever Ulster was in danger, the men would become as weak as a woman in childbirth, and they would remain in that state for five days. Only one warrior was exempt: Cú Chulainn. Thereafter he fought ferociously on behalf of the people of Ulster but thanks to the curse, he always fought alone.

Cú Chulainn in Love

Despite his horrifying appearance, Cú Chulainn was irresistible to women, and he had many lovers. The love of his life was his wife Emer, a beauty who possessed wisdom, chastity, skill with the needle, and a melodious voice. When Cú Chulainn asked for her hand, her father, Fogall, told Cú Chulainn that before he married Emer, he would have to travel and gain more experience. So Cú Chulainn spent a year and a day in the Land of Shadows, studying the arts of war with Scathach, the warrior queen. During that time, he became lovers first with Scathach's daughter Uathach and then with her sister, Aoifa, who gave birth to his son Conlaí.

When he returned to Emer, Fogall was still unwilling to accept him as a son-in-law. A battle broke out between them in the course of which Fogall accidentally leaped to his death. Emer and Cú Chulainn married. The wedding did not mark the end of his amatory adventures.

Cú Chulainn's most famous extramarital affair was with Fand, the Pearl of Beauty, who had been abandoned by her husband, the sea god Manannan Mac Lir. Cú Chulainn stayed with her for an entire month. When Emer discovered what was going on, she prepared to murder Fand. Manannan also learned about the affair, and he had a different response. Seeking a reconciliation, he asked his wife to choose between her lover and himself.

In truth, Fand preferred Cú Chulainn. But she knew that he would never leave Emer. So she chose her husband. "Farewell to you, dear Cú!," she says in a twelfth-century manuscript. "I wish that I were not going." She couldn't stop thinking about him, though, and Cú Chulainn felt similarly. He gave up food and drink, withdrew into the mountains, and remained until the Druids came to save him. They gave both Emer and Cú Chulainn a magic potion, which enabled them to put the whole episode behind them. Afterwards, to make certain that there would be no further assignations, Manannan stood between Fand and Cú Chulainn and shook his magic cloak, assuring that the two adulterous lovers would never see each other again.

The Cattle Raid of Cooley

Of all Cú Chulainn's enemies, the most formidable was Queen Medb of Connacht, a sorceress known for her promiscuity. During the period written about in *The Cattle Raid of Cooley*, she was married to King Ailill, one of her many husbands. One day, they compared possessions. The lists were equal with one exception: Ailill owned a great white-horned bull that had originally been hers. But the animal, unwilling to be a woman's prize bull, walked away from Medb's herd and voluntarily joined Ailill's. Medb wanted an equally magnificent bull for her own herd. There was only one candidate: the brown bull of Cooley. But the owner of the brown bull, a man of Ulster, refused to sell. So Medb gathered her forces and invaded.

Cú Chulainn, chief defender of Ulster, killed many of Medb's soldiers. Among them was a warrior named Cailidín whose widow gave birth to three girls and three boys. Medb sent them abroad to study sorcery, and the war raged on.

Cú Chulainn fought valiantly. At first he killed his opponents in batches of a hundred. After Medb complained, he reduced the carnage by fighting a single warrior at a time. This allowed Medb's forces to capture the brown bull. She immediately sent it to Connacht, home of the white-horned bull. Inevitably, the animals came face to face. They snorted, pawed the ground, lowered their horns at each other, and began to fight.

The battle ranged all over Ireland. The bulls were well-matched but the brown bull, which was so large that fifty boys could frolic on its back, proved stronger. It killed the white-horned bull, hoisted its considerable bulk up on its horns, and carried it back to Ulster. However, in Cooley, something terrible happened. Some say the bull ran head-on into a mountain; others say its heart burst. Either way, the brown bull died, and peace came to the people of Ulster and Connacht.

But Medb did not forgive Cú Chulainn—and she wasn't the only one. Years before, the shape-shifting triple goddess of war known as the Morrigan took the form of an appealing young woman and tried to seduce Cú Chulainn. When he rejected her advances, they came to blows and he wounded her. That incident, so long ago, still rankled her. Her anger sealed his fate.

The Death of Cú Chulainn

Years passed. Cailidín's children, trained by sorcerers under the direction of Medb, returned with a mission: to kill Cú Chulainn. When word of this plan got out, everyone who loved Cú Chulainn, including his mistress, Niamh, and all the Druids of Ulster, tried to protect him. But the children of Cailidín were determined to lure him into a fight.

First, they surrounded him with sound. Everywhere he went, he brought the clamor of battle and the clanging of swords with him. No one could stand the noise. Like a bad smell, it accompanied Cú Chulainn everywhere. It was so unpleasant that Conchobar banished Cú Chulainn to the valley of the deaf, where he bothered no one.

Cailidín's children quickly located him. This time, they surrounded him with the sights of war. They crafted soldiers out of puffballs, thistles, and dry leaves and they covered the hills and valleys with them. Then they filled the countryside with the sounds of invasions, with lamentations, the cries of wounded men, and the bleating of trumpets and horns. Cú Chulainn refused to fight.

Finally, Badb, one of Cailidín's daughters and one aspect of the Morrigan, took on the appearance of Niamh and urged him into battle. Moved by the power of love, Cú Chulainn assented. Niamh—the real Niamh—tried to tell him that he had succumbed to an illusion and that she would never send him into battle. He had been beguiled and did not believe her. So Cú Chulainn prepared to go to war.

The omens were bad. Weapons fell from the wall and clattered on the floor. A glass of wine (or milk) turned to blood in his hand. His brooch fell off and pierced his foot. And as he tried to mount his chariot, one of his horses, the Gray of Macha, balked and shed tears of blood. The worst thing was that for the only time in his life, he was forced to break his magical and mutually exclusive geissi. According to one such injunction, whenever he passed a hearth where someone was cooking, he had to share the meal. According to another, he was forbidden to eat dog. The fighting hadn't even begun when he passed three old women—yet another form of the Morrigan—roasting a dog on a spit of rowan wood. Forced to participate in the feast, he nibbled part of the shoulder, which weakened him. He was further weakened, in a classic Celtic manner, when a poet threatened to satirize him. Cú Chulainn could not allow that to happen. He threw his spear so hard that it killed not only the poet but the nine men standing behind him.

Then a warrior named Lugaid, the son of a sorcerer whom Cú Chulainn had killed in his youth, hurled a spear at Cú Chulainn's charioteer. Another warrior grabbed the spear and heaved it at the Grey of Macha. Then Lugaid threw it at Cú Chulain and the spear found its target. Cú Chulainn's guts spilled out. He scooped them up and went to the river to wash. When an otter, or water-dog, tried to drink the bloodied water, he killed it with a stone. This was the final sign, for a prophecy made in his youth had said that his first and last acts would be the killing of a dog.

Knowing that he was about to die, Cú Chulainn stumbled over to a standing stone and strapped himself to it so he could die in an upright position. For three days, he remained there as his life force ebbed away. At last a black crow, the Morrigan in one of her forms, perched on the stone, signaling that Cú Chulainn was dead. Lugaid beheaded him. Thus the words of Cathbad the Druid came true, for Cú Chulainn had a short life—he was twenty-seven when he died—but he gained eternal fame.

As for his enemy Medb, the warrior queen, she died when her nephew, using a sling, hit her with a lump of hard cheese.

The Heroic Lover

The quest for love is part of the hero's journey but heroes don't always acquit themselves well on the fields of Eros. Noble Odysseus returned to his faithful Penelope (after spending seven years with the goddess Calypso) and wept when he took her in his arms. But Theseus deserted Ariadne, Heracles killed his family, Jason married Medea and then—worse idea yet—divorced her, and the Celtic hero Finn MacCool, a great warrior in his youth, made a complete hash of things in his old age.

Finn MacCool, also known as Fionn Mac Cumhail, was raised by a female Druid. But he gained his greatest wisdom, not to mention his clairvoyance, while working for the poet Finnegas.

The Salmon of Knowledge

The Book of Genesis speaks of the Tree of Knowledge. Carlos Casteñada refers to the Moth of Knowledge. And the Celts tell about the Salmon of Knowledge. Originally the sagacious fish was a man named Fintan who turned into a salmon during the primordial flood. Later, he ate the Hazelnuts of Knowledge which dangled over the Well of Knowledge. He possessed all knowledge, and Finnegas longed to catch him. After seven years of effort, he succeeded.

Anxious to eat the fish and gain its wisdom, Finnegas instructed his student Finn MacCool, then known as Demhne, to cook it over the flames and to be certain not to eat any of it. The boy tended the fire carefully, but by accident he touched the roasting fish and, without thinking, put his thumb in his mouth. When he reported this transgression Finnegas, the poet realized that the knowledge he sought would be given to his student, not to him. He named the boy Finn and told him to eat the rest of the fish. After that, whenever Finn needed information, he sucked his thumb and all was revealed.

Finn's Pursuit of Love

As a young man, Finn was known for his good sense, kindness, and bravery. Those qualities seemed to desert him as he grew old. He was no longer young when he was betrothed to a beautiful woman named Grainne. She may have returned his affection, but at the wedding ceremony, her glance fell upon one of Finn's lieutenants, Diarmaid Ua Duibhne ("Of the Love Spot"), a man so appealing that anyone who glanced at a certain spot on his forehead was immediately smitten. Grainne fell deeply in love. All thoughts of Finn flew out of her head, and she turned the full force of her affection toward Diarmaid, who didn't know what to do. He thought his loyalty should belong to his commander, but Grainne bound him to her by way of a sacred geis which required him to take her away. Diarmaid turned his back on Finn MacCool and escaped with Grainne.

Finn and the Fianna, a band of elite warrios under his command, pursued the couple without success. At every turn the young lovers were aided by Diarmaid's foster father Oenghus, the god of love, and they consistently avoided capture. The chase continued for sixteen years until Finn, thoroughly exhausted, pardoned them. Yet his fine words of acceptance masked the truth. In his heart, Finn had not forgiven them.

Diarmaid and Grainne settled down at Tara and had five children, four boys and a girl. Then one day Finn invited Diarmaid to a boar hunt. This assured his rival's doom, for it had been predicted that Diarmaid would be killed by a magic boar. In one variant of this story, Diarmaid is gored by the boar and dies. In another, he is scratched by one of the boar's poisonous bristles. The venom seeps through his system slowly. He lingers. He can actually be saved, and Finn has the ability to do so simply by giving him a sip of water. Finn cups his hands and fills them with water. But he lets the water trickle through his fingers, and Diarmaid dies.

Finn MacCool's own death is shrouded in uncertainty. He may have died while putting down an uprising among his troops. He may have drowned in the River Boyne. Or he may have climbed into a dark cave somewhere and gone to sleep. Like Arthur, the once and future king, who boarded a ship for Avalon and was never seen again, Finn MacCool may one day return—presumably with the wisdom of his youth restored.

CELTIC MYTHOLOGY: THE MAJOR SOURCES

Ultimately it is impossible to separate mythology from literature, for that which is born in the oral tradition often dies unless it finds literary expression. In Gaul, for instance, the Druids knew how to write and did so regularly. But they did not believe in recording their mythology, and as a result, little survives. In Ireland and Wales, on the other hand, there is a wealth of material, though it is relatively recent and smacks of Christianity. The most important Welsh source is the *Mabinogion,* a fourteenth-century collection of tales, including several about King Arthur. Irish sources, all from the twelfth century, include the following:

- the *Book of Conquest of Ireland,* which tells of the successive invasions of Ireland, beginning with Cesair, Noah's granddaughter.
- the *Book of the Dun Cow* and *The Cattle Raid of Cooley,* both of which chronicle the deeds of Cú Chulainn.
- the *Book of Leinster,* which includes *The Interrogation of Old Men,* in which the poet Oisín spends three centuries in the land of perpetual youth before meeting Saint Patrick, whose questioning provides the opportunity to recount stories about his father, Finn MacCool, and the pagan past.

Psyche

It would be a fine thing if the great heroes of classical mythology had female counterparts who performed the kind of astonishing deeds we expect from Hercules or Xena the Warrior Princess. Alas, there is no such heroine, with the possible exception of Psyche, whose story was written down—or perhaps invented—by the Latin writer Lucius Apulius in his second-century novel *The Golden Ass.* The tale of her harrowing adventures and her marriage to Eros (or Cupid or Amor) has been interpreted as an allegory of the journey of the soul through life and death, as a myth of feminine individuation, and as an itinerary of relationship that begins in the dark and ends, many episodes later, in joy.

The ancient Greeks thought of Eros (or Cupid) as an adolescent. As time passed, he grew progressively younger. By the Renaissance, when this woodcut was made, he had become a chubby baby, a status he maintains today.

Psyche—"soul" in Latin—was so lovely that as she walked down the street, people offered her garlands of flowers, and after a while, they literally began to worship her. Their devotion was so extreme that Venus felt slighted and sought to make her powers known. She summoned her winged son Eros and asked him to use his magic arrows to make Psyche fall passionately in love with someone utterly vile. Then Venus "with parted lips kissed her son long and fervently." Her words were ineffective. The moment Eros saw Psyche, he was smitten.

Meanwhile, Psyche's parents were worried. Their other two daughters, ordinary girls, were married to kings, while Psyche was always alone. She was so beautiful that no one dared approach her. Finally, her despairing father asked the oracle of Apollo at Miletus for advice. The news wasn't good. Apollo said he must give up all hope for a mortal bridegroom, dress the girl for her funeral, and leave her on a craggy mountaintop. Weeping, Psyche's parents did as directed, leaving their youngest daughter trembling at the summit.

She wasn't there long. Along came the West Wind, which picked her up, wafted her down the slope, and deposited her in a field of flowers, where Psyche fell asleep. When she awoke, Apuleius tells us, "the tempest had passed from her soul."

Looking around, she saw a grove of tall trees, a transparent fountain, and a luxurious palace with gold columns and a roof made of sandalwood and ivory. She wandered over to the palace, and a voice told her to make herself at home. That night, Eros became her lover. Every night he made love to Psyche—in the dark. He insisted that she must never try to see his face, and she promised to obey. But such promises are made to be broken, or what's a story for?

After some time had passed, Eros told her that her sisters thought she was dead. Psyche was distraught. She found it impossible to ignore their sorrow. To reassure them, she brought them to the palace (with the help of the West Wind) and related her story. When she reached the part about never seeing her lover's face, her intuition told her to lie. Her husband was young and handsome, she said, and, thinking about his bow and arrows, she added that he was involved with hunting. Afraid of further questioning, she filled their arms with gifts and sent them on their way.

Anyone who remembers Cinderella knows that in stories like this, older sisters are bad news. Soon the sisters were eaten up with envy. It hardly seemed fair, one of them whined, that Psyche was married to a rich and handsome man when she had "a husband older than my father, balder than a pumpkin, and feebler than any child." The other voice similar complaints. Their envy turned to suspicion on the next visit, when Psyche made up a story that conflicted with the first. This time, she said her husband was middle-aged with grizzled hair. Psyche's sisters began to plot against her.

That night, Eros told her that she was pregnant and warned that she and the child were in danger from the sisters. "If you keep my secret in silence," he told her, "he shall be a god; if you divulge it, a mortal." The sisters had different ideas. It occurred to them that Psyche had no idea what her husband looked like, and they began to suggest terrible scenarios to her. Perhaps he was a snake, they said, who intended to devour her as soon as the baby was born. To protect herself, they suggested that she take a lantern into his room while he was sleeping and cut off his head. They frightened her so badly that she decided to do as they suggested. One night she took an oil lamp and a knife, and while Eros slumbered, she lifted the lamp above his bed and gazed at him for the first time.

He was not a monster, as her sisters had led her to suppose, for this is not a story about disappointment, about learning to accept reality, about sensing the soul of beauty beneath the face of the beast. No: this is a story of true love. At that climactic moment when Psyche was breaking her promise, she was overwhelmed by her beloved's tangled curls and dazzlingly, godlike beauty, and she dropped the knife. Then the lamp sputtered and a drop of oil fell on his shoulder and woke him. Thus Psyche broke her vow—and shattered the relationship. She "refused to remain in the garden of the unconscious," writes Jungian psychotherapist Connie Zweig. "Like Eve, she chose knowledge and sacrificed the innocence of the original relationship, enabling it to become something more."

Within moments, Eros spread his feathery white wings and flew away, with Psyche clinging to his leg. When she lost her grip, she tumbled to earth and, miraculously unhurt, realized she was near the home of one of her sisters. No longer in the dark, Psyche confided the whole sorry tale but now, understanding at last that her sister was not her friend, she made one guileful addition. She confided that Eros promised to marry her sister just as he had once married her.

Her sister, wed to a man who disgusted her, took the bait. She climbed to the top of the same mountain where Psyche had gone in her funeral clothes, called out to Eros, and, trusting in the West Wind, jumped. But the West Wind did not lift her up. Eros did not come to her aid. She fell to the rocks below and died. Then Psyche visited the other sister and told a similar story, with similar results.

Venus Reacts

When a white seagull related this to Venus, she was furious, first at her disobedient son, who was recuperating from the wound he received when the drop of oil fell on his shoulder, and then at Psyche. She determined to seek revenge. Just as Hera persecuted Heracles yet drove him into heroism, Venus badgered Psyche, presenting her with a series of seemingly undoable chores which are the most important part of the hero's journey. Intent on being reunited with her beloved, Psyche plunged in.

Her wanderings brought her to a deserted temple that belonged to Ceres, the goddess of grain. Psyche straightened it up, and her housekeeping efforts earned high marks from the goddess. But Ceres was loyal to Venus and refused to help Psyche. Juno refused to help for the same reason. Psyche was forced to face the goddess of love herself.

Although the artwork that this meeting has inspired is often very pretty, Apuleius reports that Venus tormented Psyche, tearing her clothes, messing up her hair, beating her, and even having her whipped. Then she gave her a series of tasks.

The Labors of Psyche

Psyche's first assignment was to separate an overflowing heap of seeds and grains into individual piles of millet, corn, barley, lentils, beans, poppy seeds, and so forth. Psyche didn't know how to begin this hopeless task. Fortunately, a parade of ants showed up and, one by one, carried each tiny seed to its proper place, thus bringing order to chaos.

Then Venus directed Psyche to retrieve some fleece from a wild herd of golden sheep whose bite was said to be poisonous. Psyche, easily discouraged, was ready to commit suicide by throwing herself over a cliff, but a green reed by the river counseled patience. Wait until the sheep leave their grazing place, the reed whispered, and it will be easy to find a few tufts of wool clinging to twigs. Psyche wandered through the meadow at dusk and found exactly what she wanted.

Her third task was to fill a crystal bottle with icy water from a stream whose black waters, guarded by long-necked dragons, gushed from a slippery mountaintop into the River Styx. Psyche climbed to the summit, only to discover that the waters were inaccessible, having worn a deep crevasse into the mountain side, and menacing. As they cascaded through the fissure and into the river, they hissed that she was doomed to die. Psyche was terrified. Once again, the world of the spirit came to her aid in the form of Jove's eagle, who claimed to be on an errand from Venus and easily obtained the water for her.

Her final task was the most dangerous. Venus gave Psyche a small casket and instructed her to go down to the underworld and ask Proserpine, queen of the dead, to fill it with beauty. Once again, Psyche considered suicide. She decided to fling herself off a tower. But the tower spoke up, giving her complicated directions to the underworld and many suggestions about what to do once she got there. It was important, the tower said, to hold barley cakes in her hands and to keep two coins in her mouth. With the cakes, she could distract the three-headed dog Cerberus who guarded the entrance to the underworld; with the coins, she could purchase a round-trip passage across the River Styx. The tower told her that she would meet a man driving a lame ass who would ask her to pick up a piece of wood for him: she must silently refuse. Crossing the river, she would see a dead man floating in the awful waters. He would ask to be lifted into the ferry: she must decline. Finally an old woman weaving a web would ask for help: again, her answer must be no. It was essential that Psyche set aside her compassion and ignore these pitiful requests, for if she did not, she was likely to drop the cakes, which she was going to need if she intended to return. She received other warnings, too: she must refuse to eat the delicious feast Proserpine would offer her and ask instead for rough bread. She must sit on the floor rather than relaxing on an irresistibly comfortable chair. And one more thing: once Proserpine filled the box with beauty, she must not look inside it.

So Psyche began the journey. She gave coins to Charon and cakes to Cerberus, she chatted with Proserpine, and she made it safely back to the light of day, casket of beauty in hand. Back on earth, she gave in to her curiosity, risked everything,

On her way to the underworld, Psyche pays Charon's fee. Wood engraving by William Morris (1834–1896). (Courtesy of the Library of Congress)

and peeked inside the box, which held a dark and Stygian sleep. Psyche fell into a stupor so deep she looked dead.

At that moment, all appears lost. Psyche fails. "But although she does not know it," writes Jungian psychologist Erich Neumann, "it is precisely this failure that brings her victory." Once she ignores the prohibition and looks into the box of beauty as a conscious choice, she is ready to meet her divine lover on equal ground.

At that moment, Eros saw that his wound had healed. He flew to Psyche's side, scraped off the sleep, and squeezed it back into the box. Then he woke her with a prick of his arrows. Psyche returned to consciousness and gave the box to Venus, thus completing her assignment.

Yet a barrier still separated the two lovers, for one was a god and one was mortal. So Eros flew to Jove to ask for assistance. Jove complained that Eros had embarrassed him on many occasions, causing him to fall prey to lust, to commit adultery, and to disfigure himself through disguises. Nonetheless, he announced to all the gods that it was time for Eros to marry, that "the wanton spirit of boyhood must be enchained in the fetters of wedlock." Then he gave Psyche a goblet of nectar to drink and she became immortal.

The wedding was spectacular. Vulcan cooked, Apollo strummed the lyre, Pan played the pipes, and the Hours, the Graces, and the Muses filled the hall with flowers and song. Even Venus kicked up her heels and danced.

Not long afterwards, Psyche had her baby. It wasn't a son, as Eros had expected. It was a daughter whom they named "Pleasure" or "Joy," which is always what you get when soul and desire, Psyche and Eros, are united in love.

GLOSSARY

Acamas: Son of Theseus and Phaedra; one of the soldiers inside the Trojan Horse.

Acca Larentia: Foster mother of Romulus and Remus; sometimes said to be a famous courtesan.

Achelous: A shape-shifting river god; father of the Sirens.

Achilles: The greatest hero of the Trojan War; son of Peleus and Thetis, who dipped him into the River Styx, rendering him invulnerable except in the spot where she held him, the heel. He withdrew from the war when Agamemmnon commandeered his war prize, the young Briseis, but re-entered the conflict after Hector slew his friend Patroclus. Achilles killed Hector and was slain by Paris, which fulfilled the prophecy that he would lead a short, heroic life.

Acrisius: King of Argos; father of Danaë; grandfather of Perseus.

Actaeon: A hunter who glimpsed Artemis while she was bathing. She turned him into a stag and he was devoured by his dogs.

Admete: Daughter of King Eurystheus.

Admetus: The husband of Alcestis; an Argonaut and a participant in the Calydonian boar hunt. Apollo served him as a slave. *See* Alcestis.

Adonis: The handsome son of Smyrna and Cinyras, adored by Aphrodite and Persephone; originally a Phoenician god ("adon" means lord in Phoenician) identified with Tammuz.

Aeacus: Leader of the Myrmidons; son of Aegina and Zeus; father of Peleus.

Aedon: Sister of Niobe; mother of Itylus, whom she accidentally killed.

Aeetes: King of Colchis; son of Helios; father of Medea and Apsyrtus; brother of Circe and Pasiphaë. Aeetes promised to give Jason the Golden Fleece but reneged on his offer.

Aegeus: Mortal father of Theseus; Medea's second husband.

Aegina: Daughter of the river god Asopus; mother of Aeacus.

Aegisthus: Clytemnestra's lover.

Aegyptus: King of Arabia; father of fifty sons, forty-nine of whom were slain on their wedding night by the daughters of his brother Danaus.

Aeneas: Hero of Virgil's *Aeneid*; son of Venus and Anchises; lover of Dido; a warrior on the side of Troy. His descendants include Romulus and Remus.

Aeolus: God of the winds.

Aerope: Wife of Atreus; mother of Agamemmnon and Menelaus. She was seduced by her brother-in-law Thyestes.

Aesir: The younger generation of gods in Norse mythology; residents of Asgard.

Aeson: Father of Jason; brother of Pelias, who usurped his throne.

Aether: "Ether" or "Brightness" of the upper atmosphere; son of Night (Nyx) and Darkness (Erebos).

Aethra: Mother of Theseus. She was abducted by the Dioscouri and given to Helen as a slave.

Afagddu: "Utter Darkness"; son of the Celtic goddess Cerridwen; the ugliest man in the world.

Agamemnon: King of Mycenae; son of Atreus; brother of Menelaus; husband of Clytemnestra; father of Iphigenia, Electra, and Orestes; Greek commander during the Trojan War. When his ships were unable to sail due to calm seas, Agamemnon sacrificed Iphigenia. After the war, he returned to Mycenae with Cassandra and was murdered by Clytemnestra and Aegisthus.

Agave (or Agauë): Daughter of Cadmus and Harmonia; mother of Pentheus.

Aglaia: The youngest Grace; according to Hesiod, the wife of Hephaestus.

Aglaurus: Lover of Ares; daughter of Cecrops; sister of Herse and Pandrosus; mother of Alcippe. According to Ovid, Hermes turned her to stone because she denied him access to her sister Herse.

Agni: Hindu god of fire; one of three primary gods in the *Rig Veda* (the others being Indra and Surya). Agni has red skin, two faces, and seven tongues, useful for licking up clarified butter at sacrifices. Once, according to the Mahabarata, he overindulged in this treat and became exhausted. He renewed his energy by consuming, as only fire can, an entire forest.

Ailill: King of Connacht; husband of Queen Medb. Seven other characters in Celtic mythology also claim this name.

Ajax: The name of two Greek warriors in the Trojan War. The Greater Ajax, renowned for his courage, was so insulted when the armor of Achilles went to Odysseus rather than himself that he attacked a flock of sheep. Ashamed of his rampage, he committed suicide by falling on his sword. The Lesser Ajax raped Cassandra and was drowned by Poseidon.

Alcestis: Wife of Admetus. She agreed to die in his place and was rescued from the underworld by Heracles.

Alcinous: Son of Poseidon; father of Nausicaa; husband of Arete. He is known for his hospitality to Odysseus.

Alcippe: Daughter of Ares and Aglaurus; raped by Poseidon's son Halir-rhothiuss.

Alcithoë: Sister of Arsippe and Leucippe. The three sisters shunned Dionysus and were driven mad as a result.

Alcmene: Mother of Heracles; last mortal woman beloved by Zeus.

Alcyone: One of the Pleiades; alternatively, the daughter of Aeolus. She and her husband Ceyx were turned into sea birds for having the affrontery to call each other Hera and Zeus. Nonetheless, they continued to mate. Once a year, Aeolus calmed the seas for a week so that Alcyone could hatch her eggs on her water-borne nest. Those seven days came to be known as halcyon.

LEOPOLD BLOOM ON HALYCON DAYS

I was in my teens, a growing boy. A little then sufficed, a jolting car, the mingling odours of the ladies' cloakroom and lavatory . . . And then the heat. There were sunspots that summer. End of school. And tipsycake. Halcyon Days.

—James Joyce, *Ulysses*

Althaea: Mother of Deineira and Meleager.

Amalthea: The nymph or goat who protected the infant Zeus.

Amaterasu: Japanese sun goddess; divine ancestor of the imperial family.

Amaunet: Egyptian goddess of hidden power; a member of the Ogdoad.

Amazons: A race of warriors who lived in all-female societies. To improve their skill with the bow and arrow, they supposedly cut off their right breasts (*maza* in Greek). *See* Hippolyta and Penthesilea.

Ame-no-Uzume: Japanese goddess of the dawn.

Amma: Supreme deity of the Dogon.

Amon (Ammon, Amun, Amen): "Hidden One"; the ram-headed supreme god of the Egyptian pantheon, later merged with the sun god Ra (or Re).

Amor: Latin name for Eros.

Ampelos: A youth beloved by Dionysus.

Amphion: Niobe's husband. He was such a fine musician that once when he strummed his lyre, the stones rolled off a mountaintop and formed the city of Thebes.

Amphissus: Son of Apollo and Dryope.

Amphitrite: A sea goddess; wife of Poseidon; sister of Thetis; mother of Triton.

Amphitryon: Husband of Alcmene; father of Iphicles; stepfather of Heracles.

Anat: Canaanite fertility goddess; sister of Baal.

Anchises: Father of Aeneas.

Andromeda: Daughter of Cepheus and Cassiopeia, who claimed to be more beautiful than the Nereids. Poseidon punished her by sending a sea monster, Cetus, to ravage the kingdom. Anxious to get rid of it, Cepheus consulted an oracle and was told to sacrifice Andromeda. She was chained to a rock by the sea and rescued by Perseus.

Angrboda: A frost giant in Nordic mythology; Loki's first wife; mother of Hel, the Midgard Serpent, and the wolf Fenrir.

Anshar: Babylonian god of the horizon.

Antaeus: A giant son of Gaia and Poseidon. Every time he touched the earth, he grew stronger. Heracles lifted him into the air and killed him.

Anticlea: Mother of Odysseus; wife of Laertes. She died of grief for her wandering boy, who visited her in the underworld.

Antigone: Daughter of Oedipus. After he blinded himself, she became his guide. Later, she was sentenced to be buried alive for demanding that her brother Polyneices be given a proper burial. She hung herself instead.

Antiope: An Amazon queen who died in battle; sister of Hippolyte and Melanippe.

Anu: Babylonian god of sun and sky; father of Ea.

Anubis: An Egyptian god of the dead, depicted as a jackal-headed human or a wild black dog. He invented embalming and brought the dead to judgment.

Anunna: Mesopotamian goddess of war.

Aoifa: A Celtic warrior princess in the Land of Shadows; lover of Cú Chulainn; mother of his son Conlái.

Apep: Cosmic serpent of Egyptian mythology, also known as Apophis.

Aphrodite: Olympian goddess of love and beauty, known in Rome as Venus.

Apollo: Olympian god of healing, music, prophecy, light. Known as Phoebus ("bright") Apollo.

Apsu: Babylonian god of fresh water.

Apsyrtus: Brother of Medea, who chopped him up and tossed the pieces overboard as she and Jason escaped on the *Argo*.

Arachne: A mortal who challenged Athena to a weaving contest and was turned into a spider.

Arcas: Son of Callisto. He was turned into the constellation Ursa Minor (the little bear).

Ares: Olympian god of war, known in Rome as Mars.

Arges: Offspring of Gaia and Uranus; one of the Cyclopes.

Argonauts: The crew of the *Argo*, Jason's ship. They included Heracles, Orpheus, Peleus, Meleager, Telamon, Atlanta, Castor, and Polydeuces.

Argus: A many-eyed monster who guarded Io after she turned into a heifer.

Ariadne: Daughter of Minos; wife of Theseus, who deserted her on Naxos. Afterwards, she married Dionysus.

Aristaeus: Son of Apollo; god of bee keeping. According to Virgil, Eurydice was trying to escape from him when she was bitten by a snake and died.

Arjuna: The warrior whose battlefield discussions with Krishna about the nature of existence and the path to spiritual perfection make up the *Bhagavad Gita*.

Arsippe: *See* Alcithoë.

Artemis: Olympian goddess of the hunt and the moon, known in Rome as Diana.

Aruru: A Mesopotamian goddess who protects the unborn and eases the pain of childbirth. She created Enkidu as a companion for Gilgamesh.

Ascalaphus: Son of Acheron, one of the rivers in Hades.

Asclepius: God of healing; son of Apollo and Koronis.

Asgard: Home of the Aesir gods in Norse mythology. It was surrounded by a wall and connected to Midgard, the home of human beings, by the Bifrost Bridge.

Asherah: A Canaanite fertility goddess condemned in the Bible; associated with Astarte.

Asinmbabbar: A Sumerian moon god, associated with the new moon.

Astarte: Phoenician goddess of love and war, equivalent to Inanna and Ishtar; referred to in the Bible as Asherah or Ashtoreth.

Asteria: Leto's sister; mother of Hecate. To escape from Zeus, she became a quail, leaped into the sea, and turned into Ortygia (Greek for quail), an island in the Aegean.

Asterius: King of Crete; husband of Europa.

Atahensic: Creator, also known as Sky Woman; celestial ancestor of the Iroquois and Huron.

Atalanta: The fastest runner on earth; the only female to sail on the *Argo* or participate in the Calydonian Boar Hunt; wife of Hippomenes.

Aten: A form of the Egyptian Ra. His symbol, representing the sun at high noon, was a red solar disk with rays ending in tiny hands. Around 1374 BCE, Amenhotep IV outlawed the worship of Amon (Amen), changed his name to Akhenaten, and elevated Aten to the position of chief and only god. Twenty years later, his successor, Tutankhamen, reverted to the worship of Amen.

Athamas: King of Thebes; husband of Nephele, Ino, and Themistos.

Athena: Olympian goddess of wisdom and strategy; Homer calls her "Queen of Tactics"; daughter of Metis and Zeus, from whose forehead she was born.

Atlas: A Titan; brother of Prometheus and Epimetheus; father of the Pleiades and the Hesperides.

Aton: *See* Aten.

Atreus: Son of Pelops, father of Agamemnon and Menelaus; brother of Thyestes, whose children he cooked and served at a banquet.

Atropos: "Inevitable"; one of the three Fates.

Attis: A Phrygian god; son and lover of Cybele.

Atum: "The All"; the Egyptian creator. Atum represented the sun at dusk and is depicted as an old man wearing a double crown and carrying an ankh. He merged with the sun god to become Atum-Ra.

Audhumla: The primeval cow of Norse mythology.

Augeas: Son of Helios; owner of the filthy stables cleaned by Hercules. After Augeas refused to pay him for his labor, Hercules killed him.

Autonoë: Sister of Agave and Ino; mother of Actaeon.

Avalokitesvara: The Buddhist image of compassion, a bodhisattva who reached enlightenment yet chose to remain on earth helping less evolved souls; transformed in China into the goddess Kuan Yin.

Avalon: The Otherworld in Celtic mythology, also known as Annwn.

Ba: The soul in Egyptian mythology, depicted as a bird with a human head. In contrast, the *ka*, or spirit, represented the personality and had the same shape and qualities as the person.

Baal: "Lord"; a Canaanite god whose death and resurrection were celebrated annually.

Bacchus: Roman god of wine, known to the Greeks as Dionysus or Bacchos.

Badb: An Irish war goddess symbolized by the crow. Along with Nemain and Macha, she is one third of the triple goddess known as the Morrigan.

Baldur: Norse god of light; son of Odin and Frigg; killed with a sprig of mistletoe by his brother Hoder.

Balor: One-eyed chief of the Celtic monsters known as the Fomorians; killed by Lugh.

Bastet: Egyptian lion-headed sun goddess, later a moon deity depicted as a cat or a cat-headed woman; daughter of Ra; wife of Ptah.

Baubo: A mortal who lifted up her skirts and made Demeter laugh.

Bel: "Lord"; another name for Marduk.

Belili: A Sumerian moon and love goddess; sister of Tammuz.

Belit-Sheri: Scribe of the Mesopotamian Underworld.

Bellerophon: A hero who killed the Chimera and fought the Amazons. When he tried to ride into heaven to join the gods, his mount, Pegasus, threw him off. He fell back to earth and spent the rest of his life as an outcast.

Bellona: Roman goddess of war, said to be the wife or sister of Mars.

Bendigeidran: *See* Brân the Blessed.

Benten: Japanese goddess of love, music, eloquence, beauty, wealth, and geishas; one of the seven deities of happiness and good fortune.

Bergelmir: Norse frost giant.

Bes: A lecherous dwarf god imported into Egypt from Nubia and associated with love, luck, marriage, music, and dreams; husband of Taueret. Shown full face, in contrast to other Egyptian deities, he was a popular household god who offered protection against evil spirits and wild animals, including the snake and the bee.

Bestla: Daughter of a frost giant; wife of Bor; mother of Odin, Vili, and Ve.

Bishamonten: Japanese god of happiness and war, shown with a pagoda and a spear; one of the seven deities of happiness and good fortune.

Blodeuwedd: Celtic goddess of spring, fabricated from oak, broom, and meadowsweet flowers.

Bochica: Founder of the Chibcha and Muisca people of Central Colombia; husband of the moon goddess Chia or Huitaca.

Bor: Husband of Bestla; father of Odin, Vili, and Ve.

Boreas: God of the north wind; a Titan; father of various horses.

Brahma: Hindu god of creation, originally known as Prajapati. With Vishnu and Shiva, he forms the basic trinity of Hinduism.

SOME OF BRAHMA'S CHILDREN

Born from Brahma's body while he was reading the Vedas:

- ten sages, all male, born from his head.
- Kama, the god of desire, born from his heart.
- Anger, born from between his eyebrows.
- Greed, born from his "lower parts."
- Delusion, born from his mind.
- Lust, born from his egotism.
- Joy, born from his throat.
- Death, born from his eyes.
- Dharma, born from his nipple.
- Bharata, Rama's brother, born from the palm of his hand.
- Angaja, a daughter, born from his limbs.
- Daksha and Prasuti, born from his thumbs. They had twenty-four daughters who gave birth to humans, gods, demons, birds, reptiles, and all living creatures.

Brân the Blessed: A Celtic giant; brother of Branwen.

Branwen: Daughter of Lyr; sister of Brân; wife of Matholwch, the king of Ireland.

Bres: Husband of Brigid; briefly leader of the Tuatha Dé Danaan.

Briareus: One of the Hecatonchires.

Brigid (or Brigit): Celtic goddess of fertility, healing, metalwork, poetry, and learning; known as Brigantia in England.

Brihaspati: Hindu god of prayer, the priesthood, and the word.

Brontes: "Thunder"; offspring of Gaia and Uranus; one of the Cyclopes.

Brynhild (or Brünhilde): Leader of the Valkyries; lover of Sigurd.

Buddha: The title achieved by Gautama Siddhartha (563–479 BCE), who renounced the life of a prince and sought enlightenment.

Buri: "Born One"; father of Bor.

Butes: One of the Argonauts. He jumped overboard to join the Sirens.

Cabeiro: Daughter of Proteus; lover of Hephaestus.

Cacus: Three-headed son of Hephaestus; killed by Heracles for stealing cattle from Geryon.

Cadmus: Brother of Europa; husband of Harmonia; founder of Thebes. He sowed the dragon's teeth and watched as armed warriors—the Spartoi or sown men—sprang up out of the ground and began to fight. The five survivors were the first citizens of Thebes. Cadmus is also credited with inventing the alphabet.

Caenis: A girl who changed into a man after Poseidon raped her.

Cailidín: A Celtic warrior slain by Cú Chulainn.

Calais: Son of Boreas, the North Wind; twin brother of Zetes; one of the Argonauts.

Calchas: Omniscient Greek prophet during the Trojan War.

Calliope: Muse of epic poetry; sometimes said to be the mother of Orpheus.

Callisto: An attendant to Artemis, who turned her into a bear; mother of Arcas.

Calypso: Daughter of Thetis and Atlas; lover of Odysseus, who spent seven years with her. She offered him immortality but Zeus commanded that she release him.

Cassandra: Daughter of King Priam and Hecuba. Apollo gave her the ability to foretell the future but cursed her so that no one would believe her; murdered by Clytemnestra.

Cassiopeia: Queen of Ethiopia; wife of Cepheus; mother of Andromeda. A minor figure in mythology, she claims one of the most striking constellations in the sky.

Castor: *See* Dioscouri.

Cathbad A Druid astrologer who inspired Cú Chulainn to take up weapons; father of Dechtire.

Cecrops: First king of Athens; father of Herse, Pandrosus, and Aglaurus.

Cenchreis: Wife of Cinyras; mother of Smyrna. She bragged that her daughter was lovelier than Aphrodite and was punished when Smyrna fell in love with Cinyras.

Centaurs: Mythical creatures with the head and torso of a man and the body of a horse. Although most centaurs were raucous lechers, Chiron, the most famous, was an educator and a physician, skilled in music, prophecy, healing, and hunting.

Cephalus: Son of Herse and Hermes; husband of Procris, who gave him a spear which always found its mark. When Eos fell in love with Cephalus, Procris hid in the woods to watch. Cephalus, thinking that the rustling sounds came from an animal, let loose the spear and inadvertently killed her.

Cerberus: The dog who guards the entrance to the Underworld, noted for his three (or fifty) heads and a tail made of snakes. When Aeneas visited the Underworld, he gained entrance by bribing Cerberus with a poisoned morsel—a sop to Cerberus.

Cercyon: Son of Poseidon; a murderer killed by Theseus.

Ceres: An Italian grain goddess identified with Demeter.

> *Ceres presents a plate of vermicelli—*
> *For love must be sustained like flesh and blood—*
> —Lord Byron, *Don Juan*

Cernunnos: A Celtic god of fertility and abundance, recognizable by his antlers.

Cerridwen: A shape-shifting Welsh goddess; keeper of the Cauldron of Inspiration and Knowledge; mother of the poet Taliesin.

Cesair: Leader of the first mythic invasion of Ireland; granddaughter of Noah.

Ceyx: Husband of Alcyone.

Ch'ang-o: Chinese moon goddess, also known as Heng-o.

Chango: Yoruban storm god. Originally a king, he cast a spell that caused a lightning bolt to hit his palace, killing his wife and children. He was so overwhelmed with guilt that he hung himself from a tree and became a god.

Chalchiuhtlicue: "She of the Jade Skirt"; Aztec goddess of birth and water.

Changing Woman: Navajo creator whose powers include the life force; daughter of Long Life Boy and Happiness Girl.

Chaos: "The Yawning Void"; the only element of existence in the beginning, according to Hesiod; mother of Gaia, Tartarus, Eros, Erobos, and Night.

Charis: One of the Graces; according to Homer, the wife of Hephaestus.

Charon: The ferryman who transports the dead across the River Styx and into Hades.

> *Here the ferryman,*
> *A figure of fright, keeper of waters and streams,*
> *Is Charon, foul and terrible, his beard*
> *Grown wild and hoar, his staring eyes all flame,*
> *His sordid cloak hung from a shoulder knot.*
> *Alone he pokes his craft and trims the sails*
> *And in his rusty hull ferries the dead,*
> *Old now—but old age in the gods is green.*
>
> —Virgil, *The Aeneid*, Book VI

Charybdis: Daughter of Gaia and Poseidon; sister of Scylla. Zeus turned her into a monstrous whirlpool.

Chimaera: A fire-breathing monster with the head of a lion, the body of a goat, and the tail of a dragon; killed by Bellerophon.

Chiminigagua: A Central American creator or sun god.

Chiron: The wise centaur who tutored Asclepius, Achilles, Heracles, and Jason. Though immortal, he was injured so grievously by one of Heracles's poison arrows that he chose to die.

Chrysaor: Son of Medusa and Poseidon; brother of Pegasus. When Perseus sliced off the head of Medusa, Chrysaor sprang from the bloody cut holding a golden sword.

Cian: Father of the Irish sun god, Lugh. He turned into a pig to escape from his enemies, but they stoned him to death.

Cihuacoatl: "Woman Snake"; Aztec goddess associated with childbirth.

Cinyras: Son of Paphos and Poseidon; husband of Cenchreis; father of Smyrna and her son Adonis.

Circe: Daughter of Helios; a witch who became Odysseus's lover, turned his men into swine, and told him how to reach the underworld.

Clip: Muse of history.

Clymene: A sea nymph; wife of Iapetus; mother of Atlas, Prometheus, Epimetheus, and Menoetius. Another character with the same name was the wife of Helios and the mother of Phaeton and Atalanta.

Clytemnestra: Wife of Agememnon, whom she killed; mother of Iphigenia, Electra, Chrysothemis, and Orestes, who killed her.

Coatlicue: "Serpent Skirt"; Aztec goddess; mother of Coyolxauhqui and Huitzilopochtli.

Coeus: A Titan; husband of Phoebe; father of Leto.

Conán the Bald: An Irish warrior known as a foul-mouthed, cowardly glutton.

Conchobar: King of Ulster; son of Nessa. After Nessa's husband died, she married his half-brother Fergus on condition that he let Conchobar rule for a year. When the year was over, the people would not let Conchobar step down.

Conlaí: Son of Cú Chulainn.

Cottus: One of the Hecatonchires.

Coyolxauhqui: "Golden Bells"; Aztec moon goddess; daughter of Coatlicue.

Coyote: Native American trickster and culture-bringer.

Crearwy: "Dear One"; the beautiful daughter of the Welsh goddess Cerridwen.

Creidhne: Celtic goldsmith; brother of Goibhniu and Luchta.

Creon: King of Thebes; brother of Jocasta; uncle of Oedipus. Another Creon was king of Corinth and father of Glauce.

Croesus: The last king of Lydia, famed for his wealth.

Cú Chulainn: Irish hero and champion of Ulster, often compared to Achilles.

Culann: A Celtic smith whose dog was killed by Cú Chulainn.

Cupid: Roman god of love, identified with Eros.

Curetes: Minor gods who protected the infant Zeus by masking his cries with the sounds of war.

Cybele: A goddess of Asia Minor who entered Greece around 700 BCE. Known throughout the Roman Empire as Magna Mater or the Great Mother, she was represented by a black meteorite which was ceremonially washed on March 27.

Cyclopes: One-eyed, cannibalistic giants, sons of Gaia and Uranus.

Cycnus: Son of Ares; slain by Heracles. He killed travelers and used their bones to construct a temple to his father.

Cyparissus: One of Apollo's lovers. He accidentally killed a sacred stag and was turned into a Cypress tree.

Daedalus: A skilled craftsman who built the wooden cow which enabled Pasiphae to mate with the bull, designed the labyrinth that housed the Minotaur, and escaped with his son Icarus on wings of wax and feathers.

Dagda: The good god; lord of knowledge, magic, and Druidism; father god of Irish mythology.

Dagon: "Corn"; a Mesopotamian fertility god. He is depicted with the tail of a fish, suggesting that he may also have been a sea god.

Daikoku: A Shinto god of prosperity, often depicted holding a hammer and standing on two sacks of rice; one of the seven deities of happiness and good fortune.

Damkina: Mother of Marduk; wife of the Babylonian god Ea.

Dana: Mother goddess of Irish mythology; mother of the Dagda and the Tuatha Dé Danaan. Also known as Danu, Anu, or Dôn.

Danaë: Daughter of Acrisius; mother of Perseus, who was conceived when Zeus entered the tower where she was imprisoned as a shower of gold.

Danaids: The fifty daughters of Danaus. At his insistence, all but one murdered their husbands on their wedding night.

Danaus: Father of the Danaids; brother of Aegyptus; king of Argos.

Daphne: Daughter of a river god. Apollo turned her into a bay laurel tree.

Dechtire: Mother of Cú Chulainn.

Deianeira: Sister of Meleager; wife of Heracles.

Delphyne: A dragon outwitted by Hermes and Pan while guarding Zeus's sinews.

Demeter: Olympian goddess of grain and fertility; mother of Persephone; central figure in the Eleusinian mysteries.

Demophon: Son of Theseus and Phaedra; brother of Acamas; king of Attica.

Demophoön: A child cared for by Demeter while she was grieving.

Despoena: Daughter of Demeter and Poseidon, conceived when they took the form of horses.

Deucalion: Son of Prometheus; husband of Pyrrha; the Greek Noah.

Devaki: Indian goddess of wisdom; mother of Krishna.

Devi: Hindu Goddess; Divine Mother; Shiva's wife. Her manifestations include Shakti, Kali, Durga, Sati, Gauri, Parvati, Uma, and Lakshmi.

Dia: Wife of Ixion; mother of Pirithous.

Dian Cecht: Irish god of healing.

Diana: An Italian goddess of the moon, the hunt, and childbirth; identified with Artemis. Revered throughout the ancient world, she was accused during the Inquisition of being a devil or witch and her worship, which persisted in many places, was denounced.

Diarmuid Ua Duibhne: "Of the Love Spot"; the handsomest warrior of the Fianna. He fell in love with Grainne and died at the hands of Finn MacCool.

Dido: Queen of Carthage. She fell in love with Aeneas, but Jupiter decreed that he must go to Italy to fulfill his destiny. Devastated, Dido committed suicide. When Aeneas visited the underworld, she still would not speak to him.

Dike: Goddess of Justice. She sits by the side of Zeus.

Diomedes: King of Thrace, killed by Heracles. Another Diomedes drove Ares off the field of battle and wounded Aphrodite.

Dione: Daughter of Gaia and Uranus; according to Homer, the mother of Aphrodite and Amphitrite.

Dionysus: Olympian god of wine and ecstasy, born from the body of Zeus; known to the Romans as Bacchus.

Dioscouri: The heavenly twins Castor and Polydeuces; sons of Leda. Polydeuces was the immortal child of Zeus, while Castor, the son of Tyndareus, was mortal. When Castor was killed, Polydeuces begged Zeus to let him share his immortality, and Zeus decreed that they could spend half their time on Olympus and half in Hades.

Dis Pater: Roman god of the dead.

Donn: Irish god of the dead.

Doris: Daughter of Oceanus and Tethys; wife of Nereus; mother of the Nereids.

Dryads: Nymphs of trees in general and the oak in particular.

Dryope: A Nymph who turned into a poplar tree.

Dumuzi: A Sumerian fertility god who spends half the year in the underworld and half the year on earth; husband of Inanna.

Durga: The warlike aspect of the Hindu goddess Devi. Durga's role is to rid the world of demons.

Ea: Babylonian creator and god of wisdom, known to the Sumerians as Enki; son of Apsu, whom he overthrew.

Earthmaker: Winnebago creator.

Ebisu: A Shinto god of work, shown holding a line and a fish; one of the seven Japanese deities of happiness and good fortune.

Echidna: A monster, part woman and part serpent; mother of the Chimaera, the Hydra of Lerna, Cerberus, the Sphinx, the Nemean Lion, and the eagle that tortured Prometheus.

Echo: A nymph. Hera limited her ability to speak so that she could only repeat what she had heard. When Narcissus rejected her, she pined away until nothing remained but her voice.

Efnisian: Branwen's half-brother. He started the war between Wales and Ireland by mutilating King Matholwch's horses.

Eileithyia: Greek goddess of childbirth.

El: Canaanite creator, similar to Yahweh; father of Baal.

Electra: Grief-stricken, vengeful daughter of Clytemnestra and Agamemnon. After her mother killed her father, Electra encouraged her brother Orestes to commit matricide, which he did.

Elphin: Foster father of Taliesin.

Emer: Wife of Cú Chulainn.

Endymion: A young man who gained immortality at the cost of wakefulness when the goddess Selene touched him with everlasting sleep so that she could visit him whenever she desired.

Enki: *See* Ea.

Enkidu: Best friend of Gilgamesh. His death inspired Gilgamesh to search for the secret of immortality.

Enlil: Babylonian chief divinity and god of air.

Ennead: The first nine gods of Heliopolis (from *Ennea*, the Greek word for nine): Atum, Shu, Tefnut, Geb, Nut, Seth, Nephthys, Isis, and Osiris.

Eos: Greek goddess of the dawn, known to the Romans as Aurora.

Ephaphus: Son of Io and Zeus; king of Egypt; husband of Memphis, father of Libya.

Ephialtes: A giant. He and his twin brother of Otus imprisoned Ares in a jar and tried to reach heaven by piling one mountain on top of another. When Artemis sent a deer scampering between them, the giants took aim and killed each other.

Epimetheus: "Afterthought"; brother of Prometheus and Atlas; husband of Pandora.

Epona: Celtic horse goddess.

Erato: Muse of the lyre.

Erebos: "Darkness"; one of the children of Chaos.

Erechtheus: King of Athens. At the suggestion of the Delphic oracle, he sacrificed his daughter Chthonia and conquered Eleusis.

Ereshkigal: Sumerian goddess of the underworld; sister of Inanna.

Erginus: King of the Minyans; killed by Heracles.

Eriboea: Stepmother of Ephialtes and Otus.

Erichthonius: A king of Athens, half snake and half man; son of Hephaestus.

Erigone: Daughter of Icarius.

Erinyes: *See* Furies.

Eris: Goddess of strife; daughter of Nyx. She brought the golden apple of discord to the wedding of Thetis and Peleus.

Eros: God of love, typically shown with bow and arrows; the attendant of Aphrodite. Also, Psyche's lover.

Eryx: Son of Aphrodite and Butes; killed by Heracles.

Eshu: A Yoruban trickster; son of Oshun.

Eumenides: *See* Furies.

Eumolpus: Son of Poseidon; music teacher of Heracles, whom he initiated into the Eleusinian Mysteries.

Euphrosyne: One of the Graces.

Europa: Sister of Cadmus; lover of Zeus, abducted her to Crete; mother of Minos, Rhadamanthus, and Sarpedon.

Eurydice: Wife of Orpheus.

Eurynome: Daughter of Oceanus and Tethys; mother of the Graces. Another Eurynome is the mother goddess of the Pelasgian invaders; a third is the mother of Bellerophon.

Eurystheus: King of Tiryns under whose direction Heracles performed the twelve labors; grandson of Perseus.

Euterpe: Muse of the flute.

Fand: Wife of the Irish sea-god Manannan Mac Lir; mistress of Cú Chulainn.

Fates: *See* Moirae.

Faunus: An Italian god of shepherds, flocks, and prophecy; associated with Pan.

Faustulus: Foster father of Romulus and Remus; husband of Acca Larentia.

Fenrir: A monstrous wolf in Norse mythology; son of Loki and Angrboda. He bit off Tyr's hand and is destined to kill Odin.

Ferdiad: A Celtic warrior; killed by his foster brother Cú Chulainn.

Fianna: Warriors, also known as Fenians, who guarded the High King of Ireland; precursors to the Knights of the Round Table.

Finn MacCool (or Fionn Mac Cumhail): A Celtic hero; leader of the Fianna; lover of Sadb; father of Oisin.

Fintan: Husband of Cesair. He survived the Flood by turning into a salmon.

Fir Bolg: "Bag Men"; the fourth mythical invaders of Ireland. In the distant past they were slaves forced to carry bags of earth: hence their name.

Flora: Roman goddess of flowering plants and Spring. Her festival was celebrated on May Day.

THE FIVE MYTHICAL INVASIONS OF IRELAND

The twelfth-century *Book of Invasions* reports that Cesair, Noah's granddaughter, led the first invasion of the Emerald Isle. She and her followers arrived forty days before the flood. Only one survived the deluge: her husband Fintan, who turned into a salmon.

Three centuries later, Partholón and his followers invaded. They introduced agriculture, brewed the first ale, and fought the Fomorians, all of whom were deformed. Five thousand years later, in the space of a week, the plague wiped out all but one of the Partholónians.

Nemed led the third invasion of Ireland, arriving with four women after six months at sea. They multiplied rapidly but only thirty survived the attack of the Fomorians. Those few left Ireland, some traveling to Greece and others sailing north.

The Fir Bolg were the fourth group to invade. They divided the land into five provinces and introduced the concept of kingship.

The Tuatha Dé Danann, the people of the goddess Danu, led the fifth mythical invasion and became the last race of gods to rule over Ireland. They defeated the Fir Bolg and the Fomorians but were driven underground by their successors, the sons of Mil, who were the Celts.

Fomorians: Deformed Celtic sea gods who battled the Partholonians, the Nemedians, and the Tuatha Dé Danaan during the mythical invasions of Ireland.

Frey (or Freyr): Norse god of peace, prosperity, fertility, love, and orgies, symbolized by a giant phallus; son of Njord and Skadi; brother of Freya; one of the Vanir.

Freya (or Freyja): Norse goddess of love, fertility, and divination; daughter of Njord and Skadi; sister of Frey; one of the Vanir.

Frigga (or Fricka): Wife of Odin; mother of Baldur; one of the Aesir. She and Freyja may be two aspects of the same deity.

Fukurokuju: Japanese god of wisdom and long life, shown with a stork; one of the seven deities of happiness and good fortune.

Furies: Avenging spirits born from the blood of Uranus after Zeus castrated him. Their function is to punish evil-doers, with emphasis on those who murder members of their own family. The furies (Erinyes in Greek) were also known ironically as the Eumenides or Kindly Ones.

Fuxi: "Bottle Gourd"; a Chinese creator god, associated with Nü Gua and, like her, shown with the tail of a serpent.

Gae Bolga: The magical spear of Cú Chulainn.

Gaia: "Earth," also known as Ge; daughter of Chaos; mother of the Titans, the Erinyes, and the Giants, plus numerous nymphs, monsters, and gods, including Uranus, her mate. In the *Iliad*, Hera swears by her, as did the citizens of ancient Greece.

Galatea: Most famously, the statue carved by Pygmalion and brought to life by Aphrodite. Another Galatea was a sea nymph.

Ganesha: Hindu elephant-headed god of wisdom and success, invoked at the beginning of endeavors, especially those of the literary sort; also the lord of obstacles; son of Parvati. He is often depicted riding, or accompanied by, a rat.

Ganesha

Ganymede: A young shepherd. Zeus fell in love with him, turned into an eagle, and transported him into the sky, where he replaced Hebe as cupbearer to the gods.

Garm: Norse equivalent of Cerberus, he guards the gates of the underworld.

Gauri: "Bright"; one aspect of the Hindu goddess Devi.

Geb: Egyptian god of the earth, often shown as a goose; son of Shu and Tefnut; husband and brother of Nut; father of Osiris, Nepthys, and Seth. When he laughed, the earth shook.

Geryon: A three-headed king whose three torsos were joined at the waist. Heracles stole his cattle as his tenth labor.

Geshtinanna: "Leafy Grapevine"; Sumerian goddess of wine; Inanna's sister.

Gilgamesh: Sumerian hero who sought the secret of immortality.

Glauce: Daughter of Creon of Corinth; Jason's second wife; killed by Medea.

Glaucus: Son of Sisyphus; father of Bellerophon; devoured by his horses after he lost a race. Another Glaucus fought the Greeks during the Trojan War.

Gnowee: Australian sun goddess.

Goibhniu: Smith god of the Irish; part of a trinity that included Luchta and Creidhne. Goibhniu's spears inflicted a fatal wound and his ale protected those who drank it from death and disease.

Gordius: The father of Midas. He became king of Phrygia when he fulfilled a prediction by arriving there by oxcart and tying it to a post using the complicated knot that bears his name.

Gorgons: Three sisters known for their snaky hairdos, bronze claws, and frightening demeanor. Two of them—Stheno and Euryale—were immortal. The third—Medusa—was killed by Perseus.

Graiae: Three weird sisters, gray-haired at birth, who possessed one tooth and one eye among them; sisters of the Gorgons.

Graces: Daughters of Zeus and Eurynome; the handmaidens of Aphrodite. They represented joy, grace, and beauty.

Grainne: Fiancée of Finn MacCool; lover of Diarmuid; daughter of Cormac Mac Art.

Gu: A West African smith god; son of the Fon gods Lisa and Mawu.

Gucumatz: A Mayan creator god, pictured as a plumed serpent and associated with Quetzalcoatl.

Gugalanna: Sumerian bull of heaven; husband of Ereshkigal.

Gullinbursti: Golden boar of Freja, charged with carrying her chariot across the sky; a symbol of good luck.

Gwawl: Rhiannon's betrothed. She jilted him in favor of Pwyll.

Gwerm: Son of Branwen; murdered by his uncle Efnisian.

Gwion Bach: *See* Taliesin.

Gwri: Son of Rhiannon and Pwyll.

Gyes: One of the Hecatonchires. He was so violent that even in Tartarus, he was guarded by his brother Briareus.

Hades: "The Invisible"; god of the dead; also the underworld. Known in Latin as Pluto or Dis Pater.

Halia: A wife of Poseidon. When her six sons, driven mad by Aphrodite, tried to rape her, she jumped into the sea and became Leucothea, the white goddess. See Ino for an alternative tale.

Halirrhothiuss: Son of Poseidon.

Harmonia: Wife of Cadmus; daughter of Ares and Aphrodite.

Harpies: Birds with the faces of women. Wonderful to behold in art but otherwise loathsome, they were screeching creatures who fouled everything and left behind a nauseating stench.

Hathor: Cow-headed Egyptian queen of heaven and goddess of love, referred to in the Pyramid Texts as the Great She. She wears a headdress made of the horns of a cow holding the disk of the sun. The protector of cemeteries, she held the ladder which led to heaven and was charged with feeding the dead upon their arrival there. The meal: bread and water.

Hauhet: Egyptian goddess of formlessness or infinity; a member of the Ogdoad.

Hebe: Goddess of youth and cupbearer to the gods, until Ganymede replaced her; daughter of Hera and Zeus; wife of Heracles after he became immortal.

Hecate: A triple goddess of the moon associated with magic, witchcraft, night, and the underworld; attendant of Persephone. Her image was fierce: she drank blood, ate excrement, and had Medusa-like hair.

Hecatonchires: The hundred-armed giants Cottus, Briareus, and Gyes, sons of Gaia and Uranus.

Hector: Commander of the Trojans; son of Hecuba and Priam; killed by Achilles. The *Iliad* ends with Hector's funeral.

Hecuba: Wife of Priam; mother of Paris, Hector, and eighteen other children.

Heimdall: Norse god of light. He guards the Bifrost Bridge and is fated to kill Loki.

Heket: Early Egyptian frog goddess who assists every morning at the birth of the sun.

Hel: Norse goddess of the underworld, called Helheim; daughter of Loki and Angrboda, a frost giant.

Helen: Daughter of Zeus and Leda; wife of Menelaus; the most beautiful woman on earth. Her affair with Paris caused the Trojan War.

> *Was this the face that launch'd a thousand ships*
> *And burn't the topless towers of Ilium?*
> *Sweet Helen, make me immortal with a kiss!*
>
> —Christopher Marlowe, *Doctor Faustus*

Helios: The Sun, noted for his ability to see everything. Homer called him Hyperion.

Helle: Daughter of Nephele and Athamas; sister of Phrixus. She fell off the ram with the Golden Fleece into the Hellespont, which was named in her honor.

Heng-o: Chinese moon goddess, sometimes represented as a three-legged toad.

Hephaestus: Olympian god of crafts and fire; associated with Vulcan in Rome.

Hera: Olympian goddess of marriage and queen of the gods; sister/wife of Zeus; mother of Hephaestus, Hebe, Eileithyia, and Ares.

Heracles: Great hero of Greek mythology; son of Zeus and Alcmene; great-grandson of Perseus; nemesis of Hera; known as Hercules in Rome.

Hermaphroditus: Son of Hermes and Aphrodite. He became a hermaphrodite when a naiad prayed to be joined with him forever.

Hermera: "Day"; child of Nyx and Erebos.

Hermes: Olympian god of roads, boundaries, travel, luck, speech, sleep, and dreams; messenger of the gods; a psychopomp who escorted the dead into their new abode; identified in Rome with Mercury.

Hermod: Norse messenger of the gods; son of Frigga and Odin; a psychopomp.

Hero: A priestess of Aphrodite. Forbidden to marry, Hero fell in love with Leander, who lived on the opposite side of the Hellespont. Every night he visited her, guided by a torch in her tower window. One night, the light blew out and Leander drowned. Hero committed suicide by jumping off the tower.

Herse: Daughter of Cecrops; sister of Aglaurus and Pandrosus; mother of Cephalus.

Hesione: Daughter of King Laomedon of Troy. He tried to sacrifice her but Heracles rescued her.

Hesperides: A group of sisters who lived in a garden at the edge of the world, where they guarded a tree with golden apples. Gaia gave those apples to Hera as a wedding present, Heracles captured them in one of his labors, and Hippomenes tossed them in front of Atalanta, who lost her foot race as a result.

Hestia: Olympian goddess of the hearth; identified in Rome with Vesta.

Hi'iaka: Pele's favorite sister.

Hine-nui-te-Po: Polynesian goddess of the underworld.

Hippolyta: Queen of the Amazons; daughter of Ares; lover of Theseus; mother of Hippolytus; killed by Heracles.

Hippolytus: Son of Theseus and Hippolyta; desired by his stepmother, Phaedra.

Hippomenes: Husband of Atalanta, whom he bested in a race.

Hoder: Blind brother of the Norse Baldur, whom he inadvertently killed.

Hoenir: Norse god of silence, known for his stupidity; companion of Loki and Odin.

Hopoe: Hawaiian hula goddess. Pele turned her into a lava rock.

Horae: *See* Seasons.

Horus: A falcon-headed solar god. Often shown in a mother-and-child tableau with Isis, Horus represented the living king, whereas Osiris was the king of the dead. Horus also fought with Seth for the Egyptian throne. In one version of the myth, Seth became a hippopotamus and Horus harpooned him, dismembered him, distributed his parts to the gods, and turned the leftovers into a cake.

Hotei Osho: Japanese god of generosity and large families, depicted as a Buddhist priest; one of the deities of happiness and good fortune.

Huh: Egyptian god of formlessness or infinity; a member of the Ogdoad.

Huitaca: a South American goddess of joy, sometimes considered evil because of her attitude towards drunkenness and rowdy behavior, both of which she espoused.

Huitzilopochtli: "Hummingbird on the Left"; Aztec god of war and the sun.

Humbaba: A monstrous giant killed by Gilgamesh and Enkidu.

Hunab: Creator of the Mayan people.

Hur: Sumerian moon god.

Hyacinthus: A beautiful mortal, beloved by Apollo, who accidentally killed him.

Hydra: A many-headed serpent killed by Heracles; child of Typhon and Echidna.

Hygeia: Goddess of health; daughter of Asclepius.

Hyllus: Son of Heracles; husband of Iole.

Hymen: God of weddings. His name was invoked at Greek nuptials.

Hyperboreans: A mythical people who lived in a distant land beyond the North Wind. Apollo went there every winter.

Hyperion: A Titan and early sun god; son of Gaia and Uranus; father of Helios, Selene, and Eos.

Hypermestra: The only one of the daughters of Danaus to spare her husband's life. She was put on trial for disobedience and acquitted.

Hypnos: "Sleep"; brother of Thanatos or Death; father of Dreams.

Hypsipyle: A woman of Lemnos. When they were temporarily afflicted with a foul odor, the men sought companionship elsewhere. As a result, the women killed them—except Hypsipyle, who saved her father, Thoas. She also had twins by Jason.

Iambe: A servant who made Demeter laugh. Her name is recalled in the word "iambic."

Iapetus: A Titan; father of Prometheus, Epimetheus, Atlas, and Monoetius.

Iasion: Demeter's lover.

Icarius: A resident of Attica who received the gift of wine from Dionysus, to his own misfortune; father of Erigone and Penelope.

Icarus: Son of Daedalus, who made him wax wings. Ignoring his father's warning, Icarus soared so close to the sun that the wax melted and he fell into the sea.

Idas: A mortal who competed with Apollo for the hand of Marpessa and won; an Argonaut and a participant the Caledonian boar hunt.

Idun: Norse goddess who supplied the Aesir with the golden apples of youth.

Ilos: Founder of Troy or Ilium.

Imhotep: Egyptian god of healing.

Inachus: A river god; father of Io.

Inanna: Sumerian goddess and queen of heaven, equivalent to Ishtar.

Indra: Supreme god in the Rig Veda; Hindu god of rain. He restored order by killing the dragon Vrtra, who had swallowed all the water on earth. He also seduced Ahalya, whose husband cursed him with impotence. Indra's testicles fell off on the spot but thanks to Agni, he received the testicles of a ram. He also had a thousand vaginas scattered over his body which eventually turned into eyes. He was defeated by the demon Ravana.

Inktomi: Trickster of the Lakota Indians. He possessed the power of invisibility and the ability to communicate with all living creatures including stones.

Ino: Daughter of Cadmus and Harmonia; wife of Athamas; foster mother of Dionysus; a heroine honored throughout Greece. Hera drove her mad and she jumped into the sea, where Dionysus turned her into the goddess Leucothea. Another story reports that Halia was transformed into Leucothea.

Io: Daughter of Inachus; lover of Zeus; mother of Ephaphus. Hera turned her into a white heifer.

Iole: Wife of Hyllus. Heracles, her father-in-law, won her in an archery contest.

Iphicles: Twin brother of Heracles. They shared the same mother, Alcmene, but Iphicles was Amphitryon's son while Heracles was the son of Zeus.

Iphigenia: Daughter of Clytemnestra and Agamemnon, who sacrificed her; sister of Orestes, Electra, and Chrysothemis.

Iphitus: brother of Iole.

Iris: Goddess of the rainbow; sister of the Harpies; messenger of the gods before Hermes.

Ishtar: Babylonian Goddess of love and war, equivalent to Inanna.

Isis: Widely worshipped Egyptian goddess; daughter of Geb and Nut; sister of Nepthys, Seth, and Osiris, who was also her husband; mother of Horus; known as queen of the gods, lady of green crops, the mother goddess, and according to the Roman Lucius, "the holy and eternal Savior of the human race." She wore a headdress in the form of a throne, a vulture, or a pair of horns holding a disc.

Itys: Son of Tereus and Procne.

Ixion: King of the Lapiths. He killed his father-in-law and became the first Greek to murder a member of the family. He lusted after Hera and was punished by being bound upon a wheel of fire.

Iyangura: Aunt and protector of the African hero Mwindo.

Iynx: Daughter of Pan and Echo.

Izanami: Japanese creator goddess; wife and sister of Izanagi.

Janus: Roman god of arches, doorways, and journeys. As the god of entrances and exits, he lent his name to the month of January.

Jari: Melanesian goddess of marriage and agriculture.

Jason: A pre-Homeric hero who sought the Golden Fleece; captain of the *Argo*; husband of Medea.

Jocasta: Wife of Laius; mother and wife of Oedipus. When she learned the truth about her situation, she hung herself.

Jormungand: The world serpent in Norse mythology; son of Loki. When Odin threw him into the ocean, he grew so large that he wrapped his body around the entire earth; also known as the Midgard Serpent.

Juno: Roman mother goddess and queen of heaven, equivalent to Hera.

> *Lids of Juno's eyes, violets. He walks. One life is all. One body. Do. But do.*
>
> —James Joyce, *Ulysses*

Jurojun: Japanese god of happiness and long life, shown with a staff and a stag; one of the seven deities of happiness and good fortune.

Jotunheim: Realm of the frost giants in Norse mythology.

Jupiter: Chief Roman sky god, known as Jupiter Optimus Maximus, equivalent to Zeus but with less power. For instance, he had three thunderbolts. He could throw the first one at will. But to let loose the second and third, he needed permission from the other gods.

Kahindo: Goddess of good fortune of the Nyanga nation in the Democratic Republic of Congo.

Kali: Hindu goddess of destruction, known as the black one. Often shown dancing on the naked body of her husband, Shiva, she is a manifestation of the Great Mother, the supreme force in the universe, and the goddess of time and life.

Kama: Hindu god of love. Like Cupid or Eros, he carries a bow (made of sugar cane) and arrows (tipped with flowers). His mount: a parrot.

Kama'pua'a: Hawaiian pig god, known for impulsive behavior.

Kamsa: Krishna's uncle.

Karora: Creator deity of the Arandan aborigines.

Kasiyembe: Village elder and enemy of the African hero Mwindo.

Kauket: Egyptian goddess of darkness; one of the divinities in the Ogdoad.

Keres: Savage spirits which control the destiny of heroes in the *Iliad*.

Khepri: Scarab-headed Egyptian god of transformation. Like the scarab beetle, which rolls a ball of dung before it, Khepri rolls the sun along its daily path.

Khnum: A ram-headed Egyptian god who created human beings on a potter's wheel; married to Heket, the frog goddess.

Khonsu: An Egyptian god of healing, originally a lunar deity.

Kishar: A Babylonian earth goddess.

Klotho: One of the three Fates. She spun the thread of life.

Kore: "Maiden" or "Daughter"; an alternative name for Persephone.

Koronis: Mother of Asclepius.

Koshar-wa-Hasis: "Adroit and Clever"; the Canaanite smith god.

Krishna: Hindu god: eighth avatar of Vishnu, known for his blue skin, his flute, his amorous conquests, and his timeless conversation with Arjuna in the *Bhagavad Gita.*

Kronos: Leader of the Titans; identified by the Romans with Saturn; son of Gaia and Uranus, whom he castrated; father of Hera, Poseidon, Demeter, Hades, and Hestia, whom he swallowed, and Zeus, who conquered him.

Kuan Yin: Buddhist goddess of compassion.

Kuk: Egyptian god of darkness; one of the divinities in the Ogdoad.

Kukalcan: A Mayan version of the plumed serpent, Quetzalcoatl.

Lachesis: One of the three Fates; the goddess of chance.

Ladon: A hundred-headed serpent who guarded the golden apples of the Hesperides; also, a river god.

Lahmu and Lahamu: Babylonian serpent gods, the children of Apsu and Tiamat; also silt and slime.

Laertes: Father of Odysseus; husband of Anticlea.

Laestrygonians: Giant cannibals encountered by Odysseus and his men in the *Odyssey.* "They speared the crews like fish/And whisked them home to make their grisly meal."

Laius: Father of Oedipus; husband of Jocasta.

Lakshmi: Hindu goddess of good fortune, beauty, and prosperity; the consort of Vishnu. She was born in the waves when the gods churned the ocean to obtain soma, the elixir of immortality.

Lamia: Daughter of Poseidon and Libya. When Zeus became infatuated with her, Hera drove her mad, causing Lamia to devour her children.

Laomedon: Father of Tithonous, Hesione, and Priam; a king of Troy, known for his bad faith dealings.

Lapiths: A tribe from Thessaly, famous for their conflict with the centaurs.

Lares: Roman household gods, originally agricultural spirits. Romans kept a shrine called a lararium, a cupboard filled with images of the dancing lares and penates.

Leander: *See* Hero.

Leda: Mother of Clytemnestra and Castor by her husband Tyndareus, and Helen of Troy and Polydeuces by Zeus, who slept with her in the shape of a swan.

Lethe: The river of forgetfulness in Hades.

Leto: Mother of Apollo and Artemis; daughter of Coeus and Phoebe.

Leuce: A nymph pursued by Hades. She turned into a white poplar tree.

Leucippe: One of the daughters of Minyas. She rejected Dionysus and suffered a typically Dionysian punishment: the dismemberment of her son, Hippasus.

Leucothea: The White (*Leuco*) Goddess (*thea*); a Greek sea goddess associated with Ino and Halia.

Liber and Libers: Italian gods of the countryside, identified with Dionysus.

Libya: Daughter of Zeus and Io; one of Poseidon's lovers.

Lilith: Adam's first wife; an Old Testament demon.

Linus: A son of Apollo, a tutor and musician who invented rhythm and melody. Heracles killed him with a lyre.

Lir or Llyr: Celtic god of the ocean; in Welsh mythology, the father of Brân, Branwen, and Manawydan; in Irish mythology, the father of Manannan and three children who were turned into swans by a jealous wife. After nine hundred years, they reverted to human form only to discover that they had grown old.

Lohiau: Pele's lover.

Loki: Trickster god of the Norse; husband of Angrboda and Sigyn; father of Vali, Narvi, Hel, Sleipnir, Jormungand, and Fenrir. He caused the death of Baldur, was chained to a rock, and is destined to kill and be killed by Heimdall.

Lotus Eaters: A people encountered by Odysseus on his journey home. They subsisted on the sweet fruit of the lotus, which induced forgetfulness.

Lowa: A Micronesian creator. He made sure that each creature was tattooed with its own special mark.

Luchta: An Irish god; part of a trio of metal-workers that includes Giobhniu and Creidhne.

Lugaid: The warrior who killed Cú Chulainn.

Lugh: "Shining One," the Irish sun god; grandson of Balor, whom he killed with a sling; a leader of the Tuatha Dé Danaan; sometimes said to be the father of Cú Chulainn.

Lugalbanda: Father of the Sumerian hero Gilgamesh; mortal king of Uruk.

Lycaon: A king who served human flesh to Zeus and was turned into a wolf.

Lycomedes: King of Scyros. He killed Theseus. During the Trojan War, he also hid Achilles by dressing him in girl's clothing.

Lycurgus: King of the Edonians. As punishment for failing to acknowledge Dionysus, he was driven mad.

Lynceus: Brother of Idas; husband of Hypermenstra.

Ma'at: Egyptian goddess of truth and justice, symbolized by a feather against which the soul of the dead would be measured; daughter of Ra; wife of Thoth.

Macha: A Celtic goddess of war; one aspect of the Morrigan.

Machaon: Son of Asclepius. A skilled surgeon, he hid inside the Trojan Horse and administered to injured Greek soldiers.

Maenads: Female followers of Dionysus.

Maera: The loyal dog of Icarius, set into the heavens as the Dog Star after his death.

Mahui-ike: A Polynesian goddess of fire and the underworld.

Maia: Mother of Hermes; daughter of Zeus and Pleione; oldest of the Pleiades.

Manannan Mac Lir: Irish god of healing, sorcery, and the sea. He gave Lugh a sword that could pierce any armor, a horse that could gallop over land or sea, and a boat that obeyed the thoughts of its sailor.

Manawydan: A Welsh hero; son of Lyr; brother of Branwen; husband of Rhiannon.

Manu: The only survivor of the flood in Hindu mythology; brother of Yama.

Manuk Manuk "Blue Chicken"; Indonesian creator.

Marduk: Main Babylonian god; son of Ea; conqueror of Tiamat.

Marpessa: Daughter of the river god Evenus; a nymph pursued by Apollo and Idas.

Mars: Roman god of war, equivalent to Ares; father of Romulus and Remus.

Marsysas: A satyr who challenged Apollo to a musical contest and was flayed alive.

Mary: Mother of Jesus Christ.

Matholwch: King of Ireland; husband of Branwen.

Matsu: Chinese goddess of the sea.

Matsya: A fish; one of the avatars of the Hindu god Vishnu.

Maui: Polynesian trickster and culture hero. He fished the islands up from the floor of the ocean, lassoed the sun to slow its passage, stole the secret of fire from the celestial chicken, and died in an effort to gain immortality.

Medb: A shape-shifting, promiscuous Irish goddess of war and fertility whose presence caused her enemies to lose two-thirds of their courage and strength; also the queen of Connacht in the saga of Cú Chulainn.

Medea: A priestess of Hecate; daughter of Aeetes; sister of Apsyrtus; wife of Jason and Aegeus. She helped Jason secure the Golden Fleece but is infamous for killing her children when he divorced her.

Medus: Son of Medea and King Aegeus.

Medusa: One of the Gorgons, known for her snake-haired head, which could turn men to stone; lover of Poseidon; mother of Chrysaor and Pegasus; decapitated by Perseus, who gave her head to Athena.

Megara: Wife of Heracles, who killed her in a fit of madness; daughter of Creon.

Meleager: The hero who killed the Calydonian boar. He died when his mother threw the log which represented his life into the fire.

Melanippus: Son of Theseus and Perigone.

Melpomene: Muse of tragedy.

Menelaus: Husband of Helen; brother of Agamemnon.

Mentor: A close friend of Odysseus. In the *Odyssey*, Athena appears in his guise to give advice.

Mercury: Roman god of commerce and communication, equivalent to Hermes.

Merope: Wife of Sisyphus; the only one of the Pleiades to marry a mortal.

Metaneira: Queen of Eleusis; mother of Demophoön; Demeter's employer.

Metis: "Wisdom"; the first wife of Zeus. He swallowed her when she was pregnant and gave birth to Athena from his forehead.

Mictecacihuatl: Aztec goddess of death; wife of Mictlantecuhtli.

Mictlantecuhtli: Aztec god of the dead and ruler of the underworld, Mictlan.

Midas: King of Phrygia. He asked for and received the golden touch.

Midgard: Middle Earth in Norse mythology; the home of human beings.

Mil or Milesius: A Spanish soldier. After his nephew was killed by the Tuatha Dé Danaan, Mil and his wife Scota planned to attack Ireland but were killed. Their sons, the Milesians or Sons of Mil, took up the cause and conquered the Tuatha Dé Danaan, thus beginning the human history of Ireland.

Min: Egyptian god of reproduction, shown wearing a plumed headdress, holding a whip, and in a state of full erection. The Greeks associated him with Pan.

Minerva: Roman goddess of the intellect, identified with Athena.

> *Dime next I found, Minerva, sexless cold & chill, ascending goddess of money—and was it the wife of Wallace Stevens, truly?*
>
> *and now from the locks flowing the miniature wings of speedy thought,*
>
> *executive dyke, Minerva, goddess of Madison Avenue, forgotten useless dime that can't buy hot dog, dead dime—*
>
> —Allen Ginsburg, "American Change"

Minos: King of Crete; son of Zeus and Europa; husband of Pasiphae; father of Ariadne, Phaedra, and Deucalion; Underworld judge.

Minotaur: The monstrous offspring, half man and half bull, of Pasiphae and a bull.

Minthe: A nymph pursed by Hades, crushed underfoot by Persephone, and turned into a mint plant.

Minyas: Father of Leucippe, Alcithoë, and Arsippe.

Mixcoatl: "Serpent Cloud"; the Aztec god of hunting; husband of Coatlicue.

Mnemosyne: "Memory"; a Titan; mother of the muses.

Moirae: The three fates: Klotho, who spun the thread of life; Lachesis, who unraveled the thread; and Atropos who cut the fiber at the time of death; daughters of Themis and Zeus. Even the gods had to bow to their demands.

Moloch: A Phoenician sun god depicted as a bull or with the head of a calf. It was said that children were sacrificed to him. John Milton called him a "horrid king, besmeared with blood/Of human sacrifice, and parents' tears."

Montu: A Theban solar deity and god of war.

Morpheus: A god of dreams; son of Hypnos.

Morrigan: A shape-shifting triple goddess of war and death; the Celtic goddesses Nemain, Macha, and Badb are aspects of the Morrigan.

Moses: Thirteenth-century BCE prophet and hero who led the Jews out of slavery and received the ten commandments.

Mot: Babylonian god of death and infertility.

Mukti: African sea serpent; husband of Iyangura, Mwindo's aunt.

Muisa: King of the Underworld in the saga of the African hero Mwindo.

Mummu: Babylonian god of mist.

Muses: The nine daughters of Zeus and Mnemosyne; companions of Apollo. Originally three in number, they were Calliope, Clio, Erato, Euterpe, Melpomene, Polyhymnia, Terpischore, Thalia, and Urania.

Mwindo: Warrior hero and mythical king of the Nyanga nation in the Democratic Republic of Congo.

Myrrha: *See* Smyrna.

Na-maka-o-ka-ha'i: Sister of Pele, a fire goddess who rules the surface of the water.

Naiads: Water nymphs. They inhabited streams and springs.

Namtar: Mesopotamian god of the plague; messenger of Ereshkigal.

Nanautzin: Aztec god who sacrificed himself and became the sun.

Nanda: Foster father of the Hindu god Krishna; husband of Yashoda.

Nanna: Sumerian moon god; father of Utu, the sun god.

Narcissus: A beautiful youth, obsessed with his own image.

Narvi: Son of the Norse trickster Loki. His entrails were used to bind his father to a rock.

Naunet: Egyptian goddess of chaos or the watery abyss; a member of the Ogdoad.

Nausicaa: The daughter of Alcinous. In the *Odyssey*, she is doing her laundry when she meets and falls for Odysseus.

Ndengei: The serpent-shaped creator of Fiji. Whenever he moves, the earth quakes.

Ndomadyrir: Divine blacksmith of Mali.

Neleus: Son of Poseidon; father of Nestor.

Nemain: Celtic war goddess, part of the trinity of the Morrigan; married to Nuada.

Nemed: Leader of the third mythical invasion of Ireland.

Nemesis: Goddess of retribution and moderation; daughter of Night. "Know your human state and its limits," wrote Socrates. "Do no expose yourself by excess to the vengeance of divine Nemesis."

Neoptolemus: One of the sons of Achilles. He hid inside the Trojan horse and killed King Priam.

Nephele: "Cloud"; wife of Athamas; mother of Phrixus and Helle.

Nepthys: Egyptian goddess and guardian of the tomb; daughter of Geb and Nut; sister of Isis, Osiris, and Seth, her husband (though she also had a child with Osiris). After Osiris died, she left Seth.

Neptune: Roman god of the sea, equivalent to Poseidon.

Nereids: "Wet Ones"; sea nymphs with mermaid tails and green hair; the daughters of Nereus and Doris. Among them were Thetis, Galatea, and Amphitrite.

Nereus: A shape-shifting deity known as the Old Man of the Sea; son of Gaia.

Nergal: Mesopotamian god of war and death; husband of Ereshkigal.

Nerites: Son of Nereus. He rejected Aphrodite and was turned into a shellfish.

Nessa: Mother of Conchobar.

Nessus: A centaur. He tried to rape Deianira and was killed by Heracles. Deianira collected his blood, which caused Heracles's death.

Nestor: King of Pylos; son of Neleus; the oldest Greek warrior at Troy.

Neti: Gatekeeper of the Mesopotamian underworld.

Niamh: "Brightness and Beauty"; Celtic goddess of the Otherworld. Another character with the same name was the mistress of Cú Chulainn.

Nibelungs: Underworld dwarfs or elves who made a golden ring for the Scandinavian hero Sigurd.

Niflheim: "World of Fog"; a frigid, dark place, the lowest part of the Norse Underworld, ruled by the goddess Hel.

Nike: Winged goddess of Victory, honored by athletes and charioteers. In Rome, she symbolized victory over death, in contrast to the Italian goddess Victoria, who represented victory in battle.

Ningizzida: Gatekeeper of the Mesopotamian heaven; servant to the sky god Anu.

Ninshubur: Inanna's servant; a Mesopotamian messenger goddess.

Ninsun: A Sumerian goddess of wisdom; mother of Gilgamesh.

Niobe: Daughter of Tantalus; wife of Amphion; mother of twelve children, all of whom were killed by Apollo and Artemis.

Njord: A Norse god of the sea and fertility; husband of Skadi; father of Freyja and Freyr.

Nkuba: Master of lightning in the mythology of Congo.

Nü Gua (or Nuwa): "Gourd" or "Melon"; a Chinese creator goddess, often depicted with the tail of a serpent.

Nuada: Leader of the Tuatha Dé Danaan. He lost a hand fighting the Fomorians and was killed by Balor's lethal gaze.

Nun: Egyptian god of watery chaos; one of the deities of the Ogdoad.

Nut: Egyptian goddess of the sky, shown as a star-spangled figure arched across the earth; mother of Osiris, Isis, Nepthys, and Seth.

Nyamitondo: A heroine in African mythology; Mwindo's sister.

Nyamwindo: Mother of Mwindo; favorite wife of Shemwindo.

Nyctimus: One of the sons of Lycaon.

Nymphs: Forces of nature personified as semi-divine young women. Among them were Nereids, Naiads, Oceanids, Dryads, and Sylphs.

Nut

Nyx: "Night," one of the original Greek deities; daughter of Chaos; mother of the Fates, among many others.

Obatala: Yoruban creator, known for his logical mind, gentleness, and inability to handle palm wine.

Oceanus: The oldest Titan; husband of Tethys; ruler of the Ocean.

Ocyrrhoe: A nymph lusted after by Apollo. Another character by the same name, the daughter of Chiron, could foretell the future so well that the fates forbade her to say more and turned her into a horse.

Odin: Supreme deity of Norse mythology, most popular in the eighth and ninth centuries; ruler of Asgard; son of Bor; brother of Vili and Ve; father of Vidar and Vali; also known as Wotan or Woden. He gave up one eye to drink at the fountain of knowledge, wounded himself with his spear and hung upside down for nine days from Yggdrasil, the cosmic tree. In exchange, he gained magical powers and learned the meaning of the Viking runes.

Odysseus: The hero of Homer's *Odyssey*, known to the Romans as Ulysses; son of Anticlea and Laertes; husband of Penelope; father of Telemachus. Odysseus feigned insanity to avoid serving in the Trojan War but his ruse failed, and off he went. A brave and crafty warrior, he fought on the side of the Greeks. He is best known for his perilous ten-year voyage back to Ithaca, during which time he blinded the cyclops Polyphemus, visited the land of the Lotus-Eaters, fell asleep in the Cave of the Winds, escaped from the Laestrygonians, rescused his men from the sorceress Circe, visited the underworld, sailed past the Sirens and between Scylla and Charybdis, and escaped the wrath of Helios. He spent seven years with Calypso, who offered him immortality. But Odysseus longed to return to Penelope, and Zeus decreed that he be released. Freed at last, he sailed to the land of the Phaeacians and then to Ithaca, where Penelope was besieged by suitors. With the help of his son Telemachus, now grown, he killed the suitors and resumed his rightful place.

Oedipus: The tragic hero of the Oedipus cycle by Sophocles; son of Laius, whom he killed, and Jocasta, whom he married.

Oeneus: King of Calydon; husband of Althaea. Dionysus slept with his wife and in exchange taught him the art of viniculture.

Oenghus: Irish god of love; son of the Dagda; foster father of Diarmuid; often shown with birds, representing kisses, fluttering around his head.

Oeno: One of three sisters captured by Agamemmnon. They were about to be hanged when Dionysus turned them into doves.

Oenopion: Son of Dionysus and Ariadne; father of Merope.

Ogdoad: Eight Egyptian deities who created the world. They were: Kuk and Kauket, Huh and Hauhet, Amun and Amaunet, Nun and Naunet.

Ogma: Celtic god of eloquence and literature; son of the Dagda. He invented the Ogham script which is used in inscriptions of the fifth and sixth century CE.

Ogun: Yoruban god of war, iron, and all who use metal in their work including blacksmiths, barbers, mechanics, and truck drivers.

Oisin (or Ossian): "Little Fawn"; son of Finn MacCool and Sadb; a great Irish warrior and poet.

Olorun: Chief Yoruban deity, also known as Oludumare.

Olympian Gods: The main Greek gods, they defeated the Titans and lived on Mount Olympus. They include Ares, Artemis, Aphrodite, Apollo, Athena, Demeter, Dionysus, Hephaestus, Hera, Hermes, Poseidon, and Zeus. Hestia may have been in this group but she was replaced by Dionysus.

Omphale: Queen of Lydia. Heracles spent a year in servitude to her during which time he ran the monsters and thieves out of her kingdom, switched clothes with her, and became her lover.

Ophion: The primeval serpent who hatched the cosmic egg in Pelasgian mythology.

Orestes: Son of Agamemnon and Clytemnestra; brother of Iphigenia and Electra. Seeking revenge for the death of Agamemnon, Orestes killed his mother and was set upon by the Furies. He was brought to trial and acquitted.

Orion: A hunter killed by Artemis, who was tricked into shooting him. Another story reports that Orion was blinded by the father of Merope, whom he raped. He went to the workshop of Hephaestus and lifted a boy named Cedalion onto his shoulders. Cedalion guided him toward the sun, and his vision was restored. Orion is one of five constellations mentioned by Homer, the others being the Pleaides, the Hyades, Ursa Major, and Boötes.

Orpheus: A musician and poet; son of Calliope and either a mortal king, a river god, or Apollo; husband of Eurydice. Many poems have been attributed to him, and Hesiod and Homer were both said to be his descendants.

Orunmiller: Yoruban god of divination.

Oshun: Yoruban goddess of love; mother of Eshu.

Osiris: Egyptian god of the underworld; son of Geb and Nut; brother and husband of Isis; wise ruler who spread civilization throughout Egypt; a fertility god, often shown with green skin; the resurrected god.

Otreus: King of Phrygia. Aphrodite pretended to be his daughter when she seduced Anchises. He also fought against the Amazons with Priam.

Otus: Brother of Ephialtes.

Oya: Yoruban goddess of lightning, tornadoes, and sudden change.

P'an Ku: Chinese creator, born inside the cosmic egg. He separated the earth from the sky and when he died, his body became the universe.

Pallas: Daughter of Triton; a childhood friend of Athena's. After Athena accidentally killed her, she took her name.

Pan: God of pastures, shepherds, flocks, and wild places, known for his ability to inspire fear and panic; the son of Hermes. He was depicted with the legs and horns of a goat. The Romans assocaited him with Faunus.

Panacea: "Cure-all"; the daughter of Asclepius.

Pandion: King of Attica; father of Procne and Philomela.

Pandora: "All gifts"; the first woman, crafted by Hephaestus, given life by Athena, and sent to earth by Zeus to punish mankind for receiving fire from Prometheus.

Pandrosus: One of the daughters of Cecrops.

Paphos: Daughter of Pygmalion and Galatea; mother of Cinyras.

Paris: Prince of Troy; son of Priam and Hecuba; lover of Helen. At the wedding of Thetis and Peleus, Paris was asked to decide which goddess was the most beautiful. Hera and Athena offered him wisdom and power, but Aphrodite, winner of the contest, offered him the love of the most beautiful woman on earth, Helen. This event, known as the Judgment of Paris, precipitated the Trojan War.

Partholon: Leader of the second mythical invasion of Ireland.

Parvati: A major Hindu goddess; a wife of Shiva; mother of Ganesha.

Pasiphaë: Wife of King Minos; queen of Crete; lover of the while bull; mother of Ariadne, Phaedra, Androgeus; and the Minotaur.

Pasithea: One of the Graces. In the *Iliad*, Hera offers her to Hypnos as his bride.

Patroclus: Best friend of Achilles, whose armor he is wearing when he is killed.

Pegasus: The winged horse; son of Poseidon and Medusa.

Pele: Hawaiian volcano goddess.

Peleus: Husband of Thetis; father of Achilles.

Pelops: Son of Tantalus, who cut him up, cooked him, and served him to the gods. After the pieces were reassembled, Pelops married Hippodamia but the family was cursed. Atreus, son of Pelops, continued the family tradition by cooking the children of his brother Thyestes.

Penates: Roman household deities, gods of the cupboard and hearth. Part of each meal was set aside for them and thrown into the flames on the hearth. *See* lares.

Peneius: A river god; son of Oceanus and Tethys; father of Daphne, Stilbe, and Cyrene.

Penelope: Wife of Odyssesus; mother of Telemachus; a symbol of wifely devotion.

Penthesilea: An Amazon queen. She helped King Priam during the Trojan war. She was slain by Achilles, who looked in her eyes as she died and fell in love.

Pentheus: Son of Agave; grandson of Cadmus. In *The Bacchae* by Euripides, Pentheus resists the rites of Dionysus and is torn to pieces by the maenads, one of whom is his mother.

Periboriwa: A moon god of southern Venezuela.

Perigone: Daughter of Sinis; lover of Theseus, who killed her father.

Periphetes: Evil son of Hephaestus; slain by Theseus.

Persephone: Queen of the underworld and goddess of vegetation; daughter of Demeter; wife of Hades; also called Kore or, in Rome, Proserpina.

Perses: Son of Andromeda and Perseus; brother of King Aeetes of Colchis, whom he deposed. He was killed by Medus.

Perseus: Son of Zeus and Danaë; ruler of Tiryns; founder of Mycenae; great-grandfather of Heracles. He killed the Medusa, saved the life of Andromeda, and fulfilled a prophecy by accidentally killing his grandfather Acrisius.

Phaedra: Daughter of Minos and Pasiphaë; sister of Ariadne; wife of Theseus; stepmother of Hippolytus, with whom she fell in love.

Phaethon: Son of Helios, the sun god, and Clymene. He drove the chariot of the sun across the sky but could not control the horses. Zeus struck him down with a thunderbolt.

Phanes: "Light"; in Orphic philosophy, the first being and the mate of Night.

Philoctetes: An expert marksman during the Trojan War; killer of Paris.

Philomela: Daughter of Pandion; sister of Procne; sister-in-law of Tereus, who raped her and cut out her tongue. Philomela wove a tapestry depicting these events and sent it to Procne.

Phineus: A blind soothsayer. He lost his sight because he revealed too much of the future to human beings and incurred the wrath of the gods.

Phoebe: "Bright Moon"; a Titan; handmaiden to her sister Themis; a goddess at Delphi. When Apollo claimed that oracle, he took her name and became Phoebus Apollo.

Pholus: A good centaur; the son of Silenus and a nymph.

Phrixus: son of Nephele and Athamas. He and his sister Helle were rescued by the ram with the Golden Fleece, which he later sacrificed to Zeus.

Pirithous: King of the Lapiths; friend of Theseus, who accompanied him into the underworld to abduct Persephone.

Pittheus: Son of Pelops; father of Aethra; grandfather of Theseus, who grew up in his home.

Pitys: A nymph adored by Pan and turned into a pine tree.

Pleiades: The daughters of Atlas and Pleione. Orion pursued them so relentlessly that they turned into stars to escape him. They are Maia, Electra, Taygete, Calaeno, Alcyone, Sterope, and Merope.

Ploutus: "Wealth"; son of Demeter and Iasion.

Plur na mBan: "Flower of Women"; daughter of Oisin and the Celtic goddess Niamh.

Pluto: Latin name for Hades, the god of the underworld. The Romans also called him Dis Pater.

Podalirius: Son of Asclepius; brother of Machaon; a skilled healer.

Pollux: Latin for Polydeuces. *See* Dioscouri.

Polydectes: *See* Danaë.

Polydeuces: brother of Castor. *See* Dioscouri.

Polydorus: The youngest son of King Priam of Troy and Hecuba.

Polyhymnia: Muse of pantomime and hymns to the gods.

Polyneices: Son of Oedipus; brother of Eteocles and Antigone. He and Eteocles were supposed to share the kingship of Thebes, with each ruling for a year at a time but Eteocles refused to give up the throne. Polyneices rounded up six champions and besieged the city in a battle known as Seven Against Thebes. After the other six succumbed, Eteocles and Polyneices fought each other and died. Creon claimed the throne but refused to let Polyneices be buried in the proper manner. Antigone insisted and was condemned to death.

Polyphemus: A one-eyed, man-eating Cyclops; son of Poseidon. He took Odysseus and his men captive and was blinded by Odysseus.

Poseidon: Olympian god of the sea; associated with Neptune.

Prajapati: Lord of creatures in the Vedic tradition; the "fiery seed" in the cosmic sea; one of the forms of the Hindu god Vishnu.

Priam: King of Troy during the Trojan War; husband of Hecuba; father of Paris, Cassandra, and Hector, who was killed by Achilles. In an unforgettable scene in the *Iliad*, Priam begs Achilles for his son's defiled corpse, and the request is granted. Later, Priam is murdered by Neoptolemus, one of the sons of Achilles.

Priapus: A fertility god and garden figure known for his erect phallus; the son of Aphrodite and any of several gods including Hermes, Pan, and Dionysus.

Procne: Daughter of Pandion; sister of Philomela; wife of Tereus; mother of Itys, whom she killed and cooked.

Procrustes: A giant who forced travelers to lie on his famous bed. Those who were too tall had their limbs amputated to fit; those who were too short were stretched on the rack. He was killed by Theseus.

Prometheus: A Titan; son of Iapetus and Clymene; brother of Epimetheus, Atlas, and Monoetius; champion of humanity. He created human beings out of clay and stole fire from the gods. As punishment, he was chained to a mountain, where every night an eagle pecked at his liver and every day it grew back.

Proserpina: Roman goddess of the underworld, equivalent to Persephone.

Prosymnus: A mortal who gave Dionysus directions to the underworld.

Proteus: A god of the sea who could, at will, turn into a lion, a dragon, a panther, a boar, a tree, or water.

Pryderi: "Care"; the son of the Celtic divinities Rhiannon and Pwyll.

Psyche: The beloved of Eros; heroine of a story told by in the second century CE by Lucius Apulius in *The Golden Ass.*

Ptah: Egyptian creator, worshipped in Memphis; husband of Sekhmet.

Purusha: The primeval man whose body became the universe in Hindu mythology.

Putana: A rakshasa or demon killed by the Hindu god Krishna as a baby.

Pwyll: Lord of Dyfed in Wales; husband of the Celtic goddess Rhiannon; father of Pryderi.

Pygmalion: King of Cyprus. He carved a statue, fell in love with it, and prayed to Aphrodite to bring it to life. His wish was granted.

Pyrrha: Daughter of Pandora, wife of Deucalion, and the only woman to survive the flood; hence, the mother of us all.

Python: A serpent or dragon who guarded Delphi for Gaia. It was slain by Apollo, who wrested control of the oracle away from the goddess and established the Pythian Games in its honor.

Qingu: Lover of the Babylonian goddess Tiamat; killed by Marduk, who created humanity from his blood.

Quies: Roman goddess of quietness.

Quetzalcoatl: "Feathered Serpent"; son of Xochiquetzal; Meso-American creator and hero whose return was anxiously awaited. When Hernando Cortés arrived in the new world in 1519, the ancient prophecy appeared to have been fulfilled.

> *My heart stirs just a little to the word Quetzalcóatl.*
> *Quetzalcóatl! Quetzalcóatl!*
>
> —D. H. Lawrence

Quirinus: A war god worshipped in Rome and identified with Romulus.

Ra (or Re): Solar deity of Heliopolis (Sun City in Greek); king of the Egyptian gods. Born from the primeval lotus, he lived on earth until he grew old and the goddess Nut carried him into the sky, where he created the stars. By day he sailed across the heavens; by night he traveled through the Underworld and battled the cosmic serpent Apep or Apophis. He became identified with Atum, under whose name he was worshipped as creator of the universe.

Radha: Krishna's lover.

Ragnorak: "Doom of the Gods"; the final battle at the end of the world fought between the Norse gods, headed by Odin, and Loki and the evil frost giants.

Raktabija: A Hindu demon defeated by Kali, who drank his blood.

Rama: Seventh avatar of Vishnu; hero of the *Ramayana*, a Sanskrti epic written by the poet Valmiki between 200 BCE and 200 CE.

Ravana: King of the Rakshasas or demons. He defeated Indra and was slain by Rama.

Raven: a hero or trickster in the mythology of the Pacific Northwest.

Re: *see* Ra.

Regin: Norse swordsmith; foster father of Sigurd; brother of Fafnir.

Remus: *See* Romulus and Remus.

Rhadamanthys: One of the judges of the dead; son of Zeus and Europa.

Rhea: Daughter of Gaia and Uranus; wife of Kronos; mother of Hera, Demeter, Hestia, Hades, Poseidon, and Zeus.

Rhea Silvia: Mother of Romulus and Remus.

Rhiannon: Celtic goddess; Queen of Dyfed; wife of Pwyll and Manawydan; mother of Pryderi. Her birds could raise the dead with their song and lull the living to sleep.

Rohini: Goddess of fortune in India; mother of Krishna's half-brother Balarama.

Romulus and Remus: Twin sons of Mars and Rhea Silvia; founders of Rome.

Rona: A Maori god in constant combat with the moon.

Rudra: "Howling One"; Vedic god of storms; precursor to Shiva.

Rukmini: One of Krishna's lovers; an incarnation of Lakshmi.

Sadb: Celtic moon goddess; lover of Finn MacCool; mother of Oisin. The Dark Druid turned her into a deer, and she raised her son in that form.

Salmacis: A nymph who fell in love with Hermaphroditus.

Samael: Lilith's son and lover; a demon who takes the form of a serpent.

Saraswati: Hindu goddess of wisdom; wife of Brahma, whose shakti or feminine aspect she represents.

Sarpedon: Son of Zeus and Europa; brother of Minos and Rhadamanthus; an Underworld judge.

Sati: Wife of Shiva. Under this name, she was a "good wife" who threw herself upon the funeral pyre, instituting the Indian custom of suttee.

Saturn: An ancient corn god, identified by the Romans with Kronos and typically shown carrying a scythe, like Father Time. The Saturnalia, celebrated at the end of December, featured a reversal of roles between servants and masters.

Scathach: A Celtic warrior princess. She gave Cú Chulainn his magic spear, Gae Bolga, and taught him how to fight and how to leap like a salmon.

Sciron: A tyrant who kicked travelers into the sea, where a monster devoured them. Sometimes said to be a son of Pelops; killed by Theseus.

Scylla: A sea monster, once a beautiful nymph until Circe turned her into a monster with six omnivorous dog heads sprouting from her abdomen. With her sister Charybdis, who became a whirlpool, she guards the straits of Messina.

Seasons: The Horae or Hours; daughters of Themis and Zeus. Among them were Eunomia (Discipline), Dike (Justice), and Eirene (Peace). They accompanied Aphrodite.

Sebek: Egyptian god of rivers, shown with a crocodile head.

Sedna: One-eyed Arctic goddess of the sea, known by various names; ruler of Adlivum, the realm of the dead.

Sekhmet: Egyptian goddess of war, known as the "lady of bright red linen" and depicted with a lion's head; daughter of Ra; consort of Ptah. She was associated with Bastet and Hathor, who turned into Sekhmet when angry.

Selene: Goddess of the moon; daughter of Hyperion and Theia; sister of Eos and Helios; lover of Endymion.

Semele: Daughter of Cadmus and Harmonia; lover of Zeus; mother of Dionysus. She was consumed in flames when Zeus revealed himself to her.

Setanta: The childhood name of the Celtic hero Cú Chulainn, perhaps taken from the Setantii, a Celtic tribe in northwestern England.

Seth: Egyptian god of disorder, darkness, and disaster; son of Geb and Nut; brother of Isis, Nephthys, and Osiris, whom he killed. He controlled the forces of heat, drought, hunger, and thirst, and defended the sun by battling the serpent Apep.

Seven against Thebes: *See* Polyneices.

Shakti: Great Hindu goddess, source of primal energy; and consort of Shiva, whose feminine aspect she represents.

Shara: Inanna's son; a Sumerian god abducted by demons and rescued by Inanna.

Shemwindo: Father of the African hero Mwindo; chief of Tubondo.

Shen I: Divine archer of Chinese mythology.

Sheng Mu: Chinese goddess known as the Princess of Streaked Clouds or the Holy Mother.

Shiva (or Siva): Hindu god of destruction, part of a trinity that included Brahma the Creator and Vishnu the Preserver; worshipped in the form of a phallus; often depicted with a third eye and a blue neck in which he holds the poison that once threatened mankind. His mount: the white bull Nandi.

Shu: Egyptian god of air whose function was to separate his children Geb (the earth) and Nut (the sky). His attribute: an ostrich feather on his head.

Shulpae: Sumerian god of feasting.

Sibyls: Priestesses able to foretell the future.

Siduri: Mesopotamian goddess of wine and wisdom who advised Gilgamesh to eat, drink, and be merry.

Sigurd: Scandinavian hero also called Siegfried; foster son of Regin, the evil smith. Regin sent him off in search of treasure guarded by the dragon Fafnir. Sigurd hid in a pit, stabbed Fafnir as he crawled over it, and roasted the dragon's heart. When he accidentally touched it, he found that he could understand the language of birds. Thus he learned that Regin planned to slay him. Instead, Sigurd killed Regin and took the treasure, including a ring that brought death to its owner. Later, Sigurd fell in love with Brynhild but was bewitched into marrying Gudrun. In a rage, Brynhild had him killed.

Sigyn: Loyal wife of Loki; mother of Narvi and Vali.

Silenus: A wise old satyr who brought up Dionysus. In contrast, the plural term Sileni refers to a notorious group of old satyrs famed for drunken, lecherous behavior.

Sinis: A robber known as the "bender of pine trees"; killed by Theseus.

Sinn: Sumerian god of the moon; son of Enlil.

Sirens: Frightening, seductive creatures, part woman and part bird; known for their irresistible song.

Sisyphus: King of Corinth; husband of Merope; a famed resident of Hades, condemned to an eternity of pushing a boulder up hill.

Sita: Wife of Rama in the *Ramayana*; a model of wifely devotion; an avatar of Laskhmi.

Skadi Norse mountain goddess, briefly married to Njord; mother of Freyja and Freyr.

Skanda: Six-headed Hindu god of war, born after Shiva's semen mixed with the water of the Ganges; associated with the planet Mars. His mount: the peacock.

Sky Woman: *See* Atahensic.

Sleipnir: Odin's eight-legged horse; son of Loki.

Smyrna: Mother of Adonis, sometimes called Myrrha.

Soma: The elixir of immortality. In Hindu literature it has been described as a bull, a bird, a plant, the juice of that plant, the moon, and even as a god. A more recent suggestion is that it was a hallucinogenic mushroom.

> *Soma, give us brightness, give us heaven,*
> *give us all good things; and make us happy*
>
> —the *Rig-Veda* (IX.1.4)

Sphinx: A monster with the head of a woman, body of a lion, and wings of an eagle.

Spider Woman: A creator deity recognized by the Pawnee, Hopi, Zuñi, Navajo, and other Native American groups.

Steropes: "Lightning"; offspring of Gaia and Uranus; one of the Cyclopes.

Stilbe: Lover of Apollo; mother of Centaurus and Lapithes, the ancestors of the warring Centaurs and Lapiths.

Styx: daughter of the Titans Oceanus and Tethys; goddess of the River Styx, which separates the world of the living from the realm of the dead.

Suataimh: A mortal sometimes said to be the father of the Celtic hero Cú Chulainn.

Susa-no-wo: Japanese god of storms and disorder; brother of Amaterasu. He was banished from heaven and ended up in the Underworld.

Sylphs: Nymphs of the air.

Syrinx: A nymph pursued by Pan.

Ta'aroa: Tahitian creator.

Taliesin: A sixth-century Welsh bard; said to be the son of Cerridwen.

Talos: A bronze giant crafted by Daedalus to guard Crete. He had a single vein which was plugged by a nail in his ankle. Medea cast a spell which caused the nail to be dislodged, whereupon all his ichor (the blood of divinities) flowed out like melted lead, and he died.

Tammuz: Babylonian vegetation god; husband of Ishtar; equivalent to Dumuzi. His annual return to the underworld occasioned great mourning among women.

Tantalus: Son of Zeus; father of Niobe and Pelops, whom he cooked and served to the gods. He was condemned to eternal hunger and thirst in the underworld. A less common story reports that he was forced to stand beneath a boulder which was always threatening to fall but never actually did.

Tara: A Hindu star goddess; wife of Brihaspati; lover of Soma. In Tibetan Buddhism, the wife of the bodhisattva Avalokitesvara. Her aspects include the peaceful White Tara and the terrifying Green Tara.

Taranis: Celtic thunder god. Julius Caesar compared him to Jupiter.

Tarqeq: Inuit moon god, also known as Igaluk.

Tartarus: The deepest region of creation, as distant from Hades as heaven is from earth; home of deposed gods.

Tatsuta-Hime: Japanese goddess of the wind.

Tefnut: Egyptian goddess of moisture; daughter of Atum; sister/wife of Shu; mother of Geb and Nut.

Telemachus: Son of Penelope and Odysseus. He left home to find his father, who had been gone for twenty years, and returned to help him slay Penelope's suitors.

Tepeu: Mayan god who helped Gucumatz create human beings.

Tereus: Son of Ares; king of Thrace; husband of Procne; father of Itys; brother-in-law of Philomela, whom he raped and mutilated.

Terpsichore: Muse of dance.

Tethys: A Titan; wife of Oceanus; mother of numerous river gods and Oceanids.

Teyrnon: Foster father of the Celtic god Pryderi.

Tezcatlipoca: "Smoking Mirror"; Aztec god of destruction, war, and night; brother and adversary of Quetzalcoatl. By looking into a mirror he could see the future.

Thalia: One of the graces; also, the muse of comedy.

Thamyras: A minstrel who challenged the muses to a contest and lost. He was punished with the loss of his sight and musical ability. He loved Hyacinthus and was considered the first homosexual.

Theia: A Titan; wife of Hyperion; mother of Helios, Selene, and Enos.

Themis: A Titan; daughter of Gaia and Uranus; mother of the Horae, the Moirae, and others. As the goddess of law, she lived on Olympus and advised Zeus.

Themistos: Third wife of Athamas. Out of jealousy, she asked her nurse to dress her predecessor Ino's children in black and her own in white. She schemed to have Ino's children murdered. But the nurse switched the clothing, with the result that Ino's children were untouched while her own were killed.

Theophane: Lover of Poseidon, who turned her into a ewe and mated with her; the mother of the ram with the Golden Fleece.

Theseus: The hero of Athens and champion of democracy; son of Aethra and Poseidon or Aegeus (his mortal father); killer of the Minotaur; husband of Ariadne, whom he abandoned, and Phaedra; father of Hippolytus.

Thetis: A sea nymph loved by Zeus and Poseidon; wife of Peleus; mother of Achilles.

Thinking Woman: Native American creator and Earth Mother.

Thjazi: A Norse giant; father of Skadi.

Thor: Norse god of thunder and war; son of Odin and Fjorgyn (Earth); enemy of the frost giants and the world serpent; friend of Loki. He owned iron gloves, a belt that increased his strength, a chariot pulled by two billy goats, and a boomerang-like hammer named Mjollnir that always returned to him.

Thoth: Ibis-headed Egyptian god of knowledge, writing, and the moon, often depicted as a baboon; scribe of the gods; judge in the underworld. He was credited with the invention of astronomy, geometry, hieroglyphics, writing, history, language, magic, music, law, and the calendar.

Thriae: Three sisters, daughters of Zeus, who could divine the future by reading the patterns of pebbles; said to be fond of honey.

Thyestes: Son of Pelops and Hippodamia; brohter of Artreus, whose wife he seduced. Artreus killed the children of Thyestes and served them to him at a banquet, causing Thyestes to pronounce a curse on the house of Atreus.

Tiamat: Babylonian serpent goddess of chaos and salt water; conquered by Marduk.

Ticciztecatl: Aztec god of the moon.

Tien-Mu: Chinese celestial goddess; recorder of births and deaths.

Tireisas: Most revered seer of Greek mythology; a transsexual who lived as a man and as a woman.

Titans: Children of Uranus and Gaia; the first group of ruling gods. After a ten-year battle with the Olympian gods, all the Titans except Atlas were imprisoned in Tartarus. They were: Hyperion, Iaepetus, Coeus, Kreius, Kronos, Mnemosyne, Oceanus, Phoebe, Rhea, Tethys, Theia, and Themis. Also considered Titans: Leto, Helios, Selene, Eos, Epimetheus, Prometheus, and Atlas.

Tithonus: Son of Laomedon; brother of Priam; lover of Eos, who asked Zeus to grant him immortality but forgot to request eternal youth.

Tityus: A giant who tried to rape Leto. He was shot by Artemis and punished by Zeus.

Tlaloc: Mesoamerican god of rain.

Tonantzin: Mesoamerican goddess; patron of midwives and healers. Her principal shrine was on Tepeyacac hill, where Juan Diego in 1531 saw a vision identified as the Virgin of Guadalupe.

Triptolemus: A young man who helped Demeter disseminate knowledge of agriculture, often identified with the child whom Demeter nursed.

Triton: Son of Neptune and Amphitrite; a merman.

Tsuki-yomi: Japanese god of the moon, born from the right eye of Izanagi; brother of Amaterasu and Susanowo.

Tuatha Dé Danaan: A race of gods known as the people of the goddess Dana (or Danu); the last gods to rule Ireland.

Tvastr: "Carpenter"; a Hindu smith; father of Vrtra. He crafted the weapons and attributes of the gods, including Vishnu's discuss and Indra's thunderbolt.

Tyndareus: Mortal husband of Leda; father of Castor and Clytemnestra.

Typhon: A monster, also called Typhoeus, with one hundred snake heads, eyes of fire, and an astonishing array of voices.

Tyr: Norse god of war.

Uathach: One of Cú Chulainn's lovers.

Uke Mochi: Japanese goddess of food.

Ulysses: "Symbol of the seeker," wrote Wallace Stevens. Latin form of Odysseus.

Uma: One of the forms of the wife of Shiva; an ascetic.

Upuaut: Egyptian wolf-headed god who helps guide the dead.

Uraeus: Sacred Egyptian cobra, an emblem of strength and sovereignty. The sun-god Ra wears it on his headdress surrounding a solar disc.

Urania: Muse of astronomy. John Milton invokes her in *Paradise Lost*, imploring her to "Govern thou my Song, Urania, and fit audience find, though few."

Uranus: Original Greek sky god; son and mate of Gaia; father of the Cyclopes, the Hecatonchires, and the Titans. His son Kronos castrated him at the request of Gaia. His severed genitals gave birth to Aphrodite.

Urshanabi: The boatman who helped Gilgamesh; equivalent to Charon.

Utnapishtim: The only mortal in Sumerian mythology to survive the deluge and be granted immortality.

Utu: Sumerian sun god; brother of Inanna; son of the moon god Nanna.

Vali: Son of Loki and Sigyn; brother of Narvi, whom he killed. Another character named Vali was Odin's son, who grew to adulthood the day he was born and killed Hoder.

Valkyries: Goddesses of fate; wartime attendants of Odin.

Vanir: The older race of gods of Norse mythology. Njord, Skadi, Freyja, and Freyr belonged to this group.

Varuna: Supreme deity in early Vedic literature. Before Indra replaced him in importance, Varuna controlled human destiny, taught the birds to fly, and kept the stars and planets in their proper places.

Vayu: God of the wind; Indra's charioteer.

Ve: Brother of Vili and Odin. The three brothers created the world from the body of Ymir and fashioned the first man and woman from two trees. Odin gave them the breath of life, Vili endowed them with the ability to think and feel, and Ve gave them sight and hearing.

Veles: Slavic earth eity; god of the Underworld.

Venus: Ancient Italian goddess of love and beauty, equivalent to Aphrodite.

Vesta: Roman goddess of the hearth, similar to Hestia but of greater importance.

Vili: *See* Ve.

Vishnu: Originally a solar god, later the supreme god. Linked with Brahma the Creator and Shiva the destroyer in the great Hindu trinity, Vishnu was the preserver who restored the world by coming to earth as an avatar whenever the need was great. Dark blue with four arms, he holds a discuss, a lotus, a club, and a conch shell. His mount: Garuda, the sun bird.

Vrtra: "Storm Cloud"; a demon symbolizing ignorance; slain by Indra.

Vulcan: Ancient Roman smith god, associated with Hephaestus.

Wahieloa: Pele's husband.

Wainkaura: A survivor of the flood in Brazilian mythology.

Wakdjunkaga: Winnebago trickster.

Waptokwa: A Brazilian god, responsible for the flood.

Wayland: Nordic smith god. Like Hephaestus, he is lame.

White Buffalo Woman: Oglala culture bringer.

Woden or Wotan: *See* Odin.

Xochiquetzal: Aztec goddess of flowers, love, and sexuality.

Yahweh: Hebrew god, also called Jehovah. In Freud's opinion, "Yahweh was unquestionably a volcano god."

Yam: Canaanite god of the sea; enemy of Baal; equivalent to Tiamat.

Yama: Hindu god of death; brother of Manu, who survived the flood, and the goddess Yami; sometimes said to be the first man.

Yambe-Akka: Underworld goddess of the Lapps.

Yanwang: Chinese god of death.

Yappan: An Aztec ascetic, turned into a Scorpion.

Yashoda: Foster mother of Krishna.

Yggdrasil: The world tree of Norse mythology. Its roots nourished Jotunheim, the land of giants, Niflheim, the land of mist, and Asgard, home of the Aesir gods. Its branches reached six other worlds inhabited by the fire giants, the Vanir, the elves, the righteous, mankind, and the dead.

Ymir: The first frost giant; killed by Odin, Vili, and Ve, who created the world from his corpse. "His scull was the great blue vault of Immensity, and the brains of it became the Clouds," Carlyle wrote. "What a Hyper-Brobdignagian business!"

Yomi: The underworld in Japanese mythology.

Zetes: Son of Boreas, the North Wind; twin brother of Calais; one of the Argonauts.

Zephyr: God of the western wind; son of Aeolus and Aurora; husband of Iris; father, with one of the harpies, of Xanthus and Balius, the immortal horses of Achilles.

Zeus: Chief god of the Greek pantheon; son of Rhea and Kronos; leader of the Olympians; brother of Poseidon, Hades, Demeter, Hestia, and Hera, his wife.

Zorya: Triple Eastern European sky goddess; a trinity comprising the goddess of dawn, the goddess of dusk, and the goddess of midnight.

Bibliography

Ackerman, Robert. *The Myth and Ritual School: J. G. Frazer and the Cambridge Ritualists.* Garland Publishing, Inc., 1991.

Aeschylus. *The Oresteia.* Translated by Robert Fagles. NY: Penguin Books, 1979.

Aghion, I., C. Barbillon, and F. Lissarrague. *Gods and Heroes of Classical Antiquity.* Flammarian Iconographic Guides. NY: Flammarian, 1996.

Ann, Martha and Dorothy Myers Imel. *Goddesses in World Mythology.* NY: Oxford University Press, 1993.

Apollodorus. *The Library.* Translated by J. G. Frazer. The Loeb Classical Library, Cambridge, MA: Harvard University Press, and London: Heinemann, Ltd., 1921.

Apollonius of Rhodes. *Jason and the Golden Fleece.* Translated by Richard Hunter. NY: Oxford University Press, 1993.

Apuleius. *The Golden Ass of Apuleius.* Translated by Robert Graves. NY: The Pocket Library, 1954.

Arlington, Richard and Delano Ames, translators. *Larousse Encyclopedia of Mythology.* Introduction by Robert Graves. NY: Barnes & Noble, 1994.

Bachofen, J. J. *Myth, Religion, and Mother Right.* Selected Writings of J. J. Bachofen. Translated by Ralph Manheim. Princeton, NJ: Princeton University Press, Bolligen Foundation, 1967.

Baldwin, Neil. *Legends of the Plumed Serpent: Biography of a Mexican God.* NY: Public Affairs, 1998.

Baring, Anne and Jules Cashford. *The Myth of the Goddess: Evolution of an Image.* NY: Penguin Books, 1991.

Barker, Stephen, editor. *Excavations and Their Objects: Freud's Collection of Antiquity.* Albany, NY: State University of New York Press, 1996.

Barthes, Roland. *Mythologies.* Translated by Jonathon Cope, Ltd. NY: Farrar, Straus & Giroux, 1972.

Bataille, Georges. *The Tears of Eros.* Translated by Peter Connor. San Francisco, CA: City Lights Books, 1989.

Belcher, Steve. *Epic Traditions of Africa.* Bloomington and Indianapolis, IN: Indiana University Press, 1999.

Bell, Robert E. *Women of Classical Mythology: A Biographical Dictionary.* NY: Oxford University Press, 1991.

Bierhorst, John. *The Mythology of Mexico and Central America.* NY: William Morrow & Co., Inc., 1990.

———. *The Mythology of South America.* NY: William Morrow & Co., Inc., 1988.

Bierlein, J. F. *Parallel Myths.* NY: Ballantine Books, 1994.

Bloomfield, Morton W., editor. *Allegory, Myth, and Symbol.* Cambridge, MA: Harvard University Press, 1981.

Bolen, Jean Shinoda, M.D. *Goddesses in Everywoman: A New Psychology of Women.* San Francisco, CA: Harper and Row, 1984.

Bonnefoy, Yves, editor. *Roman and European Mythologies.* Translated under the direction of Wendy Doniger. Chicago, IL: The University of Chicago Press, 1991.

Brockway, Robert W. *Myth from the Ice Age to Mickey Mouse.* Albany, NY: State University of New York Press, 1993.

Brunel, Pierre, editor. *Companion to Literary Myths, Heroes and Archetypes.* Translated by Wendy Allatson, Judith Hayward, and Trista Selous. NY: Routledge, 1996.

Bulfinch, Thomas. *The Age of Fable or The Beauties of Mythology.* NY: The Heritage Press, 1942.

Burkert, Walter. *Greek Religion.* Cambridge, MA: Harvard University Press, 1985.

Buxton, Richard. *Imaginary Greece: The Contexts of Mythology.* Cambridge, MA: Cambridge University Press, 1994.

Callimachus. *Hymns and Epigrams.* Translated by A. W. Mair and G. R. Mair. Cambridge, MA: Harvard University Press, 1955.

Campbell, Joseph. *The Hero with a Thousand Faces.* Princeton, NJ: Princeton University Press, 1968.

———. *The Masks of God: Primitive Mythology.* NY: The Viking Press, 1959.

———. *The Power of Myth* with Bill Moyers. NY: Doubleday, 1988.

———. *Transformations of Myth Through Time.* NY: Harper and Row, 1990.

Camphausen, Rufus C. *The Divine Library.* Rochester, VT: Inner Traditions International, 1992.

Carlyle, Thomas. *On Heroes, Hero-Worship and the Heroic in History.* NY: Wiley and Putnam, 1846.

Carpenter, T. H. *Art and Myth in Ancient Greece.* London: Thames and Hudson, 1991.

Cavendish, Richard, editor. *Mythology: An Illustrated Encylopedia.* NY: Barnes and Noble, 1993.

Chadwick, Nora. *The Celts.* NY: Penguin, 1997.

Cicero. *The Nature of the Gods.* Translated by Horace C. P. McGregor. Introduction by J. M. Ross. NY: Penguin Books, 1972.

Clark, R. T. Rundle. *Myth and Symbol in Ancient Egypt.* NY: Thames and Hudson, 1991.

Clauss, James J. and Sarah Iles Johnston. *Medea.* Princeton, NJ: Princeton University Press, 1997.

Clay, Jenny Strauss. *The Wrath of Athena: Gods and Men in the* Odyssey. Princeton, NJ: Princeton University Press, 1983.

Comte, Fernand. *Mythology.* Translated by Alison Goring. Edinburgh, NY: W & R Chambers, Ltd., 1991.

Condos, Theony. *Star Myths of the Greeks and Romans: A Sourcebook.* Grand Rapids, MI: Phanes Press, 1997.

Cott, Jonathan. *Isis and Osiris: Exploring the Goddess Myth.* NY: Doubleday, 1994.

Cotterell, Arthur. *A Dictionary of World Mythology.* NY: Oxford University Press, 1986.

———. *The Encyclopedia of Mythology.* NY: Smithmark, 1996.

———. *The Macmillan Illustrated Encyclopedia of Myths and Legends.* NY: Macmillan Publishing Company, 1989.

Davidson, H. R. Ellis. *Gods and Myths of Northern Europe.* NY: Penguin Books, 1964.

Detienne, Marcel. *The Creation of Mythology.* Translated by Margaret Cook. Chicago, IL: University of Chicago Press, 1986.

———. *The Gardens of Adonis.* Translated by Janet Lloyd. Princeton, NJ: Princeton University Press, 1994.

Deutsch, Helene, M.D. *A Psychoanalytic Study of the Myth of Dionysus and Apollo: Two Variants of the Son-Mother Relationship.* NY: International Universities Press, Inc., 1969.

Diel, Paul. *Symbolism in Greek Mythology: Human Desire and Its Transformation.* Preface by Gaston Bachelard. Boulder, CO: Shambhala, 1980.

Doob, Penelope Reed. *The Idea of the Labyrinth: from Classical Antiquity through the Middle Ages.* Ithaca, NY: Cornell University Press, 1990.

[Doolittle, Hilday]. *H.D. Selected Poems.* Edited by Louis L. Martz. NY: New Directions Books, 1988.

Doty, William G. *Mythography: The Study of Myths and Rituals.* Tuscaloosa, AL: The University of Alabama Press, 1986.

Dowden, Ken. *The Uses of Greek Mythology.* NY: Routledge, Chapman and Hall, Inc., 1992.

Downing, Christine. *The Goddess: Mythological Images of the Feminine.* NY: Crossword Publishing Co., 1992.

Dundes, Alan, editor. *Sacred Narrative: Readings in the Theory of Myth.* Berkeley, CA: University of California Press, 1984.

Eisler, Riane. *The Chalice and the Blade.* San Francisco, CA: HarperSanFrancisco, 1988.

Eisner, Robert. *The Road to Daulis: Psychoanalysis, Psychology, and Classical Mythology.* Syracuse, NY: Syracuse University Press, 1987.

Eliade, Mircea and Ioan P. Couliano with Hillary S. Wiesner. *The Eliade Guide to World Religions.* NY: HarperCollins Publishers, 1991.

Ellis, Peter Berresford. *Dictionary of Celtic Mythology.* NY: Oxford University Press, 1992.

Emerson, R. W. *The Early Lectures of Ralph Waldo Emerson, Volume II: 1836–1838.* Edited by Stephen E. Whicher, Robert E. Spiller, and Wallace E. Williams. Cambridge, MA: The Belknap Press of Harvard University Press, 1964.

Erdoes, Richard and Alfonso Ortiz. *American Indian Myths and Legends.* NY: Pantheon Books, 1985.

Euripides. *Orestes and Other Plays.* Translated by Philip Vellacott. NY: Penguin Books, 1972.

———. *The Bacchae and Other Plays.* Translated by Philip Vellacott, NY: Penguin Books, 1973.

———. *Alcestis/Hippolytus/Iphigenia in Tauris.* translated by Philip Vellacott. NY: Penguin Books, 1974.

Fagg, William, and John Pemberton 3rd. *Yoruba: Sculpture of West Africa.* Bryce Holcombe, Editor. NY: Alfred A. Knopf, 1982.

Faivre, Antoine. *The Eternal Hermes: From Greek God to Alchemical Magus.* Grand Rapids, MI: Phanes Press, 1995.

Ford, Clyde W. *The Hero with an African Face.* NY: Bantam Books, 1999.

Frazer, Sir James George. *The Golden Bough: A Study in Magic and Religion.* Abridged edition. NY: The MacMillan Company, 1960.

———. *The New Golden Bough*. Revised and edited by Theodor H. Gaster. NY: New American Library, Mentor Books, 1964.

Friedrich, Paul. *The Meaning of Aphrodite*. Chicago, IL: The University of Chicago Press, 1978.

Freud, Sigmund. *The Origins of Religion: Totem and Taboo, Moses and Monotheism and Other Works*. The Penguin Freud Library, Volume 13. NY: Penguin Books, 1990.

Freund, Philip. *Myths of Creation*. NY: Washington Square Press, 1965.

Gadon, Elinor W. *The Once & Future Goddess*. NY: HarperCollins, 1989.

Gantz, Jeffrey. *Early Irish Myths and Sagas*. NY: Penguin Books, 1981.

Gantz, Timothy. *Early Greek Myth: A Guide to Literary and Artistic Sources*. Baltimore, MD: The Johns Hopkins University Press, 1993.

Gill, Sam D. and Irene F. Sullivan. *Dictionary of Native American Mythology*. NY: Oxford University Press, 1992.

Gimbutas, Marija. *The Goddesses and Gods of Old Europe: Myths and Cult Images*. Berkeley and Los Angeles, CA: University of California Press, 1982.

Goetz, Delia and Sylvanus G. Morley. *Popul Vuh: The Sacred Book of the Ancient Quiché Maya*. Translated by Adrián Recinos. Norman, OK: University of Oklahoma Press, 1950.

Gonzales-Wippler, Migene. *Powers of the Orishas: Santeria and the Worship of Saints*. Plainview, NY: Original Publications, 1992.

Gordon, Stuart. *The Encyclopedia of Myths and Legends*. London, England: Headline Book Publishing, 1993.

Graf, Fritz. *Greek Mythology: An Introduction*. Translated by Thomas Marier. Baltimore, MD: The Johns Hopkins University Press, 1993.

Grant, Michael and John Hazel. *Gods and Mortals in Classical Mythology: A Dictionary*. NY: Dorset Press, 1979.

Grant, Michael. *Myths of the Greeks and Romans*. Cleveland and NY: The World Publishing Co., 1962.

Graves, Robert. *The Greek Myths*. NY: Penguin Books, 1960.

———. *The White Goddess*. NY: Creative Age Press, 1948.

Graves, Robert and Raphael Patai. *Hebrew Myths: The Book of Genesis*. NY: McGraw-Hill Book Company, 1964.

Green, Miranda. *Celtic Goddesses*. NY: George Braziller, 1996.

———. *Dictionary of Celtic Myth and Legend*. London, England: Thames and Hudson, 1992.

———. *Celtic Myths*. Austin, TX: University of Texas Press, 1993.

Grimal, Pierre. *The Penguin Dictionary of Classical Mythology*. NY: Penguin Books, 1991.

Guerber, H. A. *Greece and Rome*. NY: Avenel Books, 1986.

Guthrie, W. K. C. *The Greeks and Their Gods*. Boston, MA: Beacon Press, 1955.

Hallam, Elizabeth, general editor. *Gods and Goddesses*. NY: MacMillan, 1996.

Hamilton, Virginia. *In the Beginning: Creation Stories from Around the World*. Illustrated by Barry Moser. NY: Harcourt Brace Jovanovich, 1988.

Harding, M. Esther, M.D., M.R.C.P. *Woman's Mysteries, Ancient and Modern*. NY: Longmans, Green & Co., 1935.

Harrison, Jane Ellen. *Ancient Art and Ritual*. Westport, CT: Greenwood Press, 1969.

Harrison, Jane Ellen. *Prolegomena to the Study of Greek Religion*. Princeton, NJ: Princeton University Press, 1922.

———. *Themis*. NY: The World Publishing Company, 1962.

Hart, George. *A Dictionary of Egyptian Gods and Goddesses*. NY: Routledge and Kegan Paul, 1986.

Hawthorne, Nathaniel. *A Wonder Book and Tanglewood Tales*. NY: Dodd, Mead & Company, 1938.

Hendricks, Rhoda A. *Classical Gods and Heroes: Myths as Told by the Ancient Authors*. Translated and with an introduction by Rhoda A. Hendricks. NY: Morrow Quill Paperbacks, 1974.

Hesiod. *Hesiod and Theognis*. Translated and with an introduction by Dorothea Wender. NY: Penguin Books, 1973.

———. *Hesiod, The Homeric Hymns and Homerica*. Translated by Hugh G. Evelyn-White, M.A. Cambridge, MA: Harvard University Press, and London: Heinemann, Ltd., 1982.

Hillman, James. *A Blue Fire: Selected Writings by . . .* Edited and with an introduction by Thomas Moore. NY: Harper & Row, 1989.

Hillman, James. *Facing the Gods*. Dallas, TX: Spring Publications, Inc., 1980.

Homer. *The Iliad*. Translated by Robert Fagles. Introduction and Notes by Bernard Knox. NY: Penguin Books, 1990.

———. *The Iliad*. Translated by Ennis Rees. NY: The Modern Library, 1963.

———. *The Odyssey*. Translated by E. V. Rieue; revised by D. C. H. Rieu. NY: Penguin Books, 1991.

———. *The Odyssey: A Modern Translation*. Translated by Richard Lattimore. New York: Harper & Row, 1965.

Hooke, S. H. *Middle Eastern Mythology*. NY: Penguin Books, 1991.

Hornblower, Simon and Anthony Spawforth. *The Oxford Classical Dictionary, Third Edition*. Oxford, NY: Oxford University Press, 1996.

Horwitz, Silvia L. *The Find of a Lifetime: Sir Arthur Evans and the Discovery of Knossos*. NY: The Viking Press, 1981.

Houston, Jean. *The Hero and the Goddess: The* Odyssey *as Mystery and Initiation.* NY: Ballantine Books, 1992.

Howatson, M. C., editor. *The Oxford Companion to Classical Literature.* NY: Oxford University Press, 1989.

Hyde, Lewis. *Trickster Makes This World: Mischief, Myth, and Art.* NY: Farrar, Straus and Giroux, 1998.

Hyman, Stanley Edgar. *The Tangled Bank: Darwin, Marx, Frazer and Freud as Imaginative Writers.* NY: Atheneum, 1962.

Jackson, Guida M. *Traditional Epics: A Literary Companion.* NY: Oxford University Press, 1994.

Jackson, Kenneth Hurlstone, ed. *A Celtic Miscellany.* NY: Penguin Books, 1971.

Jaskolski, Helmut. *The Labyrinth: Symbol of Fear, Rebirth and Liberation.* Boston, MA: Shambhala, 1997.

Johnson, Buffie. *Lady of the Beasts: The Goddess and Her Sacred Animals.* Rochester, VT: Inner Traditions International, 1994.

Jones, Prudence and Nigel Pennick. *A History of Pagan Europe.* NY: Routledge, 1995.

Jung, C. G. *Alchemical Studies. The Collected Works of C. G. Jung.* Volume 13. Bollingen Series XX. Princeton, NJ: Princeton University Press, 1967.

Kerényi, Carl. *Eleusis: Archetypal Image of Mother and Daughter.* Princeton, NJ: Princeton University Press, 1967.

Kerényi, Carl. *The Gods of the Greeks.* NY: Thames and Hudson, 1951.

———. *The Heroes of the Greeks.* translated by H. L. Rose. NY: Thames and Hudson, 1959.

Kinsley, David R. *The Sword and the Flute: Kali and Krsna: Dark Visions of the Terrible and the Sublime in Hindu Mythology.* Berkeley, CA: University of California Press, 1975.

———. *The Goddesses' Mirror: Vision of the Divine from East and West.* Albany, NY: State University of NY Press, 1989.

Knox, Bernard. *Backing Into The Future: The Classical Tradition and Its Renewal.* NY: W. W. Norton & Co., 1994.

Knox, Bernard, editor. *The Norton Book of Classical Literature.* NY: W. W. Norton & Co., 1993.

Kramer, Samuel Noah., editor. *Mythologies of the Ancient World.* Garden City, NY: Doubleday & Co., Inc., 1961.

Larrington, Carolyne, editor. *The Feminist Companion to Mythology.* London, England: HarperCollins, 1992.

Larsen, Stephen and Robin Larsen. *A Fire in the Mind: The Life of Joseph Campbell.* NY: Anchor Books, Doubleday, 1991.

Larson, Jennifer. *Greek Heroine Cults.* Madison, WI: University of Wisconsin Press, 1995.

Leach, Maria, editor. *Funk & Wagnall's Standard Dictionary of Folklore, Mythology, and Legend.* San Francisco, CA: HarperSanFrancisco, 1984.

Leeming, David Adams. *The World of Myth.* NY: Oxford University Press, 1990.

Leeming, David and Margaret Leeming. *A Dictionary of Creation Myths.* NY: Oxford University Press, 1994.

Lefkowitz, Mary R. *Women in Greek Myth.* London, England: Gerald Duckworth & Co., Ltd., 1986.

Lévi-Strauss, Claude. *Myth and Meaning.* NY: Schocken Books, 1979.

———. *The Origin of Table Manners: Introduction to a Science of Mythology: 3.* Translated from the French by John and Doreen Weightman. NY: Harper & Row, 1979.

———. *The Raw and the Cooked: Mythologiques Volume 1.* Translated by John and Doreen Weightman. Chicago, IL: The University of Chicago Press, 1969.

Lyons, Deborah. *Gender and Immortality: Heroines in Ancient Greek Myth and Cult.* Princeton, NJ: Princeton University Press, 1997.

Mack, Sara. *Ovid.* New Haven, CT: Yale University Press, 1988.

Maher, John M. and Dennie Briggs. *An Open Life: Joseph Campbell in Conversation with Michael Toms.* Foreword by Jean Erdman Campbell, NY: Harper & Row, 1989.

Markman, Roberta H. and Peter T. Markman. *The Flayed God: The Mythology of Mesoamerica.* NY: HarperCollins, 1992.

Mascaró, Jean, translator. *The Bhagavad Gita.* London, England: Penguin Books, Ltd., 1962.

Matthews, Caitlín. *Elements of The Celtic Tradition.* Rockport, MA: Element, Inc., 1989.

Mencken, H. L. *Treatise on the Gods.* Second edition: corrected and rewritten. Baltimore, MD: The Johns Hopkins University Press, 1946.

Miller, Mary and Karl Taube. *The Gods and Symbols of Ancient Mexico and the Maya.* London, England: Thames and Hudson, 1993.

Monaghan, Patricia. *The New Book of Goddesses and Heroines.* St. Paul, MN: Lewellyn Publications, 1997.

Morford, Mark P. O. and Robert J. Lenardon. *Classical Mythology.* Fourth edition. White Plains, NY: Longman Publishing Group, 1991.

Motz, Lotte. *The Faces of the Goddess.* NY: Oxford University Press, 1997.

Murdock, Maureen. *The Heroine's Journey.* Boston, MA: Shambhala Publications, 1990.

Neihardt, John G. *Black Elk Speaks.* Lincoln: University of Nebraska Press, 1973.

Neimark, John Philip. *The Way of the Orisa*. San Francisco, CA: Harper-SanFrancisco, 1993.

Neumann, Erich. *Amor and Psyche: The Psychic Development of the Feminine: A Comentary on the Tale by Apuleius*. Bollingen Series LIV. Princeton, NJ: Princeton University Press, 1971.

———. *The Great Mother: An Analysis of the Archetype*. Translated by Ralph Manheim. Bollingen Series XLVII. NY: Pantheon Books, 1955.

———. *The Origins and History of Consciousness*. Translated by R. F. C. Hull. Bollingen Series XLII. Princeton, NJ: Princeton University Press, 1995.

Noll, Richard. *The Aryan Christ: The Secret Life of Carl Jung*. NY: Random House, 1997.

Norman, Dorothy. *The Hero: Myth/Image/Symbol*. NY: Anchor Books, Doubleday, 1990.

O'Flaherty, Wendy Doniger, translator. *The Rig Veda*. NY: Penguin Books, 1981.

———. *Hindu Myths*. NY: Penguin Books, 1975.

O'Hara, Gwydion. *Moon Lore: Myths and Folklore from Around the World*. St. Paul, MN: Llewellyn Publications, 1996.

Otto, Walter F. *Dionysus: Myth and Cult*. Dallas, TX: Spring Publications, 1993.

Ovid. *The Art of Love*. Translated by Rolfe Humphries. Bloomington, IN: Indiana University Press, 1957.

———. *Fasti*. Translated by Sir James G. Frazer. Cambridge, MA: Harvard University Press, 1989.

———. *Metamorphoses*. Translated and with an introduction by Mary M. Innes. NY: Penguin Books, 1955.

———. *The Poems of Exile*. Translated by Peter Green. NY: Penguin Books, 1994.

Pack, Robert. *Wallace Stevens: An Approach to His Poetry and Thought*. NY: Gordian Press, 1968.

Panofsky, Dora and Erwin. *Pandora's Box: The Changing Aspects of Mythical Symbol*. Bollingen Series LII. NY: Pantheon Books, 1956.

Pantel, Pauline Schmitt, editor. *A History of Women in the West. Volume I: From Ancient Goddesses to Christian Saints*. Translated by Arthur Goldhammer. Cambridge, MA: The Belknap Press of Harvard University Press, 1992.

Parke, H. W. *Festivals of the Athenians*. Ithaca, NY: Cornell University Press, 1977.

Patai, Raphael. *The Hebrew Goddess*. Third enlarged edition. Detroit, MI: Wayne State University Press, 1990.

Pausanias. *Guide to Greece: Volume I: Central Greece.* Translated and with an introduction by Peter Levi. NY: Penguin Books, 1971.

Peacock, Sandra J. *Jane Ellen Harrison: The Mask and the Self.* New Haven, CT: Yale University Press, 1988.

Pearson, Carol. *The Hero Within: Six Archetypes We Live By.* San Francisco, CA: Harper & Row, 1986.

Pelikan, Jaroslav. *Mary Through the Centuries: Her Place in the History of Culture.* New Haven, CT: Yale University Press, 1996.

Pindar. *The Odes of Pindar.* Translated by Richard Lattimore. Chicago, IL: The University of Chicago Press, 1947.

Pomeroy, Sarah B. *Goddesses, Whores, Wives, and Slaves: Women in Classical Antiquity.* NY: Schocken Books, 1995.

Powers, William K. *Oglala Religion.* Lincoln, NE: University of Nebraska Press, 1977.

Puhvel, Jaan. *Comparative Mythology.* Baltimore, MD: Johns Hopkins University Press, 1987.

Radin, Paul. *The Trickster: A Study in American Indian Mythology.* NY: Schocken Books, 1972.

Rank, Otto, Lord Raglan, and Alan Dundes. *In Quest of the Hero.* Introduction by Robert A. Segal. Princeton, NJ: Princeton University Press, 1990.

Rees, Alwyn and Brinley Rees. *Celtic Heritage: Ancient Tradition in Ireland and Wales.* London, England: Thames and Hudson, 1961.

Reid, Jane Davidson. *The Oxford Guide to Classical Mythology in the Arts, 1300–1990s.* Volumes 1 and 2. NY: Oxford University Press, 1993.

Rainer Maria Rilke, *Selected Poems of Rainer Maria Rilke.* Translated and wtih commentary by Robert Bly. NY: Harper and Row, 1981.

Rohde, Erwin. *Psyche: The Cult of Souls and Belief in Immortality among the Greeks.* Translated by W. B. Hillis. NY: Books for Libraries Press, 1972.

Rose, H. J. *A Handbook of Greek Mythology.* London, England: Methuen & Co, Ltd., 1958.

Rosenberg, Donna. *World Mythology: An Anthology of the Great Myths and Epics.* Second edition. Lincolnwood, IL: NTC Publishing Group, 1994.

Sandars, N. K., translator. *The Epic of Gilgamesh.* Introduction by N. K. Sandars. London, England: Penguin Books, 1972.

Scheub, Harold. *A Dictionary of African Mythology.* NY: Oxford University Press, 2000.

Sebeok, Thomas A., editor. *Myth: A Symposium.* Bloomington, IN: Indiana University Press, 1968.

Segal, Robert A. *Joseph Campbell: An Introduction*. NY: Penguin Books, 1997.

Seznec, Jean. *The Survival of the Pagan Gods*. Princeton, NJ: Princeton University Press, 1981.

Shuhmacher, Stephan and Gert Woerner, editors. *The Encyclopedia of Eastern Philosophy and Religion*. Boston, MA: Shambhala, 1994.

Slater, Philip E. *The Glory of Hera: Greek Mythology and the Greek Family*. Princeton, NJ: Princeton University Press, 1968.

Smith, John Holland. *The Death of Classical Paganism*. NY: Charles Scribner's Sons, 1976.

Snorri Sturluson. *The Prose Edda*. Translated by Jean I. Young. Berkeley, CA: University of California Press, 1954.

Sophocles. *The Three Theban Plays: Antigone, Oedipus the King, Oedipus at Colonus*. Translated by Robert Fagles; introduction and notes by Bernard Knox. NY: Penguin Books, 1982.

Spretnak, Charlene. *Lost Goddesses of Early Greece: A Collection of Pre-Hellenic Myths*. Boston, MA: Beacon Press, 1984.

Sproul, Barbara C. *Primal Myths: Creation Myths Around the World*. NY: HarperCollins Publishers, 1979.

Steiner, George, and Robert Fagles, editors. *Homer: A Collection of Critical Essays*. Englewood Cliffs, NJ: Prentice-Hall, Inc., 1962.

Steward, R. J. *Celtic Gods, Celtic Goddesses*. London, England: Blandford, 1990.

Stone, Merlin. *Ancient Mirrors of Womanhood*. Boston, MA: Beacon Press, 1990.

Storm, Rachel. *The Encyclopedia of Eastern Mythology*. London, England: Anness Publishing Limited, 1999.

Stoneman, Richard. *Legends of Alexander the Great*. London, England: Everyman, 1992.

Taube, Karl. *The Legendary Past: Aztec and Maya Myths*. Austin, TX: British Museum Press and University of Texas Press, 1993.

Thompson, Stith. *Tales of the North American Indians*. Bloomington, IN: Indiana University Press, 1966.

Turner, Alice K. *The History of Hell*. NY: Harcourt Brace and Company, 1993.

Vernant, Jean-Pierre. *Mortals and Immortals: Collected Essays*. Princeton, NJ: Princeton University Press, 1991.

Veyne, Paul. *Did the Greeks Believe in Their Myths?* Chicago, IL: The University of Chicago Press, 1988.

Vickery, John B. *The Literary Impact of* The Golden Bough. Princeton, NJ: Princeton University Press, 1973.

Vico, Giambattista. *The New Science of Giambattista Vico.* Translated by Thomas Goddard Bergin and Max Harold Fisch. Ithaca, NY: Cornell University, 1961.

Virgil. *The Aeneid.* Translated by David West. NY: Penguin Books, 1991.

Walker, Barbara G. *The Woman's Encyclopedia of Myths and Secrets.* NY: Harper & Row, 1983.

Warner, Marina. *Alone of All Her Sex: The Myth and the Cult of the Virgin Mary.* NY: Vintage Books, 1983.

Willis, Roy, general editor. *World Mythology.* NY: Henry Holt and Co., 1993.

Wilshire, Donna. *Virgin, Mother, Crone: Myths and Mysteries of the Triple Goddess.* Rochester, VT: Inner Traditions, 1994.

Wolkstein, Diane and Samuel Noah Kramer. *Inanna, Queen of Heaven and Earth: Her Stories and Hymns from Sumer.* NY: Harper & Row, Publishers, 1983.

Woolger, Jennifer Barker and Roger J. *The Goddess Within: A Guide to the Eternal Myths That Shape Women's Lives.* NY: Fawcett Columbine, 1987.

Young, Jonathan, editor. *Saga: Best New Writings on Mythology.* Volume 1. Ashland, OR: White Cloud Press, 1996.

Index